THE PHOENIX AGENDA

JC RYAN

By JC Ryan

Rossler Foundation Mysteries

The Tenth Cycle

Ninth Cycle Antarctica

Genetic Bullets

The Sword of Cyrus

The Skywalkers

The Phoenix Agenda

The Rowen

Termination

Vinci Books

vinci-books.com

Published by Vinci Books Ltd in 2025

1

Copyright © JC Ryan 2015

The author has asserted their moral right to be identified as the author of this work in accordance with the Copyright, Designs and Patents Act 1988. This work is a work of fiction. Names, characters, places and incidents are the product of the author's imagination or are used fictitiously. Any resemblance to actual persons, living or dead, places and incidents is entirely coincidental.

All rights reserved. No part of this publication may be copied, reproduced, distributed, stored in any retrieval system, or transmitted in any form or by any means, including photocopying, recording, or other electronic or mechanical methods, nor used as a source for any form of machine learning including AI datasets, without the prior written permission of the publisher.

The publisher and the author have made every effort to obtain permissions for any third party material used in this book and to comply with copyright law. Any queries in this respect should be brought to the attention of the publisher and any omissions will be corrected in future editions.

A CIP catalogue record for this book is available from the British Library.
Paperback ISBN: 9781036700430

The EU GPSR authorised representative is Logos Europe, 9 rue Nicolas Poussion, 17000 La Rochelle, France
contact@logoseurope.eu

Prologue

"Big-Mac, Big-Mac, this is Two-One Alpha. Can you read me?"

"Two-One Alpha, This is Big-Mac. I read you, over."

"Big-Mac, where are you? Serious shit over here! Heavy fire! Can't move our asses! Two casualties! Over."

"Two-One Alpha, you'll see me in 2 seconds. Mark the LZ, I'm close. Over."

"Big-Mac, roger, roger. Out."

John 'Doug' MacArthur tightened his grip on the control. His feet were shaking faintly on the tail rotor pedals as he took in the scene below him when his chopper broke the horizon over Hill 39 in the Shah-i-Kot Valley in Afghanistan's Paktia province.

"This valley's been a hellhole the last few months," he muttered. "Now this! Damn it!"

He curved the chopper around over the soldiers, surveying the scene rapidly before pulling away once again out of firing range.

Ten Marines, pinned down behind rocks and in shallow

ditches, were firing at an invisible group of thirty-odd Taliban fighters on the hill above them. Open ground in front with no cover behind. They were sitting ducks. Tracers and bullets from AK-47s, ancient British Lee-Enfield rifles, and a Russian RPK machine gun, created a blanket of instant death over the pinned-down soldiers.

Luckily, the Taliban fighters were not known for their marksmanship, and they didn't always understand that the skill of the person holding the weapon was what made the weapon useful. Most of their shots were missing their targets by several yards because they didn't understand that the fundamental principle of shooting downhill requires dropping your aim down. Nevertheless, some of their fire was hitting the target, and it was obvious the boys down there were in serious trouble.

"Big-Mac this is Two-One Alpha. I see you - putting out smoke now. Tell me the color!"

"Two-One Alpha, this is Big-Mac. Green?"

"Big-Mac, Two-One Alpha. That's it."

The unmistakable trace of smoke left by the rocket from an RPG 7 racing down the hill caught the co-pilot's eye. Leo McKenzie said, "Oh shiiiiit. The bastards have an RPG!"

The rocket exploded about 20 yards behind the soldiers, sending a chilling sensation through John's spine. He knew all too well how devastating an RPG could be. Even in the hands of an untrained person it could create havoc on the receiving end and was a very simple but deadly effective weapon against a helicopter. The US military learned the dire lesson in 1993 during the Battle of Mogadishu. Somali militia fighters, basically untrained armed civilians, successfully shot down two Black Hawk helicopters with RPGs and damaged three others - a battle that saw 18 American soldiers killed and 73 others wounded.

Over the past 18 months, John had survived many evac missions, also known as a DUSTOFF, the backronym for Dedicated Unhesitating Service to Our Fighting Forces. He knew what it was like to be under fire. He'd seen a few tight situations in his time here in the war zone, but this one in front of him now made the others look insignificant.

John knew there was no time to waste. He had to make the decision, land the chopper and risk the ten soldiers on the ground and the three of them in the helicopter. It was that, or get out and wait for help, which would almost guarantee the death of those on the ground.

'Unhesitation' was exactly what was happening when he shouted into his helmet's intercom system. "Those boys are in serious trouble down there. We better get them out and fast. With all that metal flying around it's a miracle they're not all dead already."

Tony, the third crew member and gunner, turned the door gun on the enemy positions and started firing. Some of their fire turned to the chopper but became sporadic very quickly when they experienced the business end of the machine gun.

"We can't wait for reinforcements. If we don't get them out now, they'll all be dead. I'm going in to put her down, Tony!" he shouted to the gunner as he maneuvered the chopper down to land. "Just keep those bastards on the hill down. And while you're at it, make sure that RPG isn't pointed at us."

"Roger that. I'll keep 'em busy - you can bet your ass on it," Tony shouted back.

"Two-One Alpha, ready for you. Move it. We're in kind of a hurry to find a quieter place!"

Two wounded men were hauled to the helicopter first by four of their buddies, with the rest strafing the hill to keep the Taliban heads down. The fright and panic in the eyes and faces of the soldiers were clearly visible. Their screams rose above the thundering noise of the engines as they pushed the wounded in and then took up position outside the chopper to provide covering fire for the remaining men to get in.

"All in. Let's get out of here!" Leo shouted.

"Grab tight. It's going to be a rough ride boys!"

John pulled the chopper into a steep climb while banking away from the hill. With no fire coming from the doorgun to keep them down, the full force and frustration of the enemy was now directed at the chopper and its occupants. They saw their prey escaping out of their hands right in front of their eyes.

A burning pain shot through John's back and legs as the body of the helicopter shuddered under the power of the two Rolls-Royce Gem turboshaft engines at full throttle. Smoke started to billow from the starboard engine. *I have to get over that hill three miles away. Why am I dizzy? I have to get these boys out of trouble. I have to level the chopper and save power. I must get over that hill. I must get out of the reach of the bullets.*

"Doug! Doug! Can you hear me? What's wrong man?" Leo screamed in a high-pitched, panicked voice. "Oh my God, you've been hit! Are you ok? Shit man, put the chopper down now. You'll crash and kill us all!"

"That hill ... I have to get over it ... out of range ... I must get us there ..." Doug stuttered.

"What was that? I can't hear you. For God's sake put the chopper down!" Leo shouted at the top of his voice.

"Going down, going down ... radio for help!" John whispered, a few seconds before everything went dark.

Chapter One

THE NIGHTMARE AND THE MATH

Doug paid little heed to his passengers as he banked away from the canyon rim. Max was back there to help them. Doug had plenty on his mind, between the flashback to his crash in Afghanistan and wondering when whoever had shot two of his passengers would show up and try to shoot the chopper down here and now, over the Grand Canyon. Not to mention nursing the aging machine to do his bidding.

Within minutes after takeoff from the canyon site, lying in the back of the chopper, JR and Roy were oblivious to their surroundings due to the morphine injection administered to them by Max Ellis – an ex-Marine medic and the third member of the Rossler boys' rescue expedition. Others on the chopper had more on their minds.

Raj was in his own world, eyes closed, wondering about his wife Sushma, their child, and the future. He and Sushma were not the outdoors adventure and camping types – living in a cave with other people was going to take some getting used to for them. They both grew up and had lived in the city all their lives. How was this going to work out for him and his family and, for that matter, for all of the Rosslerites?

Ever since the Rosslers, with his help and that of others, had discovered the wealth of ancient knowledge hidden in the Great Pyramid of Giza, It seemed no matter what good came of these discoveries, there was always a megalomaniac, or a group of them, who wanted to exploit it for their own nefarious reasons.

It was brought home to them over and over again that they could never rest. Whether their discoveries led to a fabulous hidden city in Antarctica or a way to micro-miniaturize the most sophisticated of electronic marvels, someone had designs on it and it was up to the Rossler Foundation and its leadership to thwart the evil-doers' plans. This time, it seemed they may be too late to foil the latest maniac.

Raj could not make up his mind immediately. What was worse, being ruled by a resurrected Persian Empire or by this psychopath, John Brideaux? They were now living in the new world of John Brideaux. There was no choice. From what he'd seen so far, he was sure neither he nor any of his friends were going to like it. He was sure they were not going to accept it either. He was not going to walk around with a chip in his body that controlled his life; he had never been controlled by anyone ... except perhaps by Sushma, he thought, as a smile played on his face.

Although Raj was uncertain about the future, he was very sure about a few other matters. He was definitely going to stay with the Rossler Foundation. They would rely on him – and he on them – to bring this new world to a speedy end. They had always relied on each other in the past to overcome adversity, and this time was the same. The second thing he was determined about was that he was going to find a way to seek out and activate his underground network and bring their full force down on John Brideaux. That lunatic was going down, and he fully intended to be there to witness it.

Max Ellis was wondering what the future held for him and his wife. He'd seen a bit of action in the last days of the Afghanistan war, before the troops were withdrawn. Returning to the States, he'd joined M&J Security Company in Boulder. He married Jenny a few years ago. She was a kindergarten teacher, and lately he'd been working part-time as a security guard while studying for a computer science degree.

Uncertainty and unknowns about what would happen to him and Jenny in the days and weeks to come made him nervous about today's events. He trusted Mark and John, or 'Doug' as everyone called him, though. They'd been good to him over the years, had encouraged and supported him to take up his studies. They'd also made it possible for him to work part-time so he and Jenny could still make ends meet while he studied.

Daniel, the only one in the back with his headset on, was startled by Mark's voice.

"Earth calling Doug! Doug, can you read me? ET calling Doug. Come in Doug. Anybody home?"

"Huh, what was that?"

Mark smiled. His best friend must have been deep in thought, as he hadn't responded to his chatter for the past few minutes. "Buddy, where have you been? I thought you fell asleep behind the wheel?"

"Ah man, that frickin' nightmare paid me a very unwelcome visit. This chopper and all the stuff today, wounded men and all, aren't good for forgetting memories you don't want to have."

"You ok, my friend?"

"Yea I'll survive. I'm ok."

"Nightmare? What nightmare, John?" Daniel asked.

"Long story Daniel, long story. A horrible start but a good ending."

"Hey Mark, why'd you call him Doug? I thought you introduced him as John. You are aware we have a military hero by the same name. Related, John?"

John smiled. "Yes, but I have to explain it to you."

Mark chipped in before Doug could say anything further. "Another long story, Daniel. If you understand it, you will be the first. He claims there's some relationship to General Douglas-Old-Soldiers-Never-Die-They-Just-Fade-Away-MacArthur. He's tried to explain it to me and many others many times, but none of us got it - at least not yet. Therefore, instead of listening to his complicated genealogical descriptions, we decided to call him Doug. It seems to make him happy and spares us the pain of listening to his explanation!"

John, a very good-natured person, was having a good laugh at the jokes at his expense. "Let me put it this way, Daniel - my nickname will be as close as I will ever come to fame and power."

"Doug, I'd surely like to hear your stories someday, both the nightmare and the math."

"Sure, Daniel. As soon as we can get a campfire going and get a few stiff shots of Scottish Aqua Vie under the belt, I'll tell you."

Chapter Two

TWO HOURS AGO

About two hours previously, Mark Bryant, John 'Doug' MacArthur, and Max Ellis, all of them ex-Marines, had walked into the 8th Cycle Canyon compound, sent on a rescue mission by Sarah Rossler. Her instructions were clear. "Bring our husbands back to us at the Rabbit Hole, dead or alive."

Hours before their arrival, John Brideaux had taken the four men they were to rescue hostage at gunpoint. After subduing the group, and in the process killing JR's best friend, Rossler Foundation geologist Robert Cartwright and wounding JR, he'd instructed Joseph Yazzie, a Navajo translator, to tie them all up.

He then started terrorizing Yazzie to produce the translations from the 8th Cycle information that would show him how to shut down The Beast, the fearsome device that he wanted to control and the Rosslers wanted to destroy. One of Brideaux's tactics was to threaten Joseph that if he didn't see quick progress, he would shoot one of the tied up men. That turned out to be no idle threat - in the first half hour he was not happy with the progress. He walked over to where Roy was sitting and shot him in the lower right leg. After that, he took potshots at Roy to 'encourage' Joseph.

Despite the extreme pressure, Joseph had somehow managed to complete the translation just when Brideaux's henchmen walked into the compound. They forced Roy to help them shut down The Beast, dismantled it, and moved it into the helicopters outside. They took all of Raj's computer equipment and Roy's robots and tools, tied Joseph's hands and dragged him with them, and took off. That left the remaining four - Daniel, JR, Raj, and Roy - tied up on the floor in a pool of blood, groaning from the pain.

Now, minutes later, when the rescue party walked in, JR recognized Mark first. "Hey, so good to see you guys!"

Mark Bryant answered, "We heard you might have had some trouble. Where are the bad guys? We'll take care of them."

"Gone," Daniel, answered. "You must have missed them by minutes. Did Sarah tell you what was here, what's at stake?"

"Yeah. I guess they got that Beast thing, too?" Mark answered.

"They did. Now we need to get out of here and get our people to safety."

"Already done, my friend. That's one efficient wife you've got there. She told us to bring you to the Rabbit Hole, dead or alive. I assume you want to get there alive?"

"That would be my first choice. JR?"

Daniel's dry humor made the others laugh as JR answered, "Oh, I guess."

Max Ellis saw Roy sitting on the ground in a pool of blood and ran over to him. "Hey why didn't you guys mention this?" He looked around. "So who else is injured?" He took out the first aid kit packed for them by Dr. Rebecca Rossler, JR's wife, and attended to Roy's wound.

They sobered, remembering Robert and pointing out where he'd fallen. "He has no family here," said JR. "His mom is in Australia. Should we take him with us?"

Daniel's voice was gentle as he made his regrets to his younger brother. "We won't be able to contact her, JR, and she won't be able to come and get his body. I think it's best we leave him here, outside in the canyon. We'll bury him before we go."

JR's left hand was throbbing with pain. He walked up to Max where he was working on Roy's leg, sat down on the floor, and waited his turn for medical attention.

Max glanced at him, "You too?" JR nodded.

Later, as they stood in a circle around the cairn that marked Robert's grave, they swore again to avenge his death. Sometime, somehow, even if they had to follow John Brideaux to hell to do it, they'd make sure of it.

As they were walking up to the helicopter, Mark explained to Daniel that he thought it would be best if they headed out to Farmington, New Mexico to refuel. Then from there they could fly directly to the Rabbit Hole near Bozeman, Montana.

"If we can get to Bozeman, I know a man who would store the chopper in a place where no one would question it."

"We're in your hands my friend - just get us to the Rabbit Hole as quickly as humanly possible. We need distance from here as soon as possible," Daniel replied.

As they were climbing into the helicopter, Daniel asked, "So, what's its range?"

"Oh, four hundred miles or so, depending on weight.

With our current load maybe two hundred and fifty," Mark said, grinning.

Daniel thought fast. The chopper had already flown from Flagstaff to here. They could probably make no further than Farmington on the remainder of the fuel in any event.

"Will it be able to carry all of us?" Daniel inquired.

John smiled. He knew from experience it could carry three crewmembers and up to six stretcher patients in the back. "Yes, it can, unless you think the combined weight of the four of you and your gear is over two thousand pounds."

"No, I guess we'll come in a few pounds below that, but only just. If it turns out we're a bit overweight, we can draw straws as to who gets pushed out the door midflight." Daniel's answer had them all laughing despite their dismal circumstances.

Within a few minutes, the seven of them were on their way above the Navajo reservation to Farmington. Daniel's thoughts turned to Joseph, now in the claws of that maniac Brideaux. He could just hope that Joseph would be treated well. He had no idea where to even begin to look for the elderly man for a rescue attempt. One more friend left behind among many, and this one was particularly painful.

Chapter Three

CAN WE REACH FARMINGTON?

Daniel looked at the lights on the control panel, but he couldn't make out head nor tail of it. Which one was the fuel gauge? Even if he could figure that out, he would still have no idea how to read it. "Doug, what's our fuel situation at the moment? Can we reach Farmington?"

"Yeah, no problem with that. We'll make it there in about an hour at the current cruise speed."

"Great. How many gas stops from there to Bozeman do you reckon?"

"From Farmington to Bozeman is about five hundred and fifty or so nautical miles. With our load, we might need two fuel stops. I reckon if we can get fuel when we need it, we can make it in about eight to nine hours, barring any mechanical problems."

The way the tone in Doug's voice changed when he mentioned mechanical problems caught Daniel's attention and made his ears prick up. "Any mechanical problems that you're aware of, Doug?"

"Not sure exactly what it is, but the power isn't what I

expect it to be. I'm not too worried about it for now, but we'll have to check it when we get to Farmington, before we go any further. This is an old chopper - its best-by-date is long gone - and with so many hours on the clock, mechanical failures can be expected."

Initially, they were going to Farmington for two reasons. Doug and Mark had a good friend there who owned a small aircraft pilot training school and could help them with fuel. The second was to throw off anyone who could be tracking them, making it appear as if they were making their way back to Boulder. With the emergence of the possible mechanical problems, a new reason had just become apparent.

Daniel turned the conversation to their current situation. "We have to assume that Brideaux will discover the nasty surprises waiting at the Rossler Foundation within a few hours and raise all hell. You can bet your bottom dollar that the names and faces of the four of us will be all over the news and in the hands of every law enforcement agency shortly. Brideaux will realize his mistake by not taking us hostage and will immediately send his hatchet men back to the canyon to pick us up."

Mark agreed, "Yes I guess that's about the size of it. What we can bank on for now, however, is that Brideaux won't know about Doug, Max, and myself, nor that you were rescued by helicopter. They might be under the impression that you would be on foot and could very well spend some time looking for you much closer to the canyon. Certainly not as far away as Farmington - at least not in the first day or two. However, I do agree with your earlier idea to put as much distance between the canyon and us as we can until daylight comes. Then we'll have to lay low until it's dark again."

Doug, being a bit more risk averse than Mark, pointed out, "Yes, that might be true, Mark. But we shouldn't make too many assumptions. My understanding is that this Brideaux character is a man of considerable means and influence, and it will just be a matter of time before he'll have things figured out. When he discovers our friend who sold us the chopper, he'll know who rescued them. Then our faces will be all over the news with those of Daniel and his crew. He'll also have one more way of finding us then - look for the chopper."

"Well, guys," Daniel said. "I have to agree with Doug. We shouldn't make too many assumptions - you know what they say about the word "assume". My take on it is that we don't have many options. But as much as I want to get to our new home and our families as quickly as possible, we shouldn't take any unnecessary risks. I'd rather walk and turn up there alive a few months from now than never."

Doug and Mark nodded their heads in agreement.

"For now, while we're sure Brideaux doesn't know where we are, let's stick with Plan A. Get as much distance between us and the canyon as quickly as possible. By the time Brideaux is wiser about our rescue, we'll be much closer to home. Although I have to admit, I don't have the slightest idea what 'home' looks like these days," Daniel said with a bit of smile.

That settled, they turned their discussion to a strategy for the Farmington pit stop.

"We can't take any chances," Daniel continued. "Doug and Mark will be the only ones to show up at the flight school. The rest of us with our gear should be dropped off at a safe location outside town."

Daniel reminded them they didn't have much food or water left – maybe two more days. Although they hoped to be home in less time than that, they decided to be safe rather than sorry.

Doug said, "While we're visiting our friend to refuel and check the engines, Mark can go into town while he and I look over the chopper. Mark, you'll get some supplies and hide them outside of town, to be picked up when we can resume our trip."

Mark and Daniel got busy studying the topographical and aerial maps, picking what they thought to be a safe and isolated location about fifteen miles out of Farmington.

About twenty minutes before they reached the spot, Daniel alerted everyone to switch their headsets on so he could explain the plan to them.

"Gather your stuff and be ready to evacuate quickly. We don't want to hover or sit down for more than a minute or two, as it could raise the suspicion of locals. Everyone understand the plan?" They nodded their agreement.

Daniel and Raj reminded everyone that they were incommunicado, "Under no circumstances can we use any electronic communications whatsoever. No mobile phone, no internet - nothing. Don't forget our lives and those of our families depend on it."

As they were descending to their hideout, Mark and Doug gave them some last minute instructions. "Guys, make sure you hide very well. Don't make any fires. Whatever you do, don't leave this place. We have no idea how long it's going to take to fix the engine trouble. It might even take a few days. Remember we can only pick you up at night - don't expect us during daytime. We'll be back for you, hopefully within an hour or two, but don't hold your breath."

Doug brought the chopper to within a few inches off the ground on the escarpment above the river and signaled to Mark, who moved to the back to help the others unload. They helped Roy out and led him a few paces away, where he could sit down. They unpacked their stuff, and forty-five seconds later, the chopper was airborne again. Mark and Doug gave the Rossler party and Max the thumbs up as they moved away.

In a warehouse in Denver, there was a lot of excitement and anticipation. John Brideaux's plans seemed to be working out exactly as he expected. The raid on the Rossler Foundation offices a few hours ago produced what appeared to be the precious 10th and 8th Cycle libraries and lots of additional information stored on the captured computers and servers.

The men who raided the Rossler Foundation offices were just waiting for Brideaux to arrive and give them the go-ahead. He finally turned up with his entourage and gave them the nod. As the men got busy, their excitement was quickly replaced by frustration.

First, none of the computers would boot up – none of them had a hard drive in it. John Brideaux, not used to being outwitted by anyone, descended into a foul and dangerous mood.

Next they hacked into the blade servers and were saluted by Raj's special welcome screen - every one of them with a full colored photo of his hand showing a middle finger! Each server was loaded with nothing but movies and games.

What was supposed to be his final victory, taking control

of the 10th and 8th Cycle Libraries before finally taking over the world, was turning into a horrendous nightmare for Brideaux. He couldn't recall the last time, if ever, he had been so outsmarted and utterly humiliated.

"Those fuckers knew we were coming!" he screamed

An uneasy feeling of doubt slowly crept into his stomach. The straw that broke the camel's back were the boxes from the vault, containing only rolls of toilet paper. Brideaux was in such a fit of rage that he had to be sedated before he stroked out.

After the chopper took off, Daniel and his party moved a few hundred yards away and remained quiet for about an hour. That was to make sure the noise of the helicopter hadn't alerted some of the locals who might get it into their heads to investigate or send the police their way.

All remained quiet, and they began to relax. Daniel asked Max to stay with Roy and JR, both of them still a bit shaky from the morphine, while he and Raj found a hiding place.

Given the difficulties of stumbling around in the dark with only a flashlight, the two of them were a bit surprised when, a few minutes after they left the other three, they stumbled across an old footpath, which led them down to the river. As far as they could see, there were no signs that anyone had used that path in a long while. That was good.

"Raj, I think it will be good if we can find a spot down here and get everyone settled before the sun comes up. According to the aerial maps, there's a lot more vegetation and potential hiding places than up there."

"Yes I agree, and it should also be relatively easy to move Roy down this footpath," Raj whispered.

Arriving at the riverbank and searching at the base of the cliffs for about twenty minutes, they found an overhanging rock amongst some dense bushes about twenty paces from the water. This looked promising as far as they could tell from what was visible in the light from the flashlights.

"Not sure about you, Raj, but I reckon this is perfect for now. We can do a bit of scouting in the morning to see if there's a better place, if necessary. "

"Okay, it looks ideal to me Daniel. Let's get the others down here."

They moved everyone quickly to the lair and made themselves as comfortable as possible.

Max was aware that Roy and JR's wounds needed regular attention, and as soon as everyone was resting, he checked on them again. Thanks to the first aid kit that Rebecca packed, Max had the best medicine and medical equipment a field medic could ever desire. Some of the stuff in that bag was not even supposed to be in the hands of an unqualified person. Max, however, did not think it necessary to worry about any legal repercussions. He was just very glad it was there.

"JR, I don't know what scenarios were going through your wife's mind when she packed this kit, but she surely planned for all emergencies. I'm darn grateful for that, and I reckon you and Roy should be too," he said over his shoulder to JR. He used a serious tone while he was changing the dressing on Roy's wound.

The syringes that could be injected into a wound to stop bleeding almost immediately while disinfecting it at the same time, the morphine, and the special antibacterial bandages had already proved their value. Both the wounds had stopped bleeding, and the pain was a lot more bearable for the wounded men. His main concern now was to make sure neither of their wounds became infected. He'd already given them antibiotics and would monitor the injuries and their temperatures closely.

Chapter Four

THE DURATION OF ETERNITY

"Hey, Patrick my friend. It's great to see you!" shouted Mark as he and Doug walked into the small office and surprised Patrick Roland, owner of Farmington Aviation School. They found him sitting behind a desk, burning the midnight oil on some aviation regulation paperwork.

"What the hell? Mark! Doug! What are you rascals doing here? Man, what a pleasant surprise."

The next few minutes were spent in hand shaking, back slapping and asking about each other's and families' health, wealth and well-being, and of course comments about how fat and ugly they'd all become.

Mark the eternal prankster, put a serious look on his face, and winked at Doug. "Patrick, I have to ask you something serious now. Do you know what the duration of eternity is?"

Doug could barely control himself but kept a straight face. He knew what was coming - he'd heard this one before, and it always cracked him up. Patrick had a puzzled look on his face as if he wondered what had gone wrong with his friend. But all he could get out was, "What the ..." before Mark started.

"Someone once explained it like this to me. If a bird landed on the Rocky Mountains once every thousand years and wiped his beak on the rocks, by the time the Rocky Mountains had been worn away, the first second of eternity would not have yet passed."

"Huh? What are you ... "

Mark interrupted him, "Another explanation I heard recently is that eternity is the elapse of time between arriving on Patrick's doorstep and being offered coffee!"

Patrick looked at him for a few seconds as if he were an alien being, before he finally got it.

"You crazy SOB! For a while there, I thought you'd lost your marbles! Yes, of course, let me get that plunger going right away. Or wait a minute. Before I get another lecture about some weird topic, are you guys up for something a bit stronger?"

Mark and Doug spoke in a chorus. "Coffee first, pal! We are parched!"

As Patrick got busy with the coffee, he asked the obvious, "So what brought you two cellmates to my doorstep? Not to give me a lecture about eternity and hopefully not any serious trouble?"

Doug replied with a straight face, "No more trouble than we know you can handle. We're on our way to Boulder and misjudged the fuel consumption on this gas-guzzler outside. And for the last hour or so, it looked like we might also have a little engine trouble."

"The gas is no problem. I can help you with that, but I must warn you I'm not much of a mechanic, especially choppers. You guys in a hurry?"

"Yes. Unfortunately, we have to get back to Boulder

urgently. We've got a crucial meeting scheduled for first thing in the morning."

"Okay, in that case, let's grab that pot of coffee and your mugs and move that bird into the empty hanger at the end. I have good lighting there."

When Brideaux came to his senses a few hours after he'd been sedated, he started screaming orders immediately.

"Where have those sons of bitches gone with my libraries? Go and visit every one of those fuckin' Rossler bastards, including their women and children and the idiots working for them. Make them talk, and if they don't want to speak, bring them to me! I am personally going to skin each one of them alive. They'll learn not to try and make a fool of John Brideaux!"

The frightening and painful visits from "FBI agents" to the remaining Foundation staff demanding the whereabouts of the Rosslers and other key employees produced nothing but total ignorance. No amount of torture and threatening produced any results.

Reports to Brideaux all had a common theme - "vanished into thin air, disappeared like mist before the sun, they are gone, vanished with no word to anyone" The neighbors didn't know anything, hadn't seen anything. They had no idea. Brideaux went mad. Waving his gun to prevent his people from sedating him again, he was swearing as no one had ever heard a human swear before.

That uneasy feeling of doubt in Brideaux's stomach that started earlier was nauseating by now. Fear was taking hold. He knew he had a problem. He'd never know peace as long as the Rosslers and their brilliant scientists had access to the

Tenth and Eighth Cycle libraries. Until he could find them and those libraries, he would always have to look over his shoulder.

"This is what you get for being nice to people! I did not shoot or capture those motherfuckers in the canyon when I had the chance to do so. I spared their lives. I showed them mercy, and this is how they thank me! Jason, I want them now! You go back to that canyon and get them. Let me know when you have them."

"Yes sir, immediately, I'm on my way," the man he addressed as Jason squeaked while scurrying away, obviously scared out of his wits by Brideaux's fury.

"Oh and Jason, just in case you were wondering, you have my personal authorization to shoot any motherfucker that stands in your way."

"Yes sir."

With a niggling feeling of uncertainty about his future and that of the world Eligo Rarus envisioned at stake, Brideaux barked more orders to subordinates to put out contracts on the Rosslerites in the crime world. Let police in every likely jurisdiction, the FBI, the CIA, and other alphabet-soup agencies know – they were wanted for heinous crimes. Call the NSA flunkies to track cell phones, landlines, Internet activity and every possible lead or trace.

"Find them!" he screamed.

Doug and Patrick quickly disappeared into the mechanics of the chopper, leaving Mark, who was not mechanically minded, alone with his second mug of coffee on an old motorcar seat against the wall. The sounds that came from the two crawling around under the chopper were not encouraging.

"Ahh, there's oil here, not good. Let's follow this hose and see where the oil is coming from."

Despite a few cups of coffee, Mark soon dozed off. When he opened his eyes again, the first thing he saw was the early morning sun streaming in through the hanger door. Next, he became aware Doug was standing in front of him saying something to him, but he couldn't make out what.

"Sorry, what was that?"

Doug repeated, "We have bigger problems than I hoped would be the case. Both engines."

Mark was fully awake by now and sat up when he heard those words. "Damn, that's no good. Do you have any idea how long it will take?"

"Negative," Doug replied. "But Patrick says there's a mechanic who might have a better understanding of helicopter engines. He should be here within the next hour or so."

"Damn again. The one thing we don't have on our side is time ... " Mark stopped mid-sentence for a second or two as his mind raced with thoughts of what had to be done now. He dropped his voice so Patrick wouldn't hear him. "Well, I guess we have no choice. We'll have to wait then. We'll also have to keep up our act with Patrick. I'll walk outside the hanger and make a 'call' to our offices in Boulder to let them know to postpone that 'important meeting' we were supposed to have later today."

"Yep. Let's do that," Doug replied immediately.

"Okay great. I'll ask him a bit later if I could borrow his truck to go and have a 'look around town' as I've never been to Farmington," Mark said with a little smile on his face.

Mark got up and acted out the phone call on his switched off mobile phone outside of earshot of Patrick.

The mechanic turned up about an hour later and on request from Patrick started his inspection right away. About forty minutes after he started, he stood away from the chopper shaking his head "I'm not all that familiar with the Rolls Royce engines, although I expect I know more than you two. You're right about the oil leaks, which isn't good news. Especially since it was hard to find where it was coming from. The starboard engine is the better of the two, but I need some tools from my truck to open up a few things and see what I can find.

"I'll definitely try to fix it, but I can't guarantee anything." He glanced at Doug's disappointed face and said, "If you don't have far to go, you could do pit stops to check the oil and make sure the engines don't overheat, and of course take plenty of oil with you. The only good news is that's it's highly unlikely both engines would go at the same time, so you should still be able to bring her down if need be."

He gave them a guestimate of four hours to do what he could, and they had to be satisfied with that. He collected his tools from his truck and got busy.

Chapter Five

VANISHED FROM SOCIETY

The distance from Boulder to the Rabbit Hole, as the Rosslerites baptized their hiding place, was not too far from Big Timber, and about eighty miles from Billings. Montana was a little over five hundred miles from Boulder. The challenge was for everyone to get there before dawn the next morning after they executed their bug-out plan.

Thanks to the excellent teamwork and cooperation managed with military precision by Sarah, Salome, and Luke, all groups except Sarah and Ben were on the road shortly after darkness fell. They had enough nighttime to get there, as long as they drove continuously, which meant alternating drivers.

Salome and Luke were diligent in their preparations. As far as they could, they gave each group different routes to travel. They assigned each vehicle a few alternative locations along the way so the sudden increase in demand for fuel was not reduced to just one or two gas stations and was therefore less likely to attract attention

Personal disguising techniques were also part of the

plan, changing their looks so that they were not easily recognized. To this end, Salome prepared a detailed makeup guide with complete instructions and images that she'd handed to each of the selected families weeks ago. They had to study it, buy the necessary goods and keep it ready for exactly an emergency evacuation such as this.

When the evacuation message reached them they all swung into action. Time was of the essence now. There could be no last-minute grief, no regrets. It was get out now and don't look back. Everything was packed and ready to leave the moment their transport arrived. There could be no mistakes.

They then went through complete makeovers, the results of which would have made some 'Extreme Makeover' reality TV shows jealous. Blonds became redheads and brunettes and vice versa. Wigs of all colors, shapes and sizes, body paint, fake tattoos, head and neck scarves, caps, hats, sunglasses, earrings, nose rings and the odd lip ring were in high fashion. Short hair became long; some long hair was tied up in buns and hidden under hats and baseball caps. A few ponytails, hoodies, and of course sunglasses were very popular as well. Two of the men became outright sexy with skirts and high heels! So long as they played dumb – literally – and didn't stagger around in the stilettos, they'd pass muster.

Luke and Ryan turned up sporting moustaches and beards that would make a few frontiersmen of old, Amish, Jewish Rabbis, or Muslim men proud of them. Their efforts at camouflaging themselves were so effective that by the time they boarded their transport that night they had to be introduced to each other.

The humor generated by their new looks helped to relieve the extreme stress they were suffering from leaving their homes. It was proving painful, travelling into the unknown - all of them aware that they might, in all likelihood, never return.

Salome and Luke warned everyone that the disguises would only fool a human observer, not real computer facial recognition systems. Therefore they should at all cost avoid high-tech truck stops and other places where that sort of technology could be in operation.

While things were not going well for Daniel and his six compatriots, it would have been a big relief to them to know that their families were on their way and safe.

Salome cautioned everyone not to attract any attention to themselves and to take care despite their urgency to follow every rule of the road, especially adhering to the speed limit. All of the groups managed to cover the 500 miles that night, moving themselves and their gear into the Rabbit Hole.

At sunrise the next morning, they had vanished from society.

Ben Rossler, Daniel's dad, was assigned to stay with Sarah to take care of the last bits and pieces and, as Luke quipped, to 'switch off the lights.'

They quickly packed the last few items into the van and headed to their destination, shortly before eleven o' clock that night. They had to travel as far as they could before dawn and then find a place to lie low during the day.

Over the four and a little bit hours it took them to reach Casper before dawn, they had a lot to talk and think about. Foremost in their minds were a husband and two sons as well as the others. They were painfully aware that they could not expect any news from them soon, but still hoped until the very last moment when they got into the van.

"Sarah we must believe they are all alive and well and may be waiting for us at our new home by the time we arrive there. It is more than 1,000 miles by road from Flagstaff to Big Timber. But in a helicopter, even with a few fuel stops, they should be there long before us. Let's hope and pray for that."

She put her hand on his arm, comforting him as well as herself.

Independently of Daniel and his team, the two of them drew the same conclusions about John Brideaux's possible actions.

If not already, then very soon Brideaux would become aware of their evacuation of the Rossler Foundation offices as well as their homes, He would be plotting the ways and means of finding them. To their frustration, the radio in the van did not work at all. It was as dead as the proverbial doorknob and they had no means of hearing any news.

By five o'clock the next morning, they managed to cover a little over 300 miles as they drove into Casper, Wyoming. They found a small motel on the outskirts of town. It was far enough from Boulder to feel a bit more relaxed about the distance between them and the danger posed by Brideaux or any of his collaborators.

Four hours after dispatching Jason and some helpers back to the canyon to go and fetch the Rosslerites, Brideaux got an infuriating telephone call.

"Jason make my day and tell me you got them, I can't take much more of this shit."

"Mr. Brideaux I am sorry, but there is no trace of them. They've disappeared. We've checked everything, even the trails they could have followed by foot, but nothing turned up. We have no idea where they could be."

"Don't say those words! I swear on my mother's grave, if you say those words one more time, I will personally come and kill you! They are not ghosts - they have not disappeared!" He paused for breath, fighting down the fury. He had to remind himself he'd not come this far by losing his cool all the time. "People don't disappear! People are always somewhere! I have sent you to find them! Go and find them - NOW."

"Yes, sir I'll do my best."

"Jason don't tell me about doing your best. Do it! Or you will be digging your own grave, and I'll find someone else who can do the job. Don't waste my time!" He ended the call and sat down. *This is getting me nowhere. Think man, what would I do in the same circumstances? I'm alive, I am going to vanish...*

"Disappeared?" Slowly, the rage dropped to a simmer as he gathered his thoughts.

Finally, he stood and announced, "So they've managed to evade us. Well that's not going to last." He looked around at the men who were standing nervously around. "Okay, we begin again."

His followers heard the calm in his voice and glanced fearfully at each other. This calm was far more deadly than the rages. This was the side of him that got him to the head of his game. Now it began.

By the same sunrise, with no chopper in sight, Daniel and the men in the river hideout surmised that the mechanical problems must have been worse than Doug thought. The dread that Mark and Doug had been taken into custody by Brideaux's outfit or the police, crossed Daniel's mind. It was another reason for an unexpected delay that he didn't want to entertain, and therefore he didn't voice it.

Jason, Brideaux's henchman, was scared out of his wits by his last phone call to Brideaux. Now he conferred with his men to figure out how the Rosslerites got away and where they could be.

"There's only one way Jase. It had to be by chopper," his next-in-command stated.

Jason thought a moment "You're right. The first thing is get to Flagstaff and maybe Farmington, the nearest cities of any size, and ask around. Find out if someone there knows about helicopter flights in and out today."

Jason relaxed. He had the scent again. This time he would not be calling Brideaux until he had some positive information. He would have to wait.

By midday, they'd picked up the trail when they found Mark and Doug's friend in Flagstaff, who'd sold them the helicopter the day before. According to him, there were only two of them, Mark and Doug. They'd said they wanted to use the helicopter in their security business back in Boulder and that's where they headed when they left last night after concluding the transaction.

Jason knew better. That chopper made a trip to the canyon first.

He made a few calculations about the fuel consumption

and the range they could fly before having to refuel. Assuming they were indeed heading for Boulder, there could be few places where they could refuel, Farmington being one of them.

He put his men on task to get in touch with all the airfields within that range.

Chapter Six

SHOP CRAWLING

By midday, with the mechanic still working and no end in sight, Mark borrowed a truck from Patrick under the pretense of exploring the 'metropolis' of Farmington boasting a staggering forty-five thousand inhabitants.

He drove into town camouflaged with a baseball cap and dark glasses. It was not a disguise that would fool any half-decent facial recognition system, but maybe just enough for anyone seeing him for the first time not to remember his face. He was not worried about encountering any sophisticated electronic facial recognition systems in Farmington, though.

He bought just a few items from a couple of different hardware stores and supermarkets, as well as an outdoors center. Here he stopped. It would be too easy for someone to remember a guy shopping for a big camping trip.

About two hours later, the shop crawling was over, and he had enough food supplies to last the seven of them for two additional days. Among the items were a few flashlights, lots of batteries, and three world band radios that would be able to receive signals from FM and AM radio stations as well as shortwave from around the world. Those radios would possibly be their only way to find out what was going on in the world.

Just as he was about to leave the last shop, his eye caught the image on a TV screen displaying the unmistakable red banner with the flashing words "Breaking News." He stopped to see what the news flash was, and soon felt as if an ice cube was slowly sliding down his spine.

There, right in front of his eyes on the screen, were clear images of Daniel, JR, Raj, and Roy. He moved closer so he could hear the announcement. They were wanted for the horrific killing of Robert Cartwright and the kidnapping of Joseph Yazzie. Having seen the horrible murder of Robert Cartwright, the police had reason to believe Yazzie could also be dead by now.

A man who was introduced as the detective in charge of the case appeared on the screen. "In all my thirty years of crime scene investigation, I've seen some horrific murders, but this was the worst ever."

He went on to say "Evidence at the crime scene, showed signs of a frantic struggle. There were empty shell casings everywhere. It is entirely possible that some of the fugitives were wounded. Hospitals, clinics, and doctors are asked to be on the lookout for the men as they might be seeking medical attention. Do not to approach or confront the suspects; they are armed and extremely dangerous. Just contact the nearest police station or phone 911."

The shock for Mark increased as the reporter continued with the story, next showing the pictures of the wives of the four men, Sarah, Rebecca, Salome, and Sushma. "The women have all disappeared and may be assisting the suspects or be directly involved. They are wanted for questioning by the police."

What they had feared had happened. Mark knew they were out of time. It was now just a matter of hours before Brideaux would figure out who helped Daniel and his men. And then his face, together with those of Mark and Max, would be on the news. By then, Brideaux's group would have found out about the helicopter. He had to get back to Doug and tell him. That chopper had to fly tonight, as soon as it was dark, or they had to make another plan. There were no other choices.

He decided it was too much of a risk to drive out to hide the supplies - he would put it all in the backpacks he bought and explain it all away somehow if Patrick asked.

As Mark walked into the hanger, he noticed that Patrick was not there. He called Doug, who crawled out from under the chopper where he and the mechanic were still busy. Mark caught Doug's eye and placed his finger on his lips, suspecting Doug would be able to read from his face there was a problem. The gesture was to warn him not to say anything. "Hey, Doug how is it going here? Where is Patrick?"

Doug replied, "He's out on a flying lesson with one of his students. As for the repairs, we've made some progress. She's definitely in better condition than when we brought her in last night."

"That's good news. Farmington is a very interesting little town; let me show you a few of the souvenirs I bought for the folks back home," Mark said, signaling him with his hand and heading towards the hanger door.

Doug followed him outside, and when they were out of hearing range of the mechanic Mark gave him the news.

"I just saw a news bulletin. Daniel and the others' faces

are all over the news, even the faces of their wives. The police are looking for all of them. You're not gonna believe it. They're accused of murder and kidnapping!"

"What the hell? Murder and kidnapping who?"

"Killing Robert Cartwright and kidnapping Joseph Yazzie. You called it, Doug. That John Brideaux is undoubtedly very well connected."

"Anything about us?"

"No, nothing ... at least not yet. That's the only thing in our favor at the moment, but given how quickly they discovered the disappearance of Daniel and the rest, our discovery is just a few hours away."

Many thoughts were racing through his mind when Mark continued, "I was thinking on the way back - we have to get out of here the moment the sun goes down. We have to make that chopper fly, or we'll have to find a vehicle. However, being on the roads wouldn't be my first choice. There could be roadblocks. They could pull us over, and it's just too risky for my liking. The sun will be down in the next hour or two. What's your assessment of the chopper's condition at the moment?"

"Well, we found all the visible leaks and plugged them as best we could. As I said before, it's in much better condition than when we landed last night. That much I know. So, for now I wouldn't worry about getting a vehicle. I'll get her airborne, and we'll fly out of here, even if it's on two broken legs. We either make it all the way or get a few hundred more miles closer to Bozeman."

With Mark's agreement, they walked back into the hanger, and Doug spoke to the mechanic. He indicated that he had almost reached the end of his knowledge and abilities in terms of helicopter engines. There wasn't much more he could do, but agreed with Doug that the engines were definitely in better shape than when he walked in there earlier today. They decided to wrap up the work - made sure everything was back in place and tied up properly.

In the meantime, Patrick returned, to Doug's relief. He'd feared that Brideaux would check out Farmington as soon as he thought 'chopper'. They gave Patrick an update.

Doug told him "There's nothing more that can be done. It looks like we've found all the leaks and fixed them. We'll head out and hope that we make it.

By the time Doug and the mechanic made their final inspection, refueled, and loaded a few gallons of extra oil into the back, the last rays of the sun had disappeared.

Doug and Patrick walked over to his office to fill out some paperwork, something both Doug and Mark would have liked to avoid. No paper trail of their visit would have been much better, but they didn't want to raise any suspicion with Patrick or put him in any danger. It was risky, but the best scenario was for them to make sure that Patrick 'knew' they were on their way to Boulder.

While Doug, Patrick and the mechanic walked away, Mark got the opportunity to move the stuff from the truck into the chopper and concealed it as best he could.

Chapter Seven

A 'BUT' IN THAT STATEMENT

As soon as darkness fell, the river group heard the noise of an approaching chopper. Daniel ran up the footpath, hiding behind a rock at the top to make sure it was their lift approaching and to wave them down.

Relief gave them wings, and it took a mere fifteen minutes to move all their gear plus Roy up the footpath and into the chopper. As soon as they were airborne, Doug turned the nose and set a course for Bozeman that would take them past Grand Junction, about 180 nautical miles away.

While Doug got busy setting course, Daniel voiced the unspoken thoughts of all of them who were in hiding, "You guys had us worried for a while today. We hoped you would get back within an hour from dropping us off. I suppose the mechanical problems were worse than we hoped they'd be?"

Mark replied, "Sorry to cause you more worries than you already have. Yes, you're right - the engine problems took almost all day to fix. That's nothing compared to what

I am about to tell you now, though. The shit has hit the fan. You guys are all over the news! So are your wives. And wait for it – you're wanted for murder and kidnapping!"

JR was the first one to comprehend Mark's news "That son of a bitch! Murder and kidnapping! What the fuck! Who did we kill and kidnap?"

"Apparently you guys killed Robert Cartwright and seized Joseph Yazzie. Don't tell me you can't remember?" Mark replied in a sarcastic tone.

JR hissed into the microphone, "John Brideaux I am going to first break all your fingers one by one, then your arms and legs, before I break your neck for this."

"Oh, and by the way they also mentioned that some of you might be wounded and will be trying to get medical help," Mark said as he gave them the last bit of news.

Daniel was reminded of a very similar experience a few years ago when they discovered the 10th Cycle Library. "Sounds like the time when those bastards of the Orion Society blamed us for everyone they killed and managed to have every law enforcement agency on the planet out looking for us. The difference is that John Brideaux is much better connected than the OS were. We can expect a lot more trouble from that lunatic."

Raj wanted more information, "Mark, so tell us the full story in detail. Where did you see this? What exactly did they say and show on the TV? What about you, Doug, and Max? Was there anything about you guys on the news?"

Mark went into greater detail, trying to ignore the expletives the others were punctuating his review with.

Even Roy, who was still very uncomfortable and drugged with painkillers, was lucid and annoyed enough to comment, "Why draw the women into it? If that bastard comes within a mile of Salome, he is going to find a nanonuke in his rabbit hole. Come to think of it, you guys just get me to *our* Rabbit Hole, and I'll build enough nanonukes for us to blow him and his disciples to hell!"

The ones who were there during the Sword of Cyrus crisis and knew from firsthand experience exactly what Roy meant and of what he was capable found some comfort in that comment. The others just smiled at his sudden outburst. They had no idea what happened during that crisis, nor Roy's role in it. In fact, they'd only known Daniel and JR before the rescue and had never met Roy or Raj. In due time, they would be filled in about the others' expertise.

Daniel calmed their minds a little bit with his next remark. "Guys, as I have said before, I don't like to assume things, but it seems we can take it that our people and families must have slipped away before Brideaux's people arrived at the foundation last night. If not, he wouldn't be looking for them as well as us. He obviously did not get his hands on the 10th and 8th Cycle libraries and realized his mistake of not keeping us hostage. He will be one very frustrated and very dangerous hombre by now."

Daniel's reasoning made sense and brought some relief to them all.

If it were not so dark in the back of the chopper, they would have noticed and questioned the smile on Raj's face. He was thinking about that middle finger welcome message on his servers. He would have paid a lot of money to be a fly on the wall when Brideaux discovered that.

Raj was thinking how nice it would be if his little joke caused Brideaux a heart attack that killed him. The thought that it would be good riddance of bad rubbish crossed his mind, but he did not think they would be so lucky. And after all, there were some scores to be settled with Brideaux first. He couldn't just check out like that. He might wish for that escape before they were finished with him, but it was not going to happen.

They had to agree there was not much else they could do now, other than get to the Rabbit Hole before the rest of their faces appeared on TV. A few minutes of silence followed while they were all contemplating their situation when Doug's voice came over their earphones, "Ah shit! Don't we have enough trouble already?"

"What is it? What now?" Almost all of them asked in unison.

"Oil pressure on the port engine just dropped. I will have to put her down and quick, before the engine cuts out."

"Oh, my God. Nothing is going our way lately," Daniel said.

Everyone went quiet as Doug started descending and landed in an isolated area about thirty miles west of Durango. Thanks to Mark and the five flashlights he'd acquired, Doug was able to inspect the engine and quickly find the problem. An oil leak in one of the hoses! They used duct tape from the toolbox and wrapped it around the hose.

Daniel commented "Keep in mind it may not hold. Let's cross our fingers and hope."

Doug added "Hey! It's not without good reason that duct tape is also known as '100 mile an hour tape' in the motorsports industry, where they use it all the time for emergencies. Even NASA has it as standard kit on their space missions since the Gemini days. Engineers and astronauts have used it in many emergencies. Remember the almost disastrous Apollo 13 mission?"

Daniel nodded. "Thanks, Doug. That makes me feel heaps better."

"Well it should. They reckon the duct tape they had

with them was one of the most important items that helped them fix their problems and save the lives of the three astronauts on board."

"Okay, I guess if duct tape is good enough for Formula One race cars and NASA's spacecraft, it's good enough for the Rossler Foundation's old helicopter," Daniel gibed.

They undertook a quick inspection of the rest of both port and starboard engines before they took off again.

As soon as they were at cruise level again, Doug spoke to them all. "Guys I don't want to borrow trouble, but I have to be honest with you. I don't trust this chopper to take us all the way. Those hoses are old and dilapidated. Any one or more of them can burst at any moment. We might not be so lucky to pick it up, as we just did, before an engine is damaged. We have to start thinking about alternatives if the worst case scenario happens."

"If one engine blows midflight can we still fly on the remaining one?" Mark asked, sounding a bit worried.

Doug explained, "We won't drop out of the sky, if that's what you are worried about. As long as one engine remains in operation we could still fly. However, there is a 'but' in that statement.

"Without boring you all with technical jargon, of which I only have a limited understanding in any event, these aircraft were built to handle situations like that. It boils down to the fact that the healthy engine, if we can call either of these engines healthy, will produce emergency power up to one hundred and thirty percent or more of its normal power to compensate for the inoperative engine.

"On the other hand, you have to understand that operating on hundred and thirty percent of normal power will put a lot of load on the operative engine, and obviously that won't be sustainable for an extended period of time. In other words, we won't be able to fly more than 50 or so miles on one engine. In fact, with our current load I would pretty much only be able to sit us down safely, and the bad news is that once we've landed there's no way I'll be able to get us back in the air again with this load."

Roy, more technically minded than any of the rest, said, "The way I see it, there are two things we can do to try and prevent engine failure. One is to slow down to a cruise speed that puts the least amount of stress on the engines but keeps us airborne. And the other is to make regular stops to inspect the engines and fix problems, to try and prevent a small problem from becoming bigger."

They all agreed, and Doug immediately reduced the cruise speed as suggested. He agreed to make a stop every forty minutes for preventative inspection of the engines.

Chapter Eight

TELL US WHAT IS GOING ON

The men were some miles northwest of Durango when Daniel had a lightbulb moment, which found quick approval from everyone.

"While looking at the map of where we are about now, I saw that we're approaching Montrose County. Raj and I have an old colleague and good friend from the New York Times living there on a farm in the mountains about 15 miles outside a little town called Nucla.

"Ah, of course. Owen Bell! That crazy guy who worked the astronomy beat and got married to the girl with the beautiful legs and short skirts! Can't remember her name," said Raj. "I heard he moved from New York to a small town."

"My memory is much better than yours Raj," Daniel smiled. "But then it could be because Sarah and I stayed in touch with them and visited each other regularly. Let me fill you all in. The girl with the short skirts' name is Alison, and she's a very nice person. I won't elaborate on the legs and skirts."

"So what are you saying, Daniel? Should we go there?" Doug inquired.

"No, not yet. I just think maybe we divert a little west of our current course and head for Nucla as a plan-B type of thing. It could be easier to reach Owen, who can help us if we have serious engine trouble."

"That makes sense. But are you absolutely one hundred percent sure you can trust this guy?" Mark asked.

"Yes unequivocally. He's a big prankster sometimes, but he's a good and loyal friend, and he'd do anything to help his friends, even if he had to do it with his hands tied behind his back. I also include Alison in that trust. What do you say Raj? You knew them when we worked at the Times."

"You know me. I am a little bit paranoid," Raj said.

Daniel interrupted him when everyone who knew Raj started laughing. "Only a little bit, Raj?"

That was the understatement of the year. Anyone who knew Raj for more than a few hours also knew he was the embodiment of paranoia.

"Okay, okay. Maybe a bit more than a little then," Raj conceded. "But what I was about to say was that I was not as close to Owen and Alison as you and Sarah were. But there is nothing that makes me nervous about them. In any event, we don't have much of a choice if we have a breakdown. Owen is the only person we know nearby, now."

They all agreed, and Doug made a change in course, which would take them closer to Nucla.

"Daniel, do you know where the farm is and what it looks like there? I mean can we land there and can we hide the chopper if necessary?" Mark asked.

"Yes, Sarah and I have been there a few times. I will get it on the map for you. From memory, the farm is about 300 acres. Owen and Alison call it their hideaway in the mountains. It is isolated, not much farming activities going on, most of the farm and surrounding area is covered in scrub oak. There's a beautiful house and a log cabin on the property, as well as a few sheds. Provided we can reach the farm, it will be the safest place for us that I can think of if we get more trouble in the next hour or so."

Max wanted to know how Owen ended up in this neck of the woods. Daniel explained that since he met Owen quite a few years ago, Owen had always talked about the day when he made his fortune. How he was going to buy himself a farm in the San Juan Mountains and sit there and enjoy life.

"He made his small fortune shortly after I left the Times, when he self-published a series of sci-fi novels about some weird interplanetary alien race and their adventures. His books got very popular and were on the Times' bestseller list, USA Today and a few others, for many months. By the time, he published his third novel in the series one of the big Hollywood filmmakers had noticed him and bought the movie rights for the series. He also got a very lucrative contract with a well-known publisher. He never mentioned to me how much he got for the film rights, but Alison slipped it to Sarah that he got about $15 million."

"Shit, I could get used to that sort of money with no effort very quickly," Max, said in a serious tone that had them all bursting into laughter.

"Okay guys, time for an engine check," Doug brought them back to reality.

Daniel's idea to head for Nucla turned out to be prophetical when they landed and checked the engines. They found new leaks, this time on both engines. Again, the duct tape came to the rescue. However, they knew they were fighting a losing battle. It was just a matter of time before one or both engines would be gone.

They got airborne again and headed for the farm, which was about 30 miles away. About 10 miles from the farm, all hell broke loose. Red lights flickered on the control panel and a deafening alarm sounded. Doug, cool as a cucumber, informed them that the port side engine was gone completely. They were on one engine now.

"We're ten miles away, but I am afraid we might not make it all the way. I'm going to keep up a gentle push and get as close as I can. I'm slowing down and will drop closer to the ground. Buckle up in case we have to make an emergency landing. It might be bumpy."

Before long, they saw the lights of the farmhouse, and Doug landed the chopper about two miles away. As they had the night before, they took cover and waited for an hour to see if anyone noticed them and were approaching their position.

When they were sure it was safe, Daniel decided that he and Mark would go to the farmhouse and make sure that Owen or Alison was there, and no one else, before they showed themselves.

The two of them sneaked up to the house as quietly as they could and were grateful that there were apparently no dogs. At least none made their presence known. They circled the house and saw Owen and Alison in front of the TV, but no one else.

Dogs started barking inside the house just as Daniel came up to the front door. An expression of shock was clearly visible on Owen's face when he opened the door and recognized his friend. "Daniel, what the hell is going on man? We just saw all this shit on the news! It can't be true. Tell me it's not true. Come into the house. "

"Hang on Owen, one thing at a time. This is my friend, Mark Bryant." Mark stepped out of the shadow and extended his hand to greet Owen.

Owen pushed them both into the house and closed the door. Alison, who'd heard the commotion, came to investigate. She was standing a few paces away from them by now, also pale-faced from shock.

"Let's get to the kitchen where we can make you some coffee and sit down, so you can tell us what is going on."

Chapter Nine

THE BLUE PILL OR THE RED PILL?

While Alison got busy with the espresso machine, Daniel got right to the point.

"Owen, Alison, please accept my sincerest apologies for barging in on you like this, but we are in desperate need of help. Our lives are at stake, and you were the closest people I knew of who could possibly help us."

Alison took a long look at him. He was as pale as milk with black circles around his eyes. If he'd slept at all in this past week, she'd be surprised.

Owen and Alison looked at each other, still in shock, and Daniel saw it.

"But before I continue any further let me first put your minds at ease. We didn't kill or kidnap anyone. A very powerful and influential man is framing us. The foulest and most wicked man I have ever met or heard of. A man with an agenda conceptualized in hell."

Owen held up his hand before Daniel could continue. "Daniel, I've never seen you so grave and tense, my friend. I never believed for a minute you'd killed or kidnaped anyone. Your word is good enough for me, and it has always been." Alison nodded her agreement with Owen.

"Thank you. I appreciate your trust very much. Let me continue a bit further. The reason for the situation we find ourselves in is that man and his allies are after the 10th and 8th Cycle libraries. There's nothing they won't do to get it into their possession. They've already killed one man, kidnaped another, and wounded two of my team members."

"That's awful, man. Where are the wounded people? Can we bring them in and help them?"

"Not yet Owen. Just bear with me. We'll get to that in due time. They're okay and taken care of for now."

"Did I hear you correctly? Did you say the 8th Cycle? I didn't know you'd discovered another cycle and its library," Owen said.

"Yes, we have. A few months ago, we discovered it not too far from your doorstep, in the Grand Canyon of all places. It's been there for more than 50,000 years, right under our noses."

"Wow! Shiiiit! Here in the Grand Canyon? It feels surreal," Owen exclaimed.

"You can say that again. These last few days have been a nightmare. Let me tell you, knowing what I know tonight, and if I could travel back in time, I'd go and 'un-discover' that place at a moment's notice. Even if it were the last thing I had to do on this earth, I'd do it." Daniel said and paused.

"Man you've got me worried now. Just keep going," Owen encouraged.

"Before I continue, I have to be entirely honest with you about the dangers you and Alison will face just by hearing what I have to say. You might think I'm melodramatic, but please hold your judgment for now. If I go on with the whole story, you will be in as much danger as we are now. The bad guys are out there looking for us right now, and I can assure you, they have the means to get to you."

Owen shrugged, and Alison put her arm through his. "Go on."

Daniel continued. "You have to prepare yourself for a visit from them or the police in the next 24 to 48 hours. Naturally, the less you know, the better for your safety, I'm sure you understand that. All you have to do if you decide to stop me now and don't hear the rest of the story is to tell them what you know. We were here, but we left again, and you don't know where we went. That will be the truth and will keep you out of trouble. "

Mark, who had been listening quietly to the conversation up until then said, "Owen, you do have another choice. You could pick up the phone and call the police now and let them know where we are. That would end it for you. You'd be safe."

Mark's comment immediately got Owen's nose out of joint. "Listen bud. I don't know you from Adam, but Daniel, Sarah, Alison and I go way back. They're our best friends. What you've suggested is an insult! I'm loyal to my friends, and that's it."

Mark realized his mistake and was quick to offer his apology, "I'm truly sorry Owen - and Alison. Please accept my apologies. I didn't intend to insult you. I just wanted to say you do have the option to stay safe from the consequences of having contact with us. I'm sorry."

"Apology accepted," Alison said.

Mark decided to leave all the talking to Daniel.

"Daniel there's no way on God's green earth that my best friend knocks on my door before the rooster crows, in apparent distress, and I send him away. That's not going to happen tonight, and it's not going to happen in the future. You need my help - you have my help. Alison?"

"Yes, Owen, we stand by our friends," Alison replied.

Daniel started talking again. "You don't know how much your loyalty and friendship means to us right now. But I just want to make sure you understand that if I let you in on the rest of the story, you can't 'un-ring' that bell. No pun intended, Owen. That means the two of you will become partners in our troubles, which is something I wish I could avoid, always. Especially where my friends are concerned."

At this point, Daniel paused and looked at each of them in turn to make sure they understood what he just said. Satisfied they did, he continued with a bit of a smile on his face, "Okay so what is it? The blue pill or the red pill?

They smiled as Daniel continued with a verbatim quote from that famous science fiction movie from the late nineties 'The Matrix', "You take the blue pill, the story ends. You wake up in your bed and believe whatever you want to believe. You take the red pill, you stay in Wonderland, and I show you how deep the rabbit hole goes. Remember: all I'm offering is the truth. Nothing more."

"It's the red pill my friend - we already told you so." Owen voiced his support, while Alison nodded her head in agreement.

"Thank you again. You're genuine friends. Let me fill you in, then. But I warn you - put on your seat belts. It's going to be a bumpy ride." Daniel started his hour-long chronicle of the events that brought him to their doorstep that night.

Nearing the end of his narrative, Daniel gave the events of the past few weeks in more detail. He explained how, with the help of his most trusted Foundation employees, he had come to understand the nature of the threat he was about to reveal. At last, Daniel paused a bit, took a deep breath, and then said, "Up until the point when I received that telephone call on the satellite phone two nights ago, we were all unaware of what was going on right under our noses. Now comes the horror part of this movie. You still sure you want to hear the rest?"

"We have to hear it, all of it," Owen said. Alison took in the grim expression on his face and nodded in agreement.

"Were it not for Salome's attentiveness and ingenuity with her Spiderweb, we would still be none the wiser," Daniel continued as requested. He explained how Salome discovered how some the richest of the rich had been working and operating in the shadows to get and keep control of virtually each and every industry in the world. How they never bought outright control, but the shareholding between them gave them power, and how they collaborated in secret to control the markets to their advantage.

Owen was a bit skeptical. "You mean to say in this day and age with all the government surveillance, and spying on citizens going on, there's a group of people that could escape it all?"

"Owen, I think what you don't get is that they're in control of each and every communication method you can think of. They control the Internet search engines, they control all social media, and they control all satellite, wireless, mobile and landline communications. They are the Internet and communications service providers for our planet. They decide what information they let through to the government spy agencies, not the other way round.

"That isn't all. Let me name just a few more industries, other than communications and media, which they also control - pharmaceutical, agriculture, banking, petroleum, and I can continue. What's more, as you'll soon find out, politicians live in the pockets of these people. The ones who don't eat from their hands are few. These guys can control the outcome of elections, which they definitely do. And for them to do that is as easy as organizing a beer bash in a brewery."

Hearing this made Owen's jaw drop in bewilderment. "That means they control the world!"

Daniel replied, "Almost, but here comes the horror part now. They are not happy to have only the financial control. No they want to also govern the world politically – they wish to be the world's *only* government. They believe they will create a fair, just, and prosperous worldwide society for all of us. Utopia – no poverty, no corruption, and long and happy lives for all of us. Up until now, their insurmountable obstacle was the expected resistance by security forces of any country they might try to overthrow. Up until now, they didn't have the necessary military capability to overcome such resistance."

Alison comprehended that Daniel had just said something crucial, "Daniel you make it sound as if they now have that military capability? How and when did that happen? And why didn't we hear anything about it?"

Owen got it a few seconds before her, "The Beast! They've got it don't they?"

"Yes my friend, I'm afraid so," Daniel said in a slow, soft voice.

"Oh my God!" Alison exclaimed as her hand flew to her mouth.

Daniel continued, "I take it that you're beginning to see what's at stake here? I am truly sorry to put you through this, but I have the same idea about loyalty to my friends as you two have, and I promised you the truth."

Owen, still digesting the information, stopped Daniel with another question, "So why would he let you and the rest of your men stay alive, leaving you all behind in the canyon, and then change his mind and now want to get you again?"

Daniel replied, "The 10th and 8th Cycle Libraries, as I said in the beginning. When he left us, he told us he had already ordered his people to go and pick up the libraries at the Foundation offices. Once he had those in his hands, we wouldn't pose any threat to him. What he didn't know was that Sarah and Salome would have activated Enigma immediately after that phone call to us. That means they would have evacuated the Rossler Foundation premises, taking with them those libraries and everything of value."

Owen began to nod as Daniel finished his thought.

"He made a big mistake. He realized he was ripped a new one when his people arrived at the Foundation and found nothing. That's why he's looking for us now. He wants to use us as bait to lure Sarah and the rest out of hiding and hand him the libraries in exchange for us. At least, that's our take on his sudden urge to get hold of us."

"I think I am starting to get the picture now," Owen said. "But what's so important to him in those libraries?"

"Well Owen, the 8th Cycle library contains all the information about how they created their society and the details of the technology that they used to accomplish that. We haven't translated all of it yet, by any means. There could very well be, and we believe there is, a lot more information in there that can help us understand their technologies better and perhaps find a way to neutralize it. And that's only half of the picture."

Owen interrupted him again, "There's more?"

"Yes, there is." Daniel continued, "Remember that we found the reference to the 8th Cycle in the 10th Cycle Library. We haven't delved into everything the 10th Cyclers knew about the 8th Cycle. In fact, we haven't even scratched the surface of all the information contained in it. For all we know, and again we believe this is the case, there could very well be a solution to our problems locked up inside of it."

"I can see why he'd be a very pissed off man by now," commented Owen.

"That's certainly true," Daniel said. "He isn't a man that's used to opposition. He's used to having things his way always, and I can assure you from firsthand experience he will kill anyone that gets in his way."

"We believe you, Daniel," Alison said.

Daniel continued, "A few more blows below the belt. With the unearthing of Brideaux's plan, Salome also discovered that Brideaux and his cronies have been buying up pathology labs like crazy for the last few months. They now have almost worldwide control of that as well."

"For what reason?" Owen interrupted.

"To get the DNA of every human on earth. She got confirmation of that and also that they have hacked into government records and got hold of the DNA sequences of law enforcement and military personnel, as well as political leaders and high-ranking government officials. We're convinced they are about to, or have already produced a nanobot that could kill or incapacitate people based on their DNA."

"And you believe that kind of technology is possible?" Owen inquired, a bit skeptically.

"Not only possible, it's already existed for some years

now. We have experience of that from the Sword of Cyrus crisis," Daniel replied. "Did you know that the nanospores of enough anthrax to wipe out the entire world population could be stored in a container the size of a briefcase?"

"Oh shit, what a mess!" Owen whispered with his head in his hands.

Daniel delivered one more shock, "Now maybe not the last low blow, but it is certainly going to be extremely painful. Salome's digging also uncovered that - hold your breath for this one - our beloved president is one of the seven Brideaux accomplices."

"Oh my God, we are screwed. The world is fucked!" shouted Owen.

"Daniel, do you have any idea how long it will take before they're able to put this satanic plan of theirs into action?" Alison wanted to know.

"Unfortunately no, we've only just now come to the realization that we haven't seen the tip of the iceberg of their resolve and capabilities. We have no idea what they've prepared in advance of seizing the Beast from us. We're totally in the dark as to where, when and how they're planning to initiate action. It could be months or weeks, but it could also be sooner than that. They certainly have the resources to make it happen. Of that much, I'm certain."

Chapter Ten

DON'T UNDERESTIMATE THEM

As Daniel and the others arrived at Owen and Alison's place, four sinister looking men knocked on Patrick Roland's door at his house in Farmington, one hundred and twenty miles south of Owens farm near Ridgway.

Patrick immediately sensed the men were trouble and tried to protect his friends, whom he also realized by now hadn't been entirely honest with him. When Jason and his men showed him their guns, he decided to tell them what he knew. He related the events of the previous day, the time Doug and Mark arrived, the mechanical problems, the efforts to fix it and the time they left.

Unbeknownst to him, his answers "confirmed" to Jason that he wasn't lying because it upheld what they'd heard in Flagstaff before - the escapees were heading for Boulder, and there were only the two of them. Although this didn't explain what happened to the Rosslerites, Jason figured that they must have been holed up somewhere while Doug and Mark did the fixing and refueling.

Even though Jason didn't look forward to another phone

call with Brideaux, he knew it had to be done. It was time to give Brideaux an update. He figured out how far that chopper could have been flying with six people and would suggest to Brideaux to start looking within a four hundred mile radius from Farmington. Another conversation littered with insults, abuse, screaming and profanity followed, as soon as Brideaux answered the phone.

"Mr. Brideaux, I'm pretty sure they're on their way to Boulder. I have that confirmed by two independent sources."

"Listen Jason, don't underestimate those guys for one second! Any one of them has more brains in their fuckin' toenail than the four of you have combined in your skulls! I want you to turn every stone, bush, and tree for four hundred miles around Farmington in the next two days. You'd better get back on their track. Don't make me come out there to do your fuckin' job."

"Yes, sir. I am onto it right away. I will get them."

"Jason and for fuck's sake, dress up appropriately, and get the police and every law enforcement agency in that area onto it as well. I'll send messages through their top echelons to expect you. So make sure you don't look like fuckin' hillbillies when you arrive to ask for their help."

"Yes, sir."

"You now know to look for a helicopter and you also know that two of them have bullet wounds I gave them, the younger Rossler in his left hand and James through his lower right leg. Now get your finger out of you fuckin' ass and find them. I have to have them in my custody in the next seven days. If you can't do it, say so now, so I can get rid of you and put someone competent on the job."

"I will have them before that time sir."

When the phone went dead, Jason was more stressed

and depressed than before. How the hell was he going to fine-comb more than 500,000 square miles in two days with four people? Even with the help of all the police in that area, it would take weeks. What the hell was with this seven days all of a sudden?

Jason and his crew decided first to search in a straight line from Farmington to Boulder, as that is where they 'knew' the chopper was heading.

They also knew that the helicopter could have had some engine trouble and therefore immediately arranged for air searches to look for the chopper as well as setup of roadblocks, in case the Rosslerites were in cars or on foot.

They followed Brideaux's instructions, dressed up in their FBI disguises and visited police stations demanding their help, which they got without a single complaint or argument. In fact, everyone was expecting them by the time they called or arrived in person.

A long silence of shock and doubt descended upon Alison and Owen when Daniel reached the end of his clarification.

Owen looked at Daniel and Mark in turn and said, "What do we do first? Say the word and we'll do it."

Daniel asked for the rest of the men to be brought into the house. After that, the most important of all was to move that chopper out of sight before dawn.

Owen went with Daniel and Mark to collect the rest of the team and brought them to the house, where Alison was preparing a lot more coffee, sandwiches, and snacks. They all arrived back, and while they were devouring the food and coffee, they decided how they were going to hide the chopper.

Owen had a tractor and a 4x4 truck that they could use to tow the chopper into one of the barns. They all agreed that was the best temporary solution, until they could fix it or make another plan. Whatever they did, it would have to be done within the next 24 hours, as that was the time they thought they might have before the police or Brideaux's people turned up there. Now Daniel understood Raj's frame of mind, since he was now paranoid that Brideaux had the capability to read his mind and find him anywhere he went.

While Roy and JR stayed behind with Alison, the rest of them went and towed the helicopter into the barn, stacked bales of hay around it to hide it completely, and also covered all the barn windows with bales of hay before locking the door. Early the next morning Owen would get on his quad bike and round up his cattle to herd them over all the tracks created by the chopper and towing vehicles.

When they were satisfied they had done all they could, Owen walked them to the log cabin about a mile away from the main house. It was well hidden amongst the trees and bushes, not at all visible from the main house. Owen explained that he sometimes used the cabin when he wanted to be alone to write. There was no electricity, but there were enough lamps and candles.

Max checked the wounded, changed dressings, and gave them another dose of antibiotics and anti-inflammatories as they all found a place to sleep.

The lack of sleep, stress, and the grim events that had started more than thirty hours before took its toll on all of them as they fell asleep. None of them woke up until about midday.

Chapter Eleven

JUST CUT A HOLE IN THE WALL

Soon after they were back on the road, Ben asked Sarah if she by chance also had some information about the Rabbit Hole's layout stored on her tablet.

"Yes, I have quite a lot on there. It's in a folder called 'RH Plans and Images', I think."

Ben found the folder and looked at the pictures and drawings, commenting that he could see there was plenty of space, enough potable water sources for them, and even some heated pools inside the caves where they could swim and relax. It was the perfect place - so remote as to be unknown, yet with sufficient space for the group and many more if necessary to live there for many years. They'd soon be out of sight, and after a few years, hopefully out of mind.

Ben said that from what he could see so far, once they got there, he could put heads together with anyone else that had the skills or the inclination for that sort of thing and come up with plans to change the place into a comfortable living space for all.

"That's good news," Sarah replied. "You know the idea

of living underground usually triggers thoughts of dark, damp, and cramped spaces, and I suspect our group will not be any different. So making the place less intimidating would help a lot."

"Whoever was responsible for these photos and drawings did an excellent job," Ben remarked.

"That honor belongs to Robert and Raj. They produced that after their exploration trip to the Rabbit Hole quite a few months ago. You remember them?"

"Yes, I do. I've met Raj a few times. Robert only once, though, at JR and Rebecca's wedding. He and JR are good friends I believe?"

Sarah smiled "Yes the two of them are like the biblical David and Jonathan. The unbiblical part is the shenanigans they can sometimes get up to, given the slightest opportunity."

Ben also smiled, "That's JR for you. He's been a mischief-maker from his first day."

Sarah remembered an interesting conversation she and Daniel had with Robert and said to Ben, "You should also have a look at that sub-folder in there about a place called 'Coober Pedy.' Not sure, about the correct pronunciation, but it's all about a modern underground city in Australia that Robert told us about. Apparently he's been out there a few times."

"Weird name isn't it?" Ben replied, He quickly found the folder Sarah referred to.

She laughed, "Yes it is. According to Robert it has its origins in the Aborigine language and means, 'the white man's hole.'"

She continued to give Ben more details about the conversation they had when Robert and Raj returned from their trip to the cave in Montana. He'd told them that with

Roy's laser tools at their disposal, they could turn that Rabbit Hole into America's Coober Pedy.

She remembered how Robert explained with pride about the ingenuity of his countrymen and how the Australians had turned an old opal mine in the Outback into an underground town. It was a place where more than nine people carved out very comfortable homes, and in fact an entire town, complete with underground hotels, restaurants, bars, an underground church, and a golf course. All in the middle of a harsh desert.

She chuckled when she told him how Daniel was quick to point out to Robert that he, of all people, should know better. The Australians were not the first to come up with such a plan. The idea of cutting residences in rocks and underground belonged at least to the 8th Cycle people and after them many others all over the world who have, for ages before his countrymen, been digging into rocks to create living spaces for themselves.

Robert told them that the 'building' work was done by tunneling machines. In their case, in the Rabbit Hole, it could be accomplished with Roy's laser tools. Need another shelf or walk in closet? Another room? Just cut a hole in the wall.

One of the interesting facts she remembered from the time when she had a quick glance through the information Robert provided, was the inhabitants and visitors reporting that the climate and humidity underground were excellent, irrespective of the outside temperature.

"Robert was quite diligent in assembling and collating all the information he could get his hands on and from his recollections when he visited the place. He gave it to Raj to store on the servers. There could be a lot more information about how they did it that might be of interest to you and the 'public works department,'" Sarah said.

Shortly after Owen gave the men a place to hide, about eight hundred-some-odd miles to the north, Sarah and Ben finally arrived at the Rabbit Hole, to the relief of everyone already there. Little Nicholas, ecstatic to see his mom again, had his arms around her neck, hugging and kissing her.

Sarah immediately noticed that Daniel and the others weren't there. "They haven't arrived yet?"

Salome shook her head, and Sarah's heart dropped to the floor, while Ben suddenly looked older. "We have no news about them either."

Sarah knew she couldn't dwell on that disappointment too much - she had to take the lead and get the people settled in as quickly and as efficiently as possible. As soon as they'd said all the hellos, she called together Luke, Sinclair, Salome, Ben, Ryan, and Rebecca. She'd decided they would be her core group for now. Little Nicholas was still clinging to her and would not let go.

As soon as they were all assembled, she spoke. "Ben and I have been making notes along the way, as, no doubt, have you. I guess everyone agrees that security comes first?"

They all nodded their heads in agreement.

"Salome and Luke, this is your beat. What have you got in place already, and what else is there to do for now?"

Salome explained that they'd already gathered everyone together and instructed them on the basics. Those were don't leave the caves under any circumstances, no fires, and they'd double-checked again that no one had a cellphone. All computers, laptops, tablets and anything that could produce a wireless signal had been handed over to Stuart Harding, Raj's sidekick. He removed, uninstalled, or disabled any wireless capabilities before he handed them back to the owners.

"Sarah, everyone is still a bit shell-shocked, as can be expected, but they all seem to understand our perilous situation and have been cooperating very well," Luke explained.

"Thanks Salome, Luke and everyone else. I couldn't wish for a better group of people to be at my side during the days, weeks, and maybe even years ahead.

"My next biggest concern, and I guess everyone else's, is the whereabouts and safety of our husbands."

Salome brought some painful reality when she said, "Sarah, I share your concern for our men. Roy is among them, of course. There's just no way of knowing their fate until they walk into the Rabbit Hole safe and sound. All we can do is keep our hopes up, maybe cross our fingers, and of course, pray."

Sarah shook her head and shoulders in a motion to get rid of the feeling of misery threatening to take control of her before she continued. "If everyone agrees there's nothing else that can't wait 'til tomorrow, I must check on everyone else here, let them know that Ben and I have arrived, and make sure they're all ok."

Before they all left for their places, Sarah asked them all to go around to everyone in the cave and ask them to write up a résumé of sorts that very night. "We need to know about everyone's skills, experience, hobbies, and interests."

Sarah anticipated they'd need the information when they started their planning session the next day.

Chapter Twelve

DON'T SHOOT!

While the men in the cabin were more or less in a state of unconsciousness within half an hour after their arrival, Owen and Alison were on the edge of panic and despair. The full impact of the dark reality facing them became apparent while they were still busy assimilating what they'd heard from Daniel and the others throughout the night.

"Owen I know we're in this now up to the hilt, but I have no idea where to begin and what to think," Alison said as she moved into the comforting arms of her man.

"Ali I'm as worried as you are. The one thing I do know is that we have to help them. My mind has been racing at a thousand miles an hour, but I don't have an answer yet. I think for now we start by hiding and feeding them and keeping them out of the claws of that psychopath. They're very intelligent guys. Once they're rested, we'll put all our heads together. We'll be able to work something out, I'm sure."

Although Owen's answer did not provide a solution, Alison found some comfort in it.

Later in the morning, Owen went over to the cabin to check on their guests but found them all fast asleep. He thought it best not to wake them. These guys had been barefoot through hell already, and there was no end in sight yet.

At about eleven o'clock, Owen and Alison got the fright of their lives when they saw a police car coming up the roadway to their house from about a mile and a half away. Was this just coincidence? Could it just be the police out on a normal patrol and dropping in to say hello? That was something they occasionally did. Or, were they out looking for their friends? That helicopter in the barn!

"Let's try and remain as calm and friendly as humanly possible," Owen said as he got over the effects of the initial adrenaline. "If they ask, yes, we saw the news, and yes, we know Daniel and Raj and their families. We should stick to the truth about everything except last night. Remember we haven't seen them or had any contact with them for months. We're shocked by the news. Those are our friends, and we can't believe what we've seen on the news."

Alison nodded her agreement and understanding.

When the police car stopped in front of the house, Owen was already waiting for them on the front porch. He walked down to welcome them and recognized both of them. They were from the Montrose County Sheriff's office.

The eternal joker, he stuck both hands in the air and shouted, "Don't shoot! I didn't do it! I am not guilty!"

This little act had the desired effect on the two officers as they played along, "Okay, put your hands behind your back, turn around, and spread your legs. You have the right to remain silent … " was as far as they got before they both exploded into laughter at the antics of one of their town's famous inhabitants.

"Come on in," Owen invited them. "Alison already started the espresso machine, and she's been looking for someone to share some of her home baked cookies for days now."

Owen dropped his usually loud voice to a whisper behind his hand. "To tell you the truth, you'll do me a big favor if you eat all of it. The stuff has been giving me heartburn lately, but I don't have the courage to tell her."

Montrose County had a few things to be proud of– the wild and beautiful Black Canyon of Gunnison National Park, Gunnison Gorge National Recreation and wilderness areas, Uncompaghre National Forest lands, and some thought the best sweet corn in the world was grown in the little town of Olathe.

The tiny Paradox Valley town of Nucla boasted a fiercely independent population, a gun ordinance that required the head of every household to own one 'for general safety', and, in the last few years, the famous writer of a very popular science fiction TV series had taken up residence in their midst. The police officers were not going to let up on the chance to have a coffee with their town's world famous writer.

Alison saw and heard what Owen was up to, and she rushed to get the espresso machine ready and got the home baked cookies out on the table. By the time the men walked into the house, they were all in a jovial mood.

Soon after they'd settled, Officer James cleared his throat and said, "We've been sent out this way to ask you a few questions."

Owen knew what was coming and was ready for it with another gag, "I told you I didn't do it."

James smiled, but it was obvious to Owen he wanted to be serious, "I take it you've seen the news about the people of the Rossler Foundation? We were told that you know some of them and that you could perhaps help us find them. Can you tell us about your friendship with them?"

Owen realized the time for joking was over, and he had to play this very well or it would raise suspicion, putting all of them in grave danger.

He ran a hand over his face, expressing his distress at the news "Yes, we saw the news, and let me tell you, we're shocked beyond belief. You're right; both of us have known Daniel and Sarah Rossler, as well as Rajan Sankaran and his wife Sushma for many years now. Alison, Daniel, Raj, and I worked together at the New York Times. We met their wives when they were still dating, and we have been guests at both their weddings. We met Daniel's brother JR and his wife Rebecca at their wedding a few years ago, but we don't know any of the other people mentioned on the news."

Owen's explanation immediately put the officers at ease as it correlated with the information they were given by the sheriff of Montrose County before they'd been dispatched.

Owen continued, "Over the years, since we all left the Times, we only stayed in touch with Daniel and Sarah. We've visited each other a few times."

The officers seemed to be more at ease as Owen, with Alison joining in, continued to give them more information stacking up with the information they'd been given.

"When was the last time you had contact with them?" James asked.

Owen looked questioningly at Alison, "What would you say Ali? Maybe three months or so ago, when we stayed at their place in Boulder for a couple of days on the way to your parents?"

"Yes that would be right," Alison confirmed.

James said, "Oh, one more thing. Will you please contact us immediately if you hear anything from them or if you can think of any place where they could be hiding?"

"You can bet on that," Owen replied.

The two police officers got up. "Thank you very much for your honesty and hospitality. We have a few more stops on our way back to the station, so we better get going again. Thank you for the coffee and the cookies. We enjoyed them."

Owen walked them to their car while fishing for more information. "You know Alison and I can't make head nor tail of this whole thing. It's just mindboggling to think you know people so well and for so long, and then all of a sudden their faces appear on the news accused of such horrendous crimes. Do you guys perhaps have more information than what we saw and heard in the media?"

"I wish we did. Your shock and disappointment is very understandable, but unfortunately we know no more than you do," James replied. "There's an enormous manhunt on the way at the moment. Air and land searches, roadblocks, and that sort of thing. I'm sure they'll be apprehended soon."

The two happy and honored police officers waved as they drove away from a very relieved couple whose adrenaline levels had been at absolute peak for the past hour or so.

When the deputies were gone, Owen and Alison surmised that their playact had the desired effect to buy themselves and their friends desperately needed time. The officers would in all probability not return very soon, unless they had more information that could lead them back here – such as someone who'd heard the chopper last night.

They were still talking about this when they heard the sound of a low-flying small airplane approaching from the south. They walked out onto the front porch and watched as the plane flew overhead. This could very well have been a spotter plane looking for the chopper, or it could have been coincidence, but they were not prepared to make any assumptions.

About an hour later, they heard the unmistakable sound of a helicopter approaching. Again, they walked out onto the porch and watched as the helicopter flew over and turned in the direction of Naturita just five miles to the southwest. Was this a coincidence? Not likely. It was time to wake Daniel and his men and alert them.

Owen walked over to the cabin and woke all of them. "Wakey-wakey guys!" Owen shouted as he entered the cabin. "We have some very urgent shit to deal with."

They were all up and sitting around him when Owen described to them the police visit and the sudden air traffic congestion over his farm in the last hour or so.

Daniel answered immediately, "I don't believe in coincidence, they're out looking for us and the chopper. We have to try and see if we can make that thing fly again or figure out how to get rid of it. I suggest we leave JR and Roy here with Max, get over to that barn of yours, and have a look at the chopper. Any other ideas?"

Raj had a better idea, "I think we need to get Roy over there as well. He and Doug are the best and if may I say so, the only mechanical minds we have on our team."

Owen chipped in his two cents, "Hey! Out here on the farm the past few years I've learned my way around a tractor. A helicopter can't be that different can it?"

"Good, in that case, let's all go," Daniel agreed with a wry smile.

They asked Alison to keep a look out from the house, where an observer had an unobstructed view for a few miles, including the access road leading to the house. She would let Owen know by cell phone to come and have coffee or something to eat the moment she spotted anything untoward.

They were all assembled around the helicopter in the barn thirty minutes later. Doug opened up the covers to the port engine and the mechanically minded got busy with their diagnostics.

Chapter Thirteen

WE ARE NOT THE FIRST

At the Rabbit Hole, the new arrivals had a much better day than the seven on the outside hiding from Brideaux, eight hundred miles to the south.

The group, numbering fifty-six in total, was up early, had eaten their breakfast and then attended the first 'town hall' meeting. The fanciful title was apt as they held it in the big room next to the hot pools.

Sarah, well aware of her own feelings and emotions brought on by the unfamiliar situation and surroundings, knew that everyone in the caves was probably having the same experience as she had. It was important to immediately put their minds at ease.

She gave them all a quick but encouraging overview of the prospects of cave dwelling. "I understand that our surroundings here in these caves could be very intimidating. However, it might be good to remember that we are not the first to do it. Over thousands of years, many people have done the same as we are doing now. It has been part of human history, especially during troubled times, to take up sanctuary in caves. Think of the people escaping the Romans, who lived in the Qumran caves where the Dead Sea Scrolls were discovered.

"In more recent times and closer to home, slaves living in the southern states and escaping from their masters took refuge in the Caves of St. Louis. They served as a hiding place along the Underground Railroad."

By now, Sarah had the undivided attention of everyone as she continued, "In the Philippines, indigenous people called the Tasaday have been living in caves for thousands of years and are still living there today. In Spain, near Granada, there are today nearly 3,000 people living in caves. They have dwellings ranging from a single room up to 200 rooms. They even have churches, schools, and stores in those caves. In China, it is estimated that about 30 million people prefer to live in cave homes called 'yaodongs' which they found to be superior to conventional homes."

In her element as a former professor, she ended by recounting the conversation she and Ben had the day before about the Australian town of Coober Pedy. The pictures on her tablet, when she showed and talked about them, seemed to excite everyone and lift their spirits.

This introduction had the impact she hoped for. It was apparent they were all excited and could see the possibilities of turning their current bleak surroundings into a happy place. Sarah then asked them all to start unpacking their belongings and begin to make their new home as comfortable as they could for now. She and her core group, which they called 'The Steering Committee' were going to work out priorities and get projects going right away.

Getting better lighting in place before the end of the day would get top priority. Until that could be accomplished, and dangerous areas properly barricaded and marked, everyone should keep an eye on the children and each other. She thanked them all for responding to her request to write down their skills, experience, and interests, saying it was going to help a lot in the days to come.

Sarah's dad, Ryan, who was an electronics engineer, got the first project - to make sure the caves were lit better by the end of the day. They quickly looked through the skills lists and found one qualified electrician, husband of one of Sinclair's translators, and an amateur electronics enthusiast.

Ryan left to get hold of his new team members and kick off the project while the rest of them continued with the meeting.

Ryan and his helpers had all of Roy's nanobattery and lighting technology at their disposal, which made things very easy. This included, among others, the light that was discovered during the first Antarctica expedition in the Paradise Canyon, which Roy had since reverse-engineered. Within a few hours, to the relief of the adults and delight of the few children, they had lights going throughout all of the occupied areas and had barricaded the rest. They would over time improve the system, but they were all happy that what they had was good enough for the foreseeable future.

By the time Ryan returned to report that phase one of 'Project Let There Be Light' was completed, the Steering Committee had already called Stuart Harding, Raj's sidekick, in. They gave him the names of two willing helpers and instructed him to secure the servers and computers to make sure no water, dust or anything that could cause damage got near them. They also planned how they could set up a proper server room and the internal network, so that access to the libraries they had stored on the file servers would be available to everyone. Ben and his son Aaron, who were assigned to take care of construction, would help them with that once plans were presented and were approved.

Ben and Aaron were also tasked to establish the Rabbit Hole's 'Department of Public Works.' They would first study the information produced by Raj and Robert during their expedition to see how they could best provide comfortable and secure living space for everyone. They already knew from the information supplied that the cave system was several miles in both length and width and that there were levels both above and below the main entry level. They needed to map out the entire cave system so that not only would everyone know where the entrances and dangerous places were, but also what other features and facilities the caves had to offer.

When they got to the discussion about food production, Sarah found Helen Bryant's skills list, "Hey, everyone look at this!" she exclaimed. "This is Helen Bryant. Not only is she the mother of two children and wife of Mark, the guy who led the rescue team to get our men back, she is also a horticulturist, who until a few days ago worked for The Urban Forestry and Horticulture section of the Parks and Recreation Department in Boulder."

"Now there is someone I am sure my Martha and a few others would like to team up with," Sinclair O Reilly remarked. "Shall I go and call the two of them?"

"Yes, thank you, Sinclair," Sarah replied.

A few minutes later Helen and Martha O'Reilly, who was a keen amateur gardener, arrived and were asked to set up the 'Gardeners of Gallatin Society' amongst the large number of those who indicated that they either had experience or interest in gardening and food growing. Their first task was to find a suitable place or places with the right temperature and microclimate to set up their indoor farm.

They'd ask Ben and Aaron, or any of the other handymen in the roster to help them as required.

The GGS swung into action right away. They quickly grew to be the most numerous group, which included Emma, Sally, and Bess, Sarah's mother, aunt and grandmother-in-law respectively, amongst at least seven others. To Sarah's big surprise and relief, Sushma, Raj's wife was among them. The two of them were good friends, but she never knew or would have guessed that her friend Sushma, who was a very popular glossy magazine model, would ever be interested in gardening. In fact, to be honest, prior to this, Sushma's background had Sara a bit concerned that she might find it harder than most of them to adapt to this new life. Now all she had to do was to talk to her relatives to make sure they took Sushma under their wings.

Next, they got to health and hygiene, the domain of Rebecca, an experienced and practicing medical physician and Sarah's sister-in-law, JR's wife. Roxanne MacArthur was a qualified and experienced physiotherapist and Cyndi, Rebecca's older sister who held a Doctor of Nursing Practice degree, was assigned to her Medical Center. Rebecca went and fetched the two of them.

Roxanne was married to John 'Doug' MacArthur and had years of experience, including working at a rehabilitation center for wounded soldiers during the Afghan and Iraq wars. They had three children, aged eight to twelve. She'd met her husband at the rehabilitation center when he was wounded in Afghanistan. What she didn't tell them, which they only discovered later, was that he'd sustained a crippling back injury during a skirmish in the war in Afghanistan when he had to evacuate a section of Marines under heavy enemy fire.

The wound in his back caused a lot of damage to his

spine and nerves. Paralyzed from the waist down, he'd been in rehab for almost a year. He'd had to learn how to walk again, which he'd accomplished due in large part to the unyielding encouragement and help of the physiotherapist, Roxanne. After being declared unfit for further military duty, he and Mark Bryant had established their M&J Security Company in Boulder.

Rebecca and her team were to set up a clinic and sterile area with consulting rooms, again calling on Ben and Aaron to help with any construction needs they might have. Furthermore, they would have to create a health and hygiene plan for the entire community and educate everyone about it. They were also given the assignment of making sure the food and water were tested regularly, and that the toilet and bathing areas would not cause health risks.

Rebecca also suggested that they would like to work out a first aid course and train everyone to be able to handle emergencies. She pointed out that until they could work out when and how people were allowed to go outside the caves, they would all have to be diligent about taking Vitamin D supplements to compensate for the lack of sunshine. During the Enigma planning and preparations, Rebecca had ensured that every family knew of the importance of Vitamin D and had brought a large supply of it with them.

Finally, Rebecca mentioned that she and Salome, their head of security, had already had a few discussions about what they could expect on the psychological front from the group. Salome also had a Master's Degree in Psychology and was well versed in human and group psychology.

On this topic, Salome pointed out that psychological issues were to be expected. It was part of human nature to react to new and stressful situations. Their current situation was one of the most severe imaginable, comparable if not worse, to the loss of a loved one by death. They agreed to work out a plan to bring back to the steering committee that could help solve the problems they were sure to face relatively soon.

At the conclusion of the medical project planning session, it was late afternoon, and they decided to call it the day.

Chapter Fourteen

GET RID OF IT

Doug, Owen, and Roy, as far as he was capable of moving without moaning from the pain in his leg, inspected both engines. It took them about three hours to conclude that there was no way they were going to resuscitate the dead engine with their limited skills and knowledge. This left them with one operating engine and the dilemma that their means of getting to the Rabbit Hole had been lost when that engine gave in last night. Although the chopper was instrumental in keeping them out of reach of Brideaux up until now, it was now an enormous and cumbersome millstone around their necks.

They couldn't leave it in the shed. It was vital they find a way to get rid of it quickly before someone, more diligent than the deputies from earlier today, turned up and decided to look around the farm. They debated their options. Maybe Doug could fly it out into a remote canyon, dump it there, and Owen could pick him up by car and bring him back. The problem was that they weren't sure if it would be possible to get the chopper airborne even with just Doug in it. Also, there was the danger of the remaining engine seizing up in flight. It was looking, by their assessment, somewhat unhealthy. Apart from the danger it posed to Doug, the location at the time might not be safe and could leave him out in an open space where he and it would be quickly discovered.

"Is there not perhaps a lake or dam nearby deep enough where we can dump it?" inquired Daniel.

"That might just work!" exclaimed Owen. "There's a deep ravine a few miles from here, a very isolated spot behind that ridge north of the main house. It is on private and unoccupied property. The ravine is wide enough for the chopper to descend without the blades touching the rock walls and at the bottom is a pool of water maybe twenty feet deep. If we can get it down there, no one will ever find it."

"Doug what do you think? You're the one risking getting this thing up in the air and over there?" asked Daniel.

"I can't see any other options. I reckon I can lift it. We'll just have to check and double check the remaining engine and fix anything that looks like it could be broken or leaking. A few miles shouldn't be a problem and certainly it's better to conceal it under water than leave it in the open, even in a remote area."

They got busy with the engine and did not spare the duct tape in the process. By the time twilight faded to night, they were done and ready for their mission.

About eight o'clock they were satisfied it was dark enough to get going. Doug got the chopper in the air without too much effort and gave the thumbs up as he turned the nose towards the ravine and kept it a few feet above the sparse treetops. He maneuvered very carefully and descended right into the middle of the pool of water. A few feet above the surface he cut the engine and when the body started to sink below the water, he got out and swam to the side where Daniel, Mark, and Owen were waiting for him. As they watched the chopper disappear under the water and with it, their hope of getting to the Rabbit Hole fast, they 'high-fived' and turned back to the house.

Doug noted, "At least one of our plans worked out as we expected."

They all groaned as Daniel remarked with gallows humor, "Well Doug, I guess we will all have to thank you for helping us find our feet. The only thing we have to figure out now is which would be the best route for our eight hundred mile hike home."

"Eight hundred miles to home?" Owen asked with surprise in his voice. "Where is home, Daniel? Or are you not ready to tell me yet?"

"No, I think the time for that has come," Daniel replied. He told Owen where they were heading.

Back at the house, Alison alerted them to more news about the manhunt on the TV, which she'd recorded for them.

They all gathered in the family room in front of the TV with the curtains drawn and the dogs outside the house to warn them of anyone approaching. They watched in growing apprehension as they saw not only their names and pictures, but also those of Mark Bryant and John MacArthur as well as their families and children. It was reported that the investigators became aware of the involvement of the two ex-Marines when they discovered the purchase of the helicopter in Flagstaff. From there they picked up the trail in Farmington, where they had to land with the old military Lynx helicopter for repairs and fuel the day before. It was also reported that they might be making their way to Boulder. There was still no mention of Max Ellis.

Lots of speculation by 'experts' followed the announcements. Every commentator had his or her own theory about what could have happened and why the Rossler Foundation's top structure became so corrupt and evil. It was obvious that for now and until another big newsworthy event replaced theirs, this was going to be the prime news story for all the media outlets across the country. Daniel and his men could not dare to make a move anywhere until the dust settled.

They weren't sure what to make of the fact that Max Ellis had somehow avoided the limelight. Also the other Rosslerites who were part of the Enigma group and who were supposed to all have evacuated three nights ago. Why was there no mention of Sinclair, Luke, Ben or any of the others and their families? Was this a clever ploy on Brideaux's part in the hope that one or more of those would become careless and show up somewhere, or worse, abandon the group? Could the reason be that none of them managed to get away with Sarah and the rest who were implicated on the news? Was it only them and their wives who got away in the end?

There was no way they could find that out without the risk of compromising themselves.

Chapter Fifteen

BREAKING NEWS

The lack of media contact from the outside world was a big contributing factor to the strain that everyone felt in the Rabbit Hole. Their world band radios had no reception. They all needed to know what was going on in the outside world and, hopefully, to get some news about their men still on the outside. They couldn't even find out if they were alive or not.

That night, at about the time when the chopper sunk to the bottom of the pool, Ryan, Luke and Ben, who had all grown up in the days of shortwave radios and bad reception, devised a crude but efficient gimmick by making an antenna out of an old-fashioned wire coat hanger that had somehow made the trip with one of the refugees. They then hid it very cleverly in a tree right outside the cave opening.

They laid a thin electrical cord, which they buried and covered up with leaves, from the antenna into the cave, and then connected it to the radio. The problem was solved. They got good reception on FM and shortwave and listened to the news.

At first, they were all shocked to hear what was going on. They were now not only cave dwellers trying to get away from an eminent dictatorial society, they were also real outlaws with every law enforcement agency in the world looking for them. The enormous rewards on their heads would also have inspired bounty hunters and adventurists to find them.

A wave of relief swept over Sarah, Salome, and Rebecca with the realization that their men were obviously still alive, because if that were not the case, the news would have been different. Unfortunately, their joy was relatively short-lived as the realization also dawned on them that Robert was dead and Joseph most likely in the claws of Brideaux.

When the news broadcast was over, chaos ensued with everyone asking questions. What happened? Was there a gunfight? How was Robert killed? Were some of them wounded? What about the helicopter? It sounded as if they had trouble with it? If that was the case, where were they now and how would they manage to get to the Rabbit Hole without it and avoid capture? What about the fact that Max Ellis's name was not mentioned? Does that mean he is also dead? Brideaux had figured out that Mark and John were involved in their escape, why not Max Ellis?

They asked the same questions Daniel and the rest had on their minds when they saw the news earlier – why only them? Why not the names of the other Rosslerites who escaped with them? It was Salome, a specialist ex-FBI profiler who pointed out that it could very well be a Brideaux subterfuge to get some of them to break cover.

Finally, Sinclair was the one who managed to bring them back to reality, "We will have to let Roxanne, Helen, Sushma, and Jenny know what we have heard."

Rebecca, Salome, and Sarah decided it would be best that they go and visit the four women who hadn't yet heard. They agreed that there was most probably no easy way to explain to Jenny what they'd heard, but it had to be done.

Roxanne, Helen, Sushma and those children old enough to understand, were elated to learn that their husbands and fathers were alive. Three days of constant worry and doubt were at an end – for now.

Breaking the news to Jenny turned out to be a bit easier than the three messengers expected. Maybe Jenny was in denial when she said, "It would have been nice to get the same news about Max as you got about your men. But I believe that he is alive with all of yours. I am convinced of that, and I'll keep on trusting in it until I hear otherwise."

When they returned to the radio, now accompanied by the four other wives, they decided that they would draw up a roster and take turns, with someone listening to the news broadcasts so they could stay on top of what was going on in the outside world and with their loved ones.

Over the days that followed, the media interest in the story dwindled, and soon none of the media outlets led with the story anymore. Some stopped mentioning it at all. For the Rosslerites, it soon became 'no news is good news'. If their men were captured or killed, they'd be front page news again in seconds. Nevertheless, as the days of absence went on, none of them were successful at pacifying their growing feelings of doubt and uncertainty. On quite a few occasions, Rebecca had to remind them of the first Antarctica expedition, when they all turned up alive on the day of their funeral.

"Remember, they have to keep a low profile," she urged. "We have to keep believing they are on their way. Consider this; what if the helicopter broke down totally? They might even have to walk here."

Chapter Sixteen

THE WATER HAS NOT RECEDED AS YET

With Owen and Alison joining their group as the first recruits outside the existing Rosslerites, they busied themselves with planning on how to get the original seven to the Rabbit Hole as well as strategies for the future.

They pulled out the maps they'd had in the chopper with them after Raj almost got a heart attack when Owen suggested they use online maps, "Man are you crazy? They track everything on the Internet; they store each and every search you make, they know about each and every site you visit. You will lead them right to us."

Owen, who still had to learn a lot about being paranoid, was scared out of his mind by Raj's tirade and promised that he would not even get within five yards of his computer from now on. Raj disconnected it from the Internet, along with any other devices, just to be on the safe side. It was too easy to forget unless you were Raj.

From Nucla to Billings was seven hundred and fifty-nine miles by car and a little more than three hours by air, if they'd still had that option. If their circumstances didn't change in the next week or so, they would have to consider walking all the way, given the dangers posed by roadblocks if they tried to drive it. But then that meant they would have to leave Roy behind and possibly Doug, whose back may not allow such a long hike.

It would take them at least thirty days, if not longer. The trip on foot in itself was not impossible, but it presented all sorts of issues, such as the increased risk of detection, how to get food and water and other unforeseeable problems. They decided to park that idea for now, and if nothing else happened that turned the wind in their favor shortly, it remained an option, albeit a dangerous one.

It would have been ideal if they could get there by airplane somehow, but they soon concluded that the risk of attempting that far outweighed the convenience. Owen also didn't know anyone, at least not anyone whom he could trust outright, for such an assignment. They decided that there were just too many lives at stake to give it any more consideration.

Three days after they ditched the helicopter, Owen and Alison got into their truck and went for a drive to Montrose. They needed supplies, and their route meant passing through several small towns where they could also hear the latest gossip and find out if the police had learned more about the whereabouts of their friends.

Daniel with his usual dry humor remarked, "Your trip reminds me of Noah in the Bible when he sent out the doves to find out if there was dry land somewhere."

Owen and Alison drove with no apparent hurry, passing through Naturita, Redvale, Norwood, Placerville and a couple of others on their way. Stopping often, they struck up conversations with the locals whenever they could, always steering the talk to what they knew and thought about those killers on the run. On their way back, late that afternoon, just outside Redvale, they were stopped at a roadblock. One of the police officers was James, who'd visited them on the farm a few days ago. He recognized them immediately.

Owen saw the opportunity to get more information. "What are you guys looking for?"

"Those Rosslers are still on the loose," James told them. "But between you and me, none of us think they ever came this way. If they did, they or their chopper would have been spotted by now. To be honest we are getting more than a little fed up wasting our time in these daily roadblocks. Of course, orders are orders, so we're stuck with it until they're withdrawn."

When the two of them got back to the farm, Alison continued Daniel's Biblical analogy of Noah when she told them about their trip, "Unfortunately we have to report that the water has not receded from the earth as yet. But we brought back an olive branch. The police are getting fed-up looking for you. Still, I'm afraid you'll have to be our guests for a while longer."

Mark joined in, to the amusement of all, "Well I guess we wait another seven days and send out the dove again as Noah did. Because we are still fresh out of ideas to get us all home safely."

They decided there was not much else they could do for now, other than to stay where they were until they could be sure that the search for them had lost its importance. The fact that the local cops were getting fed-up was a glimmer of hope. In the meantime, they agreed that it might be worthwhile to start thinking about the future after they managed to get home. The question was whether they should prepare themselves to mount a resistance or just accept that this was the way it was. The 11th Cycle would end, and all they could do was live out their days in isolation in the caves of the Gallatin National Forest.

It didn't take them long to reach the conclusion that none of them were willing to accept that scenario. They were in complete agreement about the necessity to at least attempt to reverse the situation. If Brideaux finally succeeded in realizing the much-feared one world government with the Beast that would control human behavior, and they didn't at least made an effort to stop him, life would not settle comfortably with them.

They acknowledged the fact that they didn't have much going for them at that moment, other than their absolute determination not to accept the new status quo. Nevertheless, they assumed that if Brideaux's plans came to fruition there would soon be many more people who would share their sentiments. They were going to have to construct a plan to reach those individuals and get them to join forces in their mission.

Their big advantage would be the possession of the 8th and 10th Cycle libraries that they believed would contain the key to their eventual success, as it had proven to so many times in the past. Roy, however, noted that as for the 8th Cycle Library, although they had the bulk of the information and Brideaux only a small part of it, he was concerned that Brideaux could very well have walked away with the most crucial part about the Beast when he confiscated their computers that night at the canyon.

Raj then remembered that he had taken a copy of that information that night without anyone of them seeing him do it. He knew he was going to be in some trouble but had no choice; he had to tell them.

He drew a breath and launch into his confession, "I

have a confession to make. I actually copied everything that Brideaux has onto a mini-flash drive as we were busy translating things all those days when we were at the canyon."

With this revelation he had his hands full stopping his teammates from kissing him at first. That was until Mark brought order and immediately convened a kangaroo court and a jury of six, with Doug as the judge and he the prosecutor. Raj was charged with withholding vital information from his comrades in arms, giving them no aid and causing a lot of discomfort, along with a few other serious crimes.

Raj, going along with the joke, tried to explain to the court that with everything he went through the last few days he forgot about the mini-flash drive, but he genuinely did not intend to withhold it from them. However, with no lawyer to state his case he was found guilty within a few minutes and sentenced to cook an Indian dinner for them the following night. The 'judge' followed his pronouncement of sentence with the stern warning not to muck it up, or he would be put on permanent kitchen duty and might even face solitary confinement.

Luckily, Indian food was one of Owen and Alison's favorite dishes and Raj found all the spices and ingredients necessary for an exquisite beef korma in her kitchen. The next night he got the last laugh when he added enough chili to bring tears to the eyes of his guests, all of them screaming for yogurt within seconds of taking the first bite.

Daniel found himself thinking that the rescue party fit right in with the rest of them, and joined in the hilarity with the knowledge that a bit of fun lowered stress and helped them keep their spirits up.

Chapter Seventeen

THE GARDENERS OF GALLATIN

The Rabbit Hole was a beehive of activity with almost everyone assigned to one or more projects by the Steering Committee.

Helen Bryant and Martha O'Reilly reported to them within a few days about the progress made by the GGS to provide fresh homegrown vegetables. It would be essential to produce vegetables with high vitamin and mineral content. Meat would not be part of their diet over the weeks ahead, as they couldn't risk the noise associated with hunting game for their tables. What the future would bring for provision of meat remained to be seen. They were already busy setting up hydroponics systems with special lighting so it wasn't necessary to plant anything outside in the sun where they could be discovered. The areas close to the thermal pools had the ideal microclimate.

A sprouting operation was in progress with stacks of sprouting trays using beans, alfalfa, sunflower, lentils, and peas, and the first harvest of sprouts would be ready in two days. Other batches would be reserved for replenishing the supply. They were also pleased to report that they would be producing healthy fresh vegetables in four to six weeks. Some of the plants would be grown for the sole purpose of harvesting the seeds to build up their seed banks and to make them self-sufficient.

"Almost everything that can be grown outside can be grown hydroponically inside," Helen explained.

With no worries about insects and pests, which eliminated the need for pesticides, they could grow their food organically. They had already started to make their own compost and would educate everyone how to sort domestic waste so that it could be recycled through the compost factory. Human-feces-based fertilizer known as biosolids could be developed and would go a long way to sustaining their soil for bigger crops like wheat and oats.

The big challenge would be to get their hands on earthworms. Then they could develop good soil and turn the Gardens of Gallatin into a paradise that would produce food for all of them and even flowers.

Salome and Rebecca informed the steering committee about the expected psychological behavior of the group that they had alluded to a few days ago. It was to be expected that the current holiday and adventure feeling would wear out relatively quickly and that irritation, depression, and desperation could set in within a few weeks amongst many of them. The children would probably be the first group to be affected, as they would soon start to miss their friends from school. The adults would follow shortly after the children. It would be much worse for them as they began to lose the connections with all they'd left behind – their properties, friends and family. They were stuck here with the prospect of being cave dwellers for the rest of their lives.

Another crucial aspect and potential contributing factor

to psychological issues amongst the people would be the close family members that were left behind without being able to tell them where they were. People such as parents, brothers, sisters, and even adult children like Sarah's sister, Meg, who lived in Florida. She was married to a police detective and had two girls, ten and twelve. Sarah and her parents were worried sick about Meg and her family. She knew that there were a few other families in the same boat. In fact, all families that were left behind would be subject to Brideaux's plans, and that was a terrifying thought. There was also the worry about the possibility that Brideaux might get it into his head to use those family members for extortion.

They all agreed that it was something that had to be addressed relatively quickly. That meant they would have to somehow get in touch with those family members and offer them the opportunity to move in with them at the Rabbit Hole. After that, how to move them unnoticed was going to be a challenge.

Salome suggested that they had to start right away to make sure that everyone was assigned to a project that would help to occupy their minds and made them feel valuable. Group activities for children and adults had to be devised, such as quiz and game nights, movies and other types of entertainment. It would go a long way toward preventing and addressing the imminent problem.

Rebecca mentioned that she was already troubled about her parents, John and Jane Mendenhall. John had been the dean of a private college, and Jane, a primary school principal. They had both retired a few years ago and had been struggling to adapt to life without young people around them. They'd become withdrawn and isolated even before moving to the Rabbit Hole. Since their arrival they had not been part of any of the activities and did not even bother to send in the skills list Sarah requested in the beginning.

Security was a standing item on the agenda of the steering committee. Sarah wanted to make sure that everyone was still following the rules. Luke and Salome reported that was the case but that they would have to look at how they could allow people to go outside fairly soon. The potential risks were that campers and hikers might spot them, and there was the possibility, though less likely, that they could be spotted by drones and satellites.

Luke and Salome explained that they had been working on a plan to try to get some of Roy's hummingbird drones in operation so that they could send them out to be their eyes in the sky. They could warn them if any of those hazards were in the vicinity.

As soon as they could get that going, they would be able to let people go out. However, with Roy not there to show them how those things worked it would take a few more days for them to figure it out. Ryan offered his help, and it was suggested that Stuart might also have some helpful ideas.

As for satellites, they explained that detection by satellites was possible, but the chances of that happening would be negligible unless the satellites 'knew' where and what to look for. As long as no one knew their location and pointed the satellites in their direction, they would not be detected. Salome said she was aware of computer programs that could keep track of satellite movements. However, that was something Raj would be able to help with when he arrived.

The meeting ended on a very positive note when Ryan invited them all for a look-see at a small steam generator that he and his team had constructed next to one of the hot pools.

On arrival and a lot of excitement from his audience, he explained how, by cutting into the rock with one of Roy's laser cutting torches, they'd diverted the already very hot water from the pool through the channels that they had cut into the rocks and turned it into steam. The steam was driving a turbine that in turn was driving the generator, an ingenious piece of work that impressed all of them. Ryan explained that it would be possible to build improved generators around the pool now that they had proved the concept.

They were about to become entirely self-sufficient in electricity supply as well. There would be no need to take the risk of putting solar panels or wind turbines outside the caves. They could now provide excellent lighting throughout the caves and run as many electrical devices as they needed off their own power source.

Chapter Eighteen

THE FIRST SAFE HOUSE

That night, after everyone was well fed on Raj's extra hot beef korma and in their beds, Alison and Owen had another brainstorming session. They were determined to figure out how to help Daniel and the rest to get to their new home. By midnight, they had what they thought could be a solution.

Owen got up early and went to call them over for breakfast and to share the plan. When they were seated at the kitchen table, he began; "Daniel, Alison and I have what we think could be a good plan. It would not only get you guys to your families, but could also be a long term solution for the inhabitants of the Rabbit Hole and the resistance."

By this time, they were all ears and encouraged Owen to continue.

"We thought that we should try and find some farmland to buy in the Big Timber area, as close as possible to the Rabbit Hole. We could then develop it into a safe house for people having to go in and out of the Rabbit Hole."

Roy was first to reply, "That sounds like a good idea, but

let's hear all the details. I'm particularly interested to hear how you think you'll be able to get us all there in the first place."

Owen continued, "Well we've given it a lot of thought. If we can find acres with an old house in need of repair or even no house, we would have a good reason to move a lot of stuff up there by truck - for construction purposes, you see. We could use a few forty-foot containers, pack them with what we need and rent a truck to move it all up there. We could easily hide you in those containers."

Daniel replied, "That plan might just have some merit as far as I am concerned. Discovery would still be the risk, but if we pack the containers carefully. I think it's much less of a risk than any other mode of transport we have considered so far."

By now, everyone was excited and wanted to say something but Owen interrupted them.

"Let me just give you the last bit of our idea. If we can get the right farmland, and set it up as we envisage, it would be a secure safe house. Also, it could act as a good place to drop off supplies that you cavemen might need from time to time," he said with a smile.

They had a lengthy discussion, and it became apparent that this could very well be the best way for them to get home. Yes, there were risks but, as Daniel noted earlier, a lot less than any of the other options.

One of the downsides of this plan, they thought, was the time it was going to take to find the land. There'd be travel up to inspect it, buy it, and go through the legal process of transferring and to take possession. On the other hand, they also knew that more time could work in their favor, as the police would probably become less vigilant about them as new emergencies required their attention.

After clearing it with Raj that in this case, where there was a perfectly logical reason to be on the Internet that wouldn't raise suspicion, they helped him search for a property. They used the online satellite and topographical maps to get a good idea of what the various properties looked like in reality.

Once they'd done that, they made a short list of some suitable places. One of the properties of interest was a few miles outside McLeod in Sweet Grass County, about twenty miles southwest of Big Timber. The almost hundred-acre property was advertised directly by the owner, which meant they didn't have to go through a real estate agent. The land had an old farmhouse, which, according to the advertisement, required a bit of TLC. This, in reality, meant it was most probably in a dilapidated state and in desperate need of repair. For them, that was ideal as it gave them the excuse to have lots of construction activities going on, with trucks coming and going to drop off building supplies.

The most alluring feature, however, was that the property bordered the Gallatin National Forest and was about 10 miles from the Rabbit Hole. The maps showed it was rather rugged terrain between the farmhouse and the Rabbit Hole, but not at all impossible for a human on foot or even on horseback. In adherence to their earlier Biblical analogies, they immediately named it Mount Ararat.

Owen and Alison made a few phone calls to set up an appointment to inspect the property. He and Alison drove up to Big Timber for three days, and as it turned out, the owner of Mount Ararat was a very motivated seller. He and Owen agreed on a purchase price and payment via bank transfer. As soon as the money cleared into the title company account, the deed would be recorded, and then

Owen and Alison could take possession. The seller was a jubilant man, and so were the buyers.

On the way to Big Timber and back, although they were in a hurry, they scouted all the little towns in the vicinity. They included all the local tourist information offices collecting as much data, maps, and brochures as they could. This information was going to become crucial to their resistance movement in the future.

Meanwhile, Daniel and the rest of the group went to the main house every night to watch the news on TV. The news about them still consisted of wild speculation and many questions. The Rossler Foundation was well known and in most cases a loved organization that had brought so much good to so many. There was a strong surge of doubt that this hype about them was indeed the truth. How could they turn so bad? Rumors of embezzlement and fraud were rife. Some even suggested that it could be about sensitive information harmful to the USA's national security. Before long, they were branded not only as killers and kidnappers but also as traitors.

Irrespective of the ludicrous allegations, the reality remained that Brideaux and his co-conspirators had absolute control of the media. It was just a matter of time before he would take over the world - there could be no doubt about it. It still bothered them that Brideaux apparently knew about each and every Rossler Foundation employee and their families who'd disappeared, but that never reached the media. The world and the Rosslerites were oblivious as to what was about to hit them.

Chapter Nineteen

LIBERTÉ EGALITÉ FRATERNITÉ

A few days after Owen and Alison were back home, the news broke.

World leaders at the G20 summit in New Delhi were taken hostage. Gunshots were heard but no one knew who, if anyone, was killed or wounded. Very little of what happened during the coup d'état was shown on the news. In fact, the details were never shown, and those who survived never spoke about it.

Only those who witnessed the event in person knew about the carnage in that room. The facts were that politicians, reporters and photographers who walked out of there alive were those who were warned ahead of time and were a hundred percent in support of the new world order.

The media showed dead bodies of more than a thousand security force personnel outside. It appeared these people had dropped dead without being able to move a finger. It was immediately apparent to the world that the group who implemented this mission had a weapon with unknown and unequalled killing power.

Within days, the death toll across the world reached hundreds of thousands as John Brideaux's forces completed their move and took control of all world governments. Brideaux's face and those of many prominent world leaders were on the news 24/7 calling for calm amongst the populace.

They kept on hammering on the fact that the world had become one of corruption, inequality, and inhumane conditions. More than eighty per cent of the world population were living in poverty and starvation, while twenty per cent owned almost ninety-five per cent of all wealth and were living in sinful luxury and abundance. This, they stated, had ended. The new order was likened to the French Revolution but this time it was for the whole world. All speeches started and ended with the quote originating in the French Revolution in the late 1700's, liberté, egalité, fraternité, - freedom, equality, and society.

The theme of all news was the end to poverty, hunger, crime, corruption, income inequality and environmental waste for everyone. Peace, health, and prosperity were the right of every human being, and under the new order that was guaranteed to everyone. The constant propaganda of the benefits of the utopia quickly expanded the ranks of the 'Kool-Aid drinkers'. It spread first amongst the journalists and broadcasters, followed by prominent political leaders, and in staggering numbers amongst the populace. Quickly, only the voices of advocates of the new order were heard. Antagonists disappeared never to be heard of again.

The dawn of the new world order caught the Rosslerites both inside and outside the Rabbit Hole by surprise. This was what they all expected- it was the reason they were all in hiding - but it certainly happened much, much faster than anyone of them could have imagined. Brideaux and his followers must have been preparing for this for much longer than they'd anticipated.

In the days following the takeover, Daniel and his group sensed that the tide might have turned and they would now have the opportunity to be reunited with their loved ones. Now, the police and everyone who were looking for them had much bigger fish to fry. The Rosslerites didn't matter anymore to anyone. Mark suggested that it might be time to send out another dove to see how far the water had receded.

Owen and Alison took another trip to town to gauge the feeling of the locals and check out what the sheriff's office was up to. They found that no one was talking or looking for the Rosslerites any longer. Only the new political climate was on their minds.

Everyone was frightened and confused. What could they expect? Who was this John Brideaux? What did the future hold for them?

Some were talking about resistance and going underground, but many more had already fallen victim to the effect of the Kool-Aid dished out so liberally in the media. Believing the new world would at last bring them long life, prosperity, and peace sounded wonderful.

Owen and Alison visited the sheriff's office in Redvale to find out what they recommended should be done, how to act, and what to expect. They found the local law enforcement community in chaos. The cops had no idea what to do. They weren't sure who their bosses were anymore or even if they'd be paid. Worse, they didn't know which laws to enforce or not. For the moment, they were focused on preventing looting and vigilante actions, and that was about it.

Owen wanted to know, "What about those killers? Are they still on the loose?"

The officer replied, "Yes, they are, as far as we know. But no one seems to care or worry about that anymore. They aren't around here anymore, even if they ever were."

When the couple got back to the farm and reported what they'd learned, everyone knew the time had come. The water had receded, and they could now put their plan into action.

They'd already decided it was best to make the move in two groups. Roy, JR, Max, and Raj would be the first group to make the trip to Mount Ararat. Daniel, Mark, and Doug would follow a few days later in the same way.

Two empty forty-foot containers and truckloads of furnishings for the new place as well as farm implements and supplies were delivered to the farm, and they started packing. Inside the containers, they constructed four small but comfortable cubicles, with enough room for a person to lie down and headroom to move. The cubicles would be entirely concealed by the building material once they were done with the packing. The next few days was a beehive of activity in Owen's shed, while JR was posted on a hill behind the house with binoculars to make sure no one approached the farm unexpectedly.

Owen arranged for a transport company to move the containers. He and Alison would be following the truck all the way and be there when they arrived to unload it at the right spot.

Since the inception of Enigma many months ago, everyone involved had gathered and stored large amounts of information on computers, external hard drives, flash drives and even Blu-ray and DVD's. In each case, it was related to their own fields of expertise and interest. With Raj and Stuart's zest to keep up with technology developments, combined with Roy's brilliance, the three of them developed a mind-boggling storage capacity. This was approaching one zettabyte, hosted on a few nanotech hard drives the size of a briefcase. When they evacuated the Rossler Foundation offices that night, the collection could easily be imagined to have copied the entire Internet, plus a few other sources. Ryan and his team of electrical experts finally had a few of their steam driven electricity generators going, and it was now time for Stuart to start up the servers.

Getting Sinclair and his translators going again was vital, and setting up the 'public library' was just as important. Everyone who provided data was responsible to create a proper file and index structure and to create master indexes to make it easy to search and find information. When Stuart reported to the steering committee that he and his team of enthusiasts had completed the program, relief swept the leadership team. Here at last was something to occupy the large majority of the group that had just been marking time until they could resume the activities they'd been hired to do. The committee decided there and then that this accomplishment called for a celebration, and arranged for a formal opening of the new library.

Bess and Sinclair, as the oldest members of the group, would have the honor of giving the opening address. The 11th Cycle Library was to be dedicated to the late Nicholas Rossler, Bess's husband, a distinguished scholar of archaeology and ex-university professor. He was Ben's father and was grandfather of Ben's three boys – Daniel, Aaron and JR – and to his high delight, great grandfather to the young Nicholas Rossler who was named after him.

As expected, the presence of the library contributed

significantly to changing the growing somber mood amongst the people in the Rabbit Hole. They now had access to vast amounts of academic and non-academic information, music, and videos that many of them didn't even know existed before they arrived at the Rabbit Hole. Sinclair was also happy to get back to the work he loved so much – the translation of the 10th and 8th Cycle Libraries.

Within a few days after Stuart had the servers up and running, Sinclair and his team were back in business. What was becoming more crucial, and something Sinclair had been wondering about for a long time, was how to speed up the translation process. He'd mentioned it on a few occasions, but up until now, they had just been poking around in the library, searching for topics of interest. Then again, in many cases, it had been done in response to some crisis or other. In other words, they'd not been working systematically through the library. He believed that the quicker they could get the full picture of what was contained there, the better for their security and safety. He and everyone else at the Rossler Foundation, and of course John Brideaux, were convinced that those libraries held information about technologies scientists and science fictionist writers hadn't even dreamt of.

That wasn't speculation; their convictions were based on their experiences of the past, when the 10th Cycle Library provided answers to many of their issues during crises. Those libraries, in all likelihood, had locked up in them the solution to the world's current and future problems. Therefore, Sinclair had the full support of the steering committee to investigate when he walked over to Stuart's computer center to discuss his ideas and requirements.

Stuart was a brilliant young mind and he agreed to immediately start looking at how it could be accomplished.

He told Sinclair that according to what he understood about the process, it could very well be possible to automate it. However, it would take time to develop the programming. If and when Raj was back, things would obviously be able to move along a lot quicker.

Chapter Twenty

EYES IN THE SKY

Luke and Salome called in Ryan's help and managed to get two of Roy's hummingbird mini-drones airborne. With a bit of practice, they learned how to control the devices, and with Stuart's help, they got them linked to a computer screen via Wi-Fi and sent the 'birds' outside. Stuart assured them that the Wi-Fi connection was secure and would only broadcast up to 2,000 feet. When they had the drones up, they found that at a thousand feet they had a very clear three hundred and sixty-degree view for more than two miles around them. This satisfied them that until Roy and Raj turned up to help expand the surveillance area, they'd be able to take short trips close to the caves.

Luke was the first to venture outside on a reconnaissance trip to gather information about the area where they thought it would be safe to wander around. On his first trip, he found a stream about three hundred yards away from the cave opening and investigated. He was smiling broadly when he got back and told them he'd found a very nice fishing spot in a secluded area amongst the trees and bushes, where the trout were standing at attention when they saw him. This was great news for all the fishing enthusiasts amongst them.

Sarah and the leadership group decided they'd have to create a timetable to let everyone have a chance, as part of a small group, to go out and enjoy the outdoors each day.

The fishermen would get their turn in the early mornings and evenings which, according to them, was prime time for trout fishing. Of course, this was with the understanding that everyone would share everything they caught. They had no problems with that, as most anglers do it for the kicks and excitement, not for the meal they might have in their hands at the end of the fight.

This new freedom to be able to move around outside notwithstanding the limitations, brought much-needed relief to Rebecca and Salome, who were responsible for the psychological health of the group. This was another significant victory in the battle against the sadness that already had firm hold of more than half of the group.

Luke and Ben went on the first fishing expedition late on the first afternoon, and by the time it was dark the two of them arrived home with a bag full of trout. The only problem was that they were anglers and, therefore, had no clue how to gut, scale, and filet a fish. This, they explained to their disgusted wives, was due to the fact they had always caught and released the fish, or someone else did the cutting part for them. It was Ben's octogenarian mother, Bess, who came to their rescue and taught them all how to do it. That night everyone in the caves had fresh trout for dinner.

Shortly after that, one of the fishing trips produced another treasure. It was Ryan and Sinclair's turn to go out fishing. When it was time to go home, they dug around to see if there were any earthworms to use as bait for any other type of fish swimming around in those waters. They quickly found some and carefully placed them in a small bucket, which they filled up with damp soil so that they could keep them alive for a day or two until it was their turn again. However, their plans were short-lived. When they got back to the caves, Martha asked about the contents of the bucket. And when they told her, she confiscated it on the spot and took it to Helen and the GGS, who were overjoyed. The two men were thunderstruck. What the hell? The audacity to rob a fisherman of his bait was a serious issue.

When Helen saw the look on their faces, she felt sorry for them and explained to that with an earthworm farm they could produce vermicompost instead of the compost they were currently making. "Vermicompost is seven times richer in plant nutrients than compost created by decomposing plant material through fungi and bacteria. It suppresses diseases, slugs, and insects. Almost all plants and definitely everything we are growing will just grow better and quicker, carrots, corn, tomatoes, potatoes, and cucumbers - you name it," she said, apparently very excited.

The two of them still felt robbed of their treasure but also realized this was a battle they could not win. Walking away Sinclair mumbled, "Taking a fisherman's bait from him is like opening an umbrella in his ass. Why can't they just go and dig their own worms. There are lots more where those came from." Ryan had a hard time controlling his laughter at Sinclair's grumpy remarks.

The next morning and afternoon there would be no fishing; they had to dig out earthworms to stock the farm.

They recognized that the quicker they got the worm count up to the satisfaction of those bait thieves from the GGS, the faster they could get back to their fishing. In no time, they had a large earthworm farm producing vermicompost, and the results were visible in the plants of the Gardens of Gallatin within days.

Chapter Twenty-One

THE SORRIEST HUMAN BEING ON THE PLANET

With Brideaux having to turn his full attention to his new found stardom and the ensuing instability caused by his proclamation of the new world order, his life became far more complex than he'd imagined. Jason was last heard of when he arrived in Prague because he had a 'hot lead' who saw two of the Rosslers there just a day ago.

The tide had finally turned in favor of the seven escapees.

During the trip to Mount Ararat, Owen and Alison didn't see a single police car between Nucla and Big Timber. The container was unloaded under the watchful eyes of Owen and Alison, who were following the truck all the way. The truck driver returned to Colorado to load the next container in five days' time.

When it was dark, Owen let the men out of the container. They were all well rested, keen, and ready to make the ten-mile trip to be with their families for the first time in more than a month. Alison made sure they were stocked with as much food and water as they could carry in their backpacks, allowing for the fact that they would have to assist Roy for much of the way. They had to reach Rabbit Hole under the cover of darkness.

As a precautionary measure to make sure that JR and his group didn't get into some trouble that would require them to come back, Owen and Alison would remain at Mount Ararat for two days before returning to Nucla.

Initially, because Roy was able to walk on his own with only a walking stick, the first part of the hike went well. But then, after covering two miles in as many hours he could go no further without assistance. They would from that point on, take turns with JR, who would carry him on his back as far as he could. After that Max and Raj would carry him on a stretcher as far as they could before JR took over again.

It became a grueling trip for all of them; not only because of having to carry Roy but also because of the rough and unfamiliar terrain they had to navigate by flashlight. Their pace soon slowed to less than a mile an hour. Despite their difficulties, they arrived at the main entry of the Rabbit Hole, utterly exhausted, when dawn broke on the thirty-third day after they had left the 8th Cycle compound in the canyon in the helicopter.

Raj, who had been to the Rabbit Hole before and knew what the main entry and inside looked like, went in first. There he met Luke and Sinclair heading out for their early morning fishing trip. At first sight and for a split second the two of them thought it was a stranger who'd found the cave opening. When they recognized Raj despite his bearded face, they made so much noise that they woke almost half of the people.

JR, Max, and Roy also found their way inside, and within seconds Sushma, with the baby clinging to her neck, Salome, Jenny, and Rebecca appeared around the corner and threw themselves into the arms of their men. Soon, there was not one single dry face as the men, women, and baby were all crying for joy that they were reunited after so much agony.

In the commotion that followed, no one noticed Sarah arriving, who took one look at the group and collapsed into a heap on the rock floor, her body shaking uncontrollably while she started crying. JR became aware when he heard Sarah repeating the words, "Daniel, oh Daniel" over and over again. He looked around and saw her. It took JR a few seconds to realize that Sarah must have been thinking Daniel and the rest did not make it and were dead or captured. He took two steps and pulled her up off the floor. He pushed his face against hers, yelling, "Sis, stop crying. Daniel is on his way. He's alive and so are Doug and Mark! Please stop crying. Nothing happened to them. They're safe, and they'll be here in the next four to five days!"

Sarah was still hanging in mid-air, her feet dangling a few feet off the ground, with JR trying to calm her down when she finally heard him. As if there was an 'off' switch, in her head she all of a sudden stopped crying and said, "Okay, now put me down."

However, as soon as her feet touched the ground, she started shaking again. JR immediately grabbed her to lift her up again, when he saw she was laughing. "Oh shit, you women are impossible!"

By now, Helen and Roxanne with their children were also there, but luckily they arrived just in time to hear what JR was telling Sarah. Mark and Doug were alive and well. When they heard that they joined in with the crying choir.

A few more minutes and the four new arrivals were dragged off to the Town Hall, where the entire group was jubilantly waiting to see them. Rebecca sent for her medical bag and examined Roy's leg after she had to physically unwrap him from Salome's embrace. She also had a quick examination of JR's hand and was happy that everything looked fine. Later, as soon as things calmed down, she would do a thorough examination of their wounds.

The four of them were shown where to sit, each with a large mug of coffee and a thick slice of home-baked bread with honey in their hands. Then they had to tell everyone what had happened to them since Salome's conversation with Daniel that fateful night thirty-three days ago. JR got very emotional when he described how Brideaux shot and killed Robert, wounded him and Roy, and abducted Joseph. His recount of the events dampened the joy created by their arrival. It was a sobering reminder to them all about the danger they faced in a future with John Brideaux and his new world order.

As they continued to describe their trials and tribulations of the past month, the group slowly returned to their former high spirits. At some stage, Sinclair stopped them and wanted to know, "Who is this Doug person you guys had been talking about for the past half an hour?"

JR said, "It's a long and complicated story. We've only recently been told, and only he can explain. His real name is John MacArthur. He's one of the two guys who came with Mark to rescue us. Apparently his wife is here. I have not met her as yet, but Doug never stopped talking about his lovely Roxanne."

This explanation by JR had them all roaring with laughter as Roxanne got up. Proud as a peacock, she said with a big smile, "JR, I am Roxanne and that guy Doug is my hero." She then turned to the group and continued, "But it is like JR said, how he got his nickname is a long story, and it's better if he tells you."

The four of them had many questions to answer. Rebecca called a halt after two hours and escorted them off to her clinic where she conducted a thorough examination of all of them. She found that Max did a sterling job with the care of the wounds, and there was not much more she had to do. It was up to Roxanne to take them under her care for rehabilitation physiotherapy, which would help them regain full use of the damaged nerves and muscles.

One thing was sure, if those four wives were able to get their hands on John Brideaux at that moment, he would very soon have been the sorriest human being on the planet. What he did to their men and their friends – Robert and Joseph – would never be forgotten.

Chapter Twenty-Two

THE SUPREME COUNCIL

The new world government's headquarters were established in Brussels.

The last President of the United States, one of the founding members of the One World Supreme Council, reassigned the United States Secret Service to the protection of the members of the Supreme Council. Air Force One was donated as a gesture of goodwill from the grateful people of America.

The Supreme Council, who had been planning their takeover for many years in minute detail, were somewhat disappointed to learn that not everyone on the planet liked the idea of being 'cared for' by them. They were all wondering what was wrong. Couldn't the people see how much good the Council could bring to them?

Peaceful protests across the world marked the beginning of what would turn violent within a few days, when the protesters discovered that no one was listening to them. For the common good, the Supreme Council quickly created a complete media blackout and dealt with the dissidents in a rapid and heavy-handed manner. This brought an abrupt end to the problem and left nearly a quarter of a million dead in its wake.

Despite the media blackout, the council discovered, as time passed, that they were not able to stop what people saw, thought, and spoke about. They had just created a few million more dissidents amongst the citizens of their new world.

A few countries mobilized their armed forces and were ready to go to war, only to find out soon after that there was no invading enemy force. They didn't know how to fight an invisible enemy. Yet, their soldiers were killed like flies within hours, which forced them into unconditional surrender very quickly.

When the armed forces were subdued, the Supreme Council started to implement their agenda. First, the world had to be made a safer place, and as long as people had guns it wouldn't be safe. Hence the disarmament of all citizens was announced.

All gun manufacturing plants and gun shops were closed overnight. Gun owners had seven days to hand in their weapons voluntarily, after which anyone who still had a gun according to registration records got a visit from law enforcement agencies that confiscated their firearms and charged them with disobedience to the Supreme Council.

There were no court hearings; fines were issued on the spot. This was the last time anyone would be treated this leniently when it came to firearms. From now on, anyone found in possession would face a long stretch in prison. In most countries of the world, the disarmament initiative was a non-event because of existing gun control laws, but in the USA it was a different story. The announcement by the Council had the pro-gun-control groups on their feet in a standing ovation while it had gun-ownership groups on their hind legs, ready to strike at anyone who dared to take their guns away. However, unlike attempts by previous governments in the USA, this time it was not going to be an election issue. There was not even going to be a debate or vote about it. The disarmament mission left thousands dead and created many dissidents, many of whom were just waiting for the right moment to get their guns back.

Some tried to hide or deny their weapons, but soon discovered when the police knocked on their doors that the government actually knew about each and every person who possessed a gun. There was no escape.

A precious tool in The Supreme Council's arsenal to win the hearts and minds of the people was their access to the secret vaults of every previous government in the world. Not only did it open up access to advanced technologies for them, but also gave them all the insider information about immorality, corruption, fraud, and outright criminal activities swept under the carpet by politicians of those former governments. They employed this treasure trove of information to their advantage as they seized all technology projects and placed them under their own supervision. They used their knowledge of the dirty secrets to either remove or control the people involved to dance to their tunes as they chose.

They made absolutely sure that the population of the world knew about all of the corruption, fraud and criminal activities of their previous governments. Those cases that they carefully selected to publish came with the guarantee that under the new world order it would never happen again. To thundering applause from many millions around the world, they announced their intention to remove from the planet each and every nuclear weapon without exception. That also included every nuclear power plant, bioweapon, and weapons of mass destruction and demobilization of armed forces, along with the destruction of their weapons.

The ranks of their supporters were boosted by hundreds of millions again when they announced free medical treatment and education for everyone. Health and education were the right of every citizen and not just a selected few. In the new world, everyone was guaranteed free and good quality education. Only a select few knew that the Council's dedicated scientists were working round the clock to finish the development and commence the mass production of the chips – biochips that would be implanted in every citizen of the new world. The seemingly benevolent world government had a very dirty secret.

Everyone would shortly be connected to one of the geostatic Skywalker satellites, about to be placed into orbit.

Chapter Twenty-Three

IT MERELY DICTATED WHERE THEY WOULD START

When the first truck and container that delivered JR, Roy, Raj, and Max left, Daniel, Mark, and Doug got busy setting up and packing the next container to transport them a few days later. Owen and Alison returned with the good news that the first four must have made it to the Rabbit Hole and that the coast was clear all the way. They hadn't seen a cop in days. It was as if the police were on strike.

The container was packed and ready. This time, not only with building materials but also with a lot of food supplies. Following the same procedure as JR and his group, Daniel arrived safely at Mount Ararat without any trouble whatsoever along the road.

Owen and Alison stayed behind at Mount Ararat for a week and worked on the house. There was always a chance the three might run into trouble and have to come back, or the people in the Rabbit Hole might have need of something from the outside. By now they had their plans for the operation of the safe house in place. They would visit there every three weeks until they were able to recruit and settle the right family on the farm to manage it for them. With Doug's encouragement, they were very excited about the idea of taking flying lessons and buying a small six-seater plane to use for commuting between their two properties.

Upon arrival at Mt. Ararat, when it was dark the three men put on their backpacks, stuffed with as much equipment and supplies they could carry, and made the trip to the Rabbit Hole. They found the trip a lot less challenging than JR's group without having to worry about wounded. They arrived at the cave entrance about four hours later – just before midnight on the thirty-eighth day after they'd left the 8th Cycle complex in the canyon.

As Daniel came in through the cave opening, Sarah was standing there as if she was expecting him, with Nicholas on her hip. She let out a shriek of joy when she recognized her bearded husband. Mark and Doug's appearance started her shouting at the top of her voice, "They're here! They're here!"

By the time Daniel had Sarah and Nicholas in his arms, Roxanne and Helen had appeared out of thin air, as if they were waiting by Sarah's side. Tears were flowing freely and shouts of joy were heard, which quickly attracted many of the others. Daniel could not help himself and had to wipe the tears from his eyes when he hugged and kissed Sarah. His sleepy little boy immediately threw his arms around his neck shouting, "Daddy, daddy," and started pulling at Daniel's beard.

The two hardened soldiers, who were at first trying their best to fight the tears from their eyes as they hugged their families, gave in, took Daniel's lead and were now openly crying.

Rebecca was on the scene very quickly and, as soon as the first wave of calm descended, she asked the three of them if they required any medical attention. They all told her that they were good, and there were no problems at all. JR and his arrivals had set a precedent a few days ago, and there was no way out. The three men with their families were unceremoniously dragged off to the Town Hall and put through two hours of telling and explaining and listening before they would be left alone with their families.

Once they'd done their duty to the community, each man spent a few minutes with his children, and then found one last reserve of energy in the arms of a loving wife.

Early the next day, they took an extensive tour of the Rabbit Hole facilities, which had their mouths hanging open in surprise when they saw how much had been achieved in such a short time. The Gardens of Gallatin, the Medical Center, IT Center and Ryan's steam turbines were impressive.

Daniel choked up when Sarah and his dad escorted him into the Nicholas Rossler Library. What would he have given at that moment for his grandfather to be there to see how much the people of the Rossler Foundation cherished and respected him?

Apart from the saddening absence of Robert and Joseph, the numbers of the Rosslerites were complete again. It quickly became evident that the arrival of Daniel and his two companions were an enormous boost to the morale of the entire group. It was as if they were all injected with a substance that instantly created a sparkle in their eyes and a new zest for life.

Their present circumstances could not determine where they would go; it merely dictated where they would start.

Chapter Twenty-Four

THE CHAIR OR THE CAGE?

When it was time for the daily gathering of the Steering Committee, Sarah and others had already brought Daniel up to speed with all that had happened since the first group landed at the Rabbit Hole. Daniel, Raj, and JR of the old core group and Mark and Doug as special guests were invited to attend the meeting, chaired by Sarah.

They worked through their agenda, calling in people as required to report about their projects' progress and to help them resolve any issues they had. JR had already informed them, shortly after he and the others arrived, about Owen and Alison's involvement, Mount Ararat and the idea of the safe house. Daniel now filled them in on the latest plans that they all welcomed, as it resolved one of their major issues – the replenishment of supplies. Without the availability of the safe house that would have been a major challenge with many risks for them.

With no more projects to discuss, the talks turned to the question on everyone's mind. What about the future? Were they going to accept the situation and live the rest of their lives out in these caves, or should they mount a resistance and attempt to overthrow the new regime?

Sarah said she had deliberately kept the discussion off the table because she didn't want the people here to make hasty decisions until they were all together. She'd had faith that the Rossler group would all be together again, and that it would then be the right time to have the discussion.

Now, she went around the table and gave everyone a chance to speak his or her mind. One after another, they told the meeting why they believed that there was no question about it; they were not willing to accept the status quo. Although they didn't know as yet how and with what they were going to do it, there was no doubt about it. They would have to attempt at least to get rid of this evil.

Daniel spoke second to last and confirmed what everyone else was saying. "I agree with everyone that spoke before. I cannot sit back and just let it be. The seven of us who were on the run for the past few weeks, as well as Owen and Alison, discussed this. We all feel the same about it."

Luke wanted to know if their discussions had brought up any ideas as to how it could be accomplished.

Daniel explained, "No we didn't go into that much detail. We felt the same as you here. We wanted to have everyone together before we start looking at a plan of action. But we did discuss what we felt we had going for us."

"I guess we'd all like to hear more about that, Daniel," Salome said as she took the words out of Sarah's mouth.

Daniel continued, explaining how they'd concluded that they didn't have much on their side at that moment. Their determination not to accept the way things were and would become wouldn't be limited to just their small group once Brideaux was in charge. "As we gathered from Owen and Alison's reports when they went on a reconnaissance trip around the area after Brideaux's takeover, we were right to think so. Many out there are not going to accept this new world order. Especially here in the western states, where gun ownership is held to be an almost sacred right. It will be up to us to find them and motivate them to join us in our undertaking."

"That might take a long time, but I agree that would be one of the things we'll have to take advantage of," Luke replied.

"Yes, it might be very slow initially, but keep in mind that Brideaux has promised the people his idea of heaven on earth so far, and I'm sure he is not done yet. As soon as the people that are now so supportive of the utopia idea realize what it really means, it can be expected the tide will start to turn in our favor. I think it will grow rapidly from there," Daniel explained.

Most agreed that it would be a natural reaction once they experienced Brideaux's utopia.

Daniel continued, "We also concluded that the 8th and 10th Cycle libraries could contain the key to our eventual success as it has done so many times in the past."

Sinclair said, "Yes, I have the same feeling about the 10th Cycle Library, but I'm not so sure about the 8th Cycle one."

"Why is that?" Daniel enquired.

"Well, my understanding is that Brideaux got away with what could be the most valuable information, That is, the foils containing the details about the Beast." Sinclair answered.

"Oh, I thought you knew?" Daniel responded.

But before anyone could get another word out Raj jumped in and said, "Before anyone says another word I need to know that all of you understand the meaning of the legal term double jeopardy."

By now Daniel, JR, Mark, Doug, and Roy all had a hard time controlling their sudden urge to laugh and keep a straight face. Sinclair and the rest sensed that something they had no knowledge of was afoot, but obviously they had no clue. Everyone else at the meeting looked perplexed.

Raj continued, "So you all know that double jeopardy means a person can't be punished twice for the same crime?"

Sinclair broke the silence that followed, "Raj, we are talking about the 8th Cycle Library. What has that got to do with double jeopardy?"

Raj answered, "I am sure that is what Daniel is going to tell you right now."

When Daniel finally got his laughter under control, he explained, "You see Sinclair, we thought the same as you do. The thing is, Raj actually made a complete copy of all the disks and translations that Brideaux took with him. He just forgot to tell us - that is until a week or so ago."

Sinclair and everyone else looked at Raj. He held up both hands as he said, "I had my punishment, and I have apologized – you can't punish me again – double jeopardy you know."

They all fell about laughing at Raj's expense when they were let in on the details of the swift justice that was measured out to him, as Daniel related their discovery of his crime, his trial, conviction and punishment.

JR commented that every time he thought about how

that beef korma had him in tears, he was not sure who were punished in the end.

After this humorous interlude, Sarah gave them her thoughts on the question of resistance or not. "I sometimes feel I just want to drop out of society, live in peace, bother no one, and have no one bothering me. But then I also realize I can't just think of my family and myself. There is my sister, Meg and her family, and there are billions of people out there who will be living in hell soon. Although they might not know it now, they will very soon.

"We are the only people I can think of who might be able to get everyone out of that hell again. I agree, it might not seem as if we have much going for us at the moment, but that has never stopped us in the past. What we have now is enough to start with."

To nods of agreement around the room, she continued.

"It will take time. It is not going to be easy, and many more might die and suffer in the process. Nevertheless, I am convinced we have no other option," she concluded as everyone applauded her.

Daniel suggested that they call everybody in the Rabbit Hole together in a town hall meeting and give them a chance to talk about this as well. After all, it affected everyone, including the children. It was only fair to give everyone a chance to air their agreement or dissent.

The final matter on the agenda was that Sarah wanted to hand the reigns back to Daniel to take over the chair.

"You asked me more than a month ago to hold the fort while you were away, and I did that."

She got a big cheer from everyone present as recognition for the brilliant job she did.

Daniel said he had no issue whatsoever if Sarah

remained in the chair. In fact, he liked it, but Sarah was not keen on that idea.

Daniel explained, "This is the new world, and seeing that the patriarchal system landed us all in this mess, maybe it's time to give the matriarchal system a go.

I am sure the matriarchs couldn't make a bigger mess than the patriarchs did. There are many examples of very successful matriarchal systems all over the world – don't forget the Amazons."

By this time, everyone was laughing.

When Sarah, who did her Ph.D. in mythology, finally got order restored, she said, "Listen, Daniel Rossler, I hope you are not insinuating that any of the women in this room, or outside, even remotely resembles an Amazon! If that is the case, I will get my tribe together immediately and kick most of the men out of our territory and put the rest of you in cages. I am not sure if you know, but in the Amazon society men were not allowed to live in their territory. The ones that they allowed were kept in cages as sex slaves. Only once or twice a year they would have sex with their slaves to prevent their race from dying out, and all male offspring would be killed at birth. So, what is it going to be? The chair or the cage?"

Under the roaring laughter of everyone Daniel said in a high-pitched voice, "You made a strong and convincing case my dear. It will be the chair."

The next night everyone gathered in the Town Hall to talk about their plans for the future. Daniel opened the discussion with an overview of what the Steering Committee discussed the day before and was quite surprised to find they all felt the same. There was no one who wanted to accept the new world order. Even the oldest members of the group, Bess, Martha, and Sinclair were very vocal about their dislike of the idea of letting Brideaux stay in control of the world.

Every one of them knew that there were going to be many sacrifices to make in the process. There was going to be suffering and risks, but they were prepared to accept that to regain their freedom.

Many of them pointed out that there was no other option. They knew that Brideaux and his new government were not only looking for the people whose names and faces were in the media. He knew about the rest of them as well, and each was in as much danger as any one of them. Their will to be free was their motivation and driving force – they would not give that up. The Steering Committee received their mandate, and would get busy right away to create their roadmap to freedom.

Ryan then brought up a matter that had been of concern to almost all of them. "Daniel, I think what I am about to say is something that has been foremost in the minds of nearly all of us and that is the well-being of our family members on the outside. Our oldest daughter, Meg, her husband and two children are down in Florida, Emma and I have not only been worried about the danger that they might face, but also the fact that we have disappeared without a word to them. I can just imagine the agony they must be going through."

Daniel responded, "Ryan, thank you for bringing that up. It is something that Sarah and I have been talking about for some time now, even during the planning stages of Enigma. It has been a major concern for us, and I am sure for everyone else in the same position. I guess many of them would have put two and two together by now and have figured out that everyone who was somehow connected with the Rossler Foundation has gone with the ones they saw on the news. But unfortunately, up till now we could not think of an easy way to resolve that problem."

Ben spoke next, "Nancy, Bess and I have been thinking about this and have talked to most of the people here already, except for the O'Reillys, the Mendenhalls, Luke and Sally and of course, the Rossler clan who all have their immediate family members here. Everyone else has immediate family members on the outside. It is imperative that we find a way to either get them here or at least get a message to them that we are alive and well."

Salome was next, "As you know, my parents passed away years ago, but I have a brother on the outside that I am concerned about. Luke and I have been considering some options over the past few days, but it is as Daniel said before, there is just no easy way to do it without putting them and us in danger. We can't just walk out of here and go and get them or phone them and tell them not to worry. I would bet everything I have that our family members and every one of our friends will be under very close surveillance by the authorities, in case we make contact with them. Furthermore, their knowing of our situation puts us all at risk should anyone forget and speak carelessly."

Daniel gave everyone a chance to speak and made notes of their suggestions and concerns. They decided the Steering Committee would try to come up with a plan and let everyone know within the next few days.

JR introduced one more topic. "I have been wondering if we could name this meeting place the Robert Cartwright Town Hall from now on, to remember and honor Robert, a close friend and loyal supporter of the Rossler Foundation cause and the first victim in the war to regain our freedom."

It was a somber topic for all of them, but it met with immediate approval from everyone. Even those who didn't know Robert personally were in favor, because those who did had only high praises for him as an honorable and trustworthy man and loyal friend who, to the end, was prepared to put himself in grave danger to save his friends.

Chapter Twenty-Five

FORTY-YEAR-OLD PROMISES

Sam Lewis, head of the CIA during President Nigel Harper's administration, retired three months after the Sword of Cyrus crisis. At the time, he was in charge of the entire operation that exposed the group of delusional men from Iran who called themselves the Sword of Cyrus and believed they were destined to restore the Persian Empire of Cyrus the Great. Sam, together with a few others, including the Rosslerites, was decorated for the outstanding work they did to avert the crisis and save the world.

On the day after his retirement, Sam, who had been a fly-fishing fanatic from the day he landed his first trout at the age of nine, packed his fishing and camping gear into his 4x4. He was on a trip with no end date in mind.

He'd been planning this trip for the last forty years while working for the CIA, and nothing was going to stop him. He deserved it. It was on his bucket list to visit the top ten fly-fishing spots in America, and time was of no concern to him.

However, one matter had precedence over the fishing. That was a promise he made to himself forty years ago. That promise was the reason the first leg of his trip took him the two thousand four hundred miles from Washington, D.C. to Boise, Idaho. That was where Susan Walker, formerly Susan Collins, his college sweetheart, lived.

Since that painful day forty years ago when Sam broke up with Susan, there'd been no contact between them. Sam could never have imagined how painful it was going to be for him to walk away from the only woman he ever loved.

There was never another woman in his life. He never got married, because he could never bear the thought of dragging anyone, let alone the person whom he loved so much, into the treacherous and dangerous world of CIA operations.

But on the day when he walked away from Susan, he made a promise to himself that if he survived until retirement, the very first thing he would do on the day after his retirement was look her up and explain to her why he'd done it. Although he'd never contacted her, Sam made sure that he always knew where she lived, what she was doing, and that she was okay. He had her address, and he knew she'd been married. He also knew that her husband passed away about five years ago and that she had two boys who were in their early thirties.

Sam couldn't be sure what to expect when he saw her again, but he had the promise to keep. He had to see her once more, and if she were prepared to listen to him, he would try to explain. If she didn't want to see him or talk to him, he would accept it, and that would be the end of it. He would have kept his promise.

Five days later, Sam was standing at the front door of

Susan's house in Boise, Idaho, too scared to ring the doorbell. His palms felt sweaty, his hands were shaking, and his throat was dry. *How is this possible?* He thought. *I am more nervous than when I asked her out on our first date.* Sam Lewis was the envy of many a male student on the campus when he and Susan started dating. Her smile, her laugh, her personality, the way she walked and talked, were all perfection personified. Her tender and caring ways and much more made the blonde and elegant Susan Walker a beautiful woman from head to toe, inside and out.

Come on Sam Lewis, pull yourself together man. You were a field agent in the CIA. What's wrong with you? Lift your hand and ring that bell. Come on, do it. Maybe it's better if you come back tomorrow? That will give you a chance to plan the thing better. What the hell, after forty years you still don't have a plan?

What happened next was not part of the scheme at all. Sam's hand was still halfway towards the doorbell in the same position, where it became frozen in mid-air three minutes ago, when the door opened. Susan Walker stood there, not a single day older than the day he last saw her forty years ago and still as breathtakingly beautiful as ever. Sam's heart missed several beats; he opened his mouth, but no sound came out. Sam Lewis, the tough CIA field operative was speechless and motionless.

Susan had that man-paralyzing smile when she spoke, "Samuel Lewis, what is your plan? Forty-two years ago, you made me watch you through the window when you stood in front of my door for fifteen agonizing minutes to ask me on a date. Are you planning to do that to me again today?"

"Well huh. You see ... Hum. I ... No ... Sorry ... Ah, shit!" was all that he could get out before the laughing Susan grabbed his still stretched-out hand and pulled him into the house and herself into his arms. This was not how he had been planning this moment for the past forty years - it was much, much better.

They stood there in each other's arms without saying a single word for what felt like an eternity. Sam finally got his emotions under control and his voice back. "Susan I made a promise to myself a very long time ago that if I could stay alive until retirement I would come back and give you the explanation I could not give you forty years ago. It has burdened my soul all these years."

Susan lifted her hand and placed her finger on his lips to stop him from talking, "Sam I know why you did it. At first, I hated you for doing that to me, but over time, I realized why you did it, and it just made me love you more than ever. I've been following your career all these years just as you've been following mine."

"What? How do you know?" Sam asked with surprise.

Susan just smiled, "You think you're the only one who knows how to be a spy? Your sources from whom you got your information about my life always told me about your inquiries. To have followed what you were doing the past few years was as easy as switching on the TV."

"You aren't mad at me? Don't you hate me? Susan, how is that possible after what I did to you?"

"Sam let's not live in the past. I've had a full and happy life. I was married to a wonderful and caring man, and I have two beautiful sons, two beautiful and loving daughters-in-law, and three grandchildren. I have been blessed in ways that would never have been possible if we were married while you were in the CIA. Looking back now, there's nothing I regret.

The last five years since John passed away I have been

lonely. I've thought a lot about you. Many times I've dreamed that one day I would again have the pleasure of watching you through the window gathering the courage to ring the doorbell and ask me on a date. "

Sam was speechless again for the second time in less than twenty minutes. But then he was not going to dwell on the past anymore. In fact, the past forty years had just been wiped out in twenty minutes.

Carpe Diem – seize the day – that was how he was going to live his life from now on, with the most amazing woman he had ever met. Can any man ever hope for a better retirement than this? What a redemption it was.

The two of them spent time over the next few days catching up. When Sam told Susan about the second item on his bucket list, there was no stopping her. She would be ready and packed in forty-eight hours. She declared she was not ever going to let him get away again. Sam didn't need any persuasion. He felt exactly the same.

They decided to postpone the trip to Henry's Fork, which was only two hundred and eighty miles away from Boise. Close to Yellowstone National Park, it was the first of the ten most favorite places on Sam's list. Instead, they gave all family and friends a bit of notice about the upcoming wedding.

Two weeks later, at a small and private ceremony, Sam became the proud husband of the most beautiful sixty-four year old woman in America, stepfather of two boys and their wives as well as grandfather of three lively and beautiful grandchildren. There could not have been a prouder and happier man in the world.

The time at Henry's Fork, was an idyllic and blissful honeymoon, after which they went to Washington, D.C. to pack Sam's stuff, put it in storage and arranged with an agency to rent out his house in DuPont Circle. They had decided they would live in Boise, which was close to the family and grandchildren and not too far away from three of the most popular fly-fishing spots on Sam's list in Oregon, Washington, and Montana.

Chapter Twenty-Six

THE MUSKETEERS

Although Sinclair was a few years older than Luke, Ben and Ryan, they found themselves in each other's company often in Boulder. They met in the late afternoons, played bridge or poker and enjoyed a shot or two of 'Irish nectar', as Sinclair called it.

On their fishing trips, they soon had a fierce competition going between them complete with 'de-liars' scales and rulers to weigh and measure their catch and determine on a weekly basis who was the winner. The winner got one extra fishing trip as a prize.

It did not take too long before they were known as the musketeers. But no one ever dared to tell them whom each of them resembled - Athos, Aramis, Porthos or D'Artagnan

When they were out of hearing range, their spouses referred to them as the four 'grumpy old men', but it was all in good spirits. They were actually delighted their men found good camaraderie amongst their peers. The women never questioned or let on that they knew exactly what the four men were up to when they disappeared in the afternoons and came back smiling and relaxed a few hours later.

During their preparation for the move to the Rabbit Hole, the four men had packed enough alcoholic beverages to last them until the first supply run was made.

After six weeks at the Rabbit Hole, as they were slowly but surely working their way through their stock and no supply run in sight, they realized that they were heading for a crisis. All but Sinclair thought it was something to worry about. The reason he was not worried they couldn't get out of him. He just kept on assuring them he had never run dry in his entire life, and had no intention of doing so now. Try as they might, he would not say anything else except that they should trust in the 'luck of the Irish'.

At one of their happy hours, Ryan made a few mathematical calculations, taking into account various scientific factors. Their rate of consumption being a heavily contributing factor in his calculations, he came to the conclusion that they would run dry in about three weeks. They had to either get an order out to Owen at Mount Ararat, or they would have to drink strong black coffee during happy hour, and that wasn't a pleasing thought to any of them.

Sinclair saw the despair on the faces of his friends, and he knew it was time to help them out of their misery. He asked that they all follow him to a room where he had stored some of his translation material. He had them help him move a few things around so he could get to two boxes in a corner, which marked very clearly "Handle with absolute care. Do not open without me present. Sinclair O'Reilly." There were skull and crossbones stickers across the top and sides of the boxes.

They all exploded in laughter when Sinclair carefully

unpacked and unwrapped the contents of the first box, a shining five-gallon copper moonshine still kit with an electric element.

"So this is what you have been smiling about all these weeks, you old coot!" Luke shouted. "You've caused us so much stress and anxiety, man!"

Sinclair just laughed, "I told you I have never run dry and don't intend to - I even blessed you all with the luck of the Irish. Okay, so now stop fretting and let's figure out how to assemble this thing and get it operational."

Ryan replied, "Well, I think between us we have the skills to get it assembled, and if we fail at first we can always read the instructions. The problem I see is where do we obtain the ingredients we need to get this thing going?"

"That's what the next box is for," Sinclair replied with a big smile.

They immediately opened the second box and found it to be neatly packed with a recipe book containing instructions to make moonshine from corn, rye, fruit, even berries, and honey. Sinclair certainly came to the Rabbit Hole adequately prepared. They were elated. That second box also had enough ingredients to make more than twenty gallons, and they reckoned that would last them until they could produce their own corn in the Gardens of Gallatin.

They were sure the ladies of the Gallatin Garden Society would not mind them growing some corn. In fact, those girls owed them a big favor because their flourishing gardens were only made possible by the earthworms that the four of them discovered and supplied.

Ben wanted to get down to business as quickly as possible, "Okay guys, now we have to be sure we avoid getting ourselves into trouble with the womenfolk. We have to find a place to set this operation up where no one can find it or smell it. There's a room Aaron and I have blocked off on the top level that could be ideal. Let's go inspect it and decide what we have to do."

They followed Ben and examined the place. It was perfect. They would have to cut a few small holes to the outside for ventilation. Ryan would build mini extraction fans to make sure the smell of fermentation didn't spread throughout the caves. The rest of them would smuggle the boxes up there, assemble the still and hook it up to the electricity.

It took three days to get the whole operation going. Luke made sure their pub was completely sealed off and marked with signs and barriers that said no one was allowed past that point. Within fourteen days, the three musketeers had their first taste of their 'Chateau de Grotte' and all agreed it was an exquisite vintage. Ben, who'd become quite handy with Roy's laser cutting tools since he arrived at the Rabbit Hole, constructed a beautiful table and benches out of the rocks inside their pub.

Chapter Twenty-Seven

NOT FORGOTTEN

Brideaux was a busy man with a lot on his plate. There was the world to govern, but despite that he very often found he was still getting a nauseating feeling whenever he thought about the 8th and 10th Cycle libraries. The Rosslerites and the humiliation they had caused him in front of his followers ate at him, always.

Jason, his detective who was supposed to have captured the Rosslerites weeks ago, was still traveling around the world following leads. Brideaux realized it was a wild goose chase. They'd licked him again, despite all his contacts and influence, and it remained as infuriating as always to have to admit it.

Though he and the Eligo Rarus council members were reasonably happy with their progress to subdue the world populace and establish the new order, his biggest and most disturbing problem was the missing Rosslerites and the libraries he so desperately needed. Both subjects were brought up over and over again at the meetings. There seemed to be no escaping them.

They were all painfully aware that as long as they didn't have those libraries it would serve as testimony to the biggest failure of their otherwise successful operation to date. Those treasured records in the hands of the Rosslerites could one day cause them a lot of trouble and even their downfall. It was time to cast the net wider. Brideaux kept reminding them the Rosslerites were all human, not ghosts. They had to be somewhere. They would have made a mistake somewhere. They would have left a trace somewhere. No human could be nowhere.

They had the names, photos and details of each and every one of the forty-five adults and fifteen children whom they suspected to be amongst the fugitives. To hide a group of sixty people without detection was not going to be a walk in the park. With the passing of time they would start to relax and their guard would drop. They would become a bit more careless and negligent and were bound to make mistakes sooner or later.

No one had to remind the council how brilliantly the Rosslerites saved the world from destruction by a group who called themselves the Sword of Cyrus a few years ago. They outsmarted the perpetrators who were armed with nanonuke technologies so advanced that the world's scientists were in total shock to learn that it was even possible to create. Not only was the prevention of global domination by a resurrected Persian Empire an astonishing feat. The very fact that the Rosslerites were capable of doing it in less than forty days was the cause of severe distress for the council members.

The longer it took to apprehend the Rosslerites the better the chances were that they could develop countermeasures and use it to destroy Brideaux's plans, and with them, every member of the council. They were also well aware that although they had the support of large parts of society because of the appeal of the utopian world promised to them, they had already made many enemies that would grow in number as time passed. The Rosslerites had to be prevented from ever being able to join forces with those enemies of the state.

They appointed James Gordon, former head of MI6, as the head of the Bureau of State Security (BOSS). He'd openly sworn allegiance to the Supreme Council on the day of the takeover in New Delhi and was now a member of the council. Their primary task was the identification and eradication of the enemies of the state.

The Rosslerites were enemy number one on their list.

Gordon had at his disposal the expertise and cooperation of every former law enforcement agency in the world. He appointed a team of experts and analysts, even clairvoyants to this task. The group working on the Rosslerite case would study not only their backgrounds and every scrap of information they could find, they would peel back the lives of all they could of the missing sixty people.

They would also study each and every person the vanished group ever came into contact with during their lives. They would keep a close watch on every one of them and if necessary use them to lure the Rosslerites out of hiding.

The second group was on the hunt for the enemies of the state. Gordon's task was made a lot easier than in the days when he controlled MI6, as he now had immediate and unrestricted access to the files of every former security and law enforcement agency in the world. It was astonishing, even to a man like Gordon, to see what information he had available to him. Not only the dirtiest of dirty secrets, but also files on every person ever placed on a watch list by their former governments.

Some of the reasons people were on those watch lists, especially in the so-called democratic countries of the world, made him smile. The whole concept of democracy, 'freedom of speech' and the 'right to privacy', all grandiose philosophies that people thought existed, but he knew didn't and didn't believe ever had.

He found the names and exact locations of every prepper group in the world, many of those which, or at least some of the members, were of interest to him. He made sure his employees paid them a visit just to let them know 'we know about you'. He would also direct drone surveillance over them. Most of the prepper groups just wanted to be left alone to live in isolation. They had no interest in politics or the rest of society, but Gordon also knew that once the bio tag implants became compulsory it would violate their principles. They could quickly become the ideal breeding ground for resistance.

In addition, the prospect that the Rosslerites could be holed up with one or more of these prepper groups made it a wise decision to keep close tabs on them. From a study of the files of the history of the Rosslerites, Gordon had no doubt in his mind that they were not idle. They were working on a plan and would eventually make their move. He was going to be ready for them. That was if he had not smoked them out before then.

Another task BOSS officials had was to visit all former high-ranking politicians, law enforcement, and security force officers, as well as government officials, with the purpose to persuade them to support the new world government initiative. In some cases, no persuasion was necessary at all. Many of them signed up and became loyal supporters right away. In other instances, it was a bit more challenging, but with the help of some of the information gathered from those secret files, the 'persuasion' process was very efficient. Those people were employed as campaigners for the new government, and many became regular faces and voices in the media.

The third group, those who didn't fall into line right away, proved to be a major headache for Gordon and his bureau staff. There was no help in those secret files. Many of these people were dead set against the new government and said so outright, while others just requested to be left alone. Gordon had to find another way to deal with them and limit their influence. He decided that he was going to personally conduct meetings with the highest-ranking people in this group.

BOSS moved swiftly to quarantine everyone of influence that could not be 'persuaded', by providing them with protection services for their security. Only when the protection services were in place did they realize that their safety and security had nothing to do with it. They were under house arrest and not allowed contact with anyone else.

They were in the state's protective custody until senior officials from BOSS or the head of BOSS could meet them. Councilor Gordon would work out a plan with them to guarantee their security in the future. As the meetings took place they found out that 'their safety' actually meant staying out of jail by doing what BOSS told them to do. They were not allowed to be in contact with anyone unless BOSS pre-approved such contact, and that included close family members.

Within a few short weeks, BOSS officials had paid visits to everyone on their list and effectively placed them in quarantine. With these measures in place and effectively enforced, BOSS officials took their time to arrange the promised meetings. There was no hurry.

Gordon was left with a few prominent people from the old era who did not want to cooperate as requested. He instructed his secretary to arrange the meetings and flights. For the next two weeks he did an around the world trip to have meetings with the world's most famous people – such as the Pope, the Dalai Lama, ex-president Harper and his wife, former head of the CIA Sam Lewis, and quite a few other former heads of state, along with a few celebrities.

Gordon's colleague in charge of the Bureau of Information and Political Affairs, Anastasia Oriov, former Russian Minister of Communications and Mass Media, had a few plans of her own for these former VIPs. She was going to use all of them, persuaded or not, to help her win the hearts and minds of the people. She intended to parade them in public at every possible opportunity to show the people that all the former famous people were in support of the new regime; everyone was going to see all of them. Of course, only those she chose would be heard.

Chapter Twenty-Eight

THE HARPERS

The year after the successful prevention of the world takeover bid by the Sword of Cyrus group from Iran, Nigel Harper and his wife Esther retired. They would be remembered as the most popular presidential couple in the history of America. Now they were living on their farm in Tennessee, not far from Cookeville.

The shock they felt when the first news about Daniel and the other Rosslerites emerged left them shaken and anxious. Over the next few days as they watched the reports and saw how the story got new legs with almost every broadcast, they both came to the conclusion that something was wrong.

The so-called facts as reported by the media created more questions than answers. They were soon convinced that the Rosslerites were framed in some conspiracy and that the 10th Cycle Library could very well have had something to do with it. Two FBI agents eventually turned up to question them about their relationship with the Rosslers and to ask their help to track them down. Nigel and Esther made it a point to speak their minds and told the agents in no uncertain terms that they were barking up the wrong tree.

Shortly after the news about their friends, the quiet and peaceful life of the Harpers was shattered to pieces by the coup d'état at the G20 summit in New Delhi. The next day the senior agent of their security detail told President Harper that Robert Wilson, head of the secret services in the USA wanted to meet with him later that afternoon. Nigel immediately agreed, as he was sure he was about to get all the details of what happened in New Delhi and how it was going to affect their safety and security.

Later that afternoon three black SUVs with tinted windows drove up the road and parked in front of the house. Robert Wilson got out, and he and one of his agents walked towards the president, who was standing outside the front door with all four of his own security detail standing beside him. The rest of the agents accompanying Wilson emerged from the vehicles, taking up stations in front of them.

"Good afternoon Robert, it's good to see you again. I didn't know you travelled with such a big entourage these days," Nigel said with a smile as he extended his hand.

Wilson stopped two paces away from the president and instead of shaking his hand, he said. "Mr. Harper, I am not here for any pleasantries. I am here to place you and Mrs. Harper under house arrest."

Nigel was immediately affronted and alarmed. "What the ... have you lost your mind, man?"

"Mr. Harper the men that came with me will be your new security detail. I will go through the rules with you shortly." He looked at the secret agents who stood next to Nigel. "Okay boys, you heard me. Get your asses over there in the SUVs. Your stuff will be packed and sent to you by your replacements."

"Robert Wilson, I demand an explanation. Now!" Nigel shouted.

"Mr. Harper, I get the impression you don't understand what's going on, but you are in no position to demand anything. I suggest you listen carefully to what I say and avoid any unpleasantness," Wilson said while his hand started moving to his gun.

Nigel's agents went for their weapons, but before any of them could touch their guns, they were overwhelmed by sudden muscle spasms and dropped to the ground clutching their throats. Nigel turned to his right and stopped as he saw blood spurting from the mouths and noses of his agents.

They were all dead within less than a minute.

Wilson had the gun in his hand pointed at Nigel when he looked up at him from the dead men by his side. "Mr. Harper, please, let's avoid any further incidents like this. I trust I can now rely on your full cooperation?" Wilson asked with raised eyebrows.

"You bastard! You killed them. Why, you son of a bitch! Why?" Nigel shouted.

"Mr. Harper, in case you haven't realized it by now, things have changed as of yesterday. You will now cooperate with me, and there will be no further dead people around here." He half turned to the agents at the SUVs and said, "You and you, go and get Mrs. Harper and bring her out here. I want them both to hear the new security rules." He spoke to the rest and said, "These bodies can be loaded in body bags and placed in the back of the SUVs. Then you can unpack your stuff."

Nigel Harper was trembling with rage and shock. "Listen you scumbags, if any of you so much as lay a finger on my wife, I will kill you all!" he shouted to the two men on their way to the front door.

Wilson erupted into evil laughter, "I'm wondering how you're planning to do that. Get going guys - I don't have all day! I'm a busy man!"

Nigel decided it was time to remain quiet.

A few minutes later, Esther Harper walked out the front door accompanied by the two men sent to fetch her. She was in time to see the last dead agent placed into a body bag next to the three others. Shocked and with her hand covering her mouth, she stifled a scream when she saw her husband's pale face. Something terrible had happened.

"Nigel, Robert what happened? What's going on? Are they dead? Why? What happened? Tell me what's going on!" She was trembling badly.

Nigel folded his arms around his shaking wife and whispered in her ear. "Esther we are in grave danger. Please, please stay calm. We'll be okay if we just listen for the moment."

Slowly the shaking stopped, and the former first lady recovered her demeanor.

Nigel looked at Wilson with hate in his eyes and said, "Judas betrayed Jesus with a kiss for thirty pieces of silver. You betrayed your people and your country to keep this job. But I guess I might as well be talking to the rocks over there in the garden. So do what you were sent to do, and then get out of here. If I never see you again, it will be too soon."

By the time Wilson left, they understood what Wilson meant when he said 'under house arrest'.

Six new agents had replaced their secret service detail. They were refused any contact with the outside world. No telephone calls, emails or meetings with anyone unless approved by Robert Wilson. They could not even get in touch with their families.

Surveillance cameras and bugs were installed throughout their house that same night. They had no privacy anymore. They had access to the news via their TV and radio, but soon realized it was not worth bothering to switch those on for the purpose of learning what was going on in their country and the world. It was extremely troubling to watch as the world descended into the darkest place in modern human history and maddening to sit by and watch without being able to lift a finger.

They were told that they would remain in limbo until the head of BOSS could see them and agree with them about their future. Of course, the Harpers were not used to this type of treatment. As President of the United States and thus the most powerful man in the world for eight years, this was a humiliation that went beyond his self-control. There was no way he could ever accept this as the new way of life for himself or for Esther.

They found that the only private time they had was when they would go for an early morning or late afternoon walk, and only as long as they kept their voices down. The agents were never more than ten paces away from them. They had to remain as calm and collected as humanly possible under these circumstances of utmost provocation and be ready when and if the right opportunity presented itself.

About three weeks later, while out on their early morning stroll, Esther whispered, "Nigel what do you consider is the real purpose of the meeting later today with that James Gordon character? What's going to happen there? Do you know him?"

Nigel replied. "I know of him. He was the former head of MI6 and has now apparently gone over to the dark side. I remember that Sam Lewis, my head of the CIA when we were in the White House, met him once or twice, but other than that, I don't know much else about him. As for what to expect later today, it's difficult to say what's going through these madmen's minds, but I have a few guesses. "

"What are you thinking?" she asked.

"I'm pretty sure they won't lock us up. At least not yet. They would have done that on day one if we were of no value to them. They'll try to get as much mileage out of us as they can, until we aren't useful to them anymore. They'll parade us in the media at every available opportunity. They'll use us as propaganda to show the public that even the former president has joined them. We will, however, never be allowed to say a word in public. Of that I am one hundred percent sure." Nigel said with sadness in his voice.

"What do you think we should do at the meeting today?" Esther asked.

"I think it isn't going to be easy to keep calm, but we'll have to. That's more of a warning to myself than you. I'm the one who's been struggling to keep my composure. I'm sure the place is going to be crowded with the media, and after all, it will be a big photo op for their propaganda machine.

I suspect he's going to offer us the moon and the stars if we come out openly and join their cause. If we don't, they will keep us more or less in our current situation until we are of no use to them anymore," Nigel said with a grim smile.

"What happens to us then, Nigel?" Esther asked with the concern noticeable in her voice.

"My dear, I suggest we cross that bridge when we come to it. For now, if we play along and don't upset them, we have time on our side. As long as we're useful to them we'll stay alive and out of jail. And as long we're alive and out of jail, we at least have the opportunity to work on a solution," Nigel said. Esther nodded in agreement.

Chapter Twenty-Nine

THE ROADMAP

The morning after the town hall meeting, the Steering Committee quickly reviewed and received progress updates of all ongoing projects as usual. And then, they got right down to the business of creating their roadmap to freedom. They decided that Mark and Doug, both ex-officers in the military, would become part of the Steering Committee, while Ben and Ryan would take on the oversight of the internal infrastructure projects.

It felt strange to find themselves on the other side of the fence, where *they* were now the bad guys, the terrorists, and infiltrators, the most wanted people in the world.

The fact that the news they had access to was under the absolute control of the new government meant that the events were not what really happened in the outside world. The seizure of people's guns, for instance, would not have happened the way the news media dished it up. Reports such as 'There was no resistance whatsoever; all people voluntarily handed in their guns' was obviously a lot of horse manure.

"A spokesperson for The Supreme Council in Brussels today expressed the council's profound gratitude for the cooperation of all. The council was particularly grateful that everyone understood the necessity of removing guns from society," just made them laugh. They knew better than that. Those who'd been with Owen and Alison in little Nucla, Colorado knew for a fact that this particular issue was a direct insult to the town ordinance requiring every head of household to own a gun. They suspected the same attitude about the Second Amendment was prevalent, at least in the Western United States, where bumper stickers declaring 'You can take my gun when you pry it from my cold, dead hand' was a common sight.

Understandably, they were also extremely skeptical about the apparent euphoria that descended upon the world. Every government on the planet, with no resistance and no demonstrations from anyone anywhere, apparently welcomed the new world order? People were dancing in the streets with joy? Interviews with people who were so excited about the amazing future in store for everyone on the planet were broadcast more or less 24/7. The Rosslerites were sure that was not the true state of affairs.

The first thing the Steering Committee had to consider was how to find a way to be better informed than by listening to the council's radio news broadcasts. They had to have access to the real situation, which not only meant having observers on the outside, but also having access to the new government's electronic data storage facilities. They understood that their situation required skills and experience they did not have.

Except for Luke, who was a retired CIA field agent and Salome, who had been an FBI profiler, they had no one who had even the slightest clue of the covert world of espionage.

Luke suggested, "I am of the opinion that we need to get hold of Sam Lewis. He's the most trustworthy man I ever met. He would be more up to date with the latest in spy technologies and counterintelligence than anyone else I can think of. Not only that, he would also have contact with some ex- and current covert operators who might want to join our cause."

Salome responded, "Yes, I agree with that, Luke. Getting in touch with Sam would be ideal, but we'll have to cross a few bridges in the process. He was a high-profile person, and he would still be, but in a different sense now. He would be under the closest surveillance you can imagine. We'll have to be more than just extremely careful."

Daniel added, "Based on my personal experience of Sam's handling of the Sword of Cyrus crisis, I agree. I'd like to have him with us for this. I can't think of anyone better. The first question, though, is where can we get hold of him? The second is, Luke, are you up for the job?"

Luke turned his somewhat surprised gaze to Daniel, "What do you mean? Up for what job?"

Daniel replied, "The way I see it, you know Sam better than anyone else here. Not only that, but you have the field craft skills to move about unnoticed and locate him. If he's incarcerated somewhere already, you're also the best candidate to break him out. I think you're the best and most logical person for the job. Wouldn't you agree?"

The full weight of the veracity of Daniel's words caused a brief silence before Luke responded, "I guess you're right about that. I *am* up for it. Let's work out how it can be done."

The unhesitating commitment by Luke, who was already approaching seventy, served as a harsh reminder to everyone present about the type of engagement required of each of them in the future.

Raj and Salome started to speak at the same time and then both stopped mid-sentence when they realized it, "You go first, Raj." Salome smiled.

Raj continued, "Thanks, Salome. I will be quick. I wanted to say that before taking the risk of sending people out there, we would have to get a few other crucial things in place. The first would be to get hold of the latest satellite tracking software so that we know where the surveillance satellites are at any given moment and take steps to avoid detection. Second, similar to the satellites, we will have to work out countermeasures against drone surveillance. Third, we will have to look at what we can do to escape the most sophisticated facial recognition systems and fourth, we will have to come up with a secure communications strategy."

"It's true then, great minds do think alike! That's more or less what I had on my list here," Salome said with another smile.

Daniel continued the discussions. "Okay, so far our analyses have highlighted some gaps. I don't think we have to find the solutions for them today. I suggest we continue our gap analysis so that we can get the full picture of what we are up against."

Sinclair was next. "We all know, and I am sure also agree that the secret ingredient with which we could eventually outmaneuver the technology of the new government could very well be locked up in those libraries. Hell, come to think of it, even Brideaux knows that, hence his relentless efforts to track us down. The problem we've had so far was that the translation process was just too slow and cumbersome. We still don't have any idea of the full extent of what those 10th Cyclers left for us to discover. We have to find a way to speed up the process."

Raj agreed, "Yes I support that idea. Sinclair has already spoken to Stuart and me, and we've had a look at it. Our initial assessment is that there are parts of the work that can be automated. We will keep on working with Sinclair and pick his brain. As we get a better grip on his processes, we might very well find more areas for automation. Nevertheless, I have to warn you, it is not going to be a quick or easy job. It will take time, and it might even at some stage require outside help."

"What you propose to do and how you start sounds good to me," Daniel said. "We'll have to cross the outside help bridge when we come to it. He then turned to Roy. "Roy you've been quiet. I'm very interested to hear your ideas."

Roy smiled, "In fact, I have a lot going on in my mind. I think we'll have to get our hands on those implants - 'The Skinwalkers' as Joseph used to call them. Then we can analyze and reverse engineer them. Once we understand how they work, we might be able to find a way to neutralize them. But then again, I guess getting hold of the Skinwalkers brings us back to the first point we discussed. We need someone on the outside who could find them for us.

"Another challenge we'll have is also to figure out how those chips are connected to the Skywalker satellites and if there is a way that we can perhaps neutralize or destroy them somehow. Due to our friend, Brideaux's abhorrent sense of timing, bad manners, and drinking habits, we never had the chance to conduct a meticulous study of exactly how that part of the 8th Cycle technology worked. I'd like to understand that in detail, because I'm sure that's what his scientists have been keeping themselves busy with lately."

Roy's sarcastic remarks about Brideaux had them all laughing. This was a side of Roy that they hadn't seen before. Salome was wondering if her husband's usually shy personality's suddenly developed humorous streak could be the side effects of the morphine given him for pain. Alternatively, maybe it could be the result of spending thirty-three days in Daniel's company, or even Owen Bell's. Roy had told her of Owen's constant joking.

Roy continued, "That would in broad terms be my approach. I've also been thinking a lot about that 'time travel' discovery that Raj made. It alerted us to the future those Sword of Cyrus crazies had in mind for us. Maybe it could do the same again. That time travel technology of the 10th Cyclers has been bugging me ever since, and I would certainly like to delve deeper into that. Who knows, I might find a way to travel back and put a gun in Daniel's hands to shoot the asshole outside the 8th Cycle facility when Daniel learned about his plans. Or even for those of us who were inside to overpower him when he walked in. Wouldn't it be great to go back and kick his ass for him before handing him off to JR for special treatment?"

All Salome could get out was, "Roy!" before her voice was drowned in the laughter.

While Roy was talking, Daniel noticed the stunned looks that passed between Mark and Doug, as if they were asking, "What the hell have we gotten ourselves into? Time travel? Have we managed to land ourselves in the looney bin?"

Daniel just smiled and decided to have a little bit more fun with them, "Mark, Doug don't worry about it. It won't happen all of a sudden, it happens gradually, you won't notice it in the beginning. And then one day, when it is too late, you'll discover it has happened - you have gone crazy."

By the looks on their faces, the two of them were now

seriously worried. Daniel thought he'd better calm them down before they ran away, "Guys let me put your minds at ease. It's true. We discovered something a few years ago in the 10th Cycle Library, which I guess you could call time travel. That discovery saved our asses big time. We haven't yet discovered how they did it, yet, but

I'll tell you the full story as soon as we finish this meeting. For now, take my word for it – we haven't gone round the bend."

Daniel couldn't help but add one extra bit. "But, please remind me if I forget to tell you what effect that discovery had on Sinclair and my grandfather when they learned about it."

That brought on another fit of laughter from those who remembered how drunk Sinclair and Nicholas got that day. Their singing and dancing up and down the hallways of the Foundation offices with a bottle of whiskey in their hands was so unlike them, but at the same time, hilarious.

Mark and Doug exchanged another puzzled look but didn't say a word.

Daniel returned to Roy to hear if he had anything else to say. "Is that it?"

"I was about to finish. We shouldn't forget the other toys I brought along. There's a large number of spyflies, hummingbird mini drones and a box or two full of other gadgets that might come in handy for us along the way. I'll be happy to give you all a demo and train you how to use all of it at some stage. We'll never know when we might need some of those gadgets, and come to think of it, I can already imagine how we can use the spyflies and hummingbirds. I'm obviously also more than happy to help with anything else we might need that I can build in my lab, including as many nanonukes as you might think we'll need."

Again, Mark and Doug passed that questioning look between them and also at Daniel when Roy talked about building nanonukes. They'd heard Roy mentioned nanonukes in the chopper that night on the way to Nucla, but they thought he was joking. Daniel explained briefly again that it was no joke. Roy actually built and tested a few of them before, devastating a warehouse in the process. He would give them more details later when he explained the time travel discovery to them.

"Salome you're up next," Daniel continued. "Raj's mention earlier of the satellites, drones, and communications had me wondering if you and Luke had any ideas about that."

Salome replied, "Yes, in fact we already had a few short discussions with Raj and Roy about those topics. So let me start with the satellites and drones."

Daniel nodded for her to proceed.

"As you know, we've already deployed some of the hummingbirds outside the caves to warn us about drones in the air and people on the ground. That has been working very well, but our movements are limited to about five hundred yards around the main entrance. We need to consider how we can expand our coverage so we can have more space available to move around undetected."

Raj and Roy explained they were already working on some ideas to achieve that and hoped to start testing in the next few days and deploy their extended surveillance system within a week or so.

Salome continued, "As for the technical aspects of satellite tracking; that's a little bit out of my league. Nevertheless, I can tell you that Luke and I know satellites are used for finding and tracking people by the use of body heat imaging and facial recognition. I guess Mark and Doug will have had firsthand experience of that during the Afghanistan and Iraqi wars, where satellites were used with great effect to track down the enemy."

Doug added, "Yes I saw how they work, and I know how accurate they can be. Those things can read the headlines of a newspaper from space. But what I think could be in our favor is the fact that there aren't that many of those satellites available. Up until now, they were used almost exclusively in the trouble zones of the world, not for domestic purposes. They certainly aren't covering the entire globe with them. Those satellites are usually only deployed when a particular area of interest has been identified, such as a war zone. The thing is, of course, you have to know where to look before you could find what you're looking for. It's not likely that there are any of those satellites deployed over the USA at the present moment and even less chance they would be looking around here."

"That's a bit of a relief," JR replied, "But I guess there's also no guarantee satellites could not be moved to another location. Of course, new ones could be launched to start tracking large parts of the USA too, couldn't they?"

"Yes, that's true. We can't assume that if they aren't over the USA now they won't be there in the future," Salome said. "Luke and I don't have enough technical knowledge about this subject. However, we had a very interesting discussion with Raj, and maybe it's best if he explains what he knows about that side of it."

"Raj?" Salome looked at Raj.

Raj smiled. Although he did not regard himself an expert on satellites, he always liked to learn more and talk about anything related to technology.

"I am not an expert in satellite technology and the tracking, but I will tell you what I have learned through one of my friends. Apparently, since the Russians launched the first satellite called Sputnik in the late fifties, another seven thousand or so have been placed into orbit. From memory, about four thousand of them are still in orbit, but only about a thousand or so are still operational. The rest have become part of space junk."

"Hmm, I always thought there were tens of thousands of them out there. So it isn't as crowded up there as I believed," Sarah quipped. "It would be useful if there was a way for us to know where they are, what each one's purpose is, and who are in control of them. I take it that most of them are there for purposes of communications, navigation, weather research, agriculture, space exploration and such, rather than spying?"

Raj continued, "Yes, that is also my understanding. There are not that many in use for spying purposes. What is good news for us is that apparently the United States Space Surveillance Networks are tracking every object in orbit over four inches in diameter, and they know exactly which country each piece out there belongs to."

"So, how does that help us?" Mark wanted to know.

Raj replied. "Well, there are many amateur and professional satellite watchers out there. With the information made available by organizations such as the SSN, many programs and mobile apps have been developed to enable people to know exactly where a satellite is at any given moment. But, as I said, those apps are all based on the information that the SSN was prepared to make available to the public. They would obviously not put any information about spy satellites in the public domain."

"That won't help us much, if we can't track the spy satellites," JR interrupted.

Raj smiled, "Yes that would be correct. But the point I was about to make was that in my network there are quite a few satellite enthusiasts. They have access to all the data of the SSN and a few other organizations, not just what they decide to put in the public domain."

Daniel immediately grasped what Raj was saying, "Aha, I got it. One problem almost solved. We just need to figure out how we're going to get hold of that software."

"Just one question, Raj," Luke said. "Do I understand you correctly? Those programs don't require an Internet connection to operate properly?"

"Yes, that's true. All they require is your current location and time zone and which satellites you want to track. They then follow the satellite's path according to your position and display it on the screen. Most are extremely accurate and reliable. There are a few more features I could tell you about, but in essence, that's what it does. So we have no worries about requiring an Internet connection."

"That's great news. I'm sure we're going to put that software to good use in the future." Daniel ended the satellite discussions.

"The next important topic I would like to introduce is our communications strategy with the outside world. Luke, Salome, Raj and anyone else, let's have it."

Luke was first, "That's another topic Salome and I've been thinking about. The problem with me is I'm too old - the methods that I am familiar with are outdated. Computers can crack an encoded message in a shorter time than I can write it. But we think that with Raj and Stuart's help we could try and modernize those old techniques. Having said that, I have to explain the two rules of secure communications, which are very simple. Rule number one is there is no such thing as secure communications, and rule number two is if you are ever in doubt, refer to rule number one."

Luke continued to explain that there were four categories of safeguarding communications.

First; hide the fact that a conversation took place. For instance, a bunch of flowers on a person's desk could mean, "Meet me at the usual place tomorrow." No one other than the people involved would know that a message has passed.

Second; hide the identities of the parties who were communicating. For example, use unregistered cell phones, Internet cafes, Internet proxies and other methods to disguise the origin and destination of messages.

Third; protect the message content through coding and encryption.

Fourth; use a technique known as steganography, which means that a message is hidden within another message, such as reading every second letter of the words in a sentence to spell out a message.

"Stega-what?" JR asked.

"Steganography," Luke replied, "Comes from Greek and means 'covered writing.' Apparently they wrote messages on wood or clay tablets and then covered it with wax and wrote something entirely different in the wax. So unless you knew to remove the wax, you wouldn't get to the hidden message."

Sinclair said, "Well, just to set the record books straight. The Greeks might have named the technique, but they certainly did not develop it first. As far as I can see, the 10th Cyclers have beaten them by at least five thousand years, if not more."

"I agree with that," Luke replied.

Salome and Raj explained that as far as encryption was concerned, everyone should be aware that the government agencies had the best decryption systems imaginable and nothing they tried to encrypt would be secret for much more than an hour or two after it landed in the hands of those agencies.

The advantage of steganography over encryption was that the real message was hidden in plain sight. In other words, unless the reader was aware of the fact that the text he or she was reading contained a hidden message and knew what to look for, it wasn't easy to discover. It wouldn't draw attention as would happen with an encrypted message.

Salome described in great detail how terrorists had for years been using steganography on the Internet. They could communicate with their followers so easily it was frightening. Tracking the messages down and then following them was impossible, even for governments, because it was an impossible task trying to monitor the entire Internet and scan every bit of text, images, and audio for potential messages.

Everyone was interested in how computers could be used with steganography, so Raj gave them a few examples.

In a picture, the color of every fiftieth pixel could be slightly changed and each of those changed pixels in the image would correspond to a letter or number that in turn spelled out a message, which could also be coded.

A human eye would not see those adjusted pixels, but a computer program could pick them up quickly. The same principle could be used in a sound file. In a text file, a comma or full stop and other punctuation marks could easily contain a hundred or more words.

Messages could also be hidden in radio signals, such as

those received on FM and shortwave radios. That was a very creative method used during the cold war and for quite a few years after, until the Internet started to dominate communications. Messages were not only hidden in the words you could hear but also in those hissing and crackling noises, especially on shortwave.

Daniel stopped the meeting at about four o'clock that afternoon. "We've covered quite a bit today, and we still have a lot more to cover in the days ahead. I think if we take a break now and continue tomorrow, it will give us all a chance to digest what we've discussed and start thinking about how we can implement some of our strategies. I think you will all agree that we have our work cut out for us?"

"No doubt about that," Raj replied with a smile.

"Well, I'm excited. Finally, we're on the way to go and kick that S.O.B.'s ass," JR added.

Before they left, Daniel asked everyone to think about ways Luke might get in touch with Sam Lewis and how a message could be sent out to family members outside without compromising anyone.

Chapter Thirty

THE LEWISES

It was also a big shock for Sam when he saw the news about his friends at the Rossler Foundation, but he immediately understood that something was amiss in the media version of what allegedly happened. By the third day, he picked up the phone and called his friend Luke Clarke. When he got no answer, he made a few calls to other former colleagues. All he could get out of them that he didn't already know from the media reports was that seemingly, the Rossler Foundation had been shut down. All the servers were gone, and a great number of the former employees with their families, including Luke and Sally Clarke had vanished.

A week later, when the constant speculation and elaboration in the media became utterly ridiculous, he made a few phone calls again, but this time he couldn't get anyone to talk to him. Phones went dead as soon as the call connected, or his calls were simply not answered or returned. Now he was sure something was really wrong, and he fully expected contact from his old friend Luke.

He wondered if this had anything to do with the conversation he and Luke had when they met in a restaurant in Boulder a short time ago. Luke told him a bit about the discovery of the facility of the 8th Cycle in the Grand Canyon.

The alarm bells rang a few decibels louder when two FBI agents turned up to question him about his relationship with Luke Clarke and other members of the Rossler Foundation. He was quite disturbed to discover how much highly classified information, intended to be known only to those who were involved, these agents had.

He had no information that could help them and told them so. He knew how to play the game and therefore made sure he gave them the truth. When he last saw Luke, where they were, what they were doing, all of it. His honesty obviously pacified the agents and he believed he'd never hear from them again. Sam and Susan's newfound peaceful, happy lives were crushed four days later. While they were staying at their favorite fishing place at Henry's Fork, three black SUVs with tinted windows stopped outside their cabin. Six men got out, and one of them approached and introduced himself as special agent Anderson.

"Mr. Lewis, I have orders to place you and Mrs. Lewis under immediate house arrest," Anderson said.

"Anderson, come on, I wasn't hatched under a turkey. Who is the joker? Is it Luke Clarke? Tell him he can come out; I know he's around here somewhere." Sam smiled while he looked around, expecting Luke to make his appearance.

"Mr. Lewis this is no joke. You have to pack your stuff now and come with us back to your home, where you will be placed under our care until further notice." Anderson said in an abrupt tone.

Sam looked at him and started to wonder if this was in

fact not a joke. Those agents looked sincere - they all had their hands on their guns.

"Would you care to tell me what this about?" Sam requested, half smiling.

"You don't know what happened at the G20 summit in New Delhi earlier today? You didn't see the news?" Anderson was surprised that Sam had obviously no clue of what was going on in the world at that moment.

"What the hell do you mean? What's with New Delhi? What's the G20 got to do with this? And why am I being placed under arrest?" Sam was getting irritated - the joke was getting a bit old now.

"Mr. Lewis, I have my orders and I intend to follow them. All I can tell you is that there is a new government, a world government. The United Sates government does not exist anymore, and neither does any other administration in the world," Anderson tried to explain, but only succeeded in causing more confusion in Sam's mind. He was now beginning to believe again that this was definitely a joke.

"Son, are you sure you haven't been out in the sun for too long lately? Now get it over with, tell Luke Clarke to come out now, so I can kick his ass for him." Sam laughed.

Anderson saw that he was not being taken seriously. He took out his gun and pointed it at Sam while the rest of his men followed suit and now had both Sam and Susan at gunpoint.

Sam realized something was wrong, terribly wrong. Crazy as it might sound to him these guys, whose weapons he and Susan were staring at, were serious. This was not a joke.

From years of experience, he knew that now was the time to play nicely. Any form of anger or resistance was going to trigger a lot of trouble. He looked at Susan who was standing right next to him and told her to do exactly what these men instructed. He could feel how her body was shaking when he put his arm around her.

"Very well then, Mr. Anderson. You and your men are holding the guns. What are we to do now?"

"My men will accompany you and Mrs. Lewis to help you pack your belongings, and you will be traveling in the SUVs with us. One of my boys will follow us in your vehicle. We'll take you back to your house in Boise, where I will explain all the rules to you. Please don't try to escape or resist. I have orders to keep both of you alive, but if that is not possible I am also authorized to kill you." Anderson said with bravado.

Chapter Thirty-One

THE TRANSLATION PROGRAM

After the Steering Committee meeting, Sinclair wasted no time to setup the translation center. He started with the automation process to translate the rest of the 10th Cycle Library, with help from Raj's team.

Sarah, who was the human resource manager and in charge of the day-to-day administration of the Rabbit Hole, found she had a bit of spare time on her hands once everyone got busy with their designated projects. She decided to pay Sinclair and his team a visit. Sinclair looked up from his computer screen when he saw Sarah entering and smiled. He loved this young woman as he would have loved his own daughter if he had one. Ever since he met her, he always thought that if he'd had a daughter, he hoped she would have been like Sarah.

"Hi, Sinclair. I thought I'd come over and see how you and the translation team are doing. I hope I'm not bothering you?" Sarah smiled.

"Sarah you will never bother me. For a beautiful young

lady like you, there is always time, and it will always be a pleasure." Sinclair said with a twinkle.

"Sinclair, flattery will get you anywhere!" She laughed.

"We're doing well. It's still a slow process, but with the help of the translation software that Raj and his team built for us we're gaining speed," Sinclair explained.

"That's good news. I believe, just like you, that there's a lot we can learn and gain from this library. I have my doubts about the 8th Cycle library, though. I got the feeling there wasn't much more we can learn from them," Sarah replied.

"I don't think I would agree with that. Remember we still don't exactly know how The Beast works. Neither do we know how the Skywalkers and Skinwalkers work. I suspect at some stage we'll have to find out if we want to overcome the new regime. However, the problem we have there is that we still need the services of Navajo translators to help us," Sinclair said.

"I never thought of it that way. It's just that the 8th Cycle library has caused so much trouble that I'm half-scared to even touch it again. Still, I guess you're right. We most probably have no choice," Sarah replied. Sinclair nodded his head in agreement.

"Would you mind showing me how the translation software works?" Sarah inquired.

Sinclair's face lit up; when it came to linguistics, he was like Raj and Roy about new technology; he liked to learn and talk about it. "Sure! I'd love to."

He described how they started by building a dictionary of words and phrases, that is, those they'd already translated. With that, it became possible to start automating the lookup process by just comparing the extracts from the original texts with what they had in the dictionary. As they kept on feeding new translations and language rules into the system, the process became easier and quicker. This in turn led them to the point where they were able to start building their own 10th Cycle translation algorithms.

He explained how the software would break down complex and varying sentence structures; identifying parts of speech; resolving ambiguities, and blending the information into the components and structure of the English language.

The fact that Raj already had the English part of the software ready, which he'd copied from one of the Internet translation sites when they started developing this, made things easier.

He showed her on his screen. "See here? When I copy this text from the 10th Cycle source to this box here, the translation software will interpret the words and structure of the sentences in the 10th Cycle language. Then it will generate a translation, based on the rules of the English language, as you can see in this box here."

"That's amazing!" Sarah exclaimed. "I can still recall how difficult it was when we did those first translations. Now you're doing it in seconds."

Sinclair continued. "Yes, we've come a long way since those days. However, you must keep a few things in mind. First; the speed of translation you saw there was because we have thousands of words and pages of translations already. Those we've done over the years and loaded into the translation database. Second, a computer will always be gisting. In other words, it can only provide the central idea to enhance the reader's understanding of the source text. It will never be able to translate as well as humans can."

"That's still real progress. Is it not?" Sarah wanted to know.

Sinclair replied, "Oh yes, what we have here is a giant leap forward and a big benefit to us. As we load more translated data and language rules into the translation database, the more 'intelligent' the software becomes, and the easier it is for laypeople to read and understand it."

"I've seen and used translation programs before, but never knew how such a thing worked. Thanks for that demonstration, Sinclair. It was very informative and encouraging," Sarah said. As a former Professor of Egyptology, she was excited about the possibilities of applying the same principles to the hieroglyphics and cuneiform writing of the 'ancients' of the 11th Cycle. What a head start that would provide to undergraduates who hadn't yet learned to read them in their original form. Sadly, there might never be an opportunity for her to teach her specialty again, or for students to study it.

Chapter Thirty-Two

THE OVAL OFFICE

By 10 o'clock, four SUVs pulled up outside the Harper's residence. The vehicles would take them to Upper Cumberland airport, less than twenty-two miles from their farm. From there they were transported in a small jet to Washington where a thunderous crowd of people and media were waiting and following them every step of the way from the moment they landed. They were not told where the meeting would take place. It also didn't matter much to them. As far as they were concerned, it might as well have been in a toilet. That would most probably be the most appropriate venue in any event, given what they thought of the whole thing.

They just wanted out as quickly as possible.

As they walked down the airstairs at Reagan National airport in Arlington, James Gordon, the head of BOSS, surrounded by secret service agents, was waiting for them. The flashing cameras and cheering people were overwhelming. On the tarmac outside the plane, the Harpers saw many familiar faces amongst the officers, but none of them was prepared to look their former president and first lady in the eye.

Gordon was an overweight, stocky, red-faced, beer-bellied creature, with beady dark eyes like a shark's. He had a big smile over false teeth as he shook hands with the Harpers, then held on to their hands while he turned in all directions so that all the cameras could get the shot. It was only later, when he had the chance to watch himself on the news broadcasts, that he saw neither of the Harpers was smiling.

Nigel knew that Gordon's decision not to meet with them on the farm was because he knew it wouldn't have the same impact as summoning him to Washington. It was all part of a message – a power play. It was a message he expected Gordon to send often and unequivocally. The message was plain and simple, "You don't count anymore, I am your superior, and you will do as you are told."

The Harpers were a bit surprised, but not overly so, when they were taken to the White House and escorted all the way to the Oval Office. It was a shock for them to see what had been done with the room. But then, what else could be expected from maniacs? There was not a single shred of Americana left in the Oval Office. It was heartbreaking.

Anastasia Oriov, the head of the Bureau of Information and Political Affairs, accompanied Gordon. Oriov was a grey-haired woman who looked like a former Olympic hammer throw champion. There was also another person, whom Nigel did not even bother or care to remember the name of. The Harpers were both relieved that Robert Wilson was not there – his presence would have created very difficult circumstances in which to stay calm.

"Mr. Harper let me start by apologizing for not

addressing you as Mr. President as protocol and good manners during the former era dictated. As you know, we have entered a new era in human history, and it is the Supreme Council's wish that all citizens be treated as equals, no matter their former or current positions.

Just another way to convey the same message, Nigel thought. But he said, "No problem with that. I never stood on protocol, and if you say this is the new protocol, so be it."

"Mr. Harper I still have a lot more of these meetings coming up today and the next few days. Please accept my apologies for having to get right to the point."

"My sentiments as well, Mr. Gordon. I like short and to the point meetings. I always believed that what can't be said in ten minutes is not worth saying. " Nigel said with a bit of sarcasm in his voice.

If Gordon was offended by that last remark, he did not show it and continued with a smile, "Good. We are in agreement then. The first point I would like to raise, Mr. and Mrs. Harper is that I have studied you and your presidency. As I understand it, you support the noble ideology of liberté, egalité, fraternité - freedom, equality and society."

Nigel Harper's blood was near the boiling point, he had to bite his tongue not to respond.

Gordon continued, "I am authorized by the Supreme Council to offer you a very prominent position if you were willing to use your influence and throw your support behind them."

Nigel was finding it difficult to gather the willpower to restrain himself from leaping over the table and ripping Gordon's throat out. "Please continue. I'm listening," he managed to say in a voice so cold it resembled an arctic wind.

Gordon, who did not realize how close he came to meeting his maker a few seconds ago, answered, "Maybe it's best if we finalize that point before we move on to the rest?"

"Very well, if that's what you prefer," Nigel said in a slow and measured tone, still far below freezing point. "I will be brief. I have always defended and fought for what I believed was right and for the sake of the people of my country. While I support the concept of liberté, egalité, fraternité, I am afraid you and your Supreme Council don't have the slightest intention of implementing that. You also don't have the slightest clue what it means. If you have indeed studied my presidency, and me, you would know better than to have the audacity to put such an offer in front of me. My answer to that is a categorical 'no'."

"Mrs. Harper, is that how you feel about it as well?" Gordon tried to turn the table in his favor. He knew if he could go back to Brussels with the signature of Nigel Harper on the pre-prepared statement in his briefcase, he was going to be a hero with a bright future.

Esther Harper slowly turned her eyes to Gordon, and he realized his mistake. She spoke in measured words, "Mr. Gordon, I had all the intentions in this world to stay calm and civilized during these proceedings. You have just crossed the line of decency. Your men turned up at our house and killed four innocent young men, the agents who were there to protect us, in front of our eyes. Liberté, egalité, fraternité? Those four boys who were prepared to give their lives to keep us safe were like children to us. They did nothing to you or your Supreme Council. You, Mr. Gordon, had them butchered in cold blood. Then you were still not satisfied. You went on and ordered that we be placed and kept under house arrest like criminals. That is your liberté, egalité, fraternité?

"Our house is infested with microphones and surveillance cameras. We have no privacy, not even in our bathroom. We cannot talk to anyone, write to anyone, or make a phone call to anyone, not even our family. Do you call that liberté, egalité, fraternité Mr. Gordon? How on God's earth can you be as stupid as to believe either one of us can ever support you? I would rather be dead. You can take your liberté, egalité, fraternité and shove it up your ass.-"

Nigel, who was afraid he would be the one to lose his temper, all of a sudden had his hands full to calm his wife down. He took her shaking hands in his and said softly, "Esther, we gave them our answer, let's not dwell on that anymore.

Let Mr. Gordon tell us what else he has to say and if we are still free after that, let's get out of here and go home."

Gordon, still showing no emotion whatsoever, continued, "I am very sorry to hear that is how both of you feel about it. I am left with no other option then. You will be taken back to your farm and return to the status quo. In other words, you will remain under our protection, and all the rules laid down by Robert Wilson remain. You will not be allowed to lecture, publish books, write articles or be in touch with anyone, unless the secret service has authorized it. You will be removed from all the positions you had on the boards and committees of all organizations on which you had been serving. For now, the state will continue to pay your pension, but we reserve the right to take that privilege under revision at any time."

"I guess that payment will depend on how nicely I play along with the Supreme Council? I don't care; I have been donating that income to charity every year in any event, so I guess that will only mean a few people would be worse off.

My second guess is you don't care about that, " Nigel replied with dripping sarcasm.

Gordon still did not show any emotion as he continued, "My colleague, Anastasia Oriov, the head of the Bureau of Information and Political Affairs, has one more point to discuss with you."

Anastasia spoke in a thick Russian accent while she tried to put on what could have been interpreted as a smile. "Mr. and Mrs. Harper, we don't intend to keep you on the farm at all times. We have many public events scheduled, which we want you to attend. Please make sure to put those in your calendars. You will not be required to say or do anything during these events. To have you with us will be a great honor."

Nigel could not help himself. "Aha, I am beginning to see what the term photo-opportunity means these days."

Nigel Harper was considering another option, and that was to say that they didn't accept that proposition to see if he could push Gordon far enough to either kill them or throw them in jail. That might just trigger a rebellion among the people that could overthrow this looming tyranny. It would not be the first time Americans would kick ass to gain their freedom. But then he decided with the control over the media these people had, it would be a stupid move. If the population of the United States ever needed a leader, it was now. For that reason he had to stay alive and out of jail as long as possible. He needed time to work out a plan.

"Mr. Gordon, it is exactly as you said. There is no other option. It would be much appreciated if we could now be excused and returned to our farm." Nigel tried to bring an end to the very unpleasant meeting, before he or his wife said or did something that did land them in jail.

Gordon remained irritatingly polite, despite the insults and blatant hostility from the Harpers, "Mr., and Mrs. Harper, thank you for your time. I hope you have a safe journey home."

Outside the Oval Office, Nigel mumbled to Esther, "You know, I am wondering if it wouldn't be better if this whole place were burned down, like the British did in 1814. It would be less painful to see the White House in ruins than seeing these horses' patoots in here."

"Shhh, Nigel, you will get us in more trouble!" Esther whispered.

Chapter Thirty-Three

SAM HAD ONE LAST THING TO SAY

The Lewises received the same treatment as the Harpers. They had secret service agents assigned to them, and their house was bugged with microphones and video cameras. Their phone line and Internet connection were cut off, and their mobile phones confiscated. All contact with other people, including family, had to be authorized.

Sam was devastated because of the danger he'd brought on his beloved Susan. What he had avoided for more than forty years, putting her in harm's way, had now happened, just when he was sure there was no danger anymore. Susan kept telling him that he had to stop blaming himself for that. She didn't see it that way, and it was not his fault.

From the news, they had gathered what was happening in the world. They experienced the same frustration as the Harpers as they had to stand by, helplessly watching the world descending into a bottomless pit of darkness.

When Sam got the message that he was summoned to Washington to meet with James Gordon, Susan insisted that she was going with him. He tried to reason with her, but she just said, "Last time when you went that way on your own, you stayed away for forty years, and that is not going to happen again." Fortunately, her request to accompany him was authorized.

When the Harpers walked into the White House foyer after their meeting with Gordon, they were surprised to see many familiar faces of former officials among the many people waiting their turn to be interviewed. Nigel, knowing what all these people were suffering, felt sorry for them. As he looked around the room, that emotion was slowly replaced by disappointment and sadness. Many of the faces he would have expected to see were absent. Those missing faces were either dead, or their owners already supported the Supreme Council. What won't some people do for a bit of glamor, power or money?

Many of those who saw them came over to greet them and ask how they were doing. The secret service agents were crawling all over them, so they were more or less restricted to small talk for most of the time. Nigel felt someone plucking at his arm. He turned to see Sam Lewis standing next to him, with his arm around an elegant blond and beautiful woman.

"Sam, am I glad to see you again," Nigel, said with a big smile on his face. He was relieved to see that Sam was alive. Here was a man he had the highest regard for, a man he could trust.

"Mr. President, it's wonderful to see you again. Please allow me to introduce my wife, Susan, to you and Mrs. Harper," Sam said with pride as he presented the joy of his life to them. He still could not believe what a lucky man he was to have Susan at his side as his wife.

"Your wife, Sam? How come I only hear about that

now? No wedding invite for Esther and me? Sam, my friend, I am hurt."

"It's a story with a forty-year history, Mr. President. I hope I can share it with you one day." Sam laughed.

"Oh, incidentally, you are not allowed to call me Mr. President anymore. We are all equal now, you know," Nigel said. His arched eyebrow said what he thought of that, even though he had always been a man of the people and cared little for formalities.

"I say screw them, Mr. President," Sam fired back immediately.

A few more people had gathered around them by now. In the process, the agents were forced to move back a few paces, which gave the two of them a bit more freedom to talk.

"Sam, I'm not taking this shit. I'll play along for now by staying on my farm and out of jail, but I'm going to spend my time working out a way to get rid of these lunatics." Nigel had not one moment's doubt about where Sam Lewis would stand on the matter.

Sam whispered, "Mr. President, I agree with you. I'm also not taking it. I'm certainly not going to sit on my butt watching how our country goes down the drain. But I have to warn you; we have to be very, very careful. They'll not hesitate to throw us in jail or kill us. In fact, if they were sure it wouldn't cost them a lot of support, they'd do it right now."

Nigel replied. "Yes we're the enemy now, but I would certainly like to make them regret making enemies out of us. I guess currently we are still useful to them for their propaganda and to get the masses on their side, but they'll get rid of us as soon as we have outlived our usefulness. "

Nigel shared the story of their arrest and the events on

that fateful day in as much detail as he could. Sam was alarmed when he heard how the four secret service agents were killed without a single bullet being fired. "What sort of weapon do you think could have done that, Mr. President?"

"Sam, I have no idea. Those boys just dropped to the ground and were dead in a minute. I haven't ever seen anything like that, not even in movies. Some beam or ray or... I just don't know. One thing's for sure; they have a weapon that can kill people like that, and my guess is they have already used it to kill millions all over the world. We may never know the truth."

Sam told him how their arrest happened, and what their current circumstances were.

"Do you know anything about the Rosslers?" Nigel inquired.

"No sir, just what was on the news. But that isn't true - I'm certain of that. All I could get from my contacts before they went quiet was that the Rossler Foundation was shut down, the servers had vanished, and the safe was empty when the FBI turned up there. Many of the staff and their families, including my old friend Luke Clarke and his wife, have disappeared."

Nigel was curious, "Why was that not reported in the news? What do you think?"

"Mr. President I have a theory. I could be over-optimistic, but I believe the Rosslers somehow got warning about what was about to happen and went into hiding somewhere. My guess is they've managed to keep that 10th Cycle Library out of the hands of these thugs, hence the big scene to get hold of them."

"Well, Sam, you have just made my day! If our friends are somewhere out there and have that library with them, there is a glimmer of hope. Just the same as you and I, they'll not accept this. I'm as certain of that as I am my own name. They might very well be our only hope."

Sam agreed, "Yes, Mr. President, those are my thoughts as well. I am sure that if Luke Clarke is out there and he is alive, he'll contact me when the time is right. I just wish I could find a way to stay in touch with you."

Nigel smiled, "Yes, between the two of us we would have been able to organize a revolt that would have been revolting and would make the French Revolution look like a Sunday school picnic."

An agent walked up and said, "Mr. and Mrs. Lewis, please follow me."

The Harpers and Lewises had to say goodbye in a hurry. Sam had one last thing to say when they shook hands, "Mr. President, I promise that I'll do everything I can to get you out. Remember the word 'sandpiper'. That will be my codename." With that, Sam turned around, took Susan's hand, and followed the agent.

Chapter Thirty-Four

DON'T MAKE ME WAIT TOO LONG

Sam knew James Gordon; he was one of the senior people in MI6 when they first met. Gordon became head of MI6 after Sam retired, and Sam was a little more than pissed off when he learned of Gordon's haste to join the new world order.

Sam and Susan's meeting with Gordon went much better than that of the Harpers, despite the massive, almost uncontrollable urge, Sam had to choke the living shit out of James Gordon. After which, he'd go ahead and kill Anastasia Oriov, as well as the other nincompoop in the room. However, he managed to stay calm and diplomatic throughout the entire proceedings.

Gordon started off, as with everyone else, with the offer of a good position in exchange for a pledge of allegiance. Sam and Susan quickly and very politely told him that they were not interested, mainly because neither of them was interested in politics or public life. They just wanted to be retired.

Gordon then moved on to the second option, "Sam, you

have made many enemies in your time, and we are concerned about you and your wife's safety. So therefore, you will remain in our protection as long as it is necessary. You already know the rules, which will continue to apply. The only addition will be that Anastasia…" (who reminded Sam of what the female version of a Japanese sumo wrestler could look like) "… has planned and scheduled public events into your calendars that you will be required to attend. You will not be required to say or do anything during these events. You just have to be there. Do you have any questions?"

"Yes, James - not so much a question, rather a friendly request. I am an old man, and as you have rightly pointed out earlier, I have made more enemies than one man can afford in a lifetime. Susan and I are grateful for your concern about our safety and welcome the protection. We just want to be left alone so that we can enjoy our old age and retirement. We have no problems attending your events. Susan has never been on TV, and I'm sure it will be great when her children and grandchildren can see her on TV from time to time. We're happy with your proposal. There is just one more request, sorry, actually two, which we hope you would give your favorable consideration." Sam managed to keep a smile on his face during that entire sarcastic dialog.

"What do you have in mind, Sam?"

"Well, the first request is that we be allowed to take up fly fishing again. We're both crazy about the sport and are starting to suffer from withdrawal symptoms lately," Sam said as seriously as he could without cracking up.

"That will not be a problem at all Sam. I am sure the agents will also welcome the opportunity to get out from time to time. What is your second request?"

Sam was struggling to stop himself from laughing and keep a serious face. "Thank you for that, James. That means a lot to us. The second request is that we be allowed to cover up the video cameras in our bedroom and bathroom when we are inside those rooms."

Gordon suspected for the first time that Sam had been making a complete ass of him the whole time. Nevertheless, he restrained himself and without showing any emotion told them that they would be allowed to cover the video cameras as requested. He got up, thanked them for their time, walked them over to the door, and wished them a safe trip back home.

As Gordon walked back to his seat, his mind was in a state of complete confusion. He'd expected this interview to be the toughest one of all. Was he wrong about that? Was it perhaps the toughest one and he just did not realize it? Had Sam been playing the fool with him, or was he serious that he just wanted to retire? Sam Lewis was a legend in the spy community; everyone knew what a genius the man was. He felt sure Sam was not going to take all this lying down. He had something up his sleeve. He, Gordon, had better make sure that security around Sam never relaxed. That was probably what Sam would be waiting for.

When Sam and Susan walked out of the Oval Office, Sam said, "Luke, my friend, don't make me wait too long."

"What was that Sam? Who are you talking about?" Susan asked.

Sam placed his finger on his mouth and whispered, "Shhh, I'll tell you later."

After the Lewises were out of the Oval Office, James Gordon picked up the phone and asked the secretary to get hold of Robert Wilson immediately.

A few minutes later, Wilson was on the phone. "Wilson,

listen carefully to me. I just had the interview with Sam Lewis and his wife. I'm convinced he has something up his sleeve. It is your responsibility to make sure he doesn't get away. Double the security guards, increase the surveillance - do whatever you have to do. I know him, and I know enough about him to be worried. It will serve you well to also be worried. Make certain your men never get sloppy around him. I don't want this man on the loose – ever."

Chapter Thirty-Five

THE ZINGERS

Salome, Luke, and Raj were working on a secure communications strategy when Roy arrived to ask her if she would like to accompany him on his daily walk. Roxanne had strictly enforced this as part of his rehabilitation treatment. Salome welcomed the opportunity to take a break and spend a bit of time in the open air with her husband.

"And the camera, Roy? What's that for?" Salome inquired when she saw the digital camera in his hand.

"Bird watching," Roy replied absent-mindedly.

"Don't you need binoculars or a telescope or something like that for bird watching?" Salome asked.

"I want to make a movie," Roy replied, but it was obvious his mind was occupied with something else. Salome knew him well enough to know something important was going on in that brilliant brain of his, and that it was best to not get in the way of that process. He would tell her when he had it figured out.

When they got outside, Roy said he wanted to see if he could find some hummingbirds. Not too far from the main entrance, Salome spotted a few ruby-throated hummingbirds hovering in mid-air around a tree with a wild honeysuckle vine entwined around it, and pointed Roy to them.

"Let's see how close we can get. I don't want to scare them, but I want to get as close as possible," Roy whispered.

They got to about five yards from the birds and sat down. Roy started taking pictures and videos. They were watching the spectacular show of acrobatics put on for them by these crafty little birds in absolute silence and amazement. The birds maneuvered in all directions - right, left, up, down, backwards, and even upside down. Sometimes it even seemed as if they were doing it all at once.

About an hour later, Roy got up and pulled Salome up. "It was incredible just to sit and watch them. We should do it more often. I love it," Salome said excitedly.

"Yes, it was mesmerizing to watch them, wasn't it?" Roy replied.

"Okay, Roy. Would you mind telling me now what's going on in that brain of yours? Has birdwatching become our new hobby, or is there something else I should know about?" Salome inquired.

"Salome, you know me too well. Although, I wouldn't mind taking birdwatching up as a hobby. It looks like it could be a lot of fun. The main reason I'm interested in the hummingbirds is to see if I can build one. I'd like to make one so close to the real bird, it would be impossible for a human to know the difference," Roy explained.

Salome was confused, "Darling that sounds nice, but I have no idea why you would want to do it. What do you have in mind? Please start at the beginning, and don't assume I know anything." Salome smiled.

Roy explained to her that he got the idea a few days ago when they were talking about getting in touch with Sam

Lewis. "One of the big issues is going to be contacting Sam, who will most probably be under heavy surveillance and maybe even guarded. That is, if he isn't already locked up somewhere. I think we can use the hummingbirds and spyflies to get close enough to Sam to observe what's going on and to get a message to him without being noticed."

Salome stared at him in awe. Only Roy would have thought of such a thing. But he had more to say.

"If I can build an improved version of my existing hummingbirds, similar to those that were instrumental in defeating the drones of the Sword of Cyrus, it might just work. I want to equip the new versions with cameras and microphones, speakers and other electronics. The birds have to mimic the real birds so closely that it would be impossible for casual observers to notice. That way, we could get the birds very close to the target person and drop a message without anyone realizing it. I guess you can call it, as Luke explained the other day, 'hide the fact that a communication took place,'" Roy concluded the explanation with a verbatim quote of Luke's words.

Salome just looked at him with admiration. His idea just solved a major headache for them, which was how to contact any of their target people, such as Sam, without putting anyone in danger. This idea, if he could make it work as he described, was brilliant!

Salome turned to head back when Roy said, "Hang on. Hang on. I have one more thing to do." He took a few small microphones out of his pocket and walked to the tree where he placed them as high and close as he could get to the flowers where the birds were feeding. The birds moved away a few yards, but when he walked back to where Salome was standing, they all returned immediately.

"What was that?" She asked.

"Our birds should not only look like real hummingbirds, they must sound like them too. I'm recording their chirping and the sound of their wings." Roy replied.

"Let's go back. I'd like to tell Luke and the others what an ingenious man I married," Salome joked, knowing what a modest man Roy was.

"No! Promise me you won't do that," Roy pleaded with her. "I need four days, I think, and then I will demo it to you and the rest. Just give me four days."

"And four nights. I know you, Roy James," Salome said with a smile. She knew from experience that when Roy got busy with something that interested him he forgot to sleep.

"A day has twenty-four hours; sunlight and darkness are part of it," Roy apologized in advance.

The next morning Roy, Ryan and Raj disappeared into Roy's lab and worked on the little messengers that they were going to call 'zingers'. They studied the pictures Roy took and played the videos in slow motion, sometimes frame by frame while they took notes and made sketches. Raj studied the natural movements of the birds very carefully and programmed that into the on-board nano computers of the zingers.

A little bit more than four days and four nights later, three exhausted but excited men walked out of the lab. They had three zingers, flying, humming and chirping exactly like real birds – it was time for a test and a demo.

After they had sent out the mini drones to scout the area outside to make sure it was safe to go out, they went straight to the tree where Roy and Salome had seen the live birds a few days before. There they found their little friends already busy humming, chirping and feeding. The first thing to know was if the hummers were going to scare the real birds away. Roy launched Zinger 1 and sent it over to the tree. At first, the real birds moved away when the zinger arrived, but only a few feet. They returned within less than a minute when they realized it was no threat to them.

He then launched Zinger 2 and 3. This time the real birds took exception to the arrival of these new rivals for their food. One male ruby-throat took it on himself to attack the newcomers, giving their operators a challenge to keep their artificial birds in the air. They'd fooled even the real hummingbirds - It was time for a high five! The little ruby-throat at last grew tired of chasing the zingers away since they wouldn't stand and fight, nor were they approaching the flowers to feed. At that point, the zingers mingled with the hummingbirds with no further trouble.

The second celebration came after Raj collected Luke and the rest of the Steering Committee to come and have a look. They could not pick one of the zingers out from among the real birds. They went up to two yards away, but still couldn't see a zinger, even knowing exactly what they were looking for. It was only when Roy brought the three of them back to him via the remote control that they recognized the dummies.

The next challenge Roy and his team had was to secure the radio signal between the remote control and the hummers. The danger was that someone could hijack their birds in mid-flight while operating it from a mile or more away.

Chapter Thirty-Six

THEY WERE STUNNED

The Harpers, Lewises and Rosslerites were all shocked when they saw and heard the media versions of the Harpers' and Lewises' interviews at the White House. It was the main news for days on end. *'Former President of the United States, his head of the CIA and many others came out in full support of the Supreme Council and New World Order'* the media headlines screamed.

In the days that followed, more and more names and faces of prominent politicians, officials, and celebrities from all over the world appeared. Among others, the Pope and the Dalai Lama were added to the media broadcasts as James Gordon and Anastasia Oriov continued their world trip.

Many, in fact, more than half of those who were reported to support the new regime were allowed to speak to the people and tell them why they were in support. People wondered why President Harper, the Pope, the Dalai Lama and many others never spoke, but the media was quiet about that.

Nigel and Esther Harper, although they were expecting something like this to happen, were severely affected when they saw it in reality. They started to wonder if it was not better for them to rather be locked up or dead. Their names and faces were used to lure thousands, if not millions, into slavery and misery. How could they ever live with that? Sam and Susan's reactions were not much different as they came to the same conclusions as the Harpers. Unless they could find a way to put an end to this and very soon. To live with the guilt of causing inconceivable suffering for multitudes of people was untenable. Something had to be done about it.

The first reactions of the Rosslerites were that of total shock and disbelief and the latter was what it remained – disbelief. They remembered that they were listening to the Supreme Council's news that had nothing to do with the truth. They were sure neither the Harpers nor the Lewises would have switched sides. It made them realize their friends were in imminent danger, and something had to be done about it – quickly.

As soon as these broadcasts began, the Rabbit Hole turned into a war room of activities as everyone who had a contribution to make got busy with their tasks on their resistance effort. They had decided on the name Project Phoenix, after the bird of the Greek legends that was reborn by rising out of the ashes of its predecessor.

It was as if they all personally heard Sam Lewis' desperate plea for help to his friend Luke Clarke.

Chapter Thirty-Seven

LET'S GET HOLD OF SAM LEWIS

As they walked back to the cave after Roy's demo, Luke was wondering how much easier life would have been back in his spy days if he'd had this type of technology available. He told Daniel that as soon as Roy had added the final touches to the hummers, they would have solved a major problem. He would be ready to go on his mission to find out what Sam Lewis' situation was and get in touch with him.

Daniel immediately called a few of the leadership team together to start finalizing the plans to smuggle Luke and Raj out on their missions, Luke to Boise to see what was going on with Sam Lewis and Raj to New York to get in touch with his underground network. Raj was sure Rube and Sombra, pseudonyms of two of his network who'd been real heroes during the Sword of Cyrus crisis, would be willing to join their cause along with many others in his network.

Luke's mission was first. The first question was how to get him to Boise. It was too dangerous to put him on a plane, and to rent a car was not a good option. The best options seemed to be if Owen and Alison drove him there, which was a ten-hour trip, or the Greyhound bus that was an eighteen-hour trip, and Alison or Owen would have to accompany him.

The idea was that Luke would be disguised as an elderly woman, either Alison's, or Owen's seventy-eight year old 'grandmother'. The story would be she'd had a stroke a few years ago, that left her with some paralysis on her left side and speech impairment and so she could not speak properly. For that they would need special effects makeup, and again they thought Owen was just the person. He could get it for them, as he was regularly on the sets in Hollywood where the TV series of his books were produced.

The next issue, Daniel thought, was to figure out where Luke would stay when he got to Boise, but Luke told him not to worry about that. He knew Boise fairly well, and besides, he knew how to go unnoticed. It wasn't something that could always be planned in advance. You had to be able to adapt to circumstances.

Raj's mission was a bit more of a headache for them. It was a trip of more than two thousand miles from Big Timber to New York. A trip like that would increase the risk of detection, not only because of the length of the trip exposing him to more people, but also because security cameras in the big cities were much more sophisticated when it came to facial recognition and identification technologies.

Raj proposed that he not go to New York just yet. It would be better if he could prepare one of the laptops with a complete encoded message using some of the steganography techniques that he, Salome and Luke had been working on. He would show Owen how to use the laptop and how to get in touch with Rube and Sombra. With a bit of luck one or both of them would be willing to cooperate. If a meeting could take place between them, Owen could give them the laptop so that they could read his message and instructions and respond.

Again, Owen's willingness and cooperation was key to the success of this plan. He was best suited for the job, as he had to travel to New York on a regular basis to meet with his publishers. Owen and Alison would still be at Mount Ararat. A delegation from the Rabbit Hole would go over the next night. They could then bring them up to speed with what had been planned and ask if they were willing to help.

The next evening, shortly after sunset, Daniel, Mark, Luke and Raj made the three-hour hike to Mount Ararat with empty backpacks, as they intended to bring back some supplies stored in the containers on the farm. When they arrived, they saw that the lights were still on and scouted around the house for a good hour to make sure there was no one else there, before Daniel knocked on the back door.

Once settled, each with a big mug of coffee and sandwiches, Daniel told them they had a maximum of three hours before they'd have to leave again to get to the Rabbit Hole before dawn.

Their conversation soon turned to what was going on in the outside world and the recent news about former President Harper and Sam Lewis, who were apparently now supporting the new order. It took them all of two seconds to agree that the story was obviously a heap of bovine droppings. It was obvious the Supreme Council was using those people for propaganda purposes. The danger was what would happen to them – the ones who were only seen but not heard – when they didn't have propaganda value anymore.

Owen and Alison filled them in regarding the rumors they'd heard around town, on some of the trips they took around the area. The gossip amongst the townsfolk was that many, many thousands of people, maybe millions, had been killed in the clampdown on gun owners. Many millions more were killed when government forces broke up peaceful demonstrations, and in countries that resisted the new regime, armed forces were apparently almost entirely wiped out.

From what Owen and Alison were telling them, two facts emerged consistently. Many people were dead, and they were killed with a mysterious weapon that made people die without one single shot being fired. People wondered what kind of device might be capable of doing that. Speculation ranged from death rays to poison, gas or maybe even some alien technology. No one knew because no one ever saw it in action.

Daniel and the rest of them in the kitchen had a very good idea what caused those deaths.

Next, Daniel laid out the plans they had for getting Luke out to Boise and for Raj to get in touch with his network. As expected Owen and Alison were onboard immediately, they required no persuasion.

They agreed that Owen and Alison would first go back to Nucla to establish the pattern, and then they'd visit the movie set in Hollywood. There Alison would make sure she showed great interest in makeup techniques, as she would like to use some of them to make up kids in a school play. She would try to record as much as she could of the process on video.

Raj would prepare the laptop as planned and have it ready when Owen and Alison got back to Mount Ararat. They arranged that when the two of them returned in two weeks' time, they would take a leisure trip to the place where Roy and Salome camped for a few days when they first discovered the Rabbit Hole. There they would drop off as much of the supplies as they could load onto the 4x4. That spot was less than a mile away from the main opening of the cave.

When everything was discussed and agreed, they all had another mug of coffee. Alison now had a shopping list they'd brought with them and a stack of cash. Owen didn't want to accept the money, but the Rosslerites prevailed.

Finally, with their backpacks full of supplies, Daniel's group made the trip back to the Rabbit Hole.

Chapter Thirty-Eight

ONLY ONE WAY TO FIND OUT

On Luke's return from Mount Ararat, he and Salome got busy with planning the Boise mission. They walked through as many scenarios as they could think of, trying to assess the environment and circumstances in which Sam and Susan could be living.

The mission would be executed in four stages. Stage one was to get Luke, Owen and Alison to Boise and to set them up in a place close to the Lewis house so that it was within the operational range of the spyflies and zingers. Stage two would be to deploy the spyflies and hummers and collect as much information about their friends and their surroundings as possible. Stage three would be to establish contact with them and set up a secure method of communication. The fourth and final stage would be to evacuate Sam and Susan and transfer them to the Rabbit Hole.

As they were stepping through each of the stages and the possible scenarios, they made a list of the equipment and technology that would be required. They already had the spyflies and zingers on the top of their list. They would have to talk to the technical minds such as Roy, Raj and Ryan about many of their requirements.

Three hours after they began their brainstorming session, they had covered as much detail of stages one to three as they could without having firsthand knowledge of what Luke would find in reality when he arrived in Boise.

Stage four remained vague, as it would depend entirely on how the preceding stages played out. However, they did discuss the scenario where special agents would be guarding the Lewises. This would require the elimination of the guards in some way or another, and they agreed that the use of firearms was not an option. It would be preferable, if there were guards to deal with, that they be incapacitated in some way rather than killed. Salome thought Rebecca might have some ideas about how that could be done.

Luke went out and asked Daniel, Raj, Roy and Ryan to join them in the planning room, where they gave them a detailed account of their plan.

Salome smiled as she looked at Roy and pushed the list across the table while she said, "Q, it is over to you, Raj and Ryan now to build this stuff for us."

"Q? Who's that?" Roy inquired with a frown of confusion on his face.

Everyone except Roy was laughing when Luke answered, "Q is 007's technical man, Roy. That guy that always builds the gadgets that saves Bond and the world. You have watched James Bond movies haven't you?"

"Aha, hmm ok ... I see, yes I have ... okay call me Q," he said while kicking Salome jokingly.

The three techies looked through the list, and Roy invited them to his lab as he indicated that he already had a few of those gadgets available and could show them how each worked. As Roy demonstrated some of the gadgets, his audience shook their heads in admiration for the genius of this man.

Roy was in seventh heaven. This was his world. Only Salome ranked higher on his list of priorities than his nanotechnology projects.

"Small earphones? Okay how about this?" he asked while he presented two small objects, each the size of the head of a matchstick. "Put it in your ear." He gave Salome and Luke one each. "Ready?" he asked. He walked away a few paces and spoke into a microphone in his hand.

Luke and Salome smiled immediately; this was exactly what they had in mind. Roy explained that he could make them smaller if they wanted, and he could change the color so that it would not be easy to see when inside the ear. He also explained that it could be operated from up to half a mile away from the microphone. Next, he showed them a mini microphone that was even smaller than the earphones, which could be concealed in the fabric of clothing.

Roy stopped at the next item on the list, "Cone of silence? What is that?"

Ryan explained how some years ago he had developed a device that would effectively block any sound for a few yards around people having a conversation. No bug or any device could penetrate that invisible wall of protection. The CIA, FBI, and other agencies were his biggest clients. He'd brought a few of them, with the blueprints, to the Rabbit Hole. Daniel explained to Roy how they'd used it during their discovery of the 10th Cycle, and how it helped to keep them out of the claws of the evil guys then. Of course, Roy was all ears right away. Ryan gave him the blueprints and devices, and they would work together to see if they could produce a better and much smaller version.

Next on the list were the hummers. Luke and Salome

wanted to know if they would, with a few modifications, be able to carry small physical items. This would be along with the existing video and voice recording and broadcasting capabilities. That wasn't a problem for Roy at all. In fact, he could have the first prototype ready in two to three hours for them.

Luke and Salome had one more requirement. They wanted to know if Roy would be able to build a device that would resemble the size and looks of a mosquito that would be able to inject a target with a small quantity of fluid. They were not exactly sure what the fluid was going to be yet - that was something they hoped Rebecca would be able to advise them on. They were also not sure in which circumstances they were going to use it, but it would be excellent to have it on hand and ready if the opportunity presented itself.

Roy was excited; he would have a prototype ready in two to three days.

"Which includes two to three nights." Salome smiled as she explained Roy's definition of a day.

They gave him the specifications of what they wanted for the hummer modifications and the mosquitos, and Roy got busy.

Next, they moved over to Raj's computer center, where they found Stuart and Max busily working.

Max, who had been studying computer science until the bugout to the Rabbit Hole, had joined Raj's team and almost certainly learned more in the few weeks while working with Raj and Stuart than he would have in three years at university.

Luke and Salome wanted to know if Raj had the knowledge and any gadgets needed to jam and hack into computer networks and Wi-Fi signals. Like Roy, Raj had already available for demonstration some of what they wanted. To the elation of everyone in the room, he demonstrated how he could intercept and jam Wi-Fi signals and how he could take control of a Wi-Fi router.

Raj assured them that he and Roy had already ensured that the signals between the hummers, the spyflies, and the controlling devices were safe. He also assured them it was the same for the signals between the microphones and earphones.

With Raj's technology there was a bit of a problem though. It required a higher level of computer know-how than Luke currently had. Raj would have to train Luke on the essential things and show him what to look for and record after he managed to get the spyflies into the house.

At some stage it might be necessary for Raj or Stuart to go to Boise. That decision could be made at a later stage once Luke had a good understanding of what was happening in Sam's and Susan's lives.

Finally, Raj showed them a very interesting project he and Stuart had been working on. They had been building up a library of digital recordings of the voices of every one of those supporters and any other relevant people who spoke on the radio. They paid extra special attention to those of the Supreme Council and other senior staff of the new world order.

Once they had a good sample, they analyzed the sound files of the recordings from the news and even a few of the people in the Rabbit Hole. It was interesting to learn that each person in the world had a unique voice pattern, as unique as fingerprints, retina patterns, and DNA. Raj told them that authorities, including the NSA, had for years been using voice pattern recognition systems to identify people talking on electronic devices. It was nearly impossible to hide or mask them in any way.

Luke and Salome knew about that technology and the secret clearances required of the people who worked with it. They decided not to ask how and where Raj got hold of it. In fact that didn't matter to them at all. They were just very happy he had it.

Raj's objective was not to mask or hide the voices. On the contrary, he wanted to synthesize it so closely that no recognition system would be able to pick up the difference between the real person and the computer-generated voice. He had a few more tweaks before the program would be working flawlessly.

At first, Daniel could not figure out how this technology could be of use to them. Then he saw the smiles on the faces of Luke and Salome, who explained, "Just imagine the absolute havoc and consternation that could be created if we could broadcast a speech by John Brideaux in his own voice that we wrote for him! Or if we got on a phone and started issuing orders to his subordinates."

"Raj, you genius!" Daniel exclaimed as he high-fived with a smiling Raj.

Over the next two weeks, until Owen and Alison returned to Mount Ararat, Luke had to be trained to operate the spyflies, hummers and other technical equipment; he would then in turn have to train Owen and Alison later.

Next stop was Rebecca's clinic. They wanted to know what type of drugs or gasses administered in minute quantities would be able to knock a human out very quickly and for long enough to escape without killing anyone.

As background for what they wanted, Luke told them about the Moscow theater hostage crisis in 2002, when the

Russian Spetsnaz forces used a derivative of fentanyl to sedate the hostages and terrorists before they stormed the building. That was a synthetic opioid numbing agent, a hundred percent more potent than morphine and up to twenty times stronger than heroin.

The sedative effect of fentanyl had a quick onset but a short duration. It was an excellent solution for knocking out people in a hostage situation, which was what they anticipated could be the case with the Lewises.

Rebecca told them about a few drugs she knew that could fit their requirements, fentanyl being only one of them. Some of its more potent derivatives could work very well, but would require large quantities and access to the room or building's ventilation system to administer. But it would possibly knock out everyone in the house. They decided to park that idea for a while and asked her to continue.

Scopolamine was a drug made famous by Colombian criminals. It caused amnesia and susceptibility. In other words, the drug would make the victim do anything suggested to him or her, and the best thing was, the next day the victim would have no idea what had happened. The drug came in a powder form and could be blown into the faces of targets.

The problem was that not much information was available about the drug, the onset or its effects or their duration. As far as Rebecca knew, it was not available in the USA, not even at universities or other research facilities.

Bromo-dragonfly, so named because its molecular structure resembled a dragonfly, was the supercharged version of LSD, producing severe hallucinations lasting up to three days. A minuscule dose would produce seizures, spasms in the veins and constriction of the blood vessels in the first number of hours after the drug was administered. The trip described by some victims, was like being 'dragged to hell and back'.

This drug *was* available in the USA. It was a Schedule 1 drug, which meant it would be under the strictest possible control. Only authorized university and medical research facilities would have access to it.

Etorphine, registered in the USA under the trade name M99, was five thousand times more potent than heroin and up to three thousand times stronger than morphine, so powerful a human could be overdosed and killed simply through skin contact with the drug. It was used for sedation of animals, and 1/100th of a gram of the stuff could knock out a six thousand pound elephant. As with bromo-dragonfly, it was available in the USA as a Schedule 1 drug entrusted only to authorized universities, medical and animal research facilities.

Bromo-dragonfly or etorphine would solve their problem of quickly overpowering their targets. They only had to think of a way to get hold of it. However, during their discussions of how they could potentially get their hands on the drug, it became evident it was going to be easier said than done.

Daniel had a brainwave, "Hang on. I think there might be a way. Rebecca, you said that etorphine stuff is used to sedate wild animals, right? What are the chances that places like a zoo or a wildlife park might have the stuff in their possession?"

Everyone saw where he was going and shouted in a chorus, "Places such as Yellowstone!"

"Only one way to find out, I guess," said Daniel with a smile.

Chapter Thirty-Nine

LAW AND ORDER

The Supreme Council had already announced the very popular decision to provide free education for everyone on the planet. They'd appointed their head of the Bureau of Education, and she was already busy implementing the plan. Her colleague Anastasia Oriov made sure that the opening of every school under the new plan received as much public exposure as possible, locally, nationally and internationally. The media shouted it from the rooftops - these schools were state of the art facilities with the widest possible curriculum choices and the best teachers. Funding would never again stand in the way of education.

The Bureau of Education could not keep ahead of the demand for New World Order schools; waiting lists had thousands of hopeful students. The Supreme Council were extremely pleased their education reform program was working like a charm and bagged many millions of supporters for the regime.

It was still early days for them, and there were still a

long list of agenda items that had to be addressed, but now law and order were next on the agenda. They'd learned a few useful lessons from the gun control operation about swift and efficient law enforcement. There were just too many criminal activities going on in too many countries and it was time to curtail that. The first step was to introduce the death penalty for possession of firearms. It did not involve a long court process, as the police were authorized to shoot to kill anyone found in possession of a firearm. No due process or trial was necessary. Possession was a de facto guilty verdict. People had already had enough warning and grace – now the Council showed themselves to be dead serious about it.

The police received sweeping powers, were heavily armed and authorized to arrest and detain without trial anyone suspected of committing or capable of committing a crime. Police could stop and frisk anyone anywhere at any time, no suspicion was required. They called it preventative law enforcement.

The media trumpeted the statistics of dwindling crime figures, and some were even predicting a crimeless society within two to three years. No one ever dared to say that this was not law enforcement but rather terrorization of the citizens.

A one-strike rule was introduced. For the first offence, irrespective of the nature or severity, the culprit would be shipped off to a reorientation facility. There they would be taught how to be a loyal and useful citizen to society. The second crime carried either the death penalty or, if the criminal were lucky, a minimum five-year mandatory sentence plus the penalty for the actual crime.

By now the biochip factories were in full production and every criminal found guilty of any offence received a biochip. It was a quick and easy procedure, which was completed at courthouses and police stations, where trained staff would inject a small capsule-shaped device, about half an inch long, underneath the right collarbone. It was part of the preventative law enforcement philosophy.

All law enforcement agencies were also authorized to perform the implants on anyone whom they suspected of committing a crime or whom they suspected might commit a crime in the future. The procedure quickly became known as 'chipping'. The police did not hesitate to use this method often. After all, they were all chipped for their own security and protection before they could assume or continue their duties in the new police forces. They knew it to be safe and harmless, so why not apply it for the good of society to known and potential criminals?

Everyone was given very explicit instructions not to tamper with the chips in any manner, and informed of the dire consequences if they did so. Nevertheless, thousands just did not listen or believe what they were told and were dead within seconds from attempting to remove the chips.

Many new crimes appeared on the books. One such crime had legal experts scratching their heads. Corruption against humanity, which had a description and interpretation so wide it could mean anything from jaywalking, spitting on the street, making any derogatory remarks about, or criticizing the Supreme Council or any of its appointed officials, to not having a likeable face or acceptable appearance. The crime carried sentences from jail time to the death penalty, all at the discretion of the judges.

The entire legal process was streamlined. Courts were supplied with more judges and prosecutors and were open for business 24/7. The Supreme Council's instructions were very clear; get rid of all backlogs within six months. Trial by jury was abolished; a single judge would preside and the appeals process was abolished. Everyone who appeared in court was provided with a lawyer, appointed and paid for by the state. If a private lawyer was preferred, the accused was welcome to that, but the state would not contribute to the costs.

Mindful that the 'War on Drugs' begun in the US more than fifty years before had been a complete failure, the Eligo Rarus regime took a different approach. Law enforcement agencies were instructed to summarily execute anyone involved in the drug trade, from the heads of cartels to the petty dealers on street corners – and their customers – whenever they were caught in the act (a de facto guilty plea) or reported by a credible witness and found guilty by due process of law. With their customers too frightened to buy and their distribution networks disrupted by the deaths of key personnel, the drug cartels soon folded.

After the initial six months of clearing the backlog, a rule was introduced that cases had to be brought to court and finalized within no more than seven days from being charged. The process of charging suspected offenders, however, could take as long as the police decided to investigate. No bail was granted to anyone. All accused remained in custody until trial.

Soon the comprehensive law enforcement reform initiative, the media was happy to report that the new world had become the safest society in the history of humankind.

James Gordon followed the entire process of law enforcement and the pleasing results of chipping with intense interest. He wondered if he would sleep better if he issued an order that all of his and Anastasia's superstars who resisted his proposals would be chipped. Those people were a source of constant worry for him. It would be good for their security and protection and, of course, would give him much better control over them. It was something he had to think about, and maybe he would give it a little more time to see how things worked out with those that were already chipped.

Chapter Forty

IF HE COULD ONLY HEAR WHAT THEY WERE SAYING

Sam and Susan were not allowed to stop and talk to anyone in the park at all. They knew all the faces in the park - it was a favorite place in their neighborhood. That morning they noticed two unfamiliar faces, one old and one young, on a bench as they smiled and said hello when they walked past. That was as much as their security guards would allow them to speak to anyone before they would step in. When Sam saw how the old woman's face was deformed, his first thought was that she must have had a stroke and that the younger woman was probably her granddaughter or caretaker.

Like the Harpers, the Lewises also found the morning and afternoon walk in the park across from their house very relaxing and liberating. It was the only time when they could have a private conversation without fear of being overheard and recorded, as long as they kept their voices down.

Neither Sam nor Susan noticed when two flies landed

on her baseball cap, shortly after they passed the women on the bench.

"Sam, I just remembered you were still going to tell me about your friend," Susan said.

"I don't have many of those anymore. Even James Gordon knows that," Sam quipped.

Susan smiled, "There must be at least two then, I am one of them and the other you mentioned when we walked out of the Oval Office after that interview. I can't remember exactly, but I think you said his name was Luke."

Sam was serious now, "Yes, his name is Luke Clarke. He's an old friend from the CIA, and the best friend I ever had. He retired a few years before me and moved to Boulder where he lived on a small farm until recently."

"He isn't there anymore?" Susan wanted to know.

Sam explained. "Well, that's what I don't know. He worked for the Rossler Foundation as their head of security until a year or so ago and handed the reigns to Salome James, an ex-FBI special agent. He's the uncle of Daniel Rossler's wife, Sarah. He and his wife, Sally, were part of the group of people associated with the Rossler Foundation who disappeared a few weeks ago. You remember all those reports in the news about the Rosslers?"

"Yes, I remember, but I don't remember hearing Luke Clarke's name," Susan replied.

Sam continued, "Yes, their names weren't mentioned, if I remember correctly. There were seven men and their wives named on the news. My contact in the CIA said an additional forty or so disappeared at the same time, and it was actually around sixty of them who got away. The problem is, as you know, after that first contact I had with my informant, all communications to everyone I know had been blocked. That was something I couldn't understand at the time, but it all makes sense now."

"You have no idea where they could have gone?" Susan wanted to know.

"I don't have a clue. President Harper asked me the same question when we saw him at the White House. I told him my theory is they somehow knew what was going to happen and got themselves out of the way and took that 10th Cycle Library with them, hence the authorities' eagerness to get hold of them. Both President Harper and I believe that the Rossler group, with that 10th Cycle Library in their hands, might be the one and only hope of deliverance for the world."

"One day you'll have to tell me more about that 10th Cycle Library. However, something's bothering me. I remember when we walked out of the Oval Office you were saying something like, 'Don't make me wait too long'. Do you expect Luke or any of the Rosslers to try to contact you? If so, won't that put all of us and them in a lot of danger?"

"Don't worry Susie, Luke is an old hand in the spy business, and I can assure you he will not put any of us or his people in any danger. I'm sure Luke will want to get in touch with me at some stage, which is the main reason I didn't tell Gordon to go jump in a lake and drown himself. I'd like to stay alive and out of jail, so I'm available and ready when Luke shows himself."

"Sam Lewis, promise me you are not going to walk out on me again! I'm going with you wherever you go, even if it is to hell and back. I'm staying with you."

"Susie my dear, I've learned a few things during my time in the spy game. One of them was that sometimes you have to just sit back and wait; an opportunity will present itself at some point. And yes, I promise I won't go anywhere without you." Sam took her hand and squeezed it gently to calm her.

"I hope and pray that you're right, and we'll soon hear from him. I just don't know how he's going to get past all these security guards. You must have said something that day in the Oval Office that got Gordon worried so much that he's doubled our guards," Susan said with the concern clearly audible in her voice.

"'Where there is a will, there is a way', my mother always said. Luke will find a way if there is one," Sam replied.

"Let's go back home and have a nice cup of coffee and breakfast," Sue suggested.

As they walked back to the gate of the park towards their house, they passed the couple on the bench again. The old woman smiled at them as the younger one said, "Have a nice day." The entourage of security guards following about ten yards behind them did not even look in the direction of the people on the bench.

When Sam and Susan walked into their house, the two flies still on her cap took off in different directions; one to the kitchen and one to the living room.

Sam noticed through the window of the kitchen that the old lady was helped up by her companion, who assisted her while they walked down the road past their house. The thought crossed his mind that walking was good exercise for someone who'd had a stroke.

Sam would have been dumbstruck if he could only hear what they were saying to each other.

Chapter Forty-One

THE FIFTH MUSKETEER

There was one thing that the musketeers were not successful at, and that was the fact that they were still unable to lure John Mendenhall into their group. They tried to invite him to happy hour and on their fishing trips, but he was not interested. He once went fishing with Ben, but that was just because Ben kept on asking. The trip turned out to be a bit of a social disaster as John just sat there and did not talk or respond much to Ben's conversation.

Rebecca and Cindi, who saw with growing concern how their parents were falling deeper and deeper into depression, spoke to Sarah, JR and Daniel. Daniel asked that they leave the matter to him and JR to see what they could do. By the time this conversation took place, the musketeers had just tasted the fruits of the second harvest from their still. This time they'd used honey, which they very appropriately called 'honeyshine'.

One afternoon, shortly after Luke left on the Boise mission, at the usual time of the older men's happy hour, Daniel took two tin mugs, got hold of JR and went up to the top floor. Daniel knew about the still and everything going on because some of the women had told him about the 'secret' meeting place and the activities of the four friends. Telling Daniel was just an FYI. They wanted him to know about it, but asked him to let them be as it was entirely harmless, and it was also good for them.

The musketeers were more than a little gobsmacked when Daniel and then JR appeared out of nowhere in their 'top-secret' retreat next to the poker table inside the pub. They were completely sure that no other living soul knew about the place.

"What the hell? Didn't you two snot-nosed boys read the warnings outside? And can't you knock before you walk in?" Sinclair asked in a fake angry tone. He figured the best defense was a good offense, in trying to get out of the trouble he thought they were in.

JR replied, "Yes we saw the warning signs, and that's why we came to see what danger you were in. It seems we were just in time to save you all from drinking yourself into a stupor."

Ben looked around and said, "I guess Luke should have made those warning signs to read 'adults only'. That might have kept them away."

Without saying a word, Daniel and JR placed their empty mugs on the table and sat down. "Hopefully you weren't thinking of drinking all of that on your own, were you?" Daniel asked while looking at Sinclair and pointing to the half-full bottle of honeyshine next to him on the rock table.

JR looked at the cards and said, "Deal us in. What do we use for money here?"

"Corn kernels. It keeps the lady over there in the corner

happy and bubbling," Ryan replied while jabbing with his thumb to the copper still in the corner.

As relaxation ruled and Daniel and JR proffered their mugs for a second shot, Ben, who knew his two boys better than anyone else, asked, "So would you mind telling us what brought you here? It's obvious you knew about our secret and where to find us, but you never felt the urge to join us before. There must be something bugging you now?"

"Dad, it's my in-laws, John and Jane, who are a bit of a worry to all of us. They're not doing well, and nothing we've tried so far has improved things. We *are* aware and are grateful that you all have already attempted to get them out of the hole, but without success. We were hoping we could put our heads together again and see if we can come up with another strategy," JR replied.

A lengthy discussion followed about what they could do. The Mendenhall's state of mind was indeed troublesome for all of them. While they were still throwing around ideas, Sinclair came up with one.

"I think I have a plan that might just work," he said with a smile. "I'm betting a bag of corn kernels that John's problem can be solved with a bit of Chateau de Grotte and honeyshine. The girls can take care of Jane, but as for John, this hooch will cure any ailment including depression, I am sure."

Daniel replied, "That's your plan? You've invited him before, and he wouldn't come to your happy hour. How are you going to get him here now? And even if you managed to do that, how are you going to get him to drink this stuff?"

Sinclair had that same devious smile he had when he told his friends not to worry about running dry. "Little insignificant details boyo. Never fear when Sinclair and the musketeers are near. This time tomorrow, the problem will be something of the past. Ah, wait. You better make that the morning of the day after tomorrow. This stuff does have the side effect of making people happy and sleepy, especially the uninitiated. "

Ben and Ryan looked at Sinclair, very puzzled; they'd just been committed to a plan they hadn't even heard.

"Sinclair, would you care to share our plan and then we will also know?" Ryan inquired.

"Yeah, well, if you insist. " Sinclair said as he poured another shot for all of them. "Here is what I think. I'm no trick cyclist, but my take on it is that John and Jane are ex-teachers. My guess is the cause of their malady is that they are missing the children and the school environment."

"Brilliant idea!" Daniel said very excitedly, before Sinclair could continue. "We have fifteen children here who've had no schooling since they arrived. We have a library with lots of information and curriculums for all grades. All we have to do is to convince the two of them to set up a school for us."

"Yes, exactly! What do you think?" Sinclair replied.

Ryan was a bit sceptic, "Well, I am also not a psychologist, but I know that people with depression usually don't have the motivation to do anything that looks like it might require an effort. They lose their joy, drive and motivation, and they become almost helpless. My observation of John and Jane is that they're at that point already. It's getting them over that hump that will be the trick."

Sinclair lifted his mug, as in a toast, "That is where the firewater fits into the picture."

"Shit no, you can't force the stuff down his throat, man!" JR objected, quite worried that was what Sinclair had in mind.

Sinclair laughed, "Relax boy, relax. That's not the plan.

He won't be force-fed. But I will need a bit of help – you two lads have to arrange with the women to find an excuse to drag Jane away tomorrow afternoon. That way, I can get the chance to ask John to help us with a few things."

JR replied, "No problem with that. Consider it done."

Sinclair gave the final instructions. "Oh, just one more thing. Make sure they prepare Jane to expect when John returns that he could be euphoric and moderately to severely incapacitated for the rest of the night."

The next afternoon the musketeers were all in the library. The conspirators, who now numbered at least thirteen, were all briefed in detail about what they had to do and say. Sinclair placed two full bottles on a shelf in the library, one Chateau de Grotte and one honeyshine, before he walked over to the Mendenhall's quarters.

"John and Jane, sorry to trouble you. We have a discussion going on in the library and we could use your expertise." Sinclair was saying just when Rebecca arrived.

"Sinclair, I am no expert in anything. I don't know if I can be of help to anyone with anything. What is it about?" John replied emotionless.

"Not sure that's the case. We are looking at the school curriculums that we have in the library, trying to figure out which to use for the different ages of children here. But we have no clue what we need. We thought you might be able to give us a bit of a hand. "

It was as if a little light went on in John's and Jane's eyes when they heard that.

"So, is there a plan to start a school for the kids?" John asked, with a bit of a higher tone in his voice than before.

Rebecca had to suppress a smile. This was the first in such a long time she could see a sparkle of hope in her parents' eyes.

Sinclair also saw it and continued, "Yes, that's the idea. The problem is Ben, Ryan, and I were appointed as the school committee, but we don't have any expertise. We're stuck as to which curriculum we should use and hoped you could give us some advice."

"Yeah, well like I said …" was as far as John got with an objection to get out of a commitment, when Rebecca saw what was coming and interrupted him.

"Sorry Dad, I actually came over to fetch Mom. Bess and a few of the others asked me to invite her over for a cup of tea and a taste of the first cake ever baked in these caves."

Jane responded immediately, "That sounds great, Becky. I'd love to go with you." She turned to John. "Will you be okay if I am gone for a while, dear?"

John considered for a moment what would be the worst, sitting around on his own for a few hours doing nothing or accepting Sinclair's invite. "No problem. I might as well go over to the library with Sinclair, then."

Within a minute they were ready and on their way. In the library they had the seating arranged in such a way that John would be sitting at the head of the table. He had to be 'in charge' of this meeting.

Sinclair and John arrived in the library just in time to hear a 'heated argument' between Ben and Ryan. Ben saying, "What do you want the kids to learn that stuff for? All they have to learn is how to read the Bible, calculate, ride a horse and shoot straight!"

Sinclair looked at John as they took their seats, "You see what I have to deal with here?" John nodded his head.

They laid out the plan for John; they thought it necessary to start a school for the kids and for John to agree with them. They kept on referring to their lack of knowledge and subtly heaped on the praises on John and how lucky they were to have him around to give them advice. They had many questions. A lot of them started with "John, so how would you …?" Many responses to John's answers included, "Excellent idea, never thought of it that way …" or "That will solve the problem …" or "I can see the logic of that …"

Within forty minutes, John started smiling and even made suggestions of his own without being asked. That was when Sinclair knew the time was right to roll out the big guns. He got up and fetched the bottle of honeyshine, to which they had added a bit of honey afterward for a sweet taste. Placing four tin mugs in front of them, he worked his way round the table matter-of-factly while he poured a stiff shot into each.

He sat down and shouted, "Bottoms up!" All of them except John grabbed their mugs and poured the honeyshine down their throats in one big gulp and looked at John who wasn't sure what to do. But no one was talking now, they were all staring at him. He grabbed the mug and did the same. They all smiled and continued the conversation as if there was no interruption.

Five minutes later, Sinclair did the rounds again, and this time John knew what he had to do. As they worked their way through history, geography, mathematics, science, languages and other topics, Sinclair emptied the bottle of honeyshine in their tin mugs and then started serving the Chateau de Grotte. John was now firmly in charge of the whole meeting. By the time they'd reached the halfway mark on the bottle of Chateau John had told them how much he and Jane had been missing their jobs as teachers and the school environment. By the time Ben slipped out to collect another bottle from the cellars, John had accepted the appointment as headmaster of the Gallatin Unified

School and on behalf of Jane received her appointment as a teacher.

The third bottle was empty by the time they had covered the entire curriculum. Two of them held John upright between them, while the other helped them find the way to the Mendenhall quarters, singing Gaudeamus Igitur at the top of their lungs.

When they finally managed to find the way to the Mendenhall quarters, they found a smiling Jane there, who helped them get John to bed. She thanked them as they left, now trying to whistle Beethoven's Ode to Joy while trying to find their own quarters.

A week later the Gallatin Unified School opened with fifteen students and three teachers - John and Jane Mendenhall, and Jenny Ellis, a kindergarten teacher. The youngest students were the two three-year-olds; Nicholas Joshua Rossler and Aanya Sankaran.

It was soon noticed that the new headmaster was more often than not, after school, seen in the presence of the musketeers on fishing trips. During happy hour, his wife was often observed in the presence of their spouses.

Chapter Forty-Two

I SHOULD BE THE ONE DIGGING OUT OF HERE

"Luke, please tell me you could hear them and have recorded that conversation," Alison said with excitement in her voice.

"Oh yes, I heard every word of it and recorded it. You can listen to it when we get back to the house," Luke said with as much of a smile as he could manage under all of the heavy makeup. Trying to behave like an old lady who'd had a stroke while concentrating on walking with a bit of a limp and the walking stick was not easy. "They've been waiting for us. They have all their hope pinned on us."

In a house three hundred yards down the street from the Lewises front gate, Owen, Alison and Luke quickly connected the spyflies in the Lewis house to a big computer screen. Now they could see and hear better what was going on inside the house. They made sketches of the layout of the house and captured the faces and voices of the guards as they directed the flies around the entire house.

It was heartbreaking for Luke when he saw how the guards had taken over more than half of the house, occupying three of the four bedrooms. One they used for an office and kept the Lewises in what could only be described as a prison. That afternoon it was Owen's turn to accompany the old lady on her walk to the park, and two more spyflies got smuggled in on Susan's cap. Another very informative and sometimes romantic private conversation was recorded while the Lewises walked around the park.

Luke had to smile when he heard Sam telling Susan that if his friend didn't show up in the next few weeks he had plans. He'd either storm the guards or dig a tunnel out of the house for them to escape. Susan's frantic objections followed. He was sure Sam was teasing her, but he wasn't entirely sure Sam wasn't in earnest. He had to stop himself from catching up with his friend to tell him the Marines had landed, and they should just hang on.

Two days later, they had eight spyflies roaming the house and an excellent idea of the routine of its inhabitants. That included every move of the security guards, when and what and to whom they reported. They recorded the keystrokes of the passwords that the guards typed in to access their computers. They also figured out that the surveillance microphones and cameras were interconnected by a wireless network. They carefully made recordings of each report the guards phoned in every day to their control center, which they ascertained was located in Washington.

The Lewis' shopping was done for them by one of the guards, who would also exchange their library books when required. The two prisoners did not have much to do other than watch TV, read and go for walks twice a day. It seemed though, from time to time they were also allowed to go flyfishing.

Luke and his team also knew the layout of the garden and the Lewises habit of having breakfast under a pergola in the middle of their flower garden. Here was where real hummingbirds were seen sucking nectar out of the flowers and hunting for insects.

After four days of observation, Luke was satisfied that they had enough information to be able to kick off the next stage. It was time to roll the zingers out, as there was no way he would be able to meet with Sam or Susan in person. The guards were constantly around them, and it was obvious that they were not allowed any contact with anyone else. The circumstances in which his friends were held were a source of constant annoyance to him.

The next morning, after their walk in the park, Sam and Susan carried their breakfast out to the pergola, also rigged with surveillance equipment, and noticed there were a few more hummingbirds that joined the group. They enjoyed watching these little marvels that did not mind humans so close to their feeding grounds.

While they were still talking about the birds, they saw two of them approach them and hover over their table looking for something to feed on. Susan was as excited as a little girl when the birds came so close. She'd seen videos where they would eat out of people's hands. Wouldn't that be exciting if she could get them to do that? But what happened next made her think again about that idea. The one of them closest to Sam had a little accident and left a big black and white colored gooey heap on Susan's beautiful white tablecloth. Sam saw the disgust on her face and grabbed a paper napkin to wipe it up, at the same time wondering at the size compared to the size of the birds themselves. Something wasn't right.

When he placed the napkin over the heap and picked up the bundle, he felt something solid inside. For a split second, he wanted to ignore it, but his earlier observation made him want see what it was. When he got it all gathered in the napkin, he turned it around and saw a metal tube the size of a vitamin capsule sticking out of the rest, he folded it up. "What the hell? Hummingbirds wouldn't ever eat that!" Sam didn't know much about hummingbirds, but he knew enough to be sure that they wouldn't eat a metal capsule. He had to see what it was.

"Don't worry Susie. I'll get a wet cloth to clean up the mess and throw this away," Sam said as he got up.

On his way into the house, while he had his back to the surveillance camera, he slipped the capsule out of the napkin and into his shirt pocket. He would go to the bathroom later and with the camera covered, as he was allowed to do by the grace of James Gordon, he would have the chance to inspect that capsule.

Luke and his team down the street were high-fiving and had to control themselves not to start screaming with joy when they saw on the spyfly screen when Sam put the capsule into his pocket.

With the camera covered, Sam took the capsule out of his shirt pocket and pulled it apart. His heart skipped some beats when he found a tiny piece of paper the size of a postage stamp rolled up inside. He looked at the picture of a bronze coin with a robin embossed on it and a very visible green border around the edge of the coin. He turned the stamp around and read the words - More Coming. *What was this?* He turned the stamp around and stared at the picture again. *How did it get into the bird's stomach? Hummingbirds won't eat stuff like that. Hummingbirds ... wait a minute ... I saw Roy James use hummingbirds against those nanonuke-carrying drones of the Sword of Cyrus terrorists a few years ago. Can it be?* He turned to the picture again and said the words slowly and silently to himself, *bronze coin ... robin in the middle ... green border* and it was as if something struck him between the eyes. His heart almost stopped – *Green Robin Bronze! "Oh my God! He's here!* Sam had to restrain himself from running down the hall shouting to Susan.

There were only two people in the entire world who used those code words to identify themselves to each other in situations where they could not meet face to face. He was the handler at that time, and the agent was Luke Clarke. One of them would challenge with one or two of the words, and the responder had to provide the missing word or words. Sam grinned broadly as he turned the paper around and read the words "More Coming." Again he gave himself a thumbs up in the mirror. He and Luke were back in business.

Luke and his two companions could not help but laugh when they saw that smile on Sam's face and the thumbs up on their screen.

Sam couldn't wait to go on their afternoon stroll through the park. Being sure he couldn't be heard, Sam whispered with a huge smile on his face, "My dear, I really like those hummingbirds in our garden every morning, even if they mess up your table cloth. I wonder if we could maybe put a paper towel or something on the table and let them be around us. I'd like to see if we could perhaps get them to eat out of our hands, too. I think they could have a message for us."

"I like them, too. It would be exciting if we could get them to trust us that much, but I don't like them making a mess on my table. I'll see what I can do about the table cloth," Susan replied. Then she stopped and pondered for a moment why Sam thought the birds might have some sort of message. "What type of message do you imagine they could have for us, Sam?"

Sam could not hold it any longer, "Susie, please make sure you keep your voice down when you hear what I'm about to say."

Susan nodded her head in agreement.

"My friend Luke is here! That dropping on the table this morning had a capsule with a message for me in it."

"What? How is that possible? How could a bird be trained to do that? I don't …" Susan wanted to believe him but had serious doubts.

Sam explained, "Don't worry, I'm not going crazy. One or more of those hummingbirds we saw this morning weren't real. I can't be sure how he did it, but I'm not surprised. I saw how Roy James, that nanotech scientist I told you about that works with the Rosslers, saved the world from annihilation with imitation hummingbirds. The hummingbirds I saw back then were built for a different purpose, but I suspect they have modified them to look so real we couldn't see the difference. The message Luke sent me in the capsule said there will be more coming."

Susan was excited and worried at the same time, "How can you be sure it was Luke? Won't the guards be able to find out what's going on? I'm very excited, but I am also worried, Sam."

"Okay, one thing at a time my dear. I know the message came from Luke because it contained a passcode that he and I used more than twenty years ago on a mission. There is no other person in the world who knows that passcode. We never used it again; we never used passcodes for more than one mission. As for the guards spotting the imitation birds, let's see tomorrow morning if we can spot one of them. Now that we know some of them weren't real, we could pay close attention. If we can spot them, then we know the guards can as well. But if we can't, the guards can't either," Sam said, calming her down.

Susan drew a few conclusions of her own, "If he is here, then I get the feeling that he must know what we're doing and perhaps is even watching us. How do you think he managed to avoid detection by the guards up till now?"

"You can bet that beautiful bottom of yours that he is watching us." Sam smiled.

"Sam Lewis, I am shocked! My bottom? What is going on in that wicked mind of yours?" She laughed.

Sam just ignored that question. "There's a lot more about the spy business I have to teach you, Susie. You're right - he knows what we're doing, and he'll make sure that he won't be detected. Luke was one of the best, if not *the* best, field agent I ever worked with, and he is alive today only because he was always very careful."

As they walked past the two on the bench, Sam looked straight at the old woman, and he could swear he saw her wink at him as he said 'hi'. *That was Luke Clarke! I know it, that's him! The old fox had been here for days watching us.* The guards were too close to them, so he couldn't tell Susan about it until the next morning's walk. How he would have loved to go and kiss that old woman! On second thought, maybe he would rather ask Susan to do the kissing when the time came, under his watchful eye, of course.

The next morning when they went for their walk they both noted that their 'friends' on the bench weren't there. Sam's heart dropped to the ground when he saw that. *Was that just a figment of my imagination yesterday?* Sam told Susan what he thought he saw the day before, not so sure anymore now that the bench was empty, but he was almost sure the old woman was Luke.

Susan got a cunning little smile on her face, "How long

have we been married now, Sam? Not even two years, and you are already looking at other women? Winking at you? Maybe I should be the one digging out of here, not you."

Sam just laughed - his Susie always had a good sense of humor. If this were how he had to spend the rest of his days, it would also be ok with him, as long as he was with her.

Sam's hopes came right back when they sat down at the table under the pergola for breakfast, and three hummingbirds soon hovered over the table. Susan had covered the cloth with a few paper towels in preparation for another accident like yesterday. But the birds all behaved themselves very well. Soon there were a few more of them around the table trying to get their beaks into the cups and sugar bowl.

Sam laughed as he said to Susan, "Look at this little bugger, he has his beak right into my coffee! I bet the caffeine is going to keep him awake the rest of the day." Both Susan and Sam knew that one had dropped something in his coffee. They were astounded that it was impossible to tell the difference between the real and fake birds, although they knew there were fake ones among them.

Sam carried the breakfast tray to the kitchen, and while loading the dishwasher, he slipped two metal capsules, one out of each coffee cup, into his shirt pocket. His hopes were sky-high again as he looked at Susan who was watching him with a smile on her face. "You are very domesticated, for a man who was a bachelor until recently."

Sam turned around and gave her a hug while he whispered in her ear. "Two capsules," and then so the audience could hear, "I guess I'm still afraid of my mother, who always insisted I clean up what I've used."

The first message read "get a bird feeder," and on the flip side it read, "I am the old lady," with a tiny smiley face in the corner. They had a hard time not laughing aloud when they read that. The second message read, "No tunnel - will get you out," and on the other side, "will send in earphones soon."

Susan immediately spoke to one of the guards to see if it would be a problem to get her a hummingbird feeder and extra sugar to make some nectar for it. "No problem, Mrs. Lewis. I'll get it for you tomorrow morning when I go shopping," he replied. The guards always treated them with respect, which was one thing, despite their circumstances, they both appreciated.

Susan was so excited she could barely keep her voice down as they walked into the park that afternoon. Both she and Sam had to use all their willpower not to rush up to the two people on the bench. "Sam, how on earth did they manage to do that? This is like a spy movie! I just can't believe what's happening! It's as if they can hear every word we say. Is that even possible? They really are here to get us out."

"I told you there's a lot you have to learn about the spy business. But then, I have to be honest and admit that I've also learned a few new things in the last few days," Sam replied.

Susan peppered him with questions, and Sam had a hard time to get her to keep her voice down and act normal. He'd just remembered about the spyflies Roy had constructed and used to catch the Sword of Cyrus conspirators just in time to avoid the disaster they were planning. He explained to her that possibly Luke was using those spyflies now inside and outside the house, and somehow when they are out here on their walks. That might explain why the young man and girl who always accompanied the old woman were always busy typing on their cell phones when they saw them.

When Sam thought he had figured out how Luke could know what they were saying to each other, he told Susan he was going to test his theory. "Luke, I think you can hear me. If that's the case, hold your walking stick in your left hand when we walk past you on our way home."

When they walked past the bench on their way home, the old lady had the walking stick in her left hand, and the young man beside her winked at Susan when he caught her eye.

When they got home after their morning walk, the hummingbird feeder was waiting for them with the groceries they ordered. The two of them were like children with new toys, but for an entirely different reason than the guards thought while watching them on the monitors.

Chapter Forty-Three

LIGHT A CRACKER UNDER YOUR BROTHER'S BOTTOM

Soon after Luke left on the Boise mission, Daniel gathered JR, Mark, Doug and Aaron and explained to them the urgent requirement to locate etorphine. The four of them required no encouragement. They were too happy to get involved in something a bit more adventurous than life in the caves. Daniel told them there was a good chance that one of the Yellowstone ranger offices could have etorphine that they would use to sedate animals such as wolves, bears, mountain lions and others. Mark was placed in charge of the group and asked to work out a plan to be presented to the Steering Committee.

A few days later, the quartet of excited adventurists returned with their plan. There were two likely park offices within a reasonable distance from the Rabbit Hole, one a ranger station and the other Park Headquarters. Two groups of two would venture forth to visit them armed with spyflies and zingers to see if they could find a place that held etorphine and what the security conditions were. They would then come back and finalize their plans before going in to obtain the drugs.

Since the almost calamitous 9th Cycle expedition when they thought JR and many others were dead, Daniel was ever vigilant when his younger siblings were involved in dangerous situations, and he cross-examined them like a trial lawyer. "What will you do if you encounter bears or wolves? What are your plans to avoid contact with other people? How much food will you take with you? Do you know how to operate the spyflies and hummingbirds? Do you even know what etorphine looks like?"

They had their answers ready, and in answer to the last question Mark produced a few pictures of what etorphine, or M99 as it was labeled in the USA, looked like. After a few more minutes of intensive questioning, Daniel was happy that if he left his two brothers in the care of Mark and Doug they should be reasonably safe. The next few days they had rainy weather, but when the bad weather cleared they were ready to go - Mark and JR in one team to the west, while Doug and Aaron headed south.

The cave-dwellers were all gathered in the big hall at the exit of the cave to wish them well. Rebecca noticed her older sister, Cindi, helping Aaron with a last minute check of his backpack. She could see they were talking and smiling, but could not hear what was said. She didn't miss the winks they gave each other or the sparkle in her sister's eyes when she smiled and said goodbye to Aaron. He turned, shook Daniel's hand, and walked out. Rebecca hadn't seen that sparkle in a long time. She wondered if Aaron or anyone else noticed it.

Outside the caves, the teams launched the zinger hummingbirds and would keep them in the air about five hundred feet above them. That would warn them of other people or dangerous animals, and they would help find the best routes all the way to their target destinations and back.

As the group at the cave turned back to their tasks, Rebecca could not control her curiosity any longer as she got hold of Cindi and dragged her to the side. "Sis, tell me about it!"

Cindi had no clue what Rebecca was talking about, "Tell you about what?"

"That sparkle I saw in your eyes when you spoke to Aaron earlier," she said very excitedly.

"Oh my God, Becky. Was it that obvious?" a worried Cindi asked.

"To me it was, but then I'm your sister. I haven't seen that sparkle for way too long. I thought you'd lost it, sis." Rebecca said.

"Becky, I like him very much. I'm happy and excited when he's around, but I don't have a clue about how he feels. I'm not going to tell him or ask him," Cindi said as her cheeks reddened.

"Don't worry about that, sis. I have firsthand experience with the Rossler boys. You must remember they grew up in an all-boys house with no sisters around to teach them about us. They're a bit clumsy with women. That was from my own experience with JR, and Sarah has told me it was the same with Daniel. They're slow movers, but I can tell you, once they get into action there's no stopping them." Rebecca laughed.

"Tell you, Becky, if I can figure out how to get him into action, I'm not the one who'll be stopping him. I've been on my own for way too long." Cindi, now sporting a full blush on her face and neck, laughed.

Rebecca decided to have a quiet word with Sarah at the first opportunity. She would have to see if Daniel could find out how Aaron felt, or what had to be done to kick some life into him. The two sisters would have leaped over the moon, had they known what Aaron said to his oldest brother when they shook hands earlier.

Mark and JR had a shock on the second day of their trek when they were not keeping a close eye on their hummingbird's monitor. It was a close encounter of the bear kind. They almost walked straight into a grizzly with cubs, which is not recommended as bear mothers are very aggressive around their cubs. The two of them followed every protocol in the book as they stood close together, looked straight at the bear and slowly, but very surely, retreated the way they came, walking backwards. Once they reached safety, the two of them were all bravado again trying to prove who was the braver of the two.

Doug and Aaron's trek was not as eventful as the others' were. They reached their destination first and quickly deployed the spyflies. They found a safe hiding place and lay quiet for the rest of the day while they maneuvered the flies around the park rangers' buildings.

It took them about three hours to find what they were looking for – the animal research facility. An hour later they had located the room where the M99 could be kept, but they could not get spyflies in - the door was closed, and soon after the offices closed. They fine-combed the rest of the office complex to get information about the alarm system, locks and computers before they retreated into the forest to a safe place where they would camp overnight. They would return for more observation early the next morning.

Mark and JR reached their target and found that it was just an information office with only a few administrative staff in attendance. Their spyflies quickly showed them there was no chance of finding the M99 there, after which they returned to the Rabbit Hole.

Doug and Aaron returned to the office complex very early the next morning to make sure they had the spyflies in position as the staff arrived. They were determined to capture the access codes for entry into the building and deactivation of the alarm. Shortly after the first employee arrived, one of the Rangers turned up and went through to his office, where they saw a glass-door cabinet with veterinary pharmaceuticals. They carefully maneuvered the flies over to the cabinet and recorded the labels on each of the bottles and packets inside. To their great disappointment, they could not find anything with an M99 tag.

At about midday they started the return trip to the Rabbit Hole. When they arrived back home, the sad-faced Mark and JR were there already.

While the four men were out on their assignments, Rebecca had found an opportunity to have a chat with Sarah about Cindi and Aaron. Sarah, the eternal matchmaker, with the matches between Sinclair and Martha, JR and Rebecca, and a few others to her credit was onto it immediately. Rebecca knew she would have an answer back in no time.

"Daniel, what is it with the Rossler boys and women? Why do you take forever to tell a girl that you like, how you feel about her?" she asked later.

Daniel was on alert immediately. "Maybe it's because we have been raised always to think and consider things before we act and to be modest at all times. Why are you asking? Are you thinking about my clumsiness around you when we were dating?" Daniel replied, knowing that his wife was up to something.

"Yes, that came to mind. I would have thought that your

younger brothers would have learned from your experience and would do better, but then JR arrived, and he was much worse than you. In the process he almost missed Rebecca."

Daniel sensed he would soon know what the real purpose of this conversation was.

Sarah continued, "Now, if it wasn't enough that the two of you were so inept, along comes Aaron, and he's just as bad, if not worse, than the two of you."

Daniel got it; Sarah was up to her matchmaking antics again, and he knew exactly what she was talking about. He had the advantage of knowing what Aaron said to him before he and Doug left. Even so, he was not going to tell Sarah about it yet – he was going to make her work for it.

He kept a straight face. "Sarah, my dear, you've lost me. Have I missed something I was supposed to know?"

"Daniel, don't tell me you haven't noticed the look in your brother's eyes?" Daniel frowned and shook his head. "I'm talking about that far-away look, you know?" Daniel, still frowning and shaking his head, was struggling to keep his composure.

"You know, it's like you said; the Rossler boys are a weird bunch. I don't know anything about far-away looks and stuff like that. Did I have a look like that back in the day? That far-away look you're talking about? What does it look like – can you show me?" Daniel asked, knowing he was going to crack up in another second or two.

"Daniel Rossler, I know ... " was as far as she got before Daniel threw in the towel and surrendered to the urge to laugh out loud.

"Sarah my love, I know all about that, and I know about Aaron and Cindi. I guess it's Rebecca who put you up to this, right?"

Sarah was smiling while she nodded her head. "Yes,

Rebecca and I had a talk this morning," Sarah admitted with a half-guilty shrug.

"Okay, I won't torture you anymore. I'll tell you what I know. When Aaron left, he said to me, 'Please take care of my girl while I'm gone.' He didn't say who the girl was, but I've seen him and Cindi together often, and I've been wondering."

Sarah responded immediately, "Now, you see! That's what I mean about you Rossler boys! Cindi is getting older, and time is a girl's worst enemy if she wants a family. And your brother is too shy to tell her he likes her?"

"But does she like him?" Daniel wanted to know.

"Of course she does! Do you think she'd be spending so much time with him if she didn't? And have you not seen the look on her face when she's with Aaron?" Sarah questioned.

"Sarah, you know I only have eyes for you. I'm not studying the looks on other women's faces, and even if I did, I wouldn't know what it meant!" Daniel quipped.

"Okay, now you know what that look means, and what you have to do is to light a firecracker under your brother's bottom. There's a beautiful girl waiting to hear from him." Sarah concluded the discussion with a big smile.

Chapter Forty-Four

ROBIN BRONZE GREEN

The hummingbirds, real and fake, just loved the feeder on the breakfast table. Soon the guards could hear Susan's ecstatic laughs as she enticed one of the birds to come and investigate what she had in her fist. Not long after that, Sam managed to perform the same magic. It was difficult to tell who enjoyed the game the most, the birds or the humans. The humans almost forgot to eat their breakfast.

When they went back to the kitchen they had collected four capsules. They took turns to go to the bathroom to read the messages, and then waited for their afternoon walk.

When they entered the park, they immediately noticed the bench was empty. They had nearly invisible tiny earphones in their ears, sent to them in the same way as he got the paper messages there – via capsules concealed in 'hummingbird poop', and microphones hidden in parts of their clothes closest to their mouths. They looked at each other briefly when they saw the empty bench and wondered if something could have happened to prevent Luke and his companion being there. That was until the moment they both almost screamed in shock when a voice that sounded as if it originated somewhere in their heads said, "Hello there, love birds." Their hearts raced. They finally had contact with Luke. The voice said, "Let's just check a few things, Robin."

Sam placed his finger on his lips to show Susan to be quiet while he silently counted, twenty-one, twenty-two, twenty-three, twenty-four, twenty-five before replying, "Bronze." He then counted another five seconds as before and said, "Green."

"Sam, my friend, what a relief to be able to finally talk to you." Luke's voice was loud and clear over the earphones. "Can I take it that the beauty queen by your side is the same Susan you've been telling me about for forty years?"

Sam laughed as he saw Susan blushing, "She can hear you, you idiot! Yes, the one and only," Sam said with pride in his voice.

"Please to meet you, Susan, I heard a lot about you, and Sam did not do you half the justice you deserve."

"Thank you, Luke," Susan said. "The pleasure is mine. I heard a lot about you, too, but I have the impression you already know what Sam told me about you, thanks to those spyflies."

"Susan, let me just warn you, don't believe everything that old coot tells you," Luke laughed.

"So my friends, from my eavesdropping on you two in the last few days, I've got the impression you're contemplating a change of venue?" Luke wisecracked.

Sam replied, "You can bet your ass on that. I've had a gutful of this shit."

"Sam, your language!" Susan reprimanded him.

Luke couldn't help but smile at Susan's reaction to

Sam's language, "In that case I have got a job offer for you, Sam."

Sam knew his friend and his sense of humor well enough after all these years, "What's the pay, working hours and conditions?"

"No salary, free board and lodging, no set working hours, no traveling, but excellent working conditions. Your residence will be in a place three hundred yards from where the trout are standing at attention to take a hook on command," Luke replied.

"Done. I'll take it," Sam said without hesitation.

Luke explained to them that they'd figured out all they needed to know about the guards and their routine. He described the four stages of the plan and that they were ready to start preparing for stage four – their evacuation.

Luke said, "One more question. Have either of you been implanted with a microchip?"

"Oh my God, no!" Sam said. "Are you telling me those sons of bitches are implanting people with microchips?"

"Yes, my friend, that's exactly what is happening. Our guesstimates are many millions have already been inserted, and billions more will follow. That's how they will eventually have total control over every living soul on this planet."

Susan was very concerned, "Luke, we need to get out of here, and so must my children and grandchildren."

"Susan, you and Sam must hang in there. I'll move as quickly as humanly possible. We didn't know what we would find here when we planned the mission, and we need to get a few more things in place before we can make the move," Luke said as he tried to calm her as best he could. He didn't know about Susan's children and grandchildren, and he couldn't tell them that there was no plan for that.

This was a new, unexpected, and not an insignificant

obstacle. To move the children and grandchildren would require more time, resources, observation and planning. He had no choice - he knew if Sam and Susan were to be evacuated without her children, the authorities would immediately incarcerate the children and force the two of them to come back.

Luke had a major problem on his hands. He had to figure out how to execute three separate evacuations at precisely the same time. He didn't have enough people and technological resources to make that happen in the next two weeks as he had planned, which meant the evacuation had to be delayed.

When the four adventurers, JR, Mark, Doug and Aaron, got back to the Rabbit Hole and reported the disappointing news, the Steering Committee suggested that they do another trip to a third location. If nothing were found there, they'd have to think about alternatives.

The four of them gathered in Roy's lab with Rebecca, Daniel, and Salome in attendance to have a good look at the spyfly recordings on a better and bigger screen. As they were watching, Rebecca said, "Roy, can you just rewind a few frames back and freeze it when I tell you?"

Roy did that, and Rebecca said, "Freeze! Okay, now can you try and zoom in on those two small bottles on the left of the screen?" Roy quickly zoomed in and adjusted the screen resolution; the labels said 'Immobilon'. "Roy please keep that screen there. I just want to go and get something from the clinic."

A moment later, she came back with her Samsung tablet in her hand and a big smile on her face, "Bingo! We've got it! Immobilon is the British version of etorphine. It must have been imported. Have a look here." She showed them the picture and description on her tablet.

"The question now is if Immobilon will have the same potency as the M99?" Daniel asked.

"I am looking at the manufacturer's specifications here and comparing the bottle on the screen with what I have here on the tablet. It looks like Immobilon is, in fact, pure etorphine, while I know M99 is diluted with other sedative substances. I think we have precisely what we've been looking for," Rebecca replied.

Mark was put in charge of the team of four again to study the recordings very carefully and work out in detail how they would go about getting the Immobilon into their hands. The rest of the operation worked out very well. Rebecca helped them by labeling two bottles that were exactly the same size and shape as the Immobilon and filling them with sterilized water.

They knew the combination of the lock on the front door as well as the deactivation code for the alarm. With those obstacles out of the way, it was easy. The office where the pharmaceuticals were kept was not locked and neither was the glass-door cabinet. They swapped the bottles that contained the water with the Immobilon. It took more than a year before one of the rangers found that a deer that he shot with a dart to tag it for research purposes did not want to go to sleep.

Chapter Forty-Five

SUSAN'S BIRTHDAY

It was part of Luke's original plan to go back to the Rabbit Hole before step four would be executed. That was to get the rest of the technical equipment and to bring Raj or Stuart back with him. The revelation about Susan's family threw a monkey wrench in the works.

He had no information about them whatsoever. He would have to get their addresses and set up a surveillance operation before he could even think about how it could be done. He had to assume that they would be under some sort of surveillance, and that it would be too dangerous to openly contact them.

Luke spoke to Alison and Owen about his dilemma, and Alison suggested that she or Owen could contact the children. Luke immediately pointed out that would be a big mistake. If they were seen with the children, their observers would put two and two together when the children disappeared and the two of them would find themselves on the Most Wanted list, with the Rosslerites, overnight.

Luke decided the best he could do would be to tell his

friends about the complications, and that they would have to give him time to get his ducks in a row. Maybe they would have some ideas that could be useful. After all, Sam was a very intelligent and experienced CIA operator.

The next morning Luke spoke frankly, as he explained his predicament to Sam and Susan. He wasn't aware before yesterday of Susan's children and grandchildren. He had no intention of leaving them behind. In fact, for obvious reasons, it was not an option. It did however, add a new layer of complexity to his original plans, not an impossible problem, but it was going to take longer to get everything organized.

"But we all know smooth seas never make a skillful sailor," Luke said with a smile.

Sam replied, "Luke, since our conversation yesterday I've had my thinking cap on, and yes, it's going to be difficult evacuating all of us at the same time from three different locations."

"That part could be a bit of a challenge, but I'll cross that bridge when I come to it. I first want to gather all the information about the children and their circumstances. So I'll need their names' addresses, and anything you can tell me about them, Susan," Luke replied.

Sam thought with a little smile, *that's the Luke Clarke I know. He'll never go half-cocked into any mission.* "Okay, Susan can give you that information in a minute. I just have one question. Do you think you can pull it all together in four weeks?"

"My plan was to break you two out in the next two to three weeks, but now I might need more time than that. Why do you ask?" Luke wanted to know.

"It's a long shot, but Susan's birthday is in four weeks. We're allowed to see the children once a month for an hour, but we have to get prior authorization for it." Sam got hot under the collar while talking. "Luke, can you imagine that? Having to get permission to see your own children from some moron asshole in Washington!"

"Okay, tell me how does that work exactly?" Luke inquired.

"Well, we have to fill in an application, and then it takes a few days to be approved or declined. They haven't declined any of our requests in the past. Then, if it's authorized, the guards will go and pick up the children and their families and bring them over to our house at the agreed time. They are only allowed one hour with us, in the presence of three of the guards at all times. It's like a prison. They might as well have us talking to the children through a glass window on a phone!" Sam was distressed having to even think about it. "I was just wondering if we could manage to get permission for the children to come and visit us on Susan's birthday. That would put us all together in the same place at the same time."

Luke got excited. "That would be the best scenario we could ever hope for! It would make things much, much easier, but I would like to work out a plan B as well. We can't assume things will play out as we wish. The guards, or their bosses, might just decide to change their minds at the last minute. I'd like to have a back door open."

"Agreed," Sam replied. "We'll get the application going as soon as we're back home, and hopefully they won't make us wait too long. I'll will let Susan give you all the details about the children you need."

Later that afternoon, Owen got into the passenger seat of the 4x4 in the garage attached to the house where they were staying. Thanks to Alison's recently acquired make-up skills, he was now an overweight man in his mid-thirties.

He had tattoos on his face, arms and legs, lip rings and enormous earrings. Ugly scars sliced down the left side of his face and a nose as big and skewed as the Leaning Tower of Pisa. He was dressed in jeans and a T-shirt, with a baseball cap, sunglasses, and a small backpack. That was the final result of the tips and tricks Alison learned from her studies at a Hollywood studio a few weeks ago, and of course, studying the facial recognition avoidance techniques in the files given to her by Raj.

Alison dropped Owen off at the Boise Bus Station on Bannock Street, where he disappeared amongst the crowd. He hailed a taxi to Southeast Boise, where Jack Walker, Susan's oldest son, his wife Anna, and their two boys lived. Jack was a lecturer in biochemistry at Boise State University.

The taxi dropped Owen off two blocks from their house. Within the next two hours, he managed to smuggle two spyflies into their house and connect them to the recorder. Once he had moved the flies around the house and recorded the layout and measurements of each room, the flies would automatically go around the house listening for voices and movement. He dropped the small recorder, about the size of a matchbox, in a shrub close to the pavement in front of the house as he walked past. Thanks to Roy's nanotech battery technology in the spyflies, it would be able to record for five to six days before a recharge was required.

Two blocks away he called a taxi that took him back to the bus station, where Alison was waiting for him. The next day they repeated the routine of the previous day, only the roles were reversed. Alison turned into a young mother with a baby in her arms. The taxi took her to North End where Shane Walker, an electronics engineer, Susan's younger son, his wife Mandy, and their two-year-old daughter lived.

When they retrieved the spyflies and recording devices after three days and studied them, they learned that both households were heavily bugged with microphones, but no cameras and no guards. Judging by the contents of some of their conversations, they knew that the inhabitants were probably not aware of the bugs. It became apparent there was no love lost between them and the new world government. They were worried about their future and the dramatic changes in society, as well as extremely frustrated about the fact that they were powerless to do anything to help their mother and Sam.

Luke had no doubt that their telephones, mobile phones and all internet activities would be closely monitored at all times. The good news for him was that there were no guards to deal with. He decided to keep the spyflies around the homes for a few more days to make sure he didn't miss anything important.

His initial thoughts were that on the day of the evacuation, if the children were not allowed to be at the Lewis' house, Owen and Alison could pick the two families up and drive them to the assembly point. He would take care of Sam and Susan's evacuation.

That meant he would have to get a message through to them a few days before, so that they were ready to move when their transport arrived. He would have to think carefully through every step, but the first priority now was to return to the Rabbit Hole to make the final preparations. The spyflies and recorders were swapped and set to activate only when people were at home and awake, which would extend the battery life to more than twelve days.

The next day Luke spoke to the Lewises and told them what he knew about their children and their circumstances. He had some ideas for how Plan-B could be executed. He also told them that he and his companions would have to go away now to finalize preparations.

"Make sure that you know where everything is that you would want to take with you so that you can pack in fifteen minutes, and don't pack anything before. We will have limited space, so unfortunately you'll have to leave the furniture behind," Luke ended, with a bit of humor.

Luke assured them, "We'll be back at the latest two days before Susan's birthday. In the meantime, keep on feeding the hummingbirds every morning. Be extra nice to the guards. We would definitely like to have that big family birthday party! Oh, and three weeks from now, you should start wearing the earphones again when you're in the park. I might be back by then."

Both Sam and Luke knew that the plan still had many holes in it, and there were just too many 'ifs' and 'buts' to feel comfortable. They tacitly agreed that it was not necessary to let Susan in on their reservations yet. She was already worrying about her children, on top of everything else.

Chapter Forty-Six

WE'RE IN

When Luke got back to the Rabbit Hole, he found that everything was ready for them to start work on the final plan for the evacuation. Everyone was worried about the new development, with Susan's children and grandchildren being included in the evacuation, but there was no choice - everyone had to be moved at the same time.

They had about two weeks to make ready. They had to allow a few days for Luke to prepare Owen and Alison before their return to Boise, and a few days after arrival in Boise to find out if anything had changed since they left.

While Luke was busy with the preparations at the Rabbit Hole, Owen and Alison would take a trip to New York to meet with his publishers, and to try to connect with Raj's friends, Rube and Sombra.

The Rosslerites were severely hampered by the fact that they had only two people who could move around freely in the outside world, as the rest of them were all on the most wanted list. Part of the contents of the laptop that Owen was to hand over to Rube and Sombra were the letters that the cave-dwellers wrote to their closest family members in the hope that they could be delivered to them.

The entire Steering Committee got involved in the planning and preparation process as they watched the recordings that Luke brought back from Boise. Then began the building scale models of the houses and neighborhoods, and stepping through both Plan-A and B.

Raj and Roy had all the essential equipment working as requested. Ben and JR tested the mosquitos, loaded with an extremely minuscule quantity of Immobilon, on a moose a week before Luke's arrival, under Rebecca's strict guidance and observation. One mosquito put the moose to sleep in less than two seconds. They stayed with the animal until it had fully recovered and took off.

All equipment was tested again and again to make sure there would be no hiccups when they went live. They conducted trial runs of each of the plans with Luke and Stuart, who was going to accompany him back to Boise, to take care of the technical side of the evacuation.

Two weeks later, Daniel, Aaron and Raj accompanied Luke and Stuart to Mount Ararat to find out about Owen and Alison's trip to New York.

It was quite an experience to listen how Owen described his encounter with Raj's friends. His narrative had them crawling on the ground with laughter at times. "Raj, those guys are crazy, man. I was told you are the most paranoid person on earth, but I know better than that after meeting with them." Raj just laughed.

Owen went on to explain what a mission it was to get Rube to see him. Apparently, Rube had the unfortunate Owen walking and taxiing all over New York to meeting places. Owen would turn up at a location at the right time, and then some weird person would drop a note on his table or whisper a new address. Sometimes it was just GPS coordinates, and then Owen had to get there. When they finally met, after Owen had relocated about six times, Rube did not say a single word. He just listened to Owen. When Owen finished talking, Rube gave him a napkin with an address, date and time – which was two days later – and then got up and walked out. He didn't utter a single word.

Owen gathered from the writing on the napkin that Rube wanted to meet again. So, two days later he turned up, and after four relocations they met again. Rube took the laptop from Owen, gave him another napkin with a new address, date and time – again for two days later – and walked away, again without saying a single word.

The next meeting went a bit better when they met after Owen's third relocation, and Rube handed the laptop back to Owen. Rube spoke for the first time when he said, "This is Sombra." Owen recognized Sombra's face from the meeting two nights ago - he was the guy sitting at a table next to where Owen and Rube were seated.

Owen continued, "And as soon as I discovered that Rube had in fact mastered the art of speaking when he introduced Sombra to me, I could not get him to stop talking."

"What did he say?" Raj wanted to know.

"Give this to Raj. We're in," Owen said in a solemn voice that had them all cracking up again.

Raj just smiled, "They will support us. They will have left me a message on the laptop. It will take me a day or so to read it."

Chapter Forty-Seven

THERE WAS A POWER DIP

"I see you two are still very happily married!" Luke's voice came over the earphones three days before Susan's birthday.

"Luke, you old rascal. I expected you back a bit earlier," Sam said, very excited to hear his friend's voice again.

"Sorry about that, we had lots to do, and we got back here only late last night. But I'm happy to tell you we are as ready as we'll ever be. Do you have news about the birthday party?" Luke wanted to know.

To his big relief, Sam told him it was approved. The children were allowed to visit for two hours from eight o'clock on the coming Sunday night to celebrate Susan's birthday. Things were looking a lot brighter.

Luke explained to them that Plan-A would be the evacuation on the Sunday night and would proceed only if and when the children were all in the house. If one or more of them were not there for some reason, the plan would be abandoned and Plan-B would come into play, to be executed three days later.

Over the next three walking sessions, Luke went through the plan with them several times, and by the Sunday morning stroll they all knew exactly what was going to happen. Shortly after nine thirty that Sunday night, about half an hour after they finished the delicious birthday dinner, all were in the family room, with the grandchildren fast asleep on the couch. There was a power dip – that was the signal. Sam looked at Susan and they looked around the room to make sure they knew where everyone in the room was, especially the three guards.

One minute later, the power tripped, which left the house in total darkness. One of the guards shouted, "Sit still. I will get a ..." followed by a dull sound, as if something solid had dropped on the floor. The first thud was followed by two more very similar sounds. Sam called out to the guards, but got no response. He heard the front door opening and saw two flashlights going down the hallway towards the bedrooms where the other guards were.

He told everyone to remain where they were, they could injure themselves in the dark, and maybe the lights will come on again soon. If not, he would get a flashlight from the kitchen.

Three minutes later, the lights went on and the sudden sharp light temporarily blinded everyone. Sam and Susan were standing in the middle of the room and indicated, with their fingers to their lips, to be quiet.

Sam spoke, "Please listen very carefully to me and your mother, and do exactly as we say. We have to move quickly now. This is all part of a plan to get us out of here and to a safe place. I know it's a shock to you, but you have to trust us. Your mother and I know precisely what is going on. I promise we will tell you what is happening in more detail soon, but for now, let's just do the important things first.

There are two men in the guards' office whom you don't know. Don't worry, they are our friends. All of the guards are under sedation and won't bother us. They are not dead. Anna and Mandy, can you stay with the children and make sure they don't see us take the guards out? Jack and Shane, please help me move the guards into one of the bedrooms. Susan, you can start packing - we'll come and help you soon."

As Sam finished the orders to everyone, Luke appeared in the doorway and helped them with the guards while being introduced by Sam. He told them the remaining three guards were fast asleep and already tied up in the office.

Stuart had already loaded the recordings prepared by him and Raj into the surveillance cameras. Then he loaded the computer with the reports that the 'guards' would be sending out every day for the next few days. Next he would remove the GPS tracking devices from the guards' SUV's and connect them to smartphones that would simulate the vehicles returning James' and Shane's families to their homes and coming back again.

Owen and Alison also arrived via the back door soon after and helped them to pack the guards' two SUV's, parked in the double garage with internal access via the kitchen. They left the packing of Owen's 4x4, which was parked at the rental property, for last.

Twenty minutes after the lights came on, the SUV's pulled out of the garage and took off in different directions. Owen was the driver for Jack and his family, while Alison drove Shane and his family in the second SUV.

At a large container yard in the industrial area of Boise Valley, there were four forty-foot containers, two of which were empty and two packed with building materials and farm equipment. That was where they were heading. Owen and Alison knew exactly where to go and what to do. When they arrived, they unpacked everything from the vehicles into the containers where the escapees would find everything had been set up to accommodate them all.

The SUV's were moved into the other two empty containers that were locked and destined for a scrap yard in San Francisco the next day.

At the Lewises house, Sam, Luke and Stuart double-checked that the guards were still sleeping and tied up properly, while Susan scraped together the last few things. The lights in the front parts of the house went out, and minutes later the four of them left one by one, a few minutes apart, through the back door. They met at the rental house where Luke and the team lived and packed Owen's vehicle.

They were at the container yard forty minutes after Owen and Alison. Stuart would join those in the containers for the trip to Mount Ararat while Owen and Alison would be in his 4x4 with Luke, who had turned into Alison's grandmother again. The two trucks that would transport the containers to Mount Ararat would arrive at six the next morning. Owen and Alison would be there to make sure everything was loaded and secured properly, and they would be at Mount Ararat when the trucks arrived and unloaded.

Chapter Forty-Eight

TECTUS

Raj was eager to see what was on the laptop that Owen brought back from New York. He expected Rube and Sombra would have loaded a message and a few nice applications for him. He was not disappointed.

He found a hidden file in the registry containing the key to the encoding they'd used. He read the report and smiled as he discovered they were already part of a resistance group, formed even before the New World Order came to power. They called themselves Tectus. Raj had no idea how they came up with that name.

The Tectus members, all of whom knew about the Rossler Foundation and the work they'd done in the past, were happy to help in any way they could. It seemed they already had more than one hundred members spread across the USA and even a few other countries, counting amongst them some of the top computer hackers in the world. They were always recruiting more members.

They were able to gain almost unfettered and untraceable access to government networks. They were now sitting on a wealth of information, which they were happy to share with the Rossler Foundation.

Just to prove that point, they included the latest satellite-tracking program including the launch date, location in space, description and purpose of every operational satellite, public and secret. As if that were not enough, they also included a document with the specifications and launch dates for those satellites planned to be placed into orbit over the next six months.

The report provided some disturbing information about the chipping program, which apparently had been gaining a lot of momentum lately, something that was not reported in the media. Tectus had their hands on the documents detailing the entire chipping program and strategy. Chipping had already been implemented for criminals, nonconformists, current and former high-ranking officials, existing and former security and law enforcement staff, and many others as part of the first phase. The plan was to speed up the program in the next few weeks with the objective to have everyone on the planet chipped within three years.

Tectus had an excellent and very secure communications system going, with proxies and free Internet access points. They discovered one of the best ways to communicate electronically was by hacking into the wireless networks and access points of educational facilities where they could remain anonymous amongst tens of thousands of students.

Their biggest concern was how to avoid chipping or neutralize the chips. They hadn't been able to get their hands on any of the chips and were quite scared to do so because of the horrible consequences when anyone tampered with them.

They also reported that they were happy to arrange for the safe delivery of the letters to family members on the outside. They would use the people in the network to make sure those family members would get printed versions of the messages, with instructions to burn them after reading.

The report ended with the request for another meeting as soon as convenient so that the details of future cooperation and information exchange could be worked out and implemented as early as possible.

Raj had the satellite tracking system up and running within less than an hour and studied it carefully. There were no surveillance satellites in operation that would be of concern to the inhabitants of the Rabbit Hole. It was frightening, though, to see how many Skywalkers had been launched since the takeover and how many more were being readied for launch. Within three months, every corner of the planet would be covered.

Chapter Forty-Nine

IT WAS TOO LATE

The great escape was discovered two days later, and the alarm was raised almost at the same time as Sam, Susan and their family received a hero's welcome when Luke led the group into the Rabbit Hole.

Luke escorted them to the Robert Cartwright Town Hall where everyone gathered to greet them. They immediately felt welcome as hugs and kisses from people they'd never seen or met before surprised them. It was going to take days to remember all their names, but the most important part was, they were free.

The welcome Sam and his family received stood in sharp contrast to the welcome James Gordon got when he walked into the chambers of the Supreme Council in The Berlaymont, the former headquarters of the European Union in Brussels, a day after the alarm was raised in Boise. If he'd had any hopes that the Supreme Council meeting was going to take place in a calm atmosphere, it disappeared with the opening words of the world's most powerful man.

"You fuckin', imbecilic moron! I have a good mind to shoot you right now. I suppose you have some inane excuse or explanation for this, but don't even try to give it to me! You useless bag of sloppy goose shit!"

Seven of the fourteen Council members knew John Brideaux and his psychotic temper tantrums and remained absolutely quiet. The rest, who were experiencing it for the first time, were shocked and scared out of their minds and remained silent for that reason.

"You and that dog-faced bitch over there thought you were smart!" Anastasia Oriov did not look up - she was staring at the glass of water in front of her, sickly as olive green linen.

"You kept Sam Lewis out of prison for your silly fuckin' propaganda games! Now you have the former head of the fuckin' CIA on the loose. Do you have the slightest idea what tornado of swill that guy can stir up?"

Gordon tried to open his mouth but could not get a word out. "Fuck you Gordon, don't even try to answer, you pea-brained, dim-witted, clumsy piece of hogwash!

"Mr. President, please I ... I ..." was as far as Gordon got before he looked up and found himself staring down the barrel of the gun in Brideaux's hands.

"Gordon, shut your yap! Don't even try to make an excuse! I will shoot you if I hear so much as another squeak from you!" Brideaux shouted at the top of his lungs.

"You have been in this job for how many weeks now, and you haven't even got the slightest fuckin' clue where the Rosslers and my libraries are! You were busy digging snot from your nose and sucking dead cocks while Sam Lewis, one of the most dangerous people in the world, who was placed under *your* care, walked out of his house with his wife and family as if they were going on a picnic. You hopeless idiot!" he yelled.

Gordon dared to glance up, only to be faced with someone he could barely recognize. Brideaux's eyes were red and bulging, his complexion verging on blue-grey, and there was saliva dribbling down his chin.

Gordon quickly dropped his head and stared at the table like a little boy.

The staff in the building could not believe what they were hearing. They had never seen or heard anything like this. They knew their boss had a short temper. But they didn't know it was this bad. He sounded exactly like what he was - a psychotic maniac.

"Listen up, Gordon; this is your last chance. You will personally fly over to Washington and you will personally stick a chip in the ass of that useless motherfucker, Robert Wilson. Then you will drive him over to the smallest police station in the most dismal ghetto there, where he will, from now on, be doing foot patrol seven days a week for the rest of his life. You can tell him if he so much as sneezes, I will personally push his button."

Gordon, who was by now too afraid to speak, just nodded his head in agreement. At least it looked as if he wouldn't be shot – not yet.

"After that you will get hold of the six guards and make them disappear. Now *you* disappear from my sight. Bugger off, and go do your job. Report back to this Council in two days!" Brideaux shouted with just a little less volume.

Not even if he were traveling at the speed of light would Gordon be able to get out of that room and as far away from that crazy man as quickly as he wanted. He was on his mobile to arrange a flight to Washington before he reached the end of the corridor. He was booked on a plane that would leave in less than two hours before he even reached his office. Gordon had just one immediate goal, and that was to get as much distance between him and President John Brideaux as possible, as fast as he humanly could.

On the flight to Washington he gave some serious thought to the idea of making a run for it and disappearing into some African or South American jungle. He would rather take his chances with some cannibalistic tribe than face the President of the Supreme Council again.

Gordon made more than hundred percent sure he executed his orders to the T as he believed that would give him a second chance. Two days later he walked back through the doors of the Supreme Council chambers, fully expecting a better reception than before. His mistake was revealed to him when he saw a nurse standing beside the seat to which he was pointed, with a chipping kit in her hand. He felt several cold shivers running down his spine. He should have made the runner when he thought about it a few days ago, and now it was too late.

The nurse opened his shirt and moved it over his right shoulder. She sterilized the area just below his right collarbone and made a half-inch incision without giving him a local anesthetic, a courtesy afforded even to criminals when they were chipped. She put the chip in place despite Gordon's screams of pain, put three stitches in the wound, sterilized it again, and put a small self-stick bandage on.

Finally, she pushed a few buttons on a small electronic device before saying, "Mr. Gordon do you want me to tell you what will happen if you try to take that out?"

Gordon, who was in agony, just shook his head.

This chipping procedure was the most gruesome and painful of the two available. They already had a much less invasive process, where the chip would be injected into place within a few seconds. Brideaux had ordered this one, without any anesthetic, as a special treat for Gordon. He wanted him to remember.

When the procedure was completed, Brideaux said with a wicked smile on his face "Gordon, we have a new assignment for you. These gentlemen will accompany you to your new offices."

The two agents had instructions to accompany him to Moscow. From there, he would be taken to one of the orientation camps in Siberia, where he would serve as a guard.

As President Brideaux saw the backside of Gordon, he turned to Anastasia Oriov and said, "You will be next, bitch. One misstep and you will be scrubbing decks on merchant ships during the day and fucking sailors at night for the rest of your life."

President Brideaux was a worried man. For the thousandth time he regretted that he hadn't killed the Rosslers when he had the chance. He didn't mention it to anyone, but he had no doubt that the Rosslers had something to do with Sam Lewis' escape. That combination of Sam Lewis, the Rosslers, and the 10th Cycle Library didn't bode well for him and the new world order.

Brideaux never slept; at least it seemed to be the case when he called the new head of BOSS, Liu Chen, former chief of Chinese Intelligence. It was three o'clock in the morning when he told Chen to make sure every person on the watch list was chipped within a week, and within two weeks all of their families, including parents, siblings, children and grandchildren.

Chapter Fifty

HELL WOULD BE TOO NICE FOR THEM

The police chief in Boise, whose department had been contacted by neighbors hearing screams coming from the Lewises house, immediately issued an APB and gave it to the radio and TV stations to broadcast.

The news headlines were "Former Head of CIA and Family Disappeared". Foul play was suspected because the guards were found drugged and tied up. The police were concerned for the safety of the whole family. People were asked to contact the police if they had any information.

It was central news for exactly one hour before the police chief appeared on TV again and withdrew the previous statement. He pointed out that it was all a mistake, reporting that the Lewises had been found at a holiday resort not far from Boise – all of them safe and in good health. There was no further mention of the incident and no one ever questioned the report about the guards that were found drugged and tied up. The police chief and the news reporters involved quietly disappeared themselves, never to be heard of again.

Esther Harper saw the first two news bulletins and told her husband about it while they were out on a walk. "Nigel, what do you make of that?"

"My guess is that Sam Lewis and his family got away, but the authorities don't want anyone to know about it. They could never admit that Sam has slipped through their fingers- that would never fit in with their propaganda. I'm afraid that if they recapture him though, he and his entire family will be killed right away. I can promise you, those who made the mistake of publicizing this story will be dead by now."

Esther was shocked, "Nigel, that's horrible! These people are so evil. Hell would be too nice for them."

"I'm wondering how Sam managed to pull it off. It wouldn't have been easy if his circumstances were anything like ours. I would think it would be near impossible without outside help. But then, on the other hand, he went through the ranks from field agent to the head of the CIA. It's not entirely impossible that he could have pulled it off on his own." Nigel speculated.

"Who do you think could have helped them?" Esther wanted to know.

Nigel had a little smile on his face as the thoughts were racing through his mind. "I'd place my bet on the Rosslers. And, if that is the case, I have new hope for the world and us. Remember what a powerful alliance the Rosslers and Sam formed during the Sword of Cyrus crisis?"

Chapter Fifty-One

TAKE CHARGE OF OPERATION PHOENIX

Sam and his family were astounded by the Rosslerites' colossal achievements in such a short timeframe, when they got the royal tour of the Rabbit Hole. They were shown the Gallatin Unified School, Gardens of Gallatin, Roy's lab and Raj's computer center. There was Rebecca's clinic, Sinclair's translation lab, the Nicholas Rossler Library, hot pools, steam electricity generators, sleeping quarters for every family, and meeting rooms. The fly-fishing spot immediately became Sam's favorite.

Sam smiled as he turned to Luke and said, "Man, am I happy I accepted your job offer."

The following day, the Steering Committee assigned each of them to different departments after the three new kids were welcomed at the Gallatin school. Jack, with his Ph.D. in biochemistry, was immediately assigned to work with Rebecca. His wife Anna, although being a homemaker the last few years to take care of their boys, had a degree in human biology and was also assigned to work with Rebecca. Shane, with his skills as an electronics engineer, was assigned to Ryan's team, and his wife Mandy, a firmware programmer, was assigned to Raj's team. Susan was assigned to Martha's garden society where she found a kindred spirit in their mutual love for gardening.

Sam was assigned to the Steering Committee, and that same afternoon during the happy hour, Sam would officially become the sixth musketeer. Susan quickly became friends with the rest of the musketeers' wives.

When everyone had received their assignments and left, the Steering Committee got right down to business when Daniel said, "We have a lot of things to do. I suggest we get right to it."

Raj had already given them all an electronic copy of the Tectus report that they were to discuss first. Luke wanted to know where the name came from and what it meant. Raj just shrugged his shoulders, but Salome explained that it was a Latin word, which meant covered, hidden, concealed, covert, closed, or hideaway.

Daniel looked at Sam and said, "Sam, it feels like old times to have you here and to work with you again. We'd very much like you to help us prioritize, plan, and execute our strategy. I guess you would have surmised by now that we didn't bring you here just for the excellent fishing?"

"I suspected you had some ulterior motives. I'm ready to do whatever it takes to get us out of this mess." Sam replied with a smile.

Daniel continued. "That's what we hoped you'd say. We'd like you to take charge of Operation Phoenix to help us rise from the ashes. The people in this room and everyone in this cave, as well as a few on the outside, are at your disposal."

Sam told them he owed the new government no loyalty and was not bound by any oath of secrecy he took in the past. He was happy to divulge any information he had. Raj was very tempted to ask him about the government covering up the contact they had with aliens and what was really going on at Area 51, but he decided to ask that at a later stage.

Sam continued, "With that out of the way, I think the best place to start will be for you to fill me in on what you've done so far. What do you have in mind for the future? I also need to understand everything about the 8th Cycle discovery."

Daniel replied, "Let me start with our current list. With you and your family here, we can tick off the first item on the list, and the second item is the return of Raj's laptop with the report from his two friends. The next few items on our list are first, to get our hands on some of those biochips so we can find out how they work and find a way to neutralize them. Second would be to start building a network of support and communications on the outside, because we are more or less cave-bound since acquiring outlaw celebrity status."

Daniel paused to roll his eyes. "You do know we aren't guilty of the crimes we're accused of, right?" When Sam smiled and nodded his head, Daniel continued."

Third, we have to look at what we could do to safeguard close family and friends, which won't necessarily mean bringing them here, but at least to a safe place. And fourth would be to recruit more people with expertise in nanotechnology, electronics, computing and any other specialty we might require. The final point would be to decide if we should break President Harper and his wife out of what we assume is house arrest similar to what yours was and bring them here. I'd say it's a pretty ambitious list," Daniel concluded.

"I can't see anything wrong with what you have on the list. None of it is going to be easy, but to make omelets, you have to break eggs. I just have to say again how impressed I am with how efficiently you've pulled off our escape, and again express our gratitude for that. You have just demonstrated that even with a deck stacked heavily against you, you didn't give up; you flawlessly executed an operation that would've been difficult even for the CIA with all their resources. That gave me hope and confidence that we will win this war," Sam replied. He got a round of applause when he stopped talking.

Daniel and the rest gave Sam a detailed account of the 8th Cycle discovery, Project Enigma, and all the events leading up to their evacuation of the Rossler Foundation headquarters, finishing with the arrival of the Lewis family the day before.

For the second time in two days, Sam just shook his head in admiration for what this small group of people had achieved through hard work and genius.

Sam told them about the conversation he had with Nigel Harper at the White House and the president's description of how the security agents were killed. He wanted to know if they had any idea what could have killed people like that.

Salome and Roy explained that it was entirely possible to cause deaths as described with the use of nanotechnology. DNA-specific nanobots, nanopoison and even a nanolaser or invisible beam could have been used.

"Aha," Sam exclaimed. "Now I remember; you told me about that during the Sword of Cyrus crisis." He continued to relate the rest of the conversation he had with President Harper.

Sam also expressed his concern that the president would

have put up stern resistance to being chipped. "You all know President Harper - he's a proud man. I'm afraid he and his wife would choose death over the humiliation of carrying the chip in their bodies."

"Oh my God, Sam!" Sarah cried. "We have to do something immediately. They're our friends, our President, we cannot wait. I'll never forgive myself if something like that happened and we did nothing about it."

Sam agreed, "Sarah, I agree and I think everyone else here agrees we have to do something to prevent that from happening. We might not be able to stop them from being chipped, but we could perhaps get a message through to them that we are all alive. We could let them know that I have escaped and am with you, and that help is on the way. Here's what the President said to me, the last time I saw him. *'They might very well be our only hope.'* Do you know to whom he was referring?" Everyone shook their heads, and Sam continued, "He was referring to you, the people of the Rossler Foundation. As long as he knows you are out there and alive, he knows you will be working on a plan to overthrow this regime."

"It's humbling to hear that, but at the same time it's frightening to know we're his only hope," Daniel said.

In the next few hours it became very clear that their decision to get Sam Lewis on board was a brilliant idea. The man was more than a fountain of information – in fact, it was more like a tsunami. He'd risen through the ranks in the CIA and got access to more and more top secret information with each promotion. He'd been accumulating treasure troves of knowledge over all those years, and by the time he was the head of the CIA he had access to everything. He had the details about every operation going on in the CIA, of course. Not only that, he'd made it his task to read as much as he could about past activities, including the reasons for failure or success.

They agreed that the two highest priorities were to get a message to the Harpers and to get hold of some of those chips. The problem was that once a person was chipped, it became extremely dangerous to contact him. They agreed that the Supreme Council would have ordered the immediate chipping of all remaining people on their watch lists, and possibly even their family members, since the Lewises escape. Chances were that the family members of the people in the Rabbit Hole would be chipped very soon, if not already, and that President Harper and his wife would be among the people on watch lists, probably first on the list.

Of course, all CIA agents, past and present, would have a record, to which the new government would have gained access. It had to be assumed the government would have placed them under watch and probably would have chipped all of them as well, which was disappointing as they could have used some of those agents.

Sam pulled the white rabbit out of the hat when he told them that he'd had four 'non-existent' officers reporting to him and him only during his time as head of the CIA. The term 'non-existent' meant only two people knew they worked for the CIA, and those were Sam and the agent. Their identities would not be anywhere on any record. They were not on the payroll of the CIA; they were not handed over to his successor, because the agents retired with him. Every CIA head had 'non-existent' agents, but successors did not inherit them - that was the rule.

Sam suggested, "Those are the agents we have to contact and activate. I have no doubts about them. I know where they are, what they are doing, and that they will help us. We just need to get messages through to them, and we can then use them to get hold of the chips and to get in touch with President Harper. After that, there will be many more missions where we could use them."

One of the agents lived in Texas; two lived in New York, and the last one in Los Angeles. Through Owen and the Tectus network contacts in New York, it would be the easiest and quickest to start with those two agents first. Sam, Luke and Salome would get into the preparations for those missions immediately.

The meeting ended with Sam giving them an overview of his strategy. "Margaret Mead said, 'Never doubt that a small group of thoughtful, committed people can change the world.' Do you know why?"

"Indeed it is the only thing that ever has," Daniel completed the quote.

Sam smiled, "Exactly. My initial thoughts are that we won't win this war with weapons. We will have to win it by outsmarting and outmaneuvering the enemy's technology. We won't need a cast of thousands - we just need a small group of smart and willing people."

Chapter Fifty-Two

THE SICARI REBELS

Nigel Harper could not help but smile when he saw the news that James Gordon had been replaced. Harper was not a man who carried grudges, but he was sure he wasn't going to lose any sleep over Gordon's fate. Worrying though, was the man who replaced him; Liu Chen. That *was* a reason for losing sleep. He'd heard the horror stories from his security advisors while he was still president – the man was a merciless butcher who had the blood of tens of thousands on his hands.

As depressing as that news was, Nigel smiled again when it struck him that the announcement had just wiped out any doubts he still had whether Sam Lewis was actually on the loose. If only Sam and the Rosslerites had been or would be able to team up.

The Harpers were out on their afternoon walk when they saw the three SUV's pull up to the farmhouse. They looked at each other, the concern clearly visible on their faces. The last time SUV's arrived at their house, their special agents were murdered before their eyes and they were placed under house arrest. They did not expect anything good from this visit either, and they weren't wrong.

When they arrived at the front door, the new head of the secret services in the USA, Jonathan Lucas, who replaced Robert Wilson, was there to greet them. After he introduced himself, he stated that he was ordered by the Supreme Council to oversee a medical check-up on both of them, and that he'd brought along two physicians for that purpose.

The Harpers were immediately alarmed; something was wrong. They had their own private physicians - why not let them do the check-up. Lucas was very abrupt and told them that he had orders to do it, and it would be done with or without their cooperation. The choice was theirs.

Nigel and Esther protested as much as they could, up to the point where Lucas ordered his agents to restrain and sedate them, Esther was clearly frightened by now. As the officers stepped forward, Nigel held his hand up and said, "Please give me a minute in private with Esther."

He led her aside while his mind flooded with questions. *What the hell is this? Why did they not just kill us? Maybe it's not the time for that yet. They still want us alive, but what do they want now?*

When they were out of hearing, Nigel whispered, "Esther, my dear. You know I love you, and I would never let any harm come to you. Please, listen to me very carefully. I don't know what this is about, but I'm sure that they're not here to kill us. They would have done that differently. I'm also worried, but I'm certain we'll still be alive after this. You and I have to survive. Our people will need us again, and we have to stay alive for them. I believe Sam Lewis is working with the Rosslers, and that they're planning to get us all out of this. We must wait for them and pray that they'll be successful."

Nigel's words and his arms around her helped Esther to calm down and as she wiped the tears from her face, she said, "Nigel, I love you too, and you know that. I trust you. Let's get this over with as quickly as possible."

They turned around and walked back to Lucas and his entourage. "Lucas, let's get this over with. Where do you want to do it?"

Lucas replied, "Thank you for your cooperation, Mr. Harper. I suggest we go into the house and find a place."

The female physician and some of the agents accompanied Esther, while Nigel was led away by the male doctor and the rest of the men. The doctor took his blood pressure and heart rate, hooked him up to an ECG machine, pricked his thumb for sugar and cholesterol tests, examined him with a stethoscope and finally took blood samples. During the blood sample procedure, Nigel felt a bit dizzy for a short while and later became conscious of a numb feeling in his right shoulder area. He looked at the spot and saw a bandage. "What is that? What did you do?" he inquired.

"It's a minuscule medical biochip that I inserted. It will continuously monitor your vital signs, blood oxygen levels and many other medical conditions that could be treated and prevented when detected early, such as heart disease, cancer and many others. This chip will warn us of that long before it becomes a problem. Before I leave, I'll give you a pamphlet that has all the information," the doctor replied without making eye contact with him.

Nigel didn't trust what he heard. *Why don't I have any recollection of that happening? Why is the man not looking at me? Why didn't he tell me what he was going to do?*

In the room next to his, Esther went through the same process, except that the doctor started with taking blood samples. She felt dizzy after the first tube was filled with blood, and by the time the doctor told her she was done, Esther could not believe how quickly the examination went. It felt like a few minutes, but in fact, it was almost half an hour. Only when she got up from the bed did she feel the numbness in her right shoulder - the doctor had already left the room and was on her way back to the SUV's.

The Harpers met in the living room and saw the three SUV's leaving. Nigel sat down and started reading the pamphlet and went pale with fury as he read and comprehended what just happened to them. Science fiction had just become reality as he and Esther had just become slaves under the total control of the Supreme Council. Their lives were worth as much as the push of a button at the whim of a lunatic in Brussels.

Esther did not get a pamphlet and didn't know what Nigel was reading. She still felt a bit queasy and sat down on the couch. Nigel had a very difficult time controlling himself and not storming the agents standing in the room. The only reason stopping him was the look on Esther's face – she obviously did not feel well. *The bastards must have given her a lot more sedatives than me. They have placed a chip in her as well. Oh my God what have I done? I am supposed to protect her, and now I have got us both tagged for death row!*

Finally, he managed to get some control over his emotions. He walked over to Esther, sat down next to her, and took her hand. They sat in silence. He decided not to tell Esther about the contents of the pamphlet yet. If she asked, he would tell her the same story the doctor told him.

He thought about the nine hundred and sixty Sicari rebels on Masada in 73 CE, who robbed their Roman conquerors of victory by setting all the buildings on fire and then committing mass suicide on the day the Roman soldiers breached the walls of their fortress. Nigel made a decision. The Sicari rebels, almost two thousand years ago, would rather be dead than serve under Rome. He would rather die than serve under the Supreme Council. He would not let them have the satisfaction of deciding when his time on this earth was over. *He* was going to choose that day and time, and it was going to be at a place and time where it would have the biggest negative impact on them. He was going to use their propaganda machines against them to leave one final message to his people. There were quite a few public events coming up soon.

He only hoped that when he was not there anymore the Supreme Council would let Esther go free. She was no risk to them or anyone. He was the threat.

Chapter Fifty-Three

A LONG LIFE

"You Can Live To Be 200 Years Old."
"Scientists Discover The Fountain Of Youth."

The news headlines proclaimed scientists had developed technology that would scan the human body and find the parts and systems that were defective or damaged and report about it. Physicians would be able to take immediate steps to rectify the issues. The new technology furthermore included the continuous monitoring of vital information, such as blood pressure, heart rate, sugar levels, oxygen, and many other risk factors, and would raise an alarm when detecting any problems.

A person's DNA would be analyzed, a report would be provided about vulnerability to diseases and preventative measures that could be taken to avoid it through medication and diet. Treatments would be individualized. The body would be continuously monitored to let the person know when it was time to take medications, as well as when and what to eat.

All of these wonderful benefits could be achieved with a painless, quick medical procedure by way of implanting a micro biochip below the right collarbone. Thousands of people had already had the procedure during the human trials, and they were giving their testimonials. It was incredible to hear the people testify how they were cured of cancer and other debilitating diseases. In some cases, conditions were detected years before conventional methods would have done so. There were thousands of testimonials from people who were rejuvenated and felt healthy and young again. A ninety-year-old was shown completing a half marathon, aged people looked young again - it was the most remarkable scientific achievement ever.

This story captured the imagination of everyone; it was heralded as the biggest scientific achievement in human history. It remained the most important news story for many months. The media hysteria was driven to even higher levels when the Supreme Council announced that all medical services would become free for everyone volunteering to be implanted with the medical biochip.

Neither Anastasia nor the Supreme Council was prepared for the chaos that followed these announcements. There were not enough personnel to deal with the demand for the implants. They had to train tens of thousands of people to perform the procedure. The media showed images of people outside clinics all over the world waiting in queues, sometimes a few miles long. Anastasia was back in the good books of the Supreme Council as hundreds of millions of people turned up to be chipped voluntarily.

Chapter Fifty-Four

ONLY TWO TYPES OF PEOPLE IN THIS WORLD

It was a Wednesday night shortly after nine o'clock. In one of the backstreets of the Bronx, an old crippled Indian man with a walking stick shuffled into a half-lit basement of an abandoned and ruined apartment block and shook hands with two men.

"Rube, Sombra, it has been a long time. I am glad you guys could make it on such short notice."

"Raj, good to see you again, my friend," Rube replied.

Sombra patted Raj on the back, "Welcome back to New York, man. Where have you been?"

Raj didn't answer the question, "We have a lot to talk about, guys. Is there a safe place where we could sit down and talk? "

Thanks to the preventative law enforcement measures, the Bronx was as safe as any of the most affluent neighborhoods anywhere in New York.

"We have a safe place in the building next door. I'll go first and make sure the tenant gets another place to sleep for the night. Give me five minutes, then go through the opening in that wall at the back. There you'll find a gap in the fence five yards to the right. Go through that and to the ground floor, second door on the right in the hallway." Sombra replied.

When they were seated at the table in the room, Raj took a little electronic device, similar to a small ballpoint pen, from his jacket pocket and placed it on the table. A little blue light was visible. Rube and Sombra were instantly suspicious. "Raj, what the fuck is that? Don't tell me you are going to record us?" Rube wanted to know.

Raj just laughed and said, "My friends you know me better than that, and you should know I would never do such a thing. Let me introduce you to the pen of silence."

It took him almost a quarter of an hour of explaining to get the two of them calmed down. In the end, they understood that the pen would block out any signal and voice going further than a few yards from them. Rube tested it and was jubilant when he stood four yards away and could not hear a single word Raj and Sombra were saying, even when they screamed. Rube and Sombra were happy they could trust Raj's pen and forthwith placed an order for a few of the devices. They explained that the place they were in was one of the many safe houses they had established in every state across the country. Rube, who was the leader of the New York cell of Tectus, gave Raj an overview of their activities and plans. Raj, without disclosing any information about the location of the Rabbit Hole, in turn gave them an overview of the Rosslerites' activities.

When he told them how they broke Sam Lewis and his family out of house arrest, his two friends were all ears. They were intensely interested in the technology Raj talked about and questioned him for almost an hour about the spyflies, mosquitos, hummers and earphones at the end of which they placed another order. He instantly became their hero when he produced a box containing some of each of the devices, including the pens of silence. He told them this was a gift from the Rosslerites, and he would show them how to use everything a bit later.

Raj explained the Rosslerites' top priorities. It was critical to get a message through to President Harper. Equally important was to find out the location of the factory or factories where the chips were produced and to get hold of some of those chips.

Rube told him that from their hacking activities, they already knew there was only one factory, located in China. From the plant the chips were shipped all over the world, escorted by a special guard force to various distribution points. There were exceptionally strict security measures in place around the chips.

That didn't mean the system was foolproof, but Tectus, even if they could get hold of those chips, didn't have the technical expertise to handle or analyze them. Despite all their hacking efforts and wealth of information gathered, they hadn't found the technical specifications for the chips yet. They were scared shitless by the idea of handling the chips, and consequently it was not part of their strategy to get hold of any.

Instead, they were thinking of blowing up the warehouses where the chips were stored. Raj told them it would not be a good idea to do that. It would not have any lasting impact, unless the Chinese plant was also destroyed. Even that wouldn't stop them from setting up another one very quickly. It would be better to look at other options. He got them excited when he explained the Rosslerites' strategy, which was to get hold of some of the chips so that they could analyze and reverse engineer them and find a way to neutralize them. If that could be achieved, it would level the playing field.

The Rosslerites were bargaining on the 'buyer's remorse' that would unquestionably begin to set in as soon as people found out what it meant to be chipped. They believed, in the not too distant future, there would only be two types of people in this world. Those who managed to avoid chipping and those who would give anything to get one out of their bodies.

They agreed that Rube and Sombra would gather all the details about the chips they could get out of their files. What the Rosslerites needed especially were the location of the Chinese factory, the shipping processes, warehouses and control measures. Rube and Sombra would hand the information to Raj when they met again.

Raj was given the names of the cities and towns where Tectus had safe houses, although none of them knew the exact addresses. It was part of their security measures to know things only on a need-to-know basis. Raj kept a poker face when he heard there were safe houses in all of the states around Montana, where the Rabbit Hole was, and almost smiled when he heard about the one in Billings.

Before they left, it was agreed they'd meet again in two nights at a different safe house.

Chapter Fifty-Five

THE EDWARDS DYNAMIC

Kelly Edwards was aware that people would stare at her whenever she appeared in public. Maybe it was because she was the political news anchor for World One News Network (WONN) in New York and the host of one of the most popular talk shows on TV, 'The Edwards Dynamic'. Maybe it was because she was a striking, six-foot-two blonde and former Miss District of Columbia.

At thirty-five, she was still single. It was not because of a lack of interest - she could pick and choose if she wanted to. The reason was that she was not ready yet to settle down and make the commitment required for a happy relationship.

Twice a month, on a Friday, she would escape the irritating public scrutiny to enjoy being one of the crowd. That was when she got an extreme makeover from the studio makeup artists who transformed her into a brunette with big dark sunglasses. She would slip away for the rest of the day into the streets of Manhattan to do the things normal people do. She would visit her favorite coffee shop, browse antique and second-hand bookshops and, before going back to the studio, top the day off with a sinful cheeseburger and vanilla soft-serve at MacDonald's.

From her table on the outside of Luigis' Espresso, she was staring at the people passing by on the street. Luigi's was her favorite coffee shop. It was never overcrowded, and she thought the coffee was exquisite. The place and the atmosphere sometimes reminded her of one of her favorite little espresso bars in Rome. Kelly had graduated with an MA in political science and international relations from George Washington University, followed by an honors degree in journalism from Yale. She worked for the Washington Post for almost seven years, for three of which she was posted in Europe.

While waiting for her coffee, she was thinking about the success of the once a week interviews she'd been conducting on her show with former heads of state from around the world. Three weeks from now, she would have an interview with former President Harper and his wife. She'd already made inquiries and discovered that the presidential pair did not support the new government; something the public didn't know and was not allowed to know. She saw the photos and video clips of the presidential couple attending past public events, and it did not escape her that they never smiled. It was not going to be easy, she knew.

She could not ask them what they thought about the new government nor discuss any politics, past or present, with them. Probably it would be best just to get them to talk about their lives and their interests. The fact that the interview was going to be recorded on the Harper's farm in Tennessee would help to create the right atmosphere for a good conversation. Fortunately, it was not going to be a live show. These days there were not many of those. If the interview were a disaster that could not be 'fixed' with editing, she would have the option to replace it with something else. She just had to record a backup show in advance.

The interview was already big news - their secret social media polls showed that it was going to be watched by many millions of Americans. That wasn't a surprise. President Harper was one of the most popular presidents ever.

She was startled out of her thoughts when an old Indian man with a walking stick, who tried to pass behind her, bumped into her handbag hanging over the back of her chair. "Sorry about that ma'am."

She smiled. "Don't worry, my mistake. I should have kept my bag on the table so there would be more space for people to pass through."

Chapter Fifty-Six

AMERICA, THEN THE REST OF THE WORLD

Since Roy had heard Luke and Salome explaining to the Steering Committee the various ways in which communications could be encoded and encrypted, he had been thinking. He felt sure he could develop a secure communications network with the outside world without having to use the Internet, landlines or mobile phones.

After the completion of his zinger and mosquito projects, he had more time to work on the communications project and already had a few ideas in the back of his head. First, he wanted to find out if he could establish a reliable and secure connection between computers by using laser beams instead of cables and wireless. His idea was to use the same principal as a fiber optic cable but without the cable. It wasn't new technology - the military, and NASA had been using it for quite a few years. It was just that he never investigated how exactly they did it.

Roy immersed himself in the material he'd collected about laser communications over the years. He found some research showing that the beam of a small pocket laser pointer could travel more than twelve miles and be seen by the naked eye without any problem. That was exciting news, as that would mean if it could be seen at that distance by the naked eye it could also be picked up by a sensor. In other words, if a signal were to be embedded in the laser beam, it could be used to communicate.

In theory, a laser beam could travel an infinite distance as long as there was no obstruction in its path. In a vacuum, such as space, it would go much further than in the earth's atmosphere, where dust and particulate matter would disperse the beam much quicker.

Thanks to the information left in their library about the advanced nanolaser technology in use during the 10th Cycle, Roy already had a lot of knowledge about the technology. His laser torches, used for cutting the rocks in the caves on a daily basis, were many thousands of times more powerful than those of a pocket laser pointer.

With Raj away on a mission in New York, he called in the help of Stuart, Max and Mandy. Soon they had two computers in the lab communicating via an invisible laser beam without any problems. The data transfer speed was mindboggling; reaching rates of multiple terabits per second instead of the kilobit, megabit or even gigabit transfer rates achieved with conventional cables or wireless connections.

Roy and his three teammates took the experiments outside the caves for testing. Their primary objective was to establish a link between the Rabbit Hole and Mount Ararat. They tested the link up to three miles, and it worked correctly as long as they had line of sight. They studied the topographical maps and found that they would require a few relay devices to overcome the obstructions between the Rabbit Hole and Mount Ararat.

While they were busy discussing the design of the relay devices Roy said, "Wait, I think I might have an idea that could make things a bit easier for us. How about we build the relay into a mini drone that we can send up high enough to have a line of sight directly to Mount Ararat?"

"Excellent idea!" Mandy blurted. "That could work very well. But how long will the drone be able to stay in the air?"

Roy explained that with the same battery technology he was using in the zingers and spyflies, the drones would be able to stay up in the air for months. The batteries would be charged by as little as one hour of sunlight a day, which would be enough to keep it flying for more than five days.

While Roy got busy with building the drone, the rest of them settled down to make the relay device. This method of communication was secure because the signal was sent in a narrow beam and straight line, which could only be intercepted by a receiver that had to be in the path of the beam. In addition, the receiver had to be able to 'understand' and interpret the embedded message.

Five days later they were ready for another test. They had two laptops fitted with laser transceivers, and a drone equipped with a relay device and a three foot wingspan. They checked the communications between the laptops three miles apart with no line of sight between them, using the drone to relay the beams, and it worked out exactly as they had planned. It was time to demonstrate this to the Steering Committee before they would deploy it between Mount Ararat and the Rabbit Hole.

The next morning, Roy and his team demonstrated their latest invention to the Steering Committee, who were blown away when they saw the messages coming through on the computer screen in front of them. Stuart, who was sending the messages was sitting more than three miles away, behind a hill.

As they walked back to the caves, Daniel wanted to know what the chances were that this network could be expanded to cover a much wider area.

"How far and wide do you want to go?" Roy asked.

Daniel was joking when he said, "I am thinking all of America to start with and then the rest of the world."

Roy was in invention mode and took it seriously. "I already thought about that and it is not impossible, I reckon. We only have to get our own satellite up. To build a satellite is straightforward. Amateurs and scientists have done it for many years. I could build one for us in a few days. The problem would be how to get our satellite into space. For that, we would have to hitch a ride with one of those companies that launch rockets for the purpose. But then, for some reason, I suspect John Brideaux won't approve our application."

Salome just smiled at Roy's wit, something he had been displaying quite often lately. She liked it.

The demonstration had stimulated everyone's thinking and there were many questions and ideas. Roy stopped and looked at Daniel for a while and said, "You know, I think there might be a way around that problem."

Everyone had stopped and was waiting for him to elaborate. He mumbled a few words to himself for a little while and then said, "If we could build a high-altitude balloon, it could be used to transport a drone into near space, about twenty miles up. With a few drones sitting at that height, we could cover all of America without a doubt."

The group looked at Roy in disbelief for a moment, wondering if he had a bump to the head recently. Then they remembered what he had just demonstrated to them, and most of them had firsthand experience with some of his brilliant inventions. If he told them it was possible, then it was worth listening to him. They knew that when Roy James set his mind on something, he seldom failed.

Daniel spoke for everyone when he said, "Roy, you just tell us what you need, and we will do it, or get it for you. If you could pull that off it would be a giant leap forward in our battle."

"Thanks, Daniel. I'm on it right away. I'll let you know when I need help," Roy said absent-mindedly as his brain was already in overdrive.

Chapter Fifty-Seven

THE RAT RACE IS OVER FOR ME

Peter Scott, a glass of whiskey and soda in his hand, was looking around the room of nearly fifty 'friends', celebrating his thirty-eighth birthday. There was a battle raging in his mind that had been raging for months now. He barely noticed the attractive girl next to him trying to get his attention.

There were always beautiful young women trying to get his attention. He knew it was not about him; he didn't have the looks of a hunk with a six-pack on the cover of glossy magazines, and he knew that. It was just that rich, single men, irrespective of their age, looks, or personality, were always the targets of ambitious and opportunistic women – gold-diggers – as he liked to call them.

He'd made a fortune on Wall Street in the last five years and had been living the Manhattan high-flyer lifestyle. However, in the last eight months he'd often find himself questioning his life and its purpose. The challenges and excitement of making it big on Wall Street were not there anymore. It was as if he had lost the drive and flair for that type of life.

Tonight those thoughts were stronger and more demanding than ever. *Is this what you want to do for the next twenty years of your life? How many of these friends would you still have if you lost everything? What else do you want to prove to yourself and the world? What do you have to show after nearly forty years of life other than your Ferrari and the skyscraper apartment? Yes, millions in cash, property and stocks, but a marriage that didn't last eighteen months, countless broken relationships, no family, and no real friends? When was the last time you were truly happy, Peter Scott?*

"I can't remember," he said aloud, to no one in particular.

"Sorry, Peter. Did you say something? You're unusually quiet tonight, dear. What's the matter?" The blonde gold-digger closest to him wanted to know.

"Apologies, I was deep in thought there for a few moments. Please excuse me, I have to go and talk to my partner quickly. I'll be back soon." Peter promised with a smile but no intention of returning.

"Don't make me wait too long, darling," she giggled.

Peter made up his mind as he covered the ten paces to reach his business partner, Mark Levinson. He was going to get out of the rat race. Life had more to offer than this. Two paces away from where Mark was standing surrounded by two of his own money suckers, a server with a tray filled with snacks in one hand and a small white envelope in the other blocked his way. While she was holding the tray out she gave him the envelope, which he placed in the inside pocket of his jacket. He wondered who the card was from, but he'd open it later. He had something much more important to do now.

"Excuse me, ladies. Mark, can I have a quick word with

you?" Peter indicated with his head to a quiet space in the corner.

The smile on the forty-five-year-old Mark's face turned into an expression of shock and confusion when he understood what Peter had to say. "My friend, I'm shocked. Aren't you making a hasty decision? You're earning two million a year and bonuses that have never been less than one and half million. How can you walk away from that? What has gotten into you?"

"Mark, you and I have been good friends and good partners. We've made a lot of money and we made many other people rich in the process as well. I have enough. I want to go out and enjoy the rest of my life. The rat race is over for me. "

Mark tried to argue and change his mind, but after thirty minutes, he gave up. He knew Peter well enough to accept that he'd made his choice and nothing would change his mind. "If you are sure there's nothing I can do to change your mind and sure that's what you want, then let's get the lawyers in tomorrow and finalize the paperwork."

Mark was looking forward to having it all for himself now.

As Peter walked out the door he felt at least half of the weight dropped off his shoulders. The other half would fall off in the next two days when he would walk out of the offices of Levinson-Scott for the last time. Ten million dollars would be transferred into his bank account, the yield of his share of the partnership and stock portfolio.

Back at his apartment with an espresso in his hand, he sat down. *What now, Peter Scott? The laptop lifestyle while traveling around America, Canada, Europe, Asia?*

In his mind he started to make a list of the things he had to do before he could lock the front door of his apartment and hit the road. That was when he remembered the small envelope handed to him at the party. He got up and found the envelope in the jacket.

The picture of a black bear next to a tree with a golden eagle in the background on the outside of the card triggered a sense of excitement. He didn't immediately understand why, until he read the words inside;

Happy Birthday!
I hope you had a good day.
Dave.
PS: The best Japanese food I had lately was on a Friday night at Harajuku Gyoza in downtown Manhattan.

The adrenaline of an unknown adventure ran through his veins. The last time he felt this excitement was when he worked for the person who sent him that birthday card – Sam Lewis, former head of the CIA.

Chapter Fifty-Eight

LET THEIR IMAGINATIONS RUN

As Sarah left the room after Sinclair's demonstration of the translation software, she had a plan taking shape in her head but wanted to discuss it with Daniel first. She told Daniel about the demonstration and then laid out her plan. "Now that the Library has become more 'readable' to people who don't have knowledge of the language, I think we could get more of us involved."

"What do you have in mind?" Daniel asked.

"If everyone can start looking for information related to his or her area of expertise and start grouping and indexing it, we could very quickly get a much better idea about the information in the library. In the past, we have always looked for specific topics related to some crisis, and most of the times it was. We have never worked through the information in an organized and systematic way," Sarah explained.

"Sarah that is why I fell in love with you within thirty minutes of meeting you. You are not only the most beautiful woman on the planet - you are also a genius!" Daniel said while taking her into his arms.

She looked at him and smiled, "Well, if you fell in love with me within thirty minutes from meeting me, why did it take you more than a year to say it?"

"Modesty, my dear, modesty." Daniel laughed.

Sarah went back to Sinclair to discuss her plan with him. She was not going to interfere with his operation. Sinclair knew what he was doing and he did it very well. The plan would only go ahead if he agreed to it. But there was no need to convince him. He stopped her before she even had the full plan on the table. "Sarah my dear, I've been thinking of exactly that for a while now. I was going to wait a little longer to give us the chance to load more translations, but I think the sooner we start, the better."

The next morning at the Steering Committee meeting, the plan was laid out and accepted by everyone with a lot of enthusiasm.

Sinclair and Sarah called a town hall meeting where they explained in detail how important it was that everyone would throw their weight in to help with the translations. Again, the plan was met with enthusiasm from everyone. Those who had no particular area of expertise were keen to help by reading through the computer-generated translations to improve the readability. They would do that by reorganizing sentences and punctuation to fit modern usage.

Roy, Raj and Rebecca were the first to turn up at the translation center to create and test the new process. They were each assigned a translator, and they started querying the 10th Cycle Library database with topics in their areas of expertise. They then organized the results into folders where the translation software picked up the files and produced the first draft of the translation. After that, they would review the first draft and, with the help of the translators, they would fill in the word for which there was no translation in the database yet. The last step was to pass it on to the helpers, who would try to improve the readability.

After four hours they stopped and reviewed what they had achieved. The unanimous conclusion was that Sarah had come up with a brilliant idea. Soon it became part of everyone's daily tasks to spend at least two hours in the translation center, a job everyone looked forward to and enjoyed.

They were now working through the library at more than four times the speed of what Sinclair's team could achieve before. The biggest advantage was that they were quickly beginning to get a much better understanding of the topics that were included by their ancient ancestors in this incredible fountain of knowledge.

Sinclair's translation team had grown from eight to forty-five adults in a week. It was necessary for Ben, Aaron and the rest of the public works department team to create more office space in the center. In a few weeks, those with the aptitude for languages had managed to learn hundreds of words and phrases. Those individuals became even more useful to Sinclair's original team of experts.

As the translation center started pumping information into the Nicholas Rossler Library, John Mendenhall introduced the children to the 10th Cycle treasure chest and showed them how to conduct research. It was heartwarming to see the youngsters competing to make the most exciting discoveries every day.

Sinclair mentioned to Sarah how thrilled he was with the progress they were making and how much he enjoyed seeing the children involved in the process. "I wish my old friend Nicholas were here to see that."

"Sinclair, I know how you miss him. We all miss him so much. He would have been a very proud man if he were here. I'm sure he would have shared your enthusiasm about the children," Sarah said with a tone of sadness in her voice.

"You know, I am willing to bet it's just a matter of time before one of them is going to make an important discovery. Children have a different way of looking at things than adults do. They aren't afraid to ask questions, to dream and let their imaginations run. That's what we need." Sinclair said.

Sarah and Sinclair would have been stunned if they knew how close to fulfilment his prophesy was, and even more so if they knew what impact it would have.

Chapter Fifty-Nine

OUTWIT AND OUTMANEUVER THEM

Raj deployed the pen of silence and said, "It's safe to talk now."

Rube and Sombra showed Raj all the information they were able to collect about the chips and handed it to him on a flash drive. The documents contained details about the plant in China and the security procedures followed during the shipping and distribution processes, from the factory to the warehouses and clinics where it was implanted. There was no technical information about the chips, however, as Raj hoped there might be.

He spent the next few hours, to their great delight, training both of them in the use of the gadgets he'd brought along for them. There was no doubt about it; these guys were real geeks and they liked their new toys. There was no lack of ideas about how and where they were going to use them.

Rube gave Raj all the information about their communications network. He explained how they were using steganography in videos and images in the *Darknet*, as it was known amongst those who operated on the fringes of the anonymous side of the Internet. It was not the surface web, which constituted only about twenty percent of the entire Internet and consisted of email, social media, search engines and websites that most people would use every day.

Below the Surface Web was the Deep Web, where, if one who knew how, one could find research and government databases, along with abandoned and pay-walled websites and many other things that weren't meant to be public.

The Dark Web was a part of the Deep Web, where the Internet's illicit activities resided. It was that part of the Internet where one could buy just about anything. Hacking tools, weapons, hire a hitman or escort; buy somebody's identity, prohibited drugs, counterfeit money, fake degrees, passports, cloned debit cards and stolen items were all on sale here.

Finding sites on the Dark Web was not easy; one had to know which online directories or websites were the gateways or have the exact IP addresses. Law enforcement agencies were well aware of the Dark Web. They were trying their best to root out the illicit part of it, but because of its size, it was a losing battle. It was in the smoke of this out-of-the-public-eye part of the Internet where Tectus operated and communicated. Raj would train a few of the people back home in the use of these methods.

The final point on the agenda was the message from Sam Lewis, which he wanted to be conveyed to the leaders of Tectus. It was his strategy not to try to grow big or to use force at any stage. For his plan to work, it was necessary to stay below the radar at all costs. They must remain small to develop the best technological countermeasures to outwit and outmaneuver the enemy when the time was right.

Sam was of the opinion that Tectus would play a vital role in Operation Phoenix by helping to locate secret information from government and other sources. He hoped they'd also take responsibility for creating and maintaining a secure communications network as well as helping with transporting and accommodating people in safe houses during missions.

Rube and Sombra both knew Sam Lewis from the time when they worked on his team during the Sword of Cyrus threat. They had the greatest respect for him and would follow his guidance. They agreed to take the message to the Tectus leadership group.

Chapter Sixty

THE THORNBIRDS

Kelly Edwards walked into her apartment just before twelve o'clock on Friday night. As she walked in, she kicked her shoes off and started undressing. She was heading for a luxurious bubble bath and would pick up her clothes later. She opened her handbag to take out her cell phone and noticed an unfamiliar small silver compact inside. She took it out and looked at it. *Whose is this? How did it get in here? Maybe the makeup girl back at the studio dropped it by accident. Wait, that can't be, my handbag was on the table in front of me when she did my makeup and, it was closed.*

As she opened the little metal box, the blood drained from her face when she saw the picture of a silver coin with a black border and the unmistakable image of a flamingo etched onto the coin. *Silver, black, flamingo – it's impossible! How can it be?* There was only one person who would have sent that to her, and she knew he was dead. At least that's what her sources at WONN TV were saying. Kelly's hands shook as she turned the picture around and saw the words 'The Thornbirds 1977'. There was no mistake. Sam Lewis was alive. She knew that because he had just contacted her.

She remembered the chaos following the announcement that Sam Lewis and his family were missing. Then had come the almost immediate retraction of the statement and the shaky explanations, followed by the deafening silence.

Sam Lewis' name was never mentioned again - they had strict orders never to talk of him unless they had authorization from the Supreme Council. The journalists told her that meant he was dead, and so were his family. They were wrong.

When Sam Lewis retired, Kelly had been released from her spy duties. That was the arrangement. 'Non-existents' became inactive when their handlers became inactive, be it by death or retirement.

What does this mean? Am I being reactivated? Could I be reactivated? Why? These and a thousand other thoughts kept her awake that night.

Saturday morning at nine o'clock when she walked into the Broadway rare and used bookshop in Upper West Side, Manhattan, the old bespectacled owner immediately recognized her. "Good morning, Miss Edwards. What an honor to have you visit my humble bookshop. How may I help you, ma'am?"

"Thank you, sir. That's very kind of you. I was wondering if you might have the 1977 edition of 'The Thornbirds', by Colleen McCullough," she asked with a big smile.

The old man's face lit up as he said, "Yes, Miss Edwards. In fact, I got one in a few days ago." He pulled the book out from the bottom shelf of a small rack behind his desk.

Back in her apartment, Kelly closed the blinds and

switched on the lights. She pulled the book out of her handbag and turned each of the pages, looking for any markings. Nothing has been marked and there was no clue, but she knew she was missing something. The clue was there - she just had to find it. She paged the book again but still couldn't find anything. She put the book down and poured herself a glass of fruit juice while she was thinking what she was missing.

She remembered that she had a small magnifying glass somewhere, rummaged around and found it. She picked up the book again and inspected the pages again carefully, and then she found it. Every few pages there was one letter on a page that was a few shades darker than the rest. Only the magnifying glass would have picked this up. It would not have been possible to see with the naked eye, not even with her reading glasses. She grabbed a piece of paper and wrote down the letters. When she reached the end of the book, she looked at the words she'd written down – *Connect It to a Computer Screen - No Computer.*

She considered the words for a while, then got up, and walked around the room, her mind racing with more questions than answers. *Connect what to a computer screen?* She picked the book up again and inspected the spine, that's when she felt a small hard object; she grabbed a sharp knife and carefully cut the spine open. Inside, neatly wrapped in a miniature Faraday bag, was the smallest USB flash drive she had ever seen. Her heart was racing when she unplugged the twenty-inch screen from her laptop and connected the little device via the micro USB cable.

When she switched the screen on, the first thing that she saw was a password box. She had no password. Could that be somewhere in the book? She had to stop and think carefully, knowing she had to get it right or she'd never know what was on that drive. It would immediately destroy everything if she entered the wrong password. The sender must have assumed she knew what the password was - there was no tip or hint. "Wait, maybe there is a tip," she said to herself as she took the silver compact out of her handbag.

She took a few sips of the fruit juice while staring at the password screen and then opened the compact, "Of course!" she whispered to herself. She entered *51lv3rBl4ck-Fl4m1ng0*. That was the password version of the code words 'silver black flamingo' between Sam Lewis and her on the last mission she worked for him, while living in Europe. They were the only two people in the world who knew those code words, and if it opened the flash drive, the message had to have come from Sam.

Chapter Sixty-One

HARAJUKU GYOZA

Peter Scott booked a table at Harajuku Gyoza. He loved Japanese food and had to try the new place before he left New York. He was led to his table while looking around the room, an old habit to always be aware of exactly what was going on in his surroundings. The place was packed and noisy. Shortly after he was seated, a youngish couple, maybe in their mid-thirties, took their seats a few tables from his. The woman had beautiful legs and a more than attractive face. The man, who was facing him, looked familiar but he couldn't place him.

He noticed that the man was looking at him and said something to the woman before he got up and walked over to his table. Peter was desperately trying to find a name for that face, "Apologies for the intrusion, but are you not Peter Scott? A former partner at Levinson-Scott?"

"Yes, that's me," he replied, still wondering who this man was and how he knew his name.

"My name is..." was as far as the man got before Peter said, "Of course, Owen Bell, the writer! You had my head spinning the last few minutes; I recognized your face but could not for the life of me remember your name." Peter laughed. "However, I have to admit my head is still spinning. How did you know my name? "

Owen smiled, "Oh, that's easy. I'm a client of Levinson-Scott and got the newsletter about you leaving the company a few days ago."

Peter laughed, "Good news can also travel fast, it seems."

Owen pointed to the empty seat in front of Peter, "Expecting company?"

Peter shook his head, "No. It's my first time; I thought I'd come and check it out first before I bring anyone else here. That way I don't ruin friendships by suggesting bad restaurants."

"Would you like to join my wife, Alison, and me for a drink while we wait for our orders?" Owen suggested.

Peter had to think quickly. He'd come to the restaurant for a different purpose. He expected some form of contact from Sam Lewis. How it would happen he had no idea. He knew Sam wouldn't show up in person. There would be a third party. He didn't want to make it difficult for that person to get to him, but he also didn't wish to attract too much attention by being the only loner in this packed place. He decided it wouldn't hurt if he joined them until the food was served.

"That's very kind of you; I would love to join you. Not every day that a man gets the opportunity to rub shoulders with a famous author," Peter responded with a smile.

Peter soon found out that Owen and Alison were extroverts, and it was impossible not to laugh and have fun when around them. Owen wanted to know why Peter said earlier that his resignation from Levinson-Scott was good news.

"I guess it's the onset of early male menopause. I'm tired of the rat race and want out, I'd like to travel the world and just do whatever I want, whenever I want." Peter smiled.

"That sounds like the two of us. A few years ago Owen and I made the discovery that, even if we managed to win the rat race, we would still be rats. That's when we did what you just did. We sold everything and moved to a little farm near Nucla, Colorado. We wouldn't swap that lifestyle for anything," Alison explained.

By the time the food arrived, they'd already had a few glasses of sake, and Alison had convinced Peter to stay with them at their table for dinner. Peter had a lot more laughs listening to Owen's witticisms, but he was also getting a little uneasy as he was still on the lookout for the messenger to turn up. He was beginning to worry that he could be in the wrong place, or maybe he'd misunderstood that message. He hadn't done this cloak and dagger stuff for quite a few years now. Maybe he'd lost his touch.

"Peter, whenever you are in the Western Slope area of Colorado, you're always welcome to come and visit us," Owen said, as if he'd read Peter's mind. He handed him a business card with their address and contact details, without saying a word about the card. When Peter felt the card in his hand, he looked at Owen and Alison and saw the smiles on their faces. He then realized that he'd been talking to Sam Lewis' messengers for almost two hours already.

"Thank you for the invite. I'll be sure to accept your offer. I've never been in those parts, but I hear it's beautiful. I'd certainly like to see it," he said as he put the card in the inside pocket of his jacket, without saying a word about it.

Back in his apartment, Peter took out the business card from his jacket pocket. It looked like an ordinary business card. It had all Owen's and Alison's contact details and address printed on the front. It certainly didn't feel like a business card, though. It was made of plastic like a credit card. On the back, a little piece of paper was stuck to it, with the words – *Connect it to a Computer Screen Only - No Computer*.

He disconnected the second screen from his laptop and connected the card via a cable. Then he entered his password - B34rTr33E4gl3 – for his code words 'bear tree eagle', which he and Sam Lewis had used on his last mission.

On the Sunday morning at ten o'clock, as per the instructions on the business card if he had accepted the mission, Peter walked into a luncheonette on 25th Street where Owen and Alison were already waiting for him.

He was to get from them all the information and tools he required. During brunch, Owen inconspicuously moved several tiny items over to him, including another business card. The last piece was a pen with a little blue light on it that Owen took out of his pocket and handed to Peter to write down his cell phone number. Peter commented on what a nice pen it was, and when he handed it back after writing down his number, Owen told him to keep it.

Chapter Sixty-Two

THE SECOND FRIDAY

Kelly was on her Friday escape, seated at Luigi's wearing a beautiful red silk scarf. She placed her order, replaced her sunglasses with her reading glasses while she took out a book, and hung her handbag over the back of the seat. One of the side pockets was unzipped.

It had been a soul searching two weeks for her since she got that first message from Sam Lewis. She did not support the new government - she never had and never would. She hated them with a passion. To her, they were the personification of evil.

In her position at the TV station she was privy to all of the inside information, gossip and potential news stories, and she was horrified at what she saw and heard. The very idea of chipping people like animals caused revulsion in her every time she thought or heard about it.

From the time the Supreme Council took control of the world, she couldn't bring herself to enjoy what she was doing anymore. There was absolutely no freedom, news bulletins were controlled, her talk shows were not recorded live, and many times the recorded shows were edited beyond recognition before they were broadcast. If, that is to say, they were broadcast at all. Broadcasts seldom contained the truth, not to mention the facts that were deliberately not reported.

Kelly Edwards was an American patriot, and she loathed the new world order. She would do anything to help bring about their downfall, but she couldn't see how it would be possible. With what she believed was the death of Sam Lewis, her last bit of hope went up in smoke. Since then, she'd been quietly preparing to resign and disappear to some small, out of the way country in South America or Asia.

That had all changed two weeks ago when she opened the message from Sam Lewis that asked her help to destroy the evil regime. That was why she made sure that she was sitting in Luigi's at ten o'clock, wearing a red scarf and reading a book – The Thornbirds, 1977 edition. That was the signal to the messenger that she had agreed to be activated.

She noticed the man with spiky hair, reading on his smartphone, sitting a few tables away when she arrived. She gave him no further thought. Until, when she opened the book and started reading, she saw from the corner of her eye the man got up and brushed past the back of her chair on his way out.

That night when she got back to her apartment, she did not follow her usual spa-bath routine. Instead, she immediately took out the small parcel from the side pocket of her handbag and unwrapped it. Within minutes, she was reading her mission instructions from the mini flash drive and making mental notes. She took out the rest of the contents of the parcel and studied them carefully. The operating instructions for each of the miniature devices in the package were in documents on the mini flash drive, displayed on the screen in front of her.

The mission instructions and other information she read required her to stay on at WONN in her current role, from where it would be necessary for her to perform various tasks from time to time. She would have preferred not to stay on at WONN, but if that was best, then that was what she would do.

Her first mission was to get a message through to former President Harper and establish a permanent communications system with him when she interviewed him and Mrs. Harper the next Tuesday.

When Raj returned to the Rabbit Hole, he was pleasantly surprised to see how much progress his team had made. They had the laser connection with Mount Ararat working and were now planning to expand the communications system to cover all of America in the not too distant future.

Roy was still working on various ideas to get relays deployed at a high altitude to cover longer distances.

His team also had the voice impersonator application working to near perfection. Computer generated impersonated voices, even those of people they'd recorded from radio broadcasts, could not be distinguished from the real voices by the human ear. There was a little bit more work to do before the voice analysis software would be incapable of distinguishing between the real and impersonated voices.

Raj reported to the Steering Committee about his trip to New York, during which he'd succeeded in contacting and activating Sam's two *non-existent* former agents. He'd also been able to establish a connection and solid relationships with the Tectus group.

Chapter Sixty-Three

NO WALK IN THE PARK

Peter read the instructions on his first mission, which was to commence in a few days. It was expected of him to be in Nashville the next Tuesday to observe what color scarf Kelly Edwards would be wearing when she and her crew returned from the much-publicized interview with the President and his wife.

No scarf, or any color other than blue or turquoise, meant he'd fly back to New York the next day. Blue or Turquoise indicated he would extend his visit by a few days. Peter looked at her pictures again and smiled. *That means the famous Kelly Edwards also worked for Sam Lewis. It's a pity I can't meet her in person.* He knew that wasn't going to happen, at least not on this mission and maybe never.

Next, he brought up the information about the biochips and studied the contents of the folder. Many hours later, he had gone through every bit of detail, from the plant in China, the shipping, and the warehouses - right down to the point where it was implanted at the clinics. He had the complete list of the locations of every warehouse and implant facility in the world and the exact stock levels for each of those locations as it was at the time of the report. He went through the processes again and paid close attention to the security measures, looking for a loophole.

The warehouses were guarded like a maximum-security prison. No one was allowed within three miles of the buildings, which were surrounded by walls, barbed wire fences and watchtowers. There was a no-fly zone for airplanes and drones of any kind within a radius of five miles from the warehouses.

Inside the warehouses, the boxes containing the chips were uniquely numbered and fitted with Radio Frequency Identification, also known as RFID, tags that were wirelessly connected to a central control unit and database. Each box contained two-hundred and fifty chips and was kept in a small, locked, safety-deposit type container. Opening the container required a command from the central control unit. The entire process of picking and packing was automated with warehouse robots. The first time a human would touch a box of chips was when it was loaded into the armored vehicles before it was transported to the implant facilities. Every worker and guard handling the boxes was chipped.

At the implant facilities, ranging from hospitals, clinics, courthouses and police stations, the security measures equaled those of the warehouses. The boxes were stored in a safe, inside carefully guarded rooms. A quartermaster was placed in charge of the stock and would make sure that the chips would only be handed out to authorized staff, who were also chipped. Stock levels were not allowed to be more than what was required for two days of implants. Stock checks were done every eight hours.

He was well aware of the fact that what he had been

reading thus far were the instructions that were supposed to be followed. With such a big and globally distributed operation, and the number of people involved, there would be a place or time when someone would not be following the instructions. His challenge was to find that place and to be there when that time came.

Warehouse stock levels were many thousands of times that of the largest implant center he could find. His first thoughts were that it would be a lot less conspicuous to let a box disappear from one of the warehouses than from an implant center. The first hurdle was going to be getting close enough to a warehouse to be able to deploy the spyflies on the inside. Of course, it would be simpler to deploy the spyflies inside an implant center such as a clinic, hospital or police station, but the danger was that missing stock would be detected much quicker.

He wouldn't dare to search for the locations of the warehouses or implant facilities online, which was why he went out to buy a few books, including a book with maps of New York and surrounding areas. This mission was not going to be a walk in the park. It was going to require a lot of surveillance and information gathering before it would be even possible to think of a plan.

Chapter Sixty-Four

I HAVE A MESSAGE FOR YOU

When Kelly arrived at the Harper's farm with her camera crew for the scheduled interview and saw the humiliating circumstances in which they were interned, she almost succumbed to tears. She had never met them before, but she'd been an unwavering admirer of the President and his wife for many years. It hurt when she had to call them Mr. and Mrs. Harper in front of the crew, rather than affording them their rightful titles, but she soon got a chance to rectify that.

The formal living room was prepared for the interview, and, as usual before recording an interview, she had time alone with the participants to explain everything and make them feel comfortable. She was well aware of where the surveillance cameras were in the room and that the agents would be watching. She would make sure that she always had her back to the cameras when she spoke to the Harpers, so that no one could read her lips. She was sure the agents would not hear a word of what she was going to say in the next few minutes.

The moment everyone was out of the room and the doors closed, she took her tablet out of her bag and in the process switched on the pen of silence, inside the bag. She walked up to the Harpers and said in a whisper, "Mr. President and Mrs. Harper please listen carefully to me. I have a message from Sam Lewis and Daniel Rossler for you. I am going to move around you to fix your earphones and microphones while I'm talking. Please trust me, no one can hear us. Please act as natural and as relaxed as you can and speak to me if you want to."

The shock and confusion showed briefly on their faces. "I think we would rather listen than talk. If you have something to say to us, say it. I don't trust you at all." Nigel said.

Kelly was prepared for that reaction; she didn't expect them just to accept what she was saying. As she moved around them and fitted their earpieces and microphones, she kept on talking. "Mr. President, I understand your hesitation, it's good enough for me if you prefer to remain quiet. I'm going to drop a small packet in the inside pocket of your jacket when I fit your microphone. Inside the box is a message from Sam Lewis and four tiny electronic devices. Mrs. Harper, I'm going to drop three capsules on your lap when I fix your microphone. They contain more of the message from Sam. Hide the capsules somewhere.

"Make sure you read the messages at a time and place where there are no surveillance cameras, then destroy the messages. Follow the instructions about how to use those electronic devices carefully. You will be very glad you did."

Nigel and Esther were looking at her, following every word she was saying, but it was obvious they were very suspicious and remained quiet. Kelly kept on talking and told them that the Rosslers had handled Lewis' escape and that he and his family were safe. They wanted her to let him and Mrs. Harper know that they were busy working on a plan for their escape. This message was the first step in the process.

Kelly finished the fitting of the earpieces and microphones and said, "Please play along during the interview. I promise I am going to make it very easy for you. Don't say anything negative about the Supreme Council." She stepped back and sat down.

Nigel and Esther were scared. They had been through enough deceit, backstabbing, intimidation and humiliation already and they did not trust anyone or anything anymore. This could very well be a setup to manufacture evidence of their dissent and a reason to throw them in jail or kill them. Nigel didn't mind the killing, but he wanted that done on his terms, not theirs.

Kelly got back to her seat, and while fitting her own microphone and earphones; she switched the pen of silence off. "Mr. and Mrs. Harper can you hear my voice coming through in your earphones?" They both confirmed, and she was happy that everything was setup correctly.

As she stepped them through the questions she was going to ask, Nigel and Esther started to get second thoughts about Kelly's trustworthiness. She was indeed making it easy; she was not going to ask any question that would call for a political opinion; she was not going to humiliate or insult them. Maybe she was who she said she was, but doubt remained.

Nigel looked at Esther, nodded his head slightly and she understood that meant they were going to play along and be as polite and friendly as possible, as Kelly had requested. They knew they had nothing to gain by being hostile. It would be edited out before the broadcast in any event, and maybe, just maybe, they had a lot to gain.

With the last bit of footage shot, Kelly and her crew got back into their vehicles and drove back to Nashville to have lunch at their hotel before they would check out and fly back to New York. Kelly took a beautiful turquoise scarf out of her handbag and draped it around her neck.

That afternoon, when the Harpers went for a walk, it was their first opportunity to talk about the interview earlier in the day. They hadn't had the chance to read the messages yet. They were both still scared and extremely suspicious. They agreed that nothing they said or did could be used as evidence against them. However, they knew that 'evidence' would have a different meaning in the courts these days than what it used to be. Nevertheless, they were cautiously optimistic and hopeful that what they'd heard from Kelly Edwards could be true.

Only that evening, when they took a bath, were they out of sight of the cameras and had the chance to read the messages. However, although they were burning to talk about it, they could not say a word to each other because of the ever-present microphones. That would have to wait for the morning walk. They read and reread the messages many times. They were both desperate to believe it was true that Sam Lewis was alive and had teamed up with the Rosslerites.

All these months, since their house arrest, that was what Nigel and Esther hoped and prayed for, but now that it seemed as if their prayers were answered, they couldn't bring themselves to believe it.

Chapter Sixty-Five

THE JEREMY PROJECT

Doug, Roxanne and the three children were having dinner in their quarters, when Doug asked the children to tell them about their day at school. The two girls gave a detailed account of the day that lasted almost fifteen minutes; covering everything from the time they left that morning until they returned home. Jeremy, the oldest of the three, said he had a great day and read stuff in the 10th Cycle library. His account of the day lasted an entire ten seconds.

"Jeremy, tell us what you read about the 10th Cycle?" Doug encouraged, hoping to get him to share a bit more.

Jeremy's mind was occupied, and he didn't hear the question. "Dad, I was wondering if those people had cell phones, and Xboxes, and the Internet like we have."

"Son, that's something I never thought of. It's an interesting question. I think Raj or Roy may be able to tell us. What do you say we go and ask them after dinner?" Doug was just as curious as his son to find out.

"Cool," said Jeremy and continued with his dinner. He

liked those two. One day he was going to be just as clever as they were.

When Doug and his son arrived at Roy and Salome's quarters, Salome invited them in. Doug asked Jeremy to explain to Roy what he wanted to know. Jeremy was a bit shy to speak in front of his idol, but in the end he succeeded in asking his question.

Roy looked at the boy in amazement and said, "You know, young man, that's a very interesting thought you have there. That's something I've thought about quite a lot, but I never had the time to investigate. Now you have me thinking again."

Salome just smiled at Roy and the boy's interaction. *That boy is how Roy would have looked and acted at the same age, very shy and many questions.* She was also pleasantly surprised to see how much he enjoyed talking to Jeremy; Roy was going to be a great dad for their children one day.

"Tell you what, let's drink up and go and see Raj. I'm sure he'll have an answer for us." Roy was excited.

The three of them left and found Raj at his quarters with Sushma and their daughter, Aanya, playing a computer game to the great delight of the little one.

Roy smiled when he saw the three of them in front of the computer laughing at the frolics of the characters on the screen. "Raj, I can see Aanya is going to follow in your footsteps one day. I hope we are not intruding, but Jeremy has a problem, which I can't solve. I told him if there's anyone who could, it would be you."

Raj laughed, "Roy, you've got me stressed before I even hear the problem."

Roy asked Jeremy to explain what his question was. When he finished, Raj looked at Roy and then at Doug and

The Phoenix Agenda

back at Jeremy. "You know, that *is* an interesting question. I have thought about it in passing a few times but never tried to figure out how the 10th Cyclers would have communicated. You've got me stumped, Jeremy."

The three surprised adults looked at each other wondering. *How did the 10th Cyclers communicate?*

Roy was the first one to emerge from bemusement, "Guys, I think Jeremy just gave us a lot to think about. This is an enormous gap in our knowledge, and it might very well be that the answer to our communication problems has been right in front of our noses all this time."

Doug was a very proud father, "Roy, Raj? What do you think? Is it worth investigating?"

"Absolutely!" both of them replied in unison.

Within twenty minutes the four of them had the entire Steering Committee gathered in the library with the young Jeremy MacArthur the center of attention.

Sinclair smiled as he turned to Sarah and said, "Remember what I told you a while ago? It was just a matter of time before one of these kids came up with something big."

Daniel took on the assignment of talking to John about putting Jeremy on a special assignment at school to allow him to work two hours a day with Roy and Raj. Jeremy was smiling from ear to ear when he heard that. Sinclair would get the entire translation effort focused on digging up and translating anything they could find on 10th Cycle communications. Roy placed the high altitude balloon ideas on hold and devoted his full attention to the Jeremy Project, as they started calling it, to the great delight of the boy.

Within a few days, the translation effort began producing useful results. The 10th Cyclers were masters of nanotechnology, and they had used that extensively in their communications networks.

When the researchers read the history of their communications evolution, it became evident that they went through more or less the same processes as our modern day society. They also used radio signals at some stage, but came to the same conclusion. It was slow, unreliable, and limited in its data transfer capacity. They also used laser beams, and found that to be far superior to radio signals.

Gemma, one of the translators, working on a piece of text describing a communications device, was struggling to find a meaningful translation for a few words and took her problem to Sinclair.

"I have an issue with this paragraph here," she said as she handed him the tablet. "To me it seems as if it says that this device was built or sewn into the fabric of clothes. Is my interpretation correct?"

Sinclair looked at the translation, "Yes, you've got it. That's how I would translate it as well."

Gemma continued, "Ok, thanks for that. Now the next part I'm struggling with is that bit there. The best I can come up with is that it says the clothes were connected in a mirror with a ray, or beam, or something."

Sinclair read the paragraph a few times, "Ah, I see what you mean. It is confusing. I wonder ... wait here is something. You are right about the clothes, the mirror and the beam, but that word in front of the word *mirror* means *sky*, not *in*. In other words, it should be translated as *sky mirror* or perhaps *mirror in the sky*. My suggestion is that the full translation of that sentence should read, '*The clothes were connected to the mirror in the sky via a beam.*'"

"That is interesting," Gemma said. "It sounds like they

had their cell phones built into their clothes? How nice is that?"

"Indeed, that's what it sounds like, and that 'mirrors in the sky' is another mystery. Time to talk to the propeller heads. They might have some ideas. I'll let you know what they have to say." Sinclair smiled.

Chapter Sixty-Six

SANDPIPER

The next morning after their interview, Nigel and Esther were anxious to get out of the house for their morning stroll around the farm. They had the earpieces and microphones set up as per the instructions in the messages by the time they walked out of the bathroom.

The agents were out of range of their whispered voices. They were startled when a voice spoke to them as if it originated inside their heads saying, "Diamond Horse."

Nigel counted seven seconds and replied, "Fish."

"Mr. President and Mrs. Harper. It is a privilege and a big relief to be able to speak to you. My name is Peter Scott, and I work for Sam Lewis."

Nigel replied, "Peter, I am sorry about this, but my wife and I have been through a lot in the last few months. We don't know who to trust and what to believe anymore. I am afraid that we will need some assurance that you are who you say you are."

"Mr. President, I understand that, and I don't blame you for being suspicious. Sam gave me three pieces of information he told me would convince you that I am indeed on assignment from him."

"Please go ahead; I will decide once I heard what you have to say," Nigel replied.

Peter continued, "The first one is; Salamander, the code word he used to let you know about the successful elimination of Ali bin Akbar. Only he and you knew that code word. The second one is; Pangolin, the codename you selected for a general inside the Chinese military who spied for the CIA. Again, only he and you knew and used that codename. The third one is Sandpiper. That is the codename he gave you the last time he saw you and Mrs. Harper, in the foyer of the Whitehouse."

A wave of relief washed over Nigel. He was convinced that Peter Scott was working for Sam Lewis. He looked at Esther, smiled, and showed a thumbs up. "Peter, I'm now convinced you are who you say you are and very happy to talk to you."

"Thank you, Mr. President. Sam told me that would do the trick. I'm happy it did," Peter said with the relief clearly noticeable in his voice.

"Peter, as you can imagine, we have many questions, but before we go any further, I have to tell you something first. Esther and I were both implanted with biomedical chips. Under the pretense of doing a medical checkup, we were sedated and the chips implanted without our knowledge or permission. Is it still safe to talk to us?" Peter could hear the distress in his voice.

"It's a nightmare Peter. I can't describe how horrible it felt to realize they'd invaded our bodies, enslaving us to this immoral regime," Esther said, clearly struggling to control her emotions.

Peter's heart sank as he heard the news; but he understood that the primary aim of this mission was to encourage the Presidential couple to hang in there and assure them that help was on the way. "Mr. President and Mrs. Harper, I understand your torment, but the fact that you were chipped is not a problem at all. I want you to know that Sam and the Rosslers anticipated this. That's the main reason they decided to get in touch with you now, so you know we're working on a solution to neutralize those chips as we speak."

The conversation continued for another half hour as Peter answered as many of the Harpers' questions as he could. He then arranged the contact schedule and explained to them that once the group had a way to neutralize the chips, they would be evacuated. Although their circumstances hadn't changed, the Harpers received a mountain of hope and rivers of encouragement for the future. They were equipped to wait until the cavalry arrived.

The first stage of Peter's mission was completed successfully.

Chapter Sixty-Seven
SKY MIRRORS

Sinclair took his tablet, with the translation he and Gemma had just completed, and walked over to Roy's lab, where he found all the technically minded, including Jeremy, hard at work.

"Ok, boys! Fasten your seatbelts! I'm going to show you a translation that might just throw you off your seats," Sinclair said in a serious tone.

Roy and Raj were immediately alerted; they recalled when Sinclair and Nicholas discovered the translation that led them to the discovery of evidence about time travel in the era of the 10th Cycle. They'd seen the impact it had on the two old-timers.

"Sinclair, have you discovered more evidence of time travel?" Raj asked nervously, remembering all too well how he was the one who first saw the pictures and the dates and what effect it had on him.

Sinclair just laughed and said, "No, don't worry. It's not that. However, I think what I have could be significant."

He read the passages to them and looked up, "What do

you say about those clothes with a cell phone or some sort of communications device woven into the fabric?"

Roy replied. "That's called electro-textiles; it's been around for a few years already. They have cell phones, music players and all sorts of gadgets built into clothes. The clothes are wire-free, washable, and powered by body heat."

Sinclair was half disappointed that the news didn't excite his audience as much as he thought it would. He continued, "Oh, okay. So no surprises there then. So what do you think about the 'sky mirrors'?"

Roy looked around at the others; the sky mirrors were obviously of much more interest to them. "Sky mirror, or mirror in the sky? What do you all think?"

Raj proposed that it could be a satellite. Sinclair thought for a moment and explained that 10th Cyclers used words for 'sky' and 'space' that were very similar. It could very well be that the translation should read, 'mirror in space'. That statement had all of them excited.

Ryan had an idea, "Ok, for the moment, let's assume it was a mirror in space. Is there any doubt that it was a mirror they were talking about, not a receiver or sender?"

Sinclair thought for a moment and replied, "No, I am sure it is a mirror or reflector. There is no doubt about that. They used different words for 'send' and 'receive'. What are you thinking?"

Ryan continued, "The Apollo and the Russian missions left mirrors on the moon. Although we call them mirrors, it's actually corner cube prisms, also known as lunar retro reflectors. They're still there today. Those optical corner-cube prisms would reflect light pointed at it back to the source. In other words, if you were to shine a light beam from a laser at those reflectors it would bounce the beam right back to you in seconds. The time it takes for the light to bounce back depends on the variable distance between the earth and moon. Scientists have been shooting laser beams at those retro reflectors to test the turnaround speed of the laser, measuring the distance to the moon, and conducting many other types of experiments ever since. I'm wondering if we're looking at something similar to that."

Roy jumped in, "You know, Ryan that could very well be the case. We know the 10th Cyclers abandoned radio waves as communication media because of its limitations. We know they'd been using laser, and that could explain the reference to a beam in that passage."

Raj was excited, "I think we're onto something here. I suggest we all start searching for 'sky mirrors' or 'space mirrors' and beams to see what we can dig up."

They didn't need any encouragement and were bubbling with excitement when Sinclair left the lab – exactly the effect he thought the translation would have on them when he first read it.

Chapter Sixty-Eight

A VISIT TO NUCLA

Peter got rid of his Ferrari a few days after he left Levinson-Scott and bought a modest Toyota Camry Hybrid. Selling the Ferrari was part of the process of getting rid of the baggage that had been weighing him down the last few months.

He made a careful study of the surrounding areas of the location of the New York chip warehouse, located about seventy-four miles north of Manhattan. It was just a few miles outside the little rural town of Wappinger in Duchess County. It was an area of the New York City Metropolis sometimes referred to as the 'exurbs'.

He packed his hiking gear and took a three-day trip through Duchess County.

On the second day, he took the eleven-mile Wappinger Greenway Trail encircling lower Wappinger Creek and Wappinger Lake. According to his maps, the warehouse was located on the north side of Wappinger Lake, in a tree-covered valley. He checked and was confident there was no one around before he left the trail and went into the woods and up a hill. From there, he would be able to view the buildings.

When he reached the top and looked down at the warehouse, he noted that he had just discovered the first nonconformity to the rules. No one was allowed within three miles of the buildings. From his location at the top of the hill, though, he was less than a mile from the warehouse.

He made sure he had enough cover and carefully studied the layout of the compound, the movement of people, guard towers, fences, access road and vehicles. He took photos and then unpacked one of the spyflies and sent it down to the buildings. Although he'd practiced controlling the spyflies in his apartment, it was the first time he had deployed one at such distance and in the open. However, within a few minutes, he had managed to get the first spyfly inside the main warehouse. He was amazed at the quality of the images and sound that was returned to the control panel in his hands.

Although the radar antenna was clearly visible on the roof of the building, it was a relief when it became evident that it was unable to detect the spyfly. That was the second loophole he discovered. He noted that there was an ongoing stream of heavily guarded trucks coming and going and he captured the entire process from the moment of arrival to departure.

Three hours later, he had a solid understanding of the layout and routine on the inside of the warehouse, as well as the picking and packing methods. He would need a lot more information, but he had enough for the first day. He scanned the hills around the compound and noted a few more spots from where he would be able to do more observations the next day.

Peter wondered where the workers he saw on the

premises lived. He was sure that not all of them were locals. Some of them, if not most, probably commuted. He retrieved the spyfly and returned to the trail to complete the first half of it with more visits to historic buildings and various parks along the route.

Early the next morning Peter drove to Poughkeepsie station to test his theory about the commuting workers. He arrived in time to see a train appear, and shortly after that, about twenty people getting into a bus marked *Bio Lab Distributors*. He'd seen the same emblem on the outside of the warehouse the day before.

After breakfast, he went back to complete the remaining part of the Wappinger Greenway Trail, this time starting on the eastern side of the lake. When he reached his destination on the northern area of the lake on top of a hill, he was on the opposing side of the valley from his previous location. There, he took more photos, studied the compound again, and deployed two spyflies.

He focused the lenses of the spyflies on the boxes. He took special care to note the shape, sizes, labeling and markings. Then he got images of the faces and nametags of every worker that came within close proximity of the spyflies. Two hours later, he had enough information and returned to the trail.

On his way back to Manhattan, Peter had a few brainstorming sessions with himself. It would be helpful to get tracking devices on those trucks to see which routes they followed. The radar didn't detect the spyflies. Would it be possible to get something bigger than a spyfly in there? What were the chances of getting the help of someone on the inside?

The electric fences and security around the compound were intimidating, but not undefeatable. The biggest obstacle was the isolated location and the single access road, which would make an escape extremely difficult and dangerous. Would it be possible to have a box disappear without the staff or computer system noticing it immediately?

Back in his apartment, Peter meticulously studied every bit of information he had collected on the trip and started building scenarios in his mind. Based on the information he had, if he had to steal the chips from the warehouse, he could see three options. The first would be to try to slip into the compound and get hold of a box after it was checked out but before it was loaded onto a truck. The second option was to get some help from the inside. The third option was to find a way to do it with a remote controlled device.

Each of the three options had its own challenges and each of them would require help from someone else. However, that was just half of the information that was required. He still had to gather information about the procedures that were followed at the implant centers. For that purpose, he picked the Bronx-Lebanon Hospital – a seventeen-story tower building with a large outpatient facility, and the New York-Presbyterian Hospital/Weill Cornell campus – one of the largest hospitals in America.

Over the next few days, with the help of the spyflies and some very clever disguises, he managed to find the exact locations where the implants were performed. He was able to record more than five hours of footage of the entire process; from the point where the chips arrived, were unloaded and stored, as well as the precise clinical procedures during the insertion of the chips, through to the activation. He managed to film the arrival of the people at the facilities, the registration process where everyone's details were recorded on computer systems, the taking of swabs from the inside of their mouths and many close-ups of the activation devices.

Peter was an emotionally strong person, but what he saw during those five days filled him with revulsion and horror. The brief for his mission contained detailed information about the chips used during the 8th Cycle and the atrocious life that followed for those who received the implants. It also included speculations of the potential capabilities of the modern day chips, but nothing in that brief could prepare him for the sickening scenes he witnessed and recorded during those five days. If he ever had to look at those images again it would be too soon, but he knew he would have no choice. At some stage, he had to.

The scenes of the people standing in a line like cattle waiting to be killed at a slaughterhouse, oblivious as to what was going to happen to them at the end of that line, would stay with him forever. It was only his realization of a higher and bigger purpose and extreme self-control that prevented him from running into the waiting rooms to save those poor souls from dehumanization. The final straw for him came on the last day when he followed one of the "butchers," as he called the nurses performing the implants, with a spyfly and ended up in the maternity ward, where he witnessed how she did the rounds and implanted all the babies born the past twenty-four hours.

When he retrieved the spyflies and left, he took an oath that even if it meant it was the very last thing he did in his life, he would not rest until he had destroyed this evil. When he returned to his apartment, he just could not bring himself to go through the information again. He was driven by the urge to commence the second part of the mission as quickly as humanly possible.

He had to get in touch with Sam Lewis, and the only way that was possible was to make a trip to Nucla to meet with Owen and Alison. Half an hour and a few telephone calls later everything was arranged. He would fly to Montrose Regional Airport, about ninety miles from Nucla, the next day. Owen and Alison would pick him up, and he'd stay on the farm with them for a few days while they showed him around Montrose County.

Chapter Sixty-Nine

THE BIBLIOGRAPHY

Roy already had experience with the 10th Cyclers' laser and battery technologies. He had them working flawlessly in his laser cutting tools and with the connection between the Rabbit Hole and Mount Ararat. He just had to study how they used them in their communications. Then, of course, there were those mirrors that fascinated him.

He knew the 10th Cyclers would have left detailed information about the mirrors in their Library - experience had taught him that they didn't try to hide information. The purpose of that Library was to pass on everything they knew. It was just a matter of finding the specific information he needed. As suggested by Raj, the focus of most of the translation effort had already shifted to the communications beams and mirrors.

Roy asked Sinclair to dedicate one of the translators to him for a few days, and over the next few days, the unfortunate Gemma learned what Roy's definition of a day was. On the afternoon of the second straight day without any sleep, Salome came to Gemma's rescue when she arrived in the lab and saw her looking like a ghost. She told Gemma to go and get some sleep and told Roy off for not giving the poor girl any rest. Roy didn't even look up. He most probably didn't hear a single word and had no idea how much time had passed since Gemma started helping him.

When Gemma walked back into the lab the next afternoon, after twelve hours of blissful sleep, she could swear that Roy didn't know she was gone. Neither had he changed his position since she left him. Her suspicions that he had not been out of the lab were reinforced by the fact that he had about fifty new files waiting for her attention.

"Gemma, I have loaded a few files with untranslated parts. Perhaps we can quickly have a look at them before you continue. I would like to start with that one that I marked 'Operations Guide'. It seems to contain some very interesting information," Roy said.

She opened her laptop, pulled up the files on her screen, and started the translation of the highlighted parts. Roy got very excited when she explained that it was a description of how the mirrors worked, which was, as Ryan suggested, optical corner-cube prisms. Instead of bouncing the beam back to the source, it would reflect or divert it to different locations.

"Those mirrors were acting as routers, exactly the same as we have on the Internet and computer networks today. I wonder where those mirrors were and how they got them there," Roy mused.

Gemma carried on with the translation while Roy continued reading. When she opened a new document he left for her, she noted a range of numbers at the beginning of the page. She'd seen numbers like that in the other documents before, and it piqued her interest. She opened a few of the other pages and found numbers in the same place as the other documents. She wondered if it could be possible that those numbers were a reference to other documents. "Roy, have a look at this. Here it shows numbers. I've seen those numbers on other pages as well, and I've been wondering if that could be references to related items in other documents. What do you think?"

Roy came over and looked at what she was explaining to him. "There must be a reason why they used the numbers. I am interested to find out. I would say the simplest way is to do a search for the numbers and see what results are returned."

Gemma executed the first search and Roy almost fell off his seat when she yelled, "Bingo! Just look at this. There is a stack of information here. Let me run it through the translator so that we can get an idea of what it says."

Roy was standing behind her again, looking over her shoulder, as she pulled up the documents and fed them through the translation software. Quickly it returned a version of about eighty percent of the original in gisted format. There were close to a hundred and fifty different documents. Roy quickly scanned a few of the rough translations and saw all of it related to the mirrors, and he realized that Gemma just made a significant discovery.

"Gemma, I think you have just revolutionized our search process! Let me get hold of Sinclair and show him this," Roy said with enthusiasm.

On the way to Sinclair, Roy stuck his head into the computer lab and asked Raj to join them. Daniel and Sarah, who were both in the translation center when Roy arrived, joined Sinclair. "Okay, Gemma. Show them what you found." Roy requested.

Gemma explained to them how she'd seen numbers on

many of the documents and wondered what they could be, the search she did and the results she got.

"Excellent work, Gemma! This is a major breakthrough! This is going to transform and speed up our translation efforts greatly," Sinclair commented, after he studied the documents and numbers. He was obviously elated.

"Raj, do you think you could automate some of this? Sarah asked. "I wonder if it would be possible to scan documents, find those numbers, and then pull out all related pages. Is that likely?"

Raj smiled, "Piece of cake, Sarah. I'll ask Stuart to make changes to the query. When we conduct a search, it will scan the documents for those reference numbers, then search for the reference numbers in the database, extract all the related documents, and dump it in one folder."

"I think that would be perfect. Sinclair?" Sarah asked.

"Yep, we can't ask for more," Sinclair confirmed.

"Good work, team. This is the type of advance that will eventually put us ahead of John Brideaux," Daniel said. His appreciation was evident in the pride of his tone and the big smile that accompanied his words.

Gemma's discovery and the improvements to the software made by Stuart certainly made a big difference in the translation process. It was now possible to start indexing and cross-referencing the library, which in turn made it easier to find and study the information. With the improved search method, Roy and the rest of the techies had mountains of information to sort through to learn about the 10th Cyclers' communication technologies. Their spouses had their hands full to get them to work realistic hours and get enough sleep.

As all their advice fell on deaf ears, Salome, Sushma and Sarah decided it was time to get Rebecca and Roxanne involved. Between the five of them they introduced a twice-daily Pilates exercise program. They used their charm and influence with their husbands, and persuaded the Steering Committee to make attendance compulsory for everyone, young and old. Understandably, there were a lot of moans and groans from some of the group. The most vocal of them all were the musketeers, who tried to explain that trout fishing was the best exercise any human can get. In fact, according to them, it was the *only* exercise that humans required. Roxanne was the appointed physical trainer, and she flatly ignored any arguments, demanding that everyone attend.

On the first morning, all objections vanished when the eighty-nine-year-old Bess Rossler was the first to turn up at the Robert Cartwright Town Hall and did her exercises under the watchful eyes of Roxanne and Cindi. Even the young Nicholas Rossler and Aanya Sankaran were there. That first morning, a lot of rumbling and grumbling was heard, but no one wanted to be put to shame by an eighty-ninety-year-old and two three-year-olds, so they toughed it out. Within a week everyone was enjoying the daily exercise routine and in fact, started looking forward to it.

Chapter Seventy

I AM GLAD YOU LIKE JAPANESE FOOD

With the pen of silence deployed, Peter, Owen and Alison had the chance to talk openly about their involvement in Project Phoenix and their backgrounds. For the next few hours, the three of them exchanged a wealth of information about the Rossler Foundation, including the discoveries of the 10th and 8th Cycles and the current situation, as well as the Boise operation that evacuated Sam Lewis and his family.

Peter in turn gave them an overview of his background and his association with Sam Lewis and ended off with a recount of the information about the chips he had been gathering the past two weeks. He explained to them the various options they had for getting their hands on the chips.

Owen replied, "I can see your need for assistance. Unfortunately, I have no skills or experience in any of the areas where you'll need help. However, don't worry, it's not a train wreck. We'll get you the help you need, but it will take a few days to organize. In the meantime, we'll show you around our beautiful part of the country."

Owen didn't disclose the location of the Rabbit Hole and the people hiding there. Peter understood the principal of 'need-to-know' and didn't ask about it either.

The next morning during breakfast, Alison told Peter about their second property close to Big Timber, but didn't fill him in what the real purpose of the property was. "Owen and I were planning to go up there the day after tomorrow and we were hoping you might like to go with us? We were thinking to drive through Yellowstone and Gallatin National Forest this time."

Peter sensed the invitation had something to do with Owen's promise to get him the help he required, but didn't mention it. "That sounds great. I've been to Yellowstone a few times, but never into Gallatin. It would be wonderful to see that, and maybe get in a little hiking. I'm just a bit concerned I could be overstaying my welcome."

Owen and Alison exchanged a secretive smile, before Owen replied, "Nonsense, we'd love to have you to come with us. You could possibly enjoy it so much that you'd want to give up your apartment in Manhattan and move there, once you have seen our place." Owen replied.

Over the next two days, Owen and Alison showed Peter around Ouray and Montrose Counties and then made the two-day trip to Big Timber through Yellowstone and Gallatin. The night of their arrival, after Peter went to bed, Owen contacted Daniel via the laser link and gave him an update. Daniel asked that Owen contact him early the next morning, as he first wanted to discuss the situation with Sam, Salome and Luke to find out how they wished to handle it.

After the call with Owen, Daniel gathered the three of

them, laid out the situation, and told them that Peter knew nothing about the location of the Rabbit Hole. If there were any doubt about him, they would have to let him go back without any contact. Sam assured everyone that he trusted Peter with his life and that it would most probably be best if he could spend a few days at the Rabbit Hole. Then they could study the information he had with him and help him build a plan of action. Salome and Luke were happy to follow Sam's advice. Daniel, Sam and Mark would fetch him the next evening.

The next morning, Daniel contacted Owen, gave him the feedback from Sam and the others, and told him to expect them in the evening. Owen decided not to tell Peter about the visitors and left it as a surprise. He pulled Alison to the side, told her about it, and asked her to prepare a backpack for Peter with a few essentials while he and Peter went for a walk around the farm.

Shortly after nine that night, Owen led Daniel, Sam and Mark into the family room, to Peter's astonishment. He and Sam were thrilled to see each other again - it had been a long time, and there was a lot of catching up to do.

"Peter, my friend, a few weeks ago I thought I would never see you again." Sam smiled as he hugged him and stood back to have a good look. "I'm glad you like Japanese food!"

Owen and Alison just laughed. "You should have seen him in the restaurant that night, Sam. He was going to have dinner all on his own while waiting for someone to drop him a secret message or something. Alison and I had a big struggle to keep him at our table."

After the introductions and a glass of whiskey, Alison had dinner ready for them, which was followed by a few strong espressos. By two o'clock the next morning, the four men were prepared to make the trip back to the Rabbit Hole. Peter would visit for three days only, as they agreed it was not wise to let him disappear for too long.

Peter received a warm welcome, like Sam and his family when they received the royal tour; he was astonished when he saw what this small group has achieved in difficult circumstances.

Daniel explained to Peter that he was not excused from Pilates. It was compulsory for every living soul in the Rabbit Hole, unless he wanted to cross swords with Roxanne MacArthur, which according to Daniel was not advisable. Naturally, Peter attended. He had the utmost respect for Daniel and his advice.

After the Pilates session, Peter met with Daniel, Sam, Salome and Luke, giving them an account of his contact with President Harper and his wife. He unfortunately had to confirm their fears that the President and his wife had been chipped. However, he assured them that under the circumstances, the Presidential couple was doing well and the conversations he had with them had the desired effect of encouragement.

Next, he gave them the details of his reconnaissance trips and the information he was able to collect. He was just about ready to show them the footage he collected when they heard someone shouting, "We've got it! We've got it!"

They all jumped up and Salome was just in time to grab Roy, who was the one making the noise, by his arm and bring him to a standstill. Roy was jabbering something about mirrors and space, but no one could make out what he was saying. Salome started dragging him down the hallway towards his lab. The flabbergasted Peter had no idea what was going on, nor did anyone else, so he just followed the procession.

Chapter Seventy-One

THE FOUR CORNERS OF THE EARTH

Roy, Ryan and Gemma were working in the lab when Roy all of a sudden jumped up, ran around the table, kissed a startled Gemma on the head, and started screaming, "Eureka! Eureka!" as he ran out of the room into the hallway.

Within seconds, Raj and his team in the computer center next-door were in Roy's lab, but he wasn't there. They only found a wide-eyed Gemma and a baffled Ryan.

Roy was doing a victory lap through the Rabbit Hole shouting; "We've got it! We've got it!"

Raj wanted to know what happened, but all the bewildered Gemma could get out was, "I ... I ... don't know ... he kissed me ... and started screaming ... I ... don't ..." Ryan just shrugged; he had no clue what just happened.

When Salome arrived back at the lab with Roy, the hallways were already crowded with people who were eager to know what was going on.

Sam grabbed Roy by the shoulders, looked at him, and

said in a composed voice, "Calm down son, tell us what's going on. What do you have? "

Roy pointed his shaking finger at the laptop screen and said, "They had four mirrors up in the sky and here are the coordinates. Here are the operating instructions. Here are all the technical details. Here is where they said they left them for us to use. They're still up there and fully functional! They left them for us to use. Can you believe it?"

Daniel, who was looking over their shoulders, had goose bumps from the excitement. "Ok wait, let's calm down. Let's take the computers out to the library and set up where we have more space. Sinclair, can you please bring all the translators over to the library?"

They quickly had the laptop linked up to the projector, and everyone was looking at the projection on the wall. Roy pulled up the documents and showed them what he'd found. With the help of all the translators, they systematically worked through the files one by one and improved the translations as they read the documents. There was more excitement than at a Superbowl. No one wanted to leave. Each new document pulled up and translated was like unwrapping a mountain of Christmas gifts, each discovery met with enthusiastic applause.

By midnight, they had the exact details of the mirrors, including the technical blueprints, the operating instructions, and the coordinates in space. The operating instructions told them the type and strength of the laser beam used by the 10th Cyclers and how the beams were routed.

Then Roy brought up a document that looked like some sort of code. Just a few words had translations, and the rest were just weird characters. Roy looked at Raj and said, "Raj, I am not much of a programmer, but I think this is the code for their communications protocols."

The Phoenix Agenda

Raj got up and walked closer to the screen while reading and asked Sinclair for the translation of a word or two. Then he asked Mandy to feed it into the translation database and refresh the page. A few more translated words and refreshes later, he was able to start reading the code.

Fifteen minutes after that, Raj started explaining, "Yes Roy, you hit it on the head. This is their communications protocol. Not too dissimilar from the TCP/IP protocol we use on the Internet today, just a lot better, I would say. You see, here is the header of the message; it tells the receiver where the message is coming from. Then how many packets of information there are in the message, the sequence of the packets, and how big the message is. Here is the body of the message, and here is the footer of the message. The footer tells the receiver how many packets have been sent."

Raj stopped for a few minutes to read the next part of the code and then continued again, "Interestingly, they have the sender and receiver acknowledging the packets. In other words, on the recipient side, packets are received and placed in the correct sequence and if a packet is missing it will request a resend. That way nothing is lost. I guess if you operate at laser speed, those are luxuries you can afford."

By now everyone was looking on in disbelief, Raj was reading the code as if he was reading a fairy story to his little daughter, Aanya. Raj told them that although the 10th Cycle programming language was different from any other languages, he and his group would be able to pick it up without too much trouble.

The next hurdle was the coordinates in space. Ryan explained to the audience, "Objects in space move. Therefore, the location of an object in space is always relative to another object. I don't think they would have used another object in space. Consequently, those coordinates will only make sense to us if we can figure out which fixed point on earth was used."

Everyone went quiet for a while and then Sarah looked at her original co-discoverers of the 10th Cycle Library - Daniel, Raj, and Sinclair - and said, "I place my bet on the Great Pyramid of Giza."

Daniel got very excited, "Of course! Sarah, you beauty! The Great Pyramid is located at the exact center of all landmass on earth; it would be the ideal fixed point. Furthermore, they have left this library for us there. I'm convinced that would be the point from which they would have determined those coordinates."

"Do we have the coordinates of the Pyramid?" Roy wanted to know.

Raj already had his laptop open, "Yep, I've got it here. But it's only the one for the center point of the construction. I imagine we need four points, one for each of the mirrors?"

"Yes, I would think so," said Sarah. She hesitated for a moment, then said, "Raj, do you have the correspondent figures for the four corners of the Pyramid?"

Raj made a few searches and smiled, "Got them! Way to go Sarah!"

"That's my girl!" shouted Daniel while everyone applauded.

"Those four mirrors remind me of those verses in the Bible that talk about the four corners of the earth," Sarah observed. "This could turn out to be the four corners of our communications for the future."

Sinclair wanted clarification, "So what does that mean? Do we have to go to the Pyramid to find out where those mirrors are and to communicate with them? That will be a slight problem."

Roy just laughed, "No, we don't need to go there. We

can determine the four coordinates relative to our position here."

"The next question is; how do we determine the distance from the base of the Pyramid to the mirror? What we have now is a line from the Pyramid to the mirror, the direction if you want to call it that. What we don't know is how long that line is," Ryan said.

"Oh, apologies Ryan. I thought I said that before. We have the distance as well. Here ..." was as far as he got, before Ryan shouted, "Then its game, set, and match!"

"Ok, I am obviously in the presence of greatness," Sam quipped. "But I have lost you guys completely a while ago. Suppose you find the precise location - and I have to admit I have no idea how you're going to do that - what are you going to do once you find it?"

"*I'm* going to shoot lasers at them. I don't know what the others are going to do." Roy's answer had them all laughing, but it was obvious many of them were as lost as Sam was.

Roy continued as if there'd been no interruption, "They didn't use the same units of measurement for distance as ours. My quick calculation shows this one is located about fifty-five thousand miles from earth. That's just about a quarter of the way to the moon. That means ... let me see, light travels at about one hundred and eighty-six thousand miles per second - in other words - the laser beam would make a turnaround trip in about point six seven of a second." Everyone was shaking their heads as Roy rattled off the figures, all calculated on the fly, in his head.

Daniel asked Roy to draw a picture so that everyone could get a visual idea of what they were discussing. Mandy had a picture ready and handed it to Roy on her tablet. He took the tablet and stylus from her, brought the picture up on the screen and slowly stepped the audience through the information.

By two o'clock in the morning, they decided that it was time to go to bed. The next few days were going to be frenetic, and they would need all their energy to turn their discovery into reality.

Peter sat through it all, thunderstruck; he could not believe what he saw and heard. He often looked at Sam and saw the look of excitement on his face. He had thousands of questions, but he knew it would slow everything down if he asked them. He resolved to sit down with Daniel at the first opportune moment, so that the enormous gaps in his knowledge about the 10th Cycle Library and other discoveries could be filled in.

As they all got up to go to bed, Sam and Susan looked at each other. Sam shook his head and whispered to her, "Susan, I have never seen anything like this in my life. It's absolutely incredible to watch these people at work. I have never had the privilege to be among so many brains. Nothing can stop them; nothing is ever too big or too complicated for them."

Susan got tears in her eyes as she heard her husband talk. She remembered how they were evacuated and brought to safety in the Rabbit Hole. Indeed, it was a privilege to be part of this family.

Sam turned to Peter and asked, "What do you think of what you've seen here tonight?"

Peter smiled, "Sam, to say that I am impressed would be the understatement of the century. My brain can't expand enough to comprehend what I've have witnessed, not only tonight, but since I arrived here. Wait, actually my astonishment started the moment I opened that birthday card from you and kept on growing when I met Owen and Alison, read the brief you sent me, and started using those gadgets."

"Yes, those techies are brilliant are they not? Much better than James Bond's Q." Sam smiled. "But let me tell you, those gadgets combined with these mirrors will be game changing. I'm convinced if those mirrors are still up there and still able to function, Roy and Raj will get the system operational. Can you even begin to realize what that would mean for us?"

Peter shook his head. "I comprehend that I've been privy to an earth-shattering discovery. I have to admit, they lost me some time back; most of it is way out of my league. I just hope there's enough time while I'm here for Daniel or someone to tell me more about the 10th Cycle, the Rossler Foundation, and all this technology."

"I'll ask Daniel to make time for that. Let's get some sleep, and then get back into that material you have collected for us. There's a lot we have to work through," Sam said.

As they were all leaving, Salome walked over to Gemma and expressed in a pretend serious tone, "Young lady, I have a bone to pick with you. I am told you kissed my husband. Is that true?" Gemma, still a bit shaky from the events, looked at Salome and shook her head in denial, "No! No! That's not true. He kissed me. On the head. I don't know why. I didn't do anything!" which had Salome cracking up with laughter.

Chapter Seventy-Two

THE TREAT OF A LIFETIME

Back in the meeting after four hours' sleep, Peter first showed Daniel, Sam, Salome, and Luke the material he collected at the Wappinger warehouse. Everyone listened carefully, made notes and asked questions. Then Daniel started mapping the warehouse process step by step, asking for clarification from Peter along the way.

A few hours later, they had it all in front of them - the delivery of the chips from China, the unpacking and storage, the distribution trucks' appearance, the order checking process, robots fetching the boxes from storage and delivering the boxes to the loading bays, and the loading of the trucks. They also had the images of the boxes with all the labeling and markings on them. There were still a few gaps in their knowledge, which Peter would fill in when he went back to New York.

Salome, a scholar of psychology and ex-FBI profiler, noticed the slight change in Peter's demeanor when he started sharing the footage of the implantation clinics. She wondered what was wrong. Could it be that he is just afraid of hospitals and blood, or was there something else? She kept a close watch and noticed how he got more and more troubled the more images and videos he showed. *Is this something to worry about? Did something happen during the mission, which he is not sharing with us?*

Salome decided to surprise him with a "full frontal attack" to see how he would react; she would know if he was hiding something or not.

"Peter, what went wrong?" Salome shot the question at him out of the blue, startling everyone else in the meeting, who turned questioningly to her.

Peter was well aware that he did not completely hide his feelings and that an experienced observer like Salome would be able to pick it up. The reason was, he had nothing to hide. These were his friends and he felt he could relax in their midst. He had enough interrogation training to recognize Salome's tactic.

He just smiled and said, "Nothing went wrong, don't worry about that. What you're observing is the aftershock of the horrors I witnessed. I made a promise to myself that if I never had to look at some of those videos and pictures again, it would be too soon. But I know I can't keep that promise."

Salome relaxed. He was not dishonest, and she could see that immediately. "Sorry we have to drag you through it again but perhaps it would help if you do share it with us. You know what they say - 'a problem shared is a problem halved.'"

"I guess you're right about that," Peter said and continued.

Two hours later, everyone in the room understood why Peter was upset by what he saw. It was appalling to see the people waiting in those lines to be chipped, everyone believing that they were doing it for a better and longer life. Sam commented that it reminded him of some documentaries he'd seen of Nazi death camps and gas chambers.

The final shock came when Peter showed them the video of the babies being chipped. At the end of that video, Daniel voiced what everyone was feeling at that stage, "I am sick to my stomach! Those bastards! How could any human be so sick and twisted?"

Salome was white in the face from shock and rage. "Peter, please accept my sincere apologies. This is one of the most ghastly atrocities I have seen in many years. I can understand your distress."

"No need to apologize, Salome. You had no way of knowing what I saw. I took an oath that I would not rest until I saw the end of these wicked people," Peter said, his tone manifesting that he was dead serious.

Sam brought everyone's attention back to the task at hand. "I suggest we do the same as before by mapping out the entire process, painful as it might be. We have to get our facts straight."

Daniel opened his laptop and started typing as they all contributed. Peter asked aloud what he'd been wondering since he saw it. "Why would they take a mouth swab from everyone?"

"To get their DNA. They own the technology, developed a few years ago, that enables them to sequence a person's DNA in a matter of minutes. My guess is that the chips are personalized with the DNA of the carrier." Salome replied.

Daniel thought for a moment and said, "Let me make a guess; if the DNA is linked to the chip, could that be the way they would prevent the carrier from taking it out?"

Salome replied, "I agree, it could very well be the way

they're doing it. I think Rebecca and Jack would be able to advise us better on that, and once we get hold of the chips, we would be able to verify that."

By the time they had the process mapped out completely, the excitement of the previous night, the little sleep they'd had, and the long day in the meeting room were taking their toll. The group agreed it was time to take a break and get back to it the next morning.

Sam and Susan had invited Peter, Daniel, and Sarah for dinner so that they could use the opportunity to provide Peter with more background information about the Rossler Foundation and the two libraries. By the end of the night, he felt he had taken a few significant steps forward in terms of his knowledge. He was blown away by the facilities and the technology. In addition, the family atmosphere, the absolute dedication, and positive attitudes of everyone involved overwhelmed him.

The next morning the group gathered again and started constructing a plan. They considered Peter's three options. The first option of trying to get into the compound unseen posed many problems and many risks and was parked for the moment. The second option of attempting to track down someone who worked at the compound warranted more consideration.

Peter thought it could be possible to get the personal details and background of everyone who worked at the warehouse. Someone among those workers could very well be open to a bribe or other gentle persuasion techniques. Everyone agreed it was an option worth more investigation.

The third, which Peter hadn't given much thought to a few days ago when he started thinking about choices, was to find a way to get inside the compound with a remote controlled device. That got everyone excited. He didn't understand the enthusiasm for that choice until Daniel and Sam explained that with Roy and Raj's combined brainpower, it would probably be the best, and certainly the safest, of the three options.

By midday, they had gone through every detail they could think of and noted all the missing information still to be collected before the final stage of the assignment could commence.

Next on their agenda was to bring Roy and Raj in and give them a chance to provide some input. The two of them were given an overview of what Peter told them and shown the process maps created the previous day, as well as some of the pictures and videos.

They said nothing, listened carefully and made a few notes.

The group had decided, intentionally, not to tell Roy and Raj about the options they'd discussed earlier. They wanted to give the two of them an opportunity to come up with their own fresh view of potential solutions. At the end of it, Roy looked at Raj as if to ask, you want to go first?

Raj said, "You go first, Roy."

Roy asked Daniel to bring up some of the pictures of the compound on the projector screen. He had another good look at some of the pictures, asked for a few to be zoomed and made a few more notes. He then asked Daniel to show him some of the footage taken inside the warehouse. He was interested in the videos that showed where the boxes were stacked at the loading bays and loaded into the trucks. Finally, he asked Daniel to bring up images of the boxes and zoom in on them as much as he could.

Everyone was quiet while staring at him, waiting to hear what he thought, although he was unaware of their scrutiny. His mind was entirely focused on the screen.

"Peter, do you know what they're doing with those empty boxes at the clinics?" Roy asked.

"No, I didn't think of that. There is a video that shows them flattening the boxes and dumping them in a bin, but I didn't follow the bins to see where the boxes end up," Peter replied.

Roy replied, "Don't worry about that for now - it should be easy to find out when you get back there. I get the impression they don't follow a strict security procedure to get rid of the boxes."

"Yes, from what I've seen that would probably be the case," Peter replied.

Roy gave them his initial thoughts. "Okay, here's what I think. We have to get hold of a few of those empty boxes and restore them back to their original state, or close to it. We know what the chips look like from the videos Peter took at the hospitals. Perhaps we can get more close-up images of them so we can build replicas. Then we could swap one or more of our boxes and chips for one or more of theirs. Inside the warehouse, the only place where humans handle the boxes is when they are loaded into the trucks. That's where and when we have to swap them. Those loading bay doors are big and wide and, it seems to me, always open. I think we could use a few drones to do the job."

Peter said, "That would be ideal, but the problem is, the radar might detect a drone of that size."

Roy answered, "Those fences are about eight feet high. The rooftop where the radar antenna is mounted is much taller and the angle of the antenna shows that it is scanning for flying objects from the roof level up. There's a gap of about twenty feet above that fence, where we can get a drone through."

Peter just shook his head in amazement; he hadn't even

noticed those things when he was there. Roy picked it up from videos and pictures in a few minutes. Sam and the others just smiled. They knew from firsthand experience what Roy could do with his drones.

Roy continued, "Even so, the radar is not a problem. The 10th Cyclers were masters of stealth technology; we built drones using their technology a few years ago. I can build one or two of them again. There isn't a radar on earth that would detect a drone equipped with that technology."

Raj was next, "I support Roy's idea and have a few ideas that could be helpful if we decide to use drones. We could hack into the Wi-Fi system that controls those robots. We can scan for the frequencies, and once we take control of the robots, we can make them do whatever we want. I would also like to find out where they get their power. Maybe we could arrange for a power outage like the one in Boise.

"As for the implant centers, I think the only thing we really need from them would be a few of those chip activators. That is, of course, if we cannot find some of them in the warehouse."

"Do you have any ideas how we could do that?" Luke wanted to know.

Raj replied, "The activators use some sort of wireless technology. It could be Bluetooth or infrared or Wi-Fi. We need to find out which. Once we know, we can take control of it remotely and jam it. We could then find out what they do with defective activators by jamming a few of them and observing with the spyflies what happens. I suspect if they discover the device is not working they will become careless and discard it or send it somewhere for repairs."

"Do you have scanning devices that can do that, which I can take back with me?" Peter wanted to know.

The Phoenix Agenda

"Yes, we have. It's built into some of the spyflies we used in Boise to scan the Wi-Fi frequency and take over the router in the house. I will have a few of them ready before you leave," Raj replied.

Sam and the rest of them were satisfied they had a plan that was beginning to take shape. Peter had one more day before he had to return to Mount Ararat, and there were still a few more things to discuss and do before he would return. Peter would spend a bit of time with Roy and Raj before he left, so they could show him all the technology devices they had and how each worked. There could very well be things he could use that they didn't think about.

During the last part of the planning session, they discussed the support Peter might need during the final preparations and execution of the operation. Raj suggested he could call in the help of Rube and Sombra. He would prepare a message for them on a nano flashdrive, and Peter could take that with him and hand it to Owen. Raj explained that Owen would have to do the introductions, as those two would be extremely hesitant to talk to anyone unless he or Owen introduced the person.

Sam started laughing when he heard the names of Rube and Sombra. Luke knew why Sam was laughing and also started laughing.

"Okay, you two now have to share that with us." Daniel requested.

Sam struggled to get his composure back, "Are those not the two guys who helped us a few years ago during the Sword of Cyrus operation?"

Raj nodded his head.

Sam continued, "If I remember correctly; both of them wanted full immunity, tax-exempt status for life, and to be removed from all government files. Oh yes, and one of them demanded to meet Elvis and John Lennon. According to his sources, the government has been hiding them."

By now, everyone was laughing loudly.

"On the other hand, I have to say, despite their crazy demands, they served us very well. I would have liked to decorate them both, but they didn't want to hear about that. They told me they would rather be dead than on TV or have their names printed anywhere, they just wanted to be left alone. They'll do, they've proved themselves before." Sam concluded, still smiling. "Come to think of it, their paranoia proved to be rather prophetic, didn't it? Raj's, too."

"So Sam, tell us now, did you meet all their demands? I am primarily interested in that meeting with Elvis and Lennon." Daniel wisecracked, bringing on another bout of laughter.

The next day, Peter had the treat of a lifetime during the four hours he spent with Raj and Roy. They showed him everything they had in their arsenal and the projects they were working on. By the time he had to go, he had a collection of nanotechnology and electronic devices that would have made him the envy of every spy in the world, past and present. He would give his collection to Owen to bring with him in the car on the next trip to New York. They couldn't take the chance of detection by scanners at airports.

On the night when Peter had to leave for Mount Ararat, he did so with a heavy heart. Over the past three days, he'd met some of the most amazing and caring people in his entire life. He had been a bachelor and a loner for many years, and had forgotten what it felt like to belong to a family. Now he missed it.

On the flight back from Billings to New York, he made

up his mind. When he had completed this mission and delivered the chips, he was going to buy a piece of land in these picturesque mountains and establish another safe house. When this war was over, and if he survived, he was going to find himself a wife and settle down. He was sure, somewhere out there, would still be a woman whom he would be able to charm and make happy. That last thought had him smiling at himself.

Until Owen turned up in New York, he had a few more things to find out and another visit to Tennessee on his to-do list. He had a personal message to deliver to President Harper.

Chapter Seventy-Three

HAVE NEVER SEEN ANYTHING LIKE THIS

After the discovery of the 10th Cycle mirrors, there was a rekindled fire of optimism and energy among the inhabitants of the Rabbit Hole. Everyone knew that if it were possible to reactivate that ancient communications system, it would be a significant step forward in the war to win back their own, and billions of other's, freedom.

Roy had no shortage of volunteers who were prepared to help with not only translations, but also anything else that was required. With all the extra hands the work progressed swiftly. Within a week they had extracted and translated all the technical details about the mirrors and recalculated the coordinates relative to the position of the Rabbit Hole.

Daniel, Sam, and Luke paid the techies a visit to see what progress they were making and were pleasantly surprised. Raj and his team had managed to fully translate and understand the 10th Cycle programming language. Mandy, the expert firmware programmer, coded the senders and receivers, tested them and confirmed that the system was working as expected. They already had a prototype communications system up and running inside the computer center, and they demonstrated it to Daniel, Sam and Luke during their visit.

"I've been wondering about a few things. The first is, won't clouds and bad weather obstruct the laser beams?" Daniel wanted to know.

Roy responded, "The 10th Cyclers used communications radar technology, which our scientists only started modeling in 2006 and is still being developed. Standard lasers would be scattered by dust, dirt, water vapor, and gasses in the air and clouds. In other words, standard laser communications depend on optical signals having a direct line of sight and no obstructions in-between. Not so with the 10th Cycle laser technology which 'punches through' the clouds and other obstructions. The 10th Cyclers were smart enough to combine electronic signal handling methods with a laser communications system to achieve a reliable, high speed and high capacity link through the clouds and into space."

"But I got the impression that the sender and receiver will have to remain in exactly the same position to be able to communicate," Sam responded. His tone indicated it was a question.

Roy explained, "No, that's not necessary. As long as the senders and receivers on earth are aware of their own position relative to the mirrors, they can move around. It works like GPS."

"We found the piece of code that the 10th Cyclers used for that purpose and have programmed that into our own senders and receivers. It is as Roy said. It works almost like GPS, except that the position is determined in relation to the four mirrors," Raj added, to the relief of his audience.

Roy said, "Okay, I'll give you a bit of a scientific explanation of how it's done. First, the signal is processed to shorten the overlapping data caused by the scattering. That process reduces the number of overlaps. Second, the system processes the residual signal, harvesting the good parts of the signal. It then assembles it into a complete signal, which eliminates the remaining echoes. This process is constant and happens in nanoseconds. The result is a high-quality laser message that arrives at the destination irrespective of whether the sender and receiver are motionless or mobile."

Daniel looked at Sam and Luke to see if they had any idea what Roy just said, but they were just shaking their heads. "Roy, I haven't a clue what you just said or how it works but does that mean we can build our own cell phone network?" Daniel asked. He was practically jumping up and down in his eagerness for the answer.

Raj just smiled and picked up two cell phones from the table, "Would you like to try it?"

"What? You have it working already?" Sam and Luke said simultaneously.

"Yes, indeed we have, but you must remember, it is only here in the lab, we still have to prove that it can work with the mirrors," Raj replied.

Raj pointed them to look overhead and explained that the device hanging from the ceiling about twenty feet off the ground was their own mini version of a 10th Cycle mirror. He gave Sam and Daniel each a cell phone and asked them to walk around in the room and talk to each other. The three of them were thrilled. If they could get this operational outside the caves, it meant they would have the freedom to talk to anyone, anywhere, whenever they chose. They wouldn't have to send people out of the Rabbit Hole on dangerous missions anymore. This was major progress.

"Roy, Raj. Do you think it would be possible to connect

this with those micro earphones and microphones that Luke used during the Boise mission?" Sam wanted to know. The thought had just crossed his mind how helpful it would be to speak directly to President Harper.

"Yes, Stuart and Mandy are already working on that. We think it's entirely possible." Raj replied to a very pleased Sam.

"Okay guys, this is all exhilarating stuff but what about security? Would it be possible to intercept the communications?" Luke wanted to know.

Roy explained, "Raj will tell you that no communications system is absolutely secure, but there are some things working in our favor that should put your mind at ease. First, laser is invisible."

Before Roy could continue, Daniel said, "Wait, what about those laser beams we see in the movies and even on handheld laser pointers?"

Roy laughed, "Daniel, you should know better than to believe what you see in the movies! If you can see a laser beam from the side, as in the Star Trek and other sci-fi movies, then something is wrong. That means the laser light is being scattered out of the beam. As for those laser pointers, have a good look next time you use one. You will only see the red or green dot where you are pointing at the time. There is no ray of light between the pointer and the dot. However, if there is smoke or dust between you and the dot, you will see the beam because the light is reflecting off the smoke or dust particles in the air. The technology we'll be using will punch through that. Besides, not all lasers use visible light. Some emit infrared light, which is definitely invisible to the human eye. Finally, you can't see a laser beam traveling from the source to the target because it goes at the speed of light. All those sci-fi movies showing the laser flashes zipping by the superman's head are total fiction."

Daniel laughed. "Okay, okay Roy. I'm convinced. Sorry for the interruption. Please continue."

"Therefore, the first thing in our favor is that the laser beam is invisible. To intercept the beam, the person would have to know where the beam is. It isn't like radio signals, which spread out. Laser travels in an extremely narrow channel," Roy explained. Then he looked to Raj to clarify the rest of the security measures.

"The next thing is, if the signal is intercepted, the person would have to be able to interpret the message. In other words, it would have to be decoded. That is going to be extremely difficult without one of our transceivers. Remember we are using a thirty-thousand-year-old programming and encoding language!" Raj smiled.

Luke was happy with their explanation.

"So, if we start dishing out these cell phones to our agents out there, how does the numbering system work?" Sam wanted to know.

"Sorry, we forgot to mention that. It's another part of the security features. Raj is the exchange. He has the devices programmed to be able to talk only to those who are on the authorized list on that phone," Roy explained, to the delight of Sam, Luke and Daniel.

"What's the data transfer capacity and speed of this system?" Daniel asked.

Raj got enthusiastic, "We have never seen anything like this, Daniel. We are not talking kilobits and megabits or even gigabits anymore; we are talking speeds of up to three terabits per second. In other words, up to two million times faster than broadband Internet connections operating out there today. We can broadcast live TV through this system if we want to."

When the three jubilant men walked out of the lab, Sam said, "I don't know about you, but I have never seen anything like this, either. When this mess is all over, if I'm still alive, I am personally going to see to it that we build a monument for those two guys."

Luke and Daniel agreed without hesitation.

Chapter Seventy-Four

NEXT ON THE AGENDA

The Supreme Council was in session and studying the latest figures about the progress of their chipping program. They were satisfied that things were progressing exactly as they had planned, with more than half of the world's population already chipped. The most satisfying was the unexpected and ongoing success they had with their medical chipping program. More than half of the people already chipped had done so voluntarily since the announcement of the medical benefits that the chip would bring to them.

To maintain the current momentum and to prepare for their next announcement, the Council ordered that more people be trained to perform the procedure and additional facilities created. This time the chipping program was not going to be as popular as the medical program, and they knew it. They would have to use the media extensively to prepare and persuade the people.

All the staff of all law enforcements and security agencies were already chipped. It was time to expand the program to include all government employees, as well as anyone receiving welfare, a government pension, or other entitlements.

The former president of the United States, President Harper's successor and one of the seven founding members of the Supreme Council, had a brilliant idea. "Why don't we sweeten this package with tax exempt status for all government employees?"

John Brideaux smiled, "Now that's what I call an excellent idea. Let it be so."

The media announced the new initiative and explained that the Supreme Council had decided to extend the benefits of the medical biochip program to all government employees as well as anyone receiving, welfare, a government pension, or other entitlements. It was part of the Supreme Council's program to ensure that everyone had access to free medical services and could live a long and healthy life. The announcement of tax exemption for all government employees was met with enormous applause.

Over the weeks following the announcement, the medical benefits were highlighted. Of course, Anastasia had the faces of her crowd of celebrities all over the news, encouraging everyone to join the program.

The Harpers were shocked to see their faces on the TV with a statement that said they were in support of the chipping program and the health benefits they had already experienced since they were chipped. Nothing was said about the deadline. Two months after the announcement, all government employees and anyone on government support would receive an ultimatum to be chipped within the stated time or lose their job or entitlements.

The people in the Rabbit Hole followed the announcements and concluded that time was running out. It would be a matter of two to three years before the entire world population, or what was left of it by then, would be chipped.

The new program did cause another spike in the number of voluntary chippings, as a large number of government employees were more than happy to undergo the procedure to get tax-exempt status, free medical services, and a long, healthy life. After receipt of the ultimatum, the numbers spiked again because very few wanted to lose their jobs, pensions, or entitlements. The media again hailed the success of the initiative and the benefits of being chipped.

The next item on the Supreme Council's chipping agenda was education. They had already achieved massive success with their new and free education system for all, but it was not yet coupled with chipping. It was time to do so. Again, they would follow their tried and tested method of obscuring the real reasons for the program, by announcing a guarantee of employment and no taxes for anyone graduating from their educational system. Of course, that also meant free medical services and a long and healthy life. What more could any human being desire?

As before, this announcement was to be followed a few months later by an ultimatum to be chipped before a certain date or be kicked out of the educational system. That was obviously not announced in the media in the beginning of this phase. Again, the number of chippings spiked and kept the implant centers busy for many months afterward.

Chapter Seventy-Five

THE BELLS STARTED RINGING

Raj and Roy's teams tested and tweaked the prototypes until they had it working one hundred percent the same as the original program created thousands of years ago. Three weeks after Roy's eureka moment they were ready for the first live test. They didn't expect to hit their target immediately and were therefore not disappointed when they didn't get a return beam with the first attempt or quite a few attempts after that.

It was for that reason that Raj developed a program that automated the sending of the laser beam. It would send a beam and wait one second to see if a response was received. If not, it would adjust the direction of the next beam by one one-hundred-thousandths of an inch, and send another. All they could do was wait until Raj's program reported the reception of a return signal. Raj didn't tell anyone that he'd configured the program so when it received a return signal, it would activate the sound of alarm bells on the receiving computer.

When the bells started ringing, indicating the arrival of

a return signal, pandemonium erupted the moment they realized what the ringing bells signified. It took more than a few minutes for everyone to calm down again and give the techies a chance to conduct the next part of the test. The process would have to be repeated three more times to find the other mirrors. First they wanted to make sure they could send proper messages back and forth between two computers by way of the mirror about fifty-five thousand miles into space.

They started the two laptops, which they'd prepared for that purpose, and within minutes had them communicating via the mirror without any problems. This accomplishment sparked another round of chaotic scenes of elation. It was decided, unanimously, to name the first mirror after Jeremy, which made the twelve-year-old boy ecstatic and his family very proud.

It was another day before they located the rest of the mirrors and established links to them. They now had the capability to communicate with anyone anywhere on earth. As long as the sending and receiving parties were using the adapters and programs they had developed, they would be able to communicate with each other using text, voice, and video.

The next step would be to deploy their communications network across the country, starting with Owen and Peter, and expanding it from there. For that purpose, they would have to convert a few cell phones. Due to the absolute ban on cell phones when they moved to the Rabbit Hole, they only had three, which Raj had disabled completely before they were packed. Those three were already converted and in use as handsets in the technical labs.

Raj contacted Owen via the laser link, which had

everyone excited a few weeks ago but had now become old news and redundant technology.

He asked Owen to get five new cell phones with Android operating systems; they didn't require anything fancy – the simpler, the better. Raj gave Owen the specifications and a thorough lecture on how to make sure the batteries were removed and kept separate. The sim cards were never to come near the phones. In fact, Raj wanted Owen to destroy them and throw them away as soon as he walked out of the shop.

Chapter Seventy-Six

WE HAVE YOUR PLACES READY

While Peter had to wait until Owen and Alison visited New York again to deliver the rest of his gear, he completed as much of the information gathering activities as he could with the tools he already had.

He went back to the hospitals and collected more information about the empty boxes, along with close-up images of the chips. When he followed the procedures used to discard the wrappings, boxes and packing material, he discovered it was as the Rossler group expected. The staff didn't care about the boxes once they were empty, and there were no set procedures to follow. It wasn't going to be difficult to get his hands on them.

With that completed, he prepared to travel to Tennessee. Part of the preparations for the trip was to stop in Richmond, Virginia where he visited an old friend of Sam Lewis, Jeremiah Shelby. Jeremiah used to work for the CIA on a contract basis years ago.

Arriving there, Peter used the spyflies to find out what Jeremiah's circumstances were; that is, if he was chipped and how he felt about the new world order. It took less than twenty-four hours to establish that Jeremiah was still doing business in his old trade. He didn't work for the CIA anymore, but he had a thriving business with clients who were desperate to get out of America unnoticed. Most of them were heading for out of the way, small and third world parts of the globe where they hoped they would never be tracked down and chipped.

The coast was clear, and Peter approached Jeremiah using the protocol as directed by Sam. Peter didn't want to escape anywhere - he just wanted to be someone else. Two days later a man in his mid-fifties with silver-grey hair and black-framed glasses left Richmond and made his way to Cookeville, in Putnam County, Tennessee, about eighty miles outside Nashville.

He was driving a second-hand Chevrolet Impala. His ID and credit cards showed that his name was John Webber. On arrival in Cookeville, he booked into a motel. The woman at the front desk asked why he was visiting, and he explained he was doing research about General Israel Putnam, after whom the county was named. He wanted more information about his heroic part in the French and Indian Wars and as a general in the American Revolutionary War. Over the next few days, he planned to drive around Putnam County to visit historical sites.

Since their last contact with Peter Scott, the Harpers had continued with their twice-daily walks. Every time they reached the bench under the two-hundred-year-old Northern Red Oak tree, they would sit down for a while. Since they'd met Peter, sitting on that bench was their favorite place. They also kept a constant lookout for a fly to come and sit on Nigel's left hand, which would then after a while move over to his right hand. It had been weeks since they'd heard anything. The two of them had been waiting eagerly for that fly to make its appearance.

This morning, while sitting on the bench, Nigel noticed the fly on his left hand. He shook his hand to get rid of it, the fly moved away but came back a few seconds later, and landed on his right hand.

He whispered, "Esther, he's back!" Pointing with his eyes to the fly on his right hand, he smiled.

"Thank God for that!" Esther whispered, equally excited.

That afternoon they were both wearing their micro earpieces and microphones when they took their afternoon walk.

"Mr. President, Mrs. Harper, its Peter," came his voice loud and clear over their earpieces. "If you can hear me, Mr. President please put your hands in your pocket."

Nigel put his hands in his pocket. "Peter, it's good to hear from you again. We have been expecting you for a while now. How are you doing?"

"Mr. President, I'm good. There's a lot I have to tell you, but I first have to know how the two of you are doing. Are both of you still healthy? Have you been treated well?"

"Yes, Peter," said Esther. "Your visit last time gave us hope and something to live for. We are both healthy, and despite the circumstances, we are happy. We are treated well."

"I'm very glad to hear that," Peter said. "Please allow me to first play a personal message for you from Sam Lewis, if that's okay with you."

"Please go ahead; it would be wonderful to hear his voice again," Nigel said.

The Harpers listened in silence to Sam's message. He told them how he and his family had been rescued and brought to safety by the Rosslerites. He elaborated on the progress the group had made with their plans to overthrow the government, and the breakthrough with the discovery of the 10th Cycle mirrors. He also explained what they were planning to do about the chips. Sam ended his recording with the promise that as long as there was life in his body he would be busy trying to set the two of them free, which had them both almost in tears.

Daniel and Sarah both had short personal messages for them as well, which were just as inspiring as Sam's was. Sarah spoke last and ended her message with a quote from the Bible, "Daniel 3:17- *'If we are thrown into the blazing furnace, the God whom we serve is able to save us. He will rescue us from your power, Your Majesty.'* Nigel and Esther, we are waiting for you, you will be saved. We have your places ready and we will see you soon."

They were running out of time, as the Harpers were nearing the house, and they agreed that they would have more conversations the next two days, until Peter had to leave again.

During the follow-up discussions, Peter gave them a complete overview of what had been happening since they last met, including his trip and experiences at the Rabbit Hole, without revealing the location. They knew not to ask – there were too many people's lives at stake. It was not that Peter didn't trust the Presidential couple, but he knew the information could be extracted from anyone under torture. Until the two of them were brought to safety, that remained a possibility.

Peter left the Harpers with a bit of sadness. On the way back to New York, he thought about the conversations he'd had with them over the last few days. They were such down to earth and normal people. It was difficult to believe they'd been a President and First Lady. He knew they'd fit well into the Rabbit Hole society, and wished he could be there the day they would arrive. He found himself laughing aloud when he thought how well President Harper would fit in with the musketeers.

However, before any of that would be possible, there were many mountains to climb, rivers and bridges to cross, and work to do. He turned his mind to the chips. He was half expecting to have received a call from Owen by now, to let him know when they would be visiting New York again. The call came two days later, just when he was getting a bit worried and bored with the lack of adrenaline-filled action.

"Peter, I hope you haven't forgotten our beautiful state and parks!" Owen enthused.

"No, my friend. I am still madly in love with the places you showed me. Don't be surprised if you find yourself with a new neighbor one of these days!" Peter laughed.

"Well, that will be exciting to have you as a neighbor. We just have to get you a good and beautiful wife like Alison, and you will be ready to go farming," Owen jested.

"Yeah, I would need one of those," Peter replied with a smile, "the problem is, I don't know if there are any left out there who would want to marry me."

"Buddy, don't you worry about that, just tell us when you're ready and let Alison take care of the rest. You'll find yourself eating home baked cookies and farm bread quicker than you can say, 'Will you marry me!'"

Peter was laughing loudly at Owen's quips. He was a real treat once he got going. He could make a successful career out of stand-up comedy if he ever decided to give up the farm and writing. However, Peter doubted that would ever happen.

"Alison and I were planning to be in New York in two

weeks' time. Maybe we could catch up while we're there. Maybe that Japanese place?" Owen said.

Peter inferred that something must have happened to delay their planned visit but did not mention it. "Yes, it would be great to see you again. Would you allow me to return the hospitality you and Alison showed me when I visited you, and accept my invite to come and stay at my place while you are here?"

"Let me just hear what my manager says about that," Owen went quiet for a few seconds and then continued, "She says she'd like that. It's agreed then - we'll crash at your place. I always wondered what it would be like to stay in one of those luxury places where you live." Owen laughed.

Chapter Seventy-Seven

BUILT TO SPECIFICATIONS

The Supreme Council's chipping program didn't do as well in the third world as in first world countries, which was understandable because of their lack of infrastructure, education, and access to the media. It was a concern for the Council, because the third world countries were the primary source of the world's overpopulation problem. This in turn caused those countries' poverty and health issues to be a serious burden on all of society.

If the people of those countries couldn't be chipped very soon, substitute measures had to be found. It was imperative for the world population to be reduced dramatically to guarantee a better quality of life for everyone. For that purpose, the Science Advisory Panel (SAP) was established. This body, comprised the world's foremost experts in genetics, biology, chemistry, physics, microbiology, cell biology, bioinformatics, and mathematics.

The SAP scientists had access to the largest collection of human genetic data on earth since the 8th Cycle, to analyze and interpret the inheritance of skills, evaluate and diagnose hereditary conditions and congenital malformations, perform genetic risk calculations, conduct mutation analysis, and to experiment to their hearts content. The Council instructed the head of the panel of scientists to find a solution for the world's overpopulation. She was given carte blanche, even if it meant a Nazi type 'Final Solution'. As long as the result was the reduction of the world population, they would be happy.

Not only did the Supreme Council find it necessary to devise measures to reduce the global population to secure a better life for everyone, they also believed that it was vital to improve the quality of the gene pool. The second part of the scientists' brief was, therefore, to construct a plan to achieve that.

They listened with great interest while the world famous geneticist, Professor Barbara Cohen, the director of SAP, gave them a progress update. As for the control and reduction of the world population, there were some possibilities. To stem and reverse the current population explosion was easy once people were chipped. It was just a matter of programming the Central Human Control Unit, known to the 8th Cyclers as 'The Beast,' to upload a small piece of code to the Skywalkers.

The CHCU would send it to all activated chips and for any future implants, and the code would already be activated at the time of implantation. Based on a person's genetic profile it would be decided if he or she would have children or not.

The situation for people who were not chipped was a bit more challenging, however not insoluble. SAP had identified genetic markers specific to people's race and descendancy, which would make it possible to develop infertility nanobots targeted at those people. Similarly, they could develop nanobots to eliminate those people if required. It was not such an elegant solution as when someone was chipped; those nanobots would indiscriminately make people infertile or kill them without regard for their genetic makeup.

The only way to control that, to a certain extent, would be to target specific regions with a limited number of nanobots that would self-destruct once their job was done. It would at least have the effect of reducing the population numbers and stemming the growth in the target area.

The Supreme Council was extremely pleased with SAP's progress and the options they presented. Brideaux instructed them to commence the development and testing of the nanobots, with the support of the rest of the Council.

The creation of a designer human being was Professor Cohen's pet project - she just loved the whole idea of ridding society of the riffraff. She explained how they had been able to identify the genetic makeup of the 'perfect' human that would be near defect-free and a good citizen. By using their criteria and making sure that only the selected were allowed to produce offspring, over time they would be able to 'build' humans to those specifications and populate the planet with a new breed of super-humans. This was a project that could be kicked off immediately for those who were already chipped.

The Central Human Control Unit would be programmed to render infertile anyone with low IQ, low EQ, criminal records, defects, disabilities, and a gene configuration that was prone to disease, psychological issues, or antisocial behavior.

Again, the Supreme Council was extremely pleased to hear about it and gave Professor Cohen the go ahead to commence the development and testing.

Chapter Seventy-Eight

PARANOID OVERDRIVE

Peter was anticipating with pleasure the opportunity to see Owen and Alison again. He liked their company. They were good people, and they could become good friends. The other reason for his anticipation was his eagerness to get his hands on the spy gadgets, which they'd bring along for him.

When they arrived, he gave them a tour of the apartment, and while they unpacked, he got the espresso machine going. They would go out for dinner later that night.

Owen came into the room with the small packages Peter was waiting for. To Peter's surprise, he noticed a cell phone among the items.

"Hey Owen, what's with this cell phone? We're not supposed to come close to those things."

Owen replied, "That cell phone, my friend, is the reason why we were delayed in coming here.

"Let me guess. Those whiz kids have solved the space mirror challenge?"

"Arrgh man, now you took all the fun out of it! Yes, that's exactly what they did," Owen said.

"Those two are incredible. Since the discovery of the mirrors in the 10th Cycle Library, I've had a gut feeling that if anyone on earth could solve this riddle, it would be them. Tell me all about it."

Owen explained how Raj and Roy located the mirrors and set up the communications system, the security and everything. "The best thing is they have built a new breed of spyflies, which they can control from the Rabbit Hole. So you just have to deploy one and link it to the mirrors – they will then take care of the rest."

"The people in that Rabbit Hole are John Brideaux's worst nightmare in the making. I'm just glad I'm on their side." Peter laughed.

"One more thing I'm sure you'll like is they have set it up so they can now communicate from their location with anyone using those micro earphones," Owen said.

"Sensational news man! That means they can talk directly to President Harper?" Peter wanted to know.

"Yes, that's what they had in mind. We just have to plant a relay somewhere within a mile from the farmhouse and voila," Owen explained, to Peter's delight.

"It will be fantastic to get that link established and get Sam to talk to the President and his wife. It would be the biggest present we can give them until we can get them out of there!" Peter replied.

They discussed the agenda for the next few days. First on Owen's list was to get in touch with Rube and Sombra to give them the nano flashdrive from Raj, which contained the request for assistance. Owen didn't look forward to the prospect of having to walk and taxi to six or more different locations all over the city to meet with two paranoid people who couldn't or wouldn't talk. Fortunately, Rube and Sombra were a bit less suspicious this time and met with Owen after two relocations. He handed them the flash drive and agreed to meet the next day at lunchtime again to decide how they would proceed - that is, if they were prepared to assist with the mission.

The next day, when they sat down in the darkest corner of the restaurant for lunch, Owen took his pen of silence out to switch it on. Rube just smiled and opened his jacket to show Owen that he already had his switched on. Over lunch, Owen discovered that they were actually nice guys and much more loquacious than he'd been led to believe by their behavior in the past.

Raj had full instructions for them about meeting with Peter and about the gadgets that he sent with Owen. They told Owen they were happy to help with whatever they could and to meet with Peter. They agreed to meet at a safe house in Brooklyn the next night, when he would also give them Raj's presents.

At seven o'clock the next evening, Owen and Peter were at the safe house where they met with the two hackers and two girls. At Rube's insistence, they were introduced but no names were exchanged. Peter smiled at one of the girls and said, "I've seen you before. Didn't you give me a card at my birthday party a while ago?"

She just smiled and nodded her head in acknowledgment.

First on the agenda was the spy tools, the gift from Raj. Owen unpacked the bundle and gave the contents to them; Raj had included the operating instructions for each of the devices on a nano flashdrive. But then, typical Raj, he always kept something as a surprise. In this case he did not tell them anything about the cellphones in advance. When

Owen took the cell phones out, Rube and Sombra were on their feet immediately.

"What the fuck! Have you lost your mind man? How the hell could you bring that in here? We'll be tracked and arrested! Are you crazy?" Sombra shouted while he and Rube were heading for the door.

Owen was befuddled; he didn't expect reactions like that. He was at a loss for words. Luckily, Peter immediately grasped what just happened. He'd had almost the same reaction a few days ago when Owen handed him his cell phone. He came to the rescue.

"Hang on guys, hang on. Just listen to me. I'll explain." Peter managed to stop them just short of the door.

Peter explained in detail how the Rosslerites had discovered the mirrors and developed the communications system, and that it was totally secure. They were still standing close to the door, not convinced that what they'd heard could be true. They'd worked with Roy and Raj before, though. It could perhaps be true, but they were skeptical.

Peter said, "Ok, I don't know what else I can do to calm you guys down and convince you that I'm not lying. How about we call Raj now, and you can talk to him?"

Rube and Sombra looked at each other. It was obvious they were worried; they wanted to believe what they'd heard, but scared out of their minds at the same time.

Rube spoke first, "Okay, let's do that, but let me be very clear – if I so much as get a sniff that there's a problem, we're gone. You won't see or hear from us ever again. Is that understood?"

Owen and Peter nodded their head in agreement.

Peter picked the phone up and pressed a few buttons. He had it on speaker. A few seconds later Raj's voice came over the speaker, "Sombra, I see you got my present. How do you like it?"

By now, Sombra and Rube were standing next to Peter. "Raj, where did we meet the last time I saw you?"

Raj realized his friends were in paranoid overdrive. "We met at the safe house in the Bronx. It was a Wednesday night, shortly after nine."

"What color shirt did I wear and what color shirt did Rube wear?" Sombra asked.

"You wore a dark red shirt and Rube a black t-shirt," Raj replied.

"Who of us was sitting at the head of the table that night? Sombra fired his last question.

"No one was sitting at the head. I was sitting opposite Rube and you were sitting to his right." Raj replied again.

Sombra and Rube both smiled from ear to ear. "Raj, you old fox! You could have warned us, man! We almost disappeared!" Rube exclaimed.

"Sorry, it must have slipped my mind," Raj said, with the smile in his voice clearly noticeable.

A short conversation followed, during which Raj gave them the assurance that Peter was telling them the truth and that they could trust him and Owen. Rube and Sombra were on cloud nine – this was the best present they could ever hope for. They were like little boys who got their first bicycles. When the call ended the two of them were calm, relaxed, and euphoric.

They settled down to continue their meeting with the discussion of Peter's requirements. He started with the chip boxes and packing materials as well as the activator and explained why they would need that. One of the girls said she had a contact that worked at one of the hospitals in the Bronx where implants were performed. She thought her contact would help with the boxes. As for better images of the chips and the activators, Peter wanted them to deploy the spy flies and link them up with Raj, who would then collect the required information. They agreed to take care of that and let him know when it was done.

Next, he asked if they could try to get the names and details of the people working at the warehouses and implant facilities. He wondered if they might be able to get the details of the electricity supply for the warehouse in Wappinger. They figured that would be fairly easy to do and would let him know when it was ready.

Finally, Peter wanted to know if they had Tectus members in Tennessee. Rube replied that they had three members in Nashville. Peter requested that they deploy six spy flies into the former president's house, and another two in the oak tree. Then set up two relays within less than a mile from the house in such a place that it would not be noticeable, yet had enough exposure to the sun during the day to charge the devices. Once they had completed that task, they just had to activate the devices and Raj would take care of it from then on.

Rube and Sombra were happy to help with that and would let Peter know when they had contact with their members in Nashville. They didn't expect any issues with the request. One of them would take the equipment to Nashville personally.

Owen asked them if they would again deliver messages to the Rosslerite family members as they did before. They were more than happy to do that.

The last request was from Owen, passed on by Raj. That was for Rube to arrange for the delivery of another nano flashdrive to the same person as before, at Luigi's Coffee Shop this coming Friday. Neither Peter nor Owen knew who the person was and didn't ask. If they were supposed to know, Raj or Sam would have told them

They were happy that they had a fruitful meeting and were excited about the breakthroughs coming from the Rosslerites on the technology front. With the mirror phones, they had direct contact with each other now and could in the future do most of their business over the phones. That meant they wouldn't have the hassle of having to run the risk of detection or to take elaborate evasive measures to meet with each other in person.

Chapter Seventy-Nine

THE FLIGHT OF OWLS

Peter had everything in place now to start collecting the rest of the information required by the team at the Rabbit Hole, other than the information about the warehouse. To collect that, he had to make another trip to Wappington to plant the new generation spyflies that would collect the information about the robots and the Wi-Fi frequencies. The day after Owen and Alison left, he made the trip, deployed the spyflies and relays, and activated them. He called Raj to confirm that the link was working and everything was setup correctly.

Raj congratulated him on a job well-done.

Within four days after the meeting, Rube called to confirm that they had deployed the spyflies at the hospitals and linked them up with Raj. They reported they'd done some surveillance of the hospital in the Bronx. They were ready to make the move to get their hands on the chip boxes, which they thought would take about a week. They also had contact with one of the Nashville members of their group who was eager to help. Sombra would take the spyflies to Nashville over the weekend and help with the deployment.

Just a week later, Peter received a call from Rube, who asked that he get himself a briefcase, a picture of which was sent to him. After getting it, he had to go to a certain restaurant. Rube told him that when he left the restaurant, a taxi would be waiting for him. Inside he would meet a woman with blonde hair, dark glasses and a cameo necklace. He should call her Emily and act as if he knew her. She would have a briefcase the same as his. They were to swap the briefcases and both get off a few blocks further on.

That afternoon, Peter followed Rube's instructions, met with Emily, and swapped the briefcases. He returned to his apartment and found five boxes neatly folded with wrapping materials and, to his big surprise, a chip activator. Seeing the activator had him on high alert straightaway. *How did they manage to get hold of that?*

Peter called Rube to get an explanation. Rube just laughed and told him not to worry about it. While they were doing surveillance at the Bronx hospital, they scanned the activators to find out what technology they were using and found it was Bluetooth, one of the easiest signals to hijack. Therefore, they hijacked the signal and jammed the device. To their surprise, the nurse threw it in the rubbish bin with the boxes and just picked up a new one. They just couldn't let that opportunity pass. Peter was relieved and happy with that explanation.

Rube also told him that the implant center at that hospital was totally drowned in work. They didn't have enough staff, because the unemployed and welfare people were lining up in queues stretching up to two miles. Rube asked if he would like to get a few chips as well, because he thought it would be very easy to do. The staff at that hospital was very careless. Peter stopped him right away and explained how strictly those chips were monitored and controlled. Stealing chips like Rube suggested would definitely be detected very soon and would raise the alarm, without any doubt.

Peter reported the contents of the package to the Rabbit Hole, to Roy and Raj's enjoyment. Having their hands on the boxes was excellent, and getting an activator with so little effort was a huge bonus. They would contact Rube to find out if he could get a few more of the activators. They wanted to be sure that they'd have enough to be able to take them apart and study them for purposes of reverse engineering.

There was big excitement the day Sombra called Raj from Tennessee to hand him control of the spyflies deployed for the Harpers. Sam was standing next to Raj the next morning at the time when the couple took their usual morning walk and saw them arriving at the bench under their beloved oak tree.

Raj launched one of the flies out of the tree and maneuvered it to land on Nigel's left hand and then shortly after that on his right hand. They could see him looking at it and heard him whispering to Esther, "I am surprised, but it seems to me Peter is back here. I didn't expect him back so soon."

Esther replied, "Let's hope its good news that brought him back so soon."

"Yes let's hope so. We will find out this afternoon." Nigel replied. Neither of them would have guessed how good the news would be.

That afternoon they almost yelled out loud when they

recognized Sam's voice. "Mr. President and Mrs. Harper, its Sam Lewis. How are you doing?"

They had a hard time keeping their excitement undetected, "Sam Lewis! I cannot believe it! How have you managed to pull this off?" Nigel stage-whispered. Esther placed her hand on his knee to quiet him.

"Sam, thank God! We thought we'd never talk to you again." Esther said warmly.

"Mr. President, I will tell you later, it's a long story. I have Daniel and Sarah here with me. They can hear you."

The next forty minutes and in the days that followed, they had regular contact and a lot to share with each other. Those conversations became the Harper's lifeline, and strangely enough, it in turn became a significant motivating factor for the people at the Rabbit Hole. Knowing their favorite president and his wife were alive and well and couldn't wait to come and help them take back their country, was a big boost to their morale.

As the links from the spyflies were established back to the Rabbit Hole, Sam and the operations team got busy with recording and analyzing the information as it streamed in. Soon they had enough information about the warehouse, the chips and activators to start fine-tuning their plans. They also carefully studied and collected information about the Harpers' residence on the inside and outside, including the routine of the special agents guarding them.

They decided that their first option would be to lift the chips from the warehouse with drones, as suggested by Roy and Raj. Roy studied the property very carefully and started building a drone that would be big enough to lift a box of chips and fly out of the warehouse. One of his challenges was to design and build that large a drone in such a way that it would create as little noise as possible during flight.

In their quest to develop a noise free drone, they had a lot of existing research and actual designs by aeronautical engineers who had been successful at constructing drones that were near silent. It was fascinating to find out that most of that research started off with the study of the flight of owls. Aero acoustics specialists found that owls fly silently due to the shape of their wings and the comb-like structure of their feathers. The airflow and their angle of approach, along with the feathers on their legs, made them silent and therefore deadly hunters. Over the years scientists had modeled owls in flight on computers and refined their developments in wind tunnels.

With this information and some of the designs, which they ordered through the Tectus network, along with material that Owen got for them, Roy and his team went to work in the lab. They constructed a drone with an undercarriage, which copied some of the strange features of owls' legs. The wings were built in such a way that the noise from air turbulence over them was almost entirely eliminated. The final result was a drone so quiet it was impossible to hear it from more than eight yards away in a quiet room. Outside the caves, the noise of nature blocked out all sound from the drone and it was completely noiseless.

While Roy and his team were busy with the owl-drone project, Rube and Sombra reported to Raj that they'd got hold of three more chip activators and would deliver them to Peter. With the delivery of the chip boxes and activators, nothing more was required from the implant centers, and the co-conspirators could focus all their attention on the warehouse. By now Sam and his team knew the warehouse and the routine inside better than the managers of the compound did.

They knew exactly who was working there, which shifts they were working on, the lunch and coffee breaks, the precise tasks each employee were assigned to, and how well they were doing it. They knew everything about the warehouse's power supply and backup generator as well as the Wi-Fi frequency of the robots inside and, they'd captured the passwords to the computers and the router. With the help of some of the more artistic people in their midst, they fashioned a scale model of the compound and surrounding areas to use during their final planning and preparations.

It was time to get Peter back to the Rabbit Hole so they could finalize their planning and equip him with the owl-drones and anything else he might need during the execution of the plan. Sam called him and made the necessary arrangements. Peter had to make his way to the Rabbit Hole in two weeks. He was looking forward to getting out of New York and back to the place he'd fallen in love with a few weeks ago.

When he started making his plans for the trip to Billings, he realized he had a bit of a problem. How was he going to get those activators smuggled through the airport scanners? He thought about it for a while and decided to give Raj a call to find out if he might have any ideas. He explained what his problem was, Raj just laughed and told him to get hold of Rube and Sombra – they would solve that little problem in no time at all.

The activators went back to Raj's friends the same way Peter received them, via the swapping of briefcases in the back of a taxi. Four days later Peter did another swapping of briefcases and found he just got a nice new laptop. Rube explained to him over the phone that they had disassembled the activators and soldered the pieces onto the motherboard of the laptop. Airport security would not be able to detect which was part of the laptop circuitry and which was part of the activators' circuitry. Raj already had the reassembly instructions.

Chapter Eighty

ANOTHER INTERVIEW

When Sam finished his call with Peter, he asked Raj to get in touch with Rube to request that another message be delivered to the woman at the coffee shop. That Friday afternoon Owen got the call from Kelly Edwards he'd been expecting for a while. He'd never met her, but knew all about her because she was a celebrity

"Mr. Bell, it's Kelly Edwards of WONN TV. Is it possible for you to talk now?" Kelly asked.

"Miss Edwards, what a surprise. Yes, it is convenient, and please call me Owen. To what do I owe the honor?" he replied.

"Thank you, Owen, the honor is all mine. And please call me Kelly. I was hoping I could persuade you to agree to an interview for my talk show. I did a bit of study on your rise to fame, and it will be a big honor for us if you would agree," Kelly added.

"Well Kelly, you don't have to persuade me at all. I'm hardly going to refuse the opportunity to be on the same TV screen as the famous Kelly Edwards!" Owen laughed.

"I have to be honest, I was actually thinking the same as I was looking forward to being seen on the same screen as the famous writer, Owen Bell." Kelly laughed as she returned the compliment.

"You just say where and when, and I will be there. Would it be okay if my wife Alison joins me?" Owen asked.

"No problem at all. I was going to ask if she would mind joining you. And I was wondering if you would mind having the interview on your farm in Nucla," Kelly inquired.

"That will be very convenient for us. We'll be more than happy to do it here. When did you have in mind?" Owen replied.

"I was wondering if we could do it the Wednesday of the week after next. How would that suit you?" Kelly asked.

"That suits us fine. I take it you'll be flying out here. Can we fetch you from the airport?" Owen wanted to know.

Kelly replied, "I'll be bringing a cameraman and sound engineer with me. We'll rent a vehicle at the airport and will stay in Naturita. The day after the interview, I'm going to disappear from society for two weeks, my yearly break. So my crew will return without me," Kelly said.

"Thank you for the call. We'll be looking forward to meeting you. Please let us know if there is anything that we have to do in preparation," Owen said as they ended the call.

Kelly went out to Naturita with her crew on the day before the interview and early the next morning they drove the few miles to Nucla and then on to the farm. Owen and Alison showed them around the farm before they went inside, where Alison had a feast of cake, cookies and freshly baked farm bread ready for them.

Kelly and her crew left after lunch, and as they walked

out the front door, Owen slipped an envelope into her handbag, unnoticed by her crew. They drove out to Montrose Airport, from where her staff would take a flight back to New York via Denver. When they left, Kelly opened the envelope and found her instructions and a ticket booked on a private chartered flight to Billings, Montana. It was the first time she learned where she was going to spend the next two weeks. She would hire a car in Billings and drive out to a farm – the map to get there was in the envelope. Before she got on the plane, she went to the restroom, where she switched her mobile phone off and removed the battery and sim card.

She was on leave. To her staff at the office that meant she would not be contactable for the next two weeks. Neither did they know where she was.

Peter arrived at Mount Ararat the day before Kelly. He was excited to meet Kelly Edwards, something he wished for a while ago, but there had never been an occasion. Sam informed him that she knew nothing about their connection, nor did she know anything about the Rabbit Hole and its inhabitants. She would know that he was at Mount Ararat and that she would get further instructions once she got there. Both of them knew what the other looked like, and just as an extra security measure, she would be wearing a gold necklace and he would be wearing a black baseball cap when they met.

When Kelly arrived, Peter was waiting for her outside, and when she got out of the car he felt his heart miss a beat - maybe even a few. He wasn't sure how many. The woman was stunning. He felt a flutter in his stomach, something that he hadn't felt in many years. He managed to keep his composure as he walked up to the car to welcome her and help her carry her luggage to her room.

He was smiling at himself when he started the espresso machine to make them coffee. He was so nervous, he felt like a schoolboy on his first date with the most beautiful and graceful girl in school. He tried to get control of his thoughts. *Man, come on, pull yourself together. We're here to do a job, that's all. Besides, she probably already has a man in her life – no woman that beautiful would be single for long.*

Kelly was watching Peter while he made the coffee. She blushed when she caught herself thinking that Sam didn't make a bad choice when he picked her handler. He was quite a good-looking man, tall, well built, and charming.

Peter showed her around the farm. Later when they returned home, she helped him to prepare dinner, which consisted of heating up prepackaged frozen meals. He again caught himself thinking how nice it would be to have her around for dinner every night. They were both surprised how easily they conversed with each other, given that they only met a few hours ago. They had many common interests and soon found themselves talking like old acquaintances.

Kelly was wondering when Peter would start talking about the reason for her visit and what was expected of her, but he didn't mention anything. Maybe he would talk about it the next day. Later that night Peter asked her if she knew anything about fly-fishing.

"No, I've watched people do it and always thought it looks like a lot of fun," she replied.

"Would you like to try it? I know of a great spot. It's a bit of a hike to get there, but I can assure you the fishing is excellent and the scenery is breathtaking. The only thing is, we'll have to camp out for a day or two to make it worthwhile." Peter smiled.

"I am a city girl and don't have much, or let me rather

say, *any* knowledge of the outdoors, but I always wanted to do it. I'm game, as long as you know what to do. I think it could be a perfect break for me. But I didn't bring any camping or fishing gear with me," she said.

"Don't worry about that. I've done it many times. I have all the gear we need, including two one-man tents and fishing gear. I suggest we head out tomorrow morning as soon as we've had breakfast. We can pack our stuff tomorrow. It's about ten miles into the Gallatin National Forest. It will take roughly five hours, if we go slowly and enjoy the scenery along the way. That's assuming the altitude doesn't bother you, but it gives us time before dark to stop and rest if it does. And it still leaves us with enough time to set up camp and get a bit of fishing done before nightfall. You could be eating fresh trout tomorrow night." He laughed.

"That sounds exciting! I just hope I won't be a burden for you with my inexperience." She said.

"We all had a first time. I am sure you'll enjoy it," he replied.

They decided it was time to get some sleep. When Kelly had gone to her room, Peter called the Rabbit Hole and told Sam to expect them by nightfall the next day.

Peter was up early in the morning and started making breakfast. The aroma of something she hadn't experienced in a very long time - bacon, eggs, toast and coffee - awakened Kelly.

She surprised Peter, who had his back turned to the kitchen door when she walked in. "Good morning. I could not believe what I smelled and had to come and see if it was true!"

Peter's heart skipped a few beats when he turned around and looked at Kelly. She was still as breathtaking without makeup and uncombed hair as she was yesterday when she stepped out of the car. "Good morning, Kelly. Did you sleep well?" was the best he could get out when he handed her a mug of coffee.

"Like a baby. I can't remember when was the last time I slept so well and awakened to the aroma of bacon and coffee. You seem very skilled around a kitchen for a bachelor," she quipped.

"I can help myself in a kitchen if it's necessary. You should see me with a microwave and a can opener." Peter laughed.

Later in the morning, they packed their gear for the camping trip and headed out.

Chapter Eighty-One

A SPINE-CHILLING SCREAM

By the time the mountains were casting long shadows on the east side, Peter and Kelly arrived at the fishing spot that was about five hundred yards from the main entrance to the Rabbit Hole. They took their backpacks off and looked around for a good place to pitch their tents. Sam had arranged that no one from the Rabbit Hole would be outside.

As soon as they unpacked their stuff, Peter took the fishing rods and asked if Kelly would like to follow him to the stream. "If we want to have trout for dinner, we'd better get our lines in the water."

Kelly went with him, and Peter demonstrated to her how it was done and told her he would be moving a little downstream from her. "How will I know when I have hooked a fish?" the worried Kelly wanted to know.

Peter laughed, "Kelly, you will know immediately, it's a feeling that you will never forget. I can't describe it to you; you have to experience it for yourself. I promise you won't catch a fish without knowing about it."

"Okay, well, so what then if it's hooked? What do I do then?" she wanted to know.

You bring it in, but don't break the line or rip the hook out of its mouth ... Wait, tell you what - instead of me trying to tell you everything that you should do, I'll be just a few yards from you. Call me and I'll come and talk you through it." Peter was struggling not to laugh too much.

He coached her to cast, and after a few attempts, she got the hang of it. "Ok, good. Now, once your line hits the water you start to reel it in ... slowly, slowly. The idea is to mimic an insect moving on the water ... that's it ... yes, you've got it. You're a natural!"

He turned around, got his fishing rod and walked a few yards away. Before he reached the spot, he was stopped in his tracks by a spine-chilling scream, "Peter! Something's trying to drag the rod out of my hands! Come quickly! What is it?" she screamed, with her eyes as wide as saucers.

He took a few steps and started giving her instructions, "You've got one! It looks like a nice big one. Ok, listen carefully. You mustn't allow the line to go slack ... reel it in slowly ... yes, like that. Now give it just a little bit of slack. Yes, let the line run out but keep it tight ... okay now reel it in again ... yes like that. Just keep the line tight, and every time he wants to make a run, let him do it. But make him fight for it ... there, it stopped ... okay now reel it in again. Kelly, you are a born angler." Peter smiled.

Slowly Kelly got over her first adrenaline shot caused by the scare and shock when the fish grabbed the hook. She got better control of her hands and a sense of the line. "Now I know why you were laughing at me when I asked how I will know that I have hooked a fish. Does it feel like that every time when you hook one?" she asked, while fighting the trout at the end of the line as Peter kept on instructing her.

'Yes, every time. I've fished, ever since I was a boy. And that excitement is still there every time it happens," Peter told her.

Kelly was smiling from ear to ear, "I can get hooked on that feeling! It's like you said, it's an indescribable feeling that I'll never forget."

Ten minutes later Peter took the net and scooped the trout out of the water, "Nice one! You have been fishing for less than an hour and you land a two pounder! I won't even tell you how small my first one was." Peter laughed, and Kelly was hooked on fly-fishing.

It was almost dark, so they decided to get back to the tents to cook their dinner.

He was delighted at having a fishing partner as enthralled as her. "Kelly, I hope you know how to gut, scale and fillet a fish. I don't know how to. My mother and other people always did that part for me," Peter joked.

"Well, in that case, let's put it back in the water, I have never caught a fish before, let alone cut it up!" She sounded concerned.

He laughed, "Don't worry. I was just pulling your leg. I'll do it. Would you like me to show you how?"

"I guess if I'm going to drag them out of the water I must be able to make a meal out of them as well." She said with a smile.

While Peter was showing her how to prepare the fish, he looked up over her shoulder where she was sitting across from him and saw Sam Lewis standing about two yards behind her. When he caught Peter's eye, he placed his finger on his mouth to show him to be quiet. Peter knew what was coming and had a hard time to keep his poise.

Sam suddenly spoke in a loud voice. "Aha! I see you discovered my fishing spot."

Kelly landed on top of Peter, crushing him to the ground. By the time he got up, she was standing two yards behind him, and Sam was sitting flat on the ground screaming with laughter.

Kelly looked at Peter, saw him laughing and then looked at the man sitting on a log, recognized him, and rushed towards him. She threw him over, pinned him down, and sat on top of him.

"Sam Lewis, you bastard! I almost wet my pants! I'll get you back for this! Where did you come from? How long have you been here?" Kelly yelled as she pounded him on the chest.

It took a while for Sam to get out of Kelly's grip. He got up and finally managed to stop laughing. "From your reaction, I guess you're not happy to see me?"

Kelly turned and looked at Peter, "You Judas! Wipe that smile off your face, you traitor! You planned it - led an innocent girl into the wilderness just to scare the living daylights out of her. I have a strong inclination to break your leg!" she yelled, while moving towards a retreating Peter, but then she gave in to the impulse to burst out laughing.

When they finally got back to normal, Sam had not answered Kelly's questions, but he had a suggestion. "Why don't you two join me at my camping place? I can assure you, it's much more comfortable than yours."

Peter smiled as he looked at Kelly questioningly. "Yes, that will be good. I guess after a shock like that, I can do with a comfortable place to sleep." Kelly replied.

If Kelly knew what the next surprise was that the two mischief-makers had in store for her, she would definitely have broken some of their limbs. They packed all their gear and followed Sam. He led them into the cave, and when they walked around the corner into the entrance hall, the lights went on. Kelly froze in her tracks and stared at the smiling faces in front of her in shock and awe.

She was speechless as she slowly turned to Peter standing a pace away from her with a big smile on his face, looking at her. She started moving towards him. He knew what was coming and tried to get away, but she caught him by the wrist and said, "I *should* have broken your leg. You planned this whole thing with that scoundrel, Sam Lewis! Who are these people?"

Sam came to Peter's rescue. "Kelly, sorry about all the scares and secrecy. Welcome to the Rabbit Hole, the home of the Rossler Foundation. Let me introduce you to everyone here and then we will answer all your questions."

Sam made her name known and like all newcomers; Kelly received a hero's welcome with hugs from all of the inhabitants. Kelly's fame preceded her arrival, there was no one who hadn't seen her on TV and knew about her. They were honored and thrilled to have her there. Within minutes, she felt relaxed and overwhelmed by the warmth and care of the people. Peter was assigned to Daniel and Sarah's quarters and Kelly to the Lewises. Sarah had dinner ready and invited the Lewises to join them for fresh trout and home grown organic vegetables.

Peter commented that he told her she would have fresh trout for dinner. Then he ducked away when she threw a playful punch at him. "Yes, you said that, but what you didn't tell me was about you and Sam's conspiracy, you scoundrel."

Kelly had a thousand questions. Daniel, Sarah, Sam and Susan had their hands full to satisfy her inquisitive mind. Little Nicholas took an immediate liking to her and occupied her lap for the entire dinner, to her delight.

Afterwards Daniel said, "Kelly, we have a few more surprises for you. Don't worry; it's going to be nothing like these two have put you through. I promise you might even enjoy it. We like to give every novice the royal tour of our facilities, so now it's your turn. If you feel up to it, let's do it."

"Absolutely, I'm burning to see all of it. After what Sam and Peter put me through, I can certainly do with a few less mortal surprises." Kelly laughed.

Sarah is our HR and facilities manager, and she'll lead the way," Daniel said as he held his hand out for Sarah to lead them.

For the next hour, Kelly's mouth was hanging open almost all of the time. Her journalistic talents were clear as she queried everything in minute detail. There was just way too much to assimilate, but there'd be more time to see it again. Peter explained that the plan was for them to stay there for the next seven days. She would have much more opportunity to revisit and spend time with Roy, Raj, Rebecca, and everyone else to familiarize herself with everything.

By the time they finished the quick tour, Kelly was drooping with exhaustion. "Folks, this is all amazing, and everything, but is there a bed for me somewhere? This joker," she continued, nodding at Peter, "force-marched me about a hundred miles before scaring the life out of me. I'm done for!"

"Of course. Oh, you poor dear." Sarah turned to Daniel. "She won't have been used to that kind of exertion, or the altitude. I'm surprised she's still standing!"

"No, it's okay," Kelly protested. "I've loved every minute

of it. Except the couple when I was having heart attacks, of course. But I'm afraid I'm going to feel it tomorrow."

Before they retired for the night, Peter informed Kelly about the compulsory Pilates sessions and that it was not a good idea to skip it. The instructor, Roxanne, apparently did not take kindly to nonappearances. Then he added, so cheerfully that Kelly was ready to punch him, "That ought to help with any soreness from that little hike."

"Little hike," she muttered. "Right."

Chapter Eighty-Two

OPERATION NIGHT OWL

After Pilates and breakfast, Sam, Luke, Daniel, Salome, Peter, and Kelly gathered to start the final plan. Preparations for Operation Night Owl, as they dubbed the mission to get hold of the chips.

Kelly's head was still spinning from all the revelations and surprises she went through in the past twenty-four hours. Like Peter on his first visit to the Rabbit Hole, she felt uninformed and overawed. Sam and the rest spent the first hour filling her in with as much background information as she could absorb. Daniel undertook to elaborate during dinner that night, the same as they did with Peter weeks ago on his first visit.

With the roadmap up on the screen, Daniel showed her the various stages of what they had in mind. "As you can see, we're still just at the beginning. It took us a long time and a lot of effort to get to where we are now, and sometimes it felt like we were fighting a losing battle. Every time we made a bit of progress, the Supreme Council announced a new initiative that would put us a few steps back. However, lately, with the discovery of the space mirrors and the establishment of our communications network, we have finally started to gain ground on them as things began to move along faster."

Kelly commented, "I think you're not giving yourselves enough credit for what you have already achieved. I've been here for only a few hours, and I still don't understand a fraction of what I have to and want to. But I can already see that you have literally moved mountains in this time. It's nothing short of amazing."

Peter joined in with her, "Daniel, I agree with Kelly. I was introduced to this place and your team only a few weeks ago, as you know. Nevertheless, since I left here and have had time to digest what I've seen and experienced, I am convinced the Rossler Foundation is the only group of people who have the ability to set the world right again. You are the only hope."

"Kelly, Peter, thanks for the encouragement. As you no doubt have seen, we're all motivated and dedicated. Everyone is happy and enthusiastic about the plans; no one will give up, no matter how long it takes and what effort it requires," Daniel replied.

Sam then got down to business as he explained to Kelly what her contribution to turn their plans into reality would be. She was to help them infiltrate the technical facilities of WONN TV. To do so, she would deploy spyflies in the computer and control rooms, the newsroom, the CEO's office, board room, and other meeting rooms. She had to keep her eyes and ears open, listen to rumors, find out what the journalists were working on and investigating. She had to identify people who were not happy with the New World Order and may be open to doing her a few favors in the future. It was important not to trust anyone; she had to operate on her own.

Salome explained that she would be trained by Roy and Raj to operate all the spy equipment, and she would also be issued with her own cell phone and all the equipment she might need.

Kelly was happy and excited to get involved with the Phoenix Project. This was an honor for her. Now that she had a new purpose again, instead of having to go and live in some remote part of the world, she was going to be part of a worthy cause.

Sam could not help but smile when he started talking, "Kelly, I'm not sure about my final request. I was wondering, in the light of what Peter did to you last night, if you would still be prepared to maintain contact with him when you're back home?"

Everyone was laughing; it was obvious Sam told them how he and Peter almost met their end the night before.

Kelly chuckled, "Sam, I noticed that you have shifted all the blame onto Peter now. Just remember you are both still in the doghouse. Another point is that I thought I'm not to trust anyone. After what you two did to me, you want me to trust him? I will answer you once I've exacted my vengeance on both of you."

Although Peter didn't say a word and managed to suppress a smile, he very much liked the idea of staying in touch with her. Nevertheless, for that to happen he first had to survive Kelly's revenge.

Salome smiled as she thought of an idea how Kelly could get her revenge. She would share it with her as soon as they were alone.

With Kelly's role covered, they fetched the scale model of the chip warehouse in Wappinger and started working on their plan. Roy and Raj were called to join them; it was their technology that would make the execution possible. By mid-afternoon, they had the first draft of the plan ready. They now had to do 'dry runs' or 'walkthroughs,' as they referred to the rehearsals, to ensure that every step had been covered in detail.

Peter would lead the execution stage; Rube and Sombra would assist him with the technology side of things. With the help of a few people with design and art skills, Roy had already developed fake chips that looked and weighed exactly the same as the real thing. The wrapping of the boxes would be restored to its original state. When they were finished, they would ask people to come into the lab and compare the photos of the original boxes with the boxes they'd prepared and see if they could find anything that looked suspicious.

Through their surveillance in the warehouse and scanning for Wi-Fi signals, they knew that the chips were not activated until after they were implanted into the carrier. That meant the chips were not electronically tracked. However, the boxes were fitted with Radio Frequency Identity tags for tracking purposes. Raj had studied the frequencies and labels on the boxes they had in their possession. He called in the help of Rube and Sombra, and within two days, they had a solution that would enable them to swap the electronic signal identity of the tags on the boxes.

Peter's training in the use of the owl-drones would be broadcast to Rube and Sombra so that they were also able to operate the drones if necessary. For the next few days, they would make daily 'dry runs' or 'walkthroughs' of the plan and adjust things that they discovered were left out or had to change.

That afternoon, Sam, to avoid Kelly's vengeance or at least soften her heart up a bit, invited her and Peter to join him and the rest of the musketeers for trout fishing. "I would definitely like to join you, but you must know, this isn't going to get the two of you out of trouble," she said. The laugh she followed her statement with was not comforting to Sam, who was beginning to believe her revenge would be painful.

Salome had already had a quiet word with Kelly, giving her what she thought was an ideal form of revenge, which Kelly liked. She knew what awaited them. Shortly before dark, they returned with their catch. Kelly was ecstatic as she managed to catch two good-sized trout. Peter continued his lesson about the preparation of the fish, which was interrupted the night before with Sam's 'shocking' appearance.

As Daniel had promised, during dinner and late into the night a lot more information about the history of the Rossler Foundation and plans for its future was imparted to Kelly. She was amazed at what she was hearing. Much of it was so surreal she had to constantly remind herself that it was, in fact, all true - she knew it was, she just had to look around her.

After a walkthrough of the plan the next morning, which took about three hours, Peter and Kelly reported to Roy and Raj to commence their technology training. Peter already had some exposure to the two geniuses from his previous visit. Kelly was in for a big treat and he told her so. She was not disappointed.

On the second night after Peter and Kelly's arrival, Sarah called a Town Hall meeting; there were a few significant and severe matters to be discussed. No one, not even Daniel, could get any more information out of her about those 'important and serious issues'. She just answered anyone who wanted to know, "Sorry, can't tell you. Just make sure you are there."

At about eight that night, everyone was gathered in the Robert Cartwright Town Hall when Sarah got up and all went quiet. "As HR and facilities manager it is my responsibility to make sure that we live and work in harmony. Where everyone is treated equally and equitably, and we are all free of harassment, discrimination and workplace bullying."

By now everyone was worried, but if they cared to look around, they would have noted a few smiling faces. Sarah sounded and looked solemn.

She continued, "A severe and disturbing matter was brought to my attention this morning and I have decided to act immediately. It is a situation that cannot be neglected and has to be addressed without delay. Therefore, I have assembled a court and will now name the offenders so that they can be charged and dealt with right now."

Everyone started looking around nervously. Who were the culprits?

"The accused are Sam Lewis and Peter Scott." Sarah continued in a somber tone.

Both of them jumped up and headed for the exit, but saw JR and Aaron standing there with arms folded over chests and big smiles on their faces. Neither of the accused wanted to take on the Rossler brothers. They slowly turned around in defeat and took their seats again. They had no escape.

The jury members were called out, Bess, Rebecca, Emma, Sally, Jane, Nancy, Martha, Susan and Sushma. The plaintiff was Kelly, the prosecutor was Salome, and Sarah was the judge. The court was in session. The accused were given five minutes to get themselves a lawyer or if they wished, two lawyers. The two of them considered for a while, looked around the hall, and decided their best bet was to employ Daniel.

The charges were; behavior unbecoming of a member of the Rossler Foundation, harassment of a staff member, gender discrimination, withholding information and conspiracy to scare a staff member. These were all serious charges that carried harsh penalties.

The charges were put to the accused and they both pleaded not guilty.

After the pleas were entered in the record, Daniel was on his feet, "Your honor, I want to object to the jury selection process. An accused is entitled to a jury of his peers, and this jury does not fulfil that definition."

"Mr. Rossler, what are you insinuating? Are you objecting because the jury consist of women only or is it because of their age?" Judge Sarah replied.

Daniel knew he had stepped right into it. If he objected on those grounds he was going to find himself accused of sexism. "Your honor, I would never object on those grounds. This is the most beautiful and elegant jury I have seen in my entire life. They look young and intelligent - no accused could ask for a better looking jury." This reply of his got him the immediate support of the jury but unfortunately, it was short-lived.

"So Mr. Rossler what exactly is your objection then?" The judge wanted to know.

Daniel had to think quickly, "Your honor, I am objecting

to the fact that the two accused had no say in the jury selection process."

"Neither had the plaintiff, Mr. Rossler. I assembled the jury. Are you calling into question the court's discretion and ability to assemble an impartial jury?"

"Your honor, in that case I withdraw my objection." Daniel said as the accused men realized they might as well have pleaded guilty.

Salome, the prosecutor, made her opening statement and swayed more than half of the audience and the jury in favor of the plaintiff. She described how the poor, lonely, defenseless and innocent girl entrusted herself to the care of that man, Peter Scott, who was supposed to protect her. How this ruthless man had led her into a wild and dangerous place under false pretenses. How he and the second accused conspired to scare her and once was not enough for them, they had to do it twice in less than half an hour.

Stating this horrendous experience has caused permanent psychological damage to the poor girl, she claimed, before reminding the jury of their solemn duty to eradicate this type of behavior. By the time, she sat down, half of the jury members were in tears and the judge had a hard time to maintain order in court. Chaos threatened to erupt among the audience, some of whom wanted to stop the trial there and then and lynch the accused.

The defense lawyer made his opening statement. He tried to convince the jury and the audience that the accused were acting in the interest of national security, and that they had no choice. However, it was clear that the jury members were not impressed, nor were the citizens.

The plaintiff was called to testify and her tears now swayed anyone who was not sympathetic to her before. It was difficult for her to relive the horrors that the accused brought upon her. The proceedings were often interrupted as the poor woman succumbed to tears and had to be calmed. During cross-examination, the prosecutor objected to every question that the defense lawyer asked the plaintiff and the judge sustained every objection, with the effect that the plaintiff did not have to answer a single question.

The accused were worried men. The hangman's noose was a shadow slowly swinging on the wall before them. The accused were both advised by their council not to take the stand to testify. He thought anything they might say would just aggravate their already calamitous situation.

The jury did not even have to leave the room to deliberate, the accused were found guilty on all the charges within ten seconds. The accused were now given the opportunity to address the court in mitigation of sentence.

Sam pleaded with the court to take into consideration his senior years, and that he'd served his country with distinction for decades. The fact that he married recently and loved his wife dearly even though she was one of the jurors who found him guilty, would surely count for something.

Peter pleaded with the court to take into consideration that he was in the prime of his life. He did not have a wife as he was still looking for someone to love him and to remember the fact that he was just following orders from his superior.

The judge was ready to hand down the sentence. She started by saying she found no extenuating circumstances and that this was one of the most horrible crimes she'd ever had in her court. It was obvious that the accused were ruthless men with no regard for others and the impact their thoughtless acts could have on a defenseless young woman.

Their sentence was as follows:

They both had to go down on their knees in front of the victim and beg for her forgiveness. They had to promise that as long as they lived they would never again do that to her or any other human being.

They were also, for the duration of the victim's stay at the Rabbit Hole to be her servants. To be beside her at all times, to fulfil all her wishes - tea, coffee, food - whatever she wanted they had to provide without delay. As part of her psychological rehabilitation program, doctor Rebecca recommended that the victim should go fly-fishing twice a day, and it was the responsibility of the convicted to see to it. Finally, once she was back in New York, Sam Lewis was sentenced to contact her once a week to talk to her and make sure she was okay. Peter was to stay in touch with her and ensure that she received a bunch of flowers at least once a week.

Everyone was happy that justice was served and that the offenders received sentences fitting their crimes. Kelly was pleased that she had exacted her revenge and was now agreeable to stay in touch with Peter when they were back in New York.

The court was adjourned and refreshments were served to everyone, including the convicted.

The people liked Kelly and Peter – it was as if they had known each other for years, and they fitted right into Rosslerite family. They felt the same and mentioned to each other how much they respected these people, what an honor and joy it was to be part of the group.

Finally, Sam and his team were happy they had the steps of the Operation Night Owl plan covered in detail. Now it was time to go outside the Rabbit Hole, measure out the distances between the warehouse and where their positions were going to be during the real operation, and start rehearsing it every night. By the time Peter and Kelly had to leave, they were all confident that everything had been covered and practiced and that they were ready to execute the plan at the first opportune moment.

For Kelly and Peter, it felt like their time at the Rabbit Hole was flying. They enjoyed the place, and neither of them wanted to return to New York. They would have liked to disappear as the Rosslerites did, with no forwarding address. On Kelly's daily therapeutic fishing trips, prescribed by Rebecca to restore the psychological damage caused by Peter and Sam's criminal behavior, she often spoke to Peter about her experience of the last few days.

"If you or anyone had told me what was going on here, I would not have believed it for one moment. I guess it's like catching your first fish you have to experience it for yourself,." she remarked.

"Yes, it is an incredible experience. It's like a beehive of activity in there, yet everyone is happy, relaxed, and somehow there is tranquility in this place. If it weren't for the work I still had to do, I would relocate immediately," Peter said.

"You know, it's the largest collection of geniuses in one place I have ever seen. Yet Sarah, Daniel, Rebecca, Salome, Roy, Raj, Sam, Luke - everyone here are such nice, down-to-earth people. There are no pretenses; nothing has gone to their heads. They are truly WYSIWYG - what-you-see-is-what-you-get. They're serious about their work, but they have time for fun and humor and each other. It's such a contrast to the place where I live and work, where you have to look out a window to see if it really was morning when someone said 'good morning' to you. I agree with you. If I could have it my way, I would just ask Ben and Aaron to cut me a few holes in the rock. That way, I'd have a place to sleep and I would simply not turn up at WONN next Monday morning." Kelly laughed as she described to Peter how she felt.

Sarah noticed that Sam was not the one who took Kelly on the fishing trips ordered by the court. It was only ever Peter who accompanied her. She wondered if Sam had delegated his duties to Peter or if he knew something she didn't. She started watching them a bit more carefully and saw there was some dynamic at work, but it was apparent from her observations that neither of them was aware of the other's body language. Sarah smiled. Here was another challenge for the Rosslerites' master matchmaker.

Sarah didn't let the grass grow under her feet. "Daniel, I like Kelly and Peter. They are really a nice couple. What do you think of them?"

"They're good people Sarah. It's great to have them on our side. It looks like they have fit right in with all of us, and it seems to me everyone here likes them as well." Daniel said as he looked up and saw the smile on Sarah's face. "Wait, wait, wait, hang on for just one second. Did you say 'nice couple'? I didn't know they were a couple."

"Not yet," Sarah replied, still smiling.

"Now let me guess. You are on a matchmaking mission again. Right, Sarah Rossler?" Daniel wanted to know.

"Well, you know me. I just can't stand by and see two people meant for each other miss their opportunity to be happy ever after!" Sarah laughed.

"So what makes you think they are even interested in each other, madam matchmaker?" Daniel inquired.

"The whole dynamic, the looks and body language between them says it all. They definitely like each other, but have not said it as yet," Sarah replied.

"Oh, I see, it's that 'looks' thing again. Well, as you know, I've no idea what those 'looks' look like or mean." Daniel just shook his head. "Good luck with your quest. Just remember, tomatoes are not ripened by applying pressure," Daniel laughed. He knew that once Sarah had set her head on making a match she would see it through to the end.

On the last day of Peter and Kelly's stay, a final walk-through was conducted. All their equipment was checked and tested. Shortly after dark, the two of them left for Mount Ararat, where Owen and Alison were waiting for them. It was with sadness that they said goodbye to everyone and promised to be back as soon as circumstances would permit them. On the way back, they had a lot to talk about, including Peter's idea of buying land somewhere close and setting up another safe house.

"That sounds like a great idea, Peter." She smiled up at him.

Chapter Eighty-Three

IT WAS SHOW TIME

Peter and Kelly took a flight from Billings back to New York, where they had to wait for Owen to deliver the equipment they couldn't pass through airport security. Owen was scheduled for a final studio interview with Kelly three weeks later, for which he and Alison had to be in New York.

In the meantime, after arriving back in New York, Peter made sure that he strictly adhered to the conditions of his sentence. He was to stay in touch with Kelly and see to it that she got a bunch of flowers once a week. Sometimes he had the flowers delivered to her office and sometimes he brought them in person when they would meet for lunch or dinner.

It caused a bit of confusion when Peter met her the first time, as she was disguised to avoid public attention. She had to introduce herself to him, and only when she started talking did he recognize her voice and the laughter in it.

While waiting for the equipment to arrive, Peter reviewed the plans on a daily basis. He made a few preparations and contacted Rube and Sombra to make sure they understood the plan and were ready to go on short notice. He admired the two, who were real nerds and city dwellers all their lives, but didn't hesitate to offer their help for a very dangerous mission.

Owen delivered the equipment to Peter, who then met with Rube and Sombra, passed on their gear, and conducted a few walkthroughs with them. They checked the weather forecast for the next five days and decided to execute the plan the next night, when there would be clear skies. He and his team were ready.

It was a Thursday, one of the busiest days at the warehouse. That was the day when hospitals and clinics would stock up on chips for the weekend, preparing for the rush of people who could not make it during the week due to work commitments. It was also two days after full moon, which meant they'd have enough light and didn't have to use flashlights to find their way.

Late the next afternoon, Peter drove to a safe house outside New York, parked his car on the street, and entered the apartment building where Rube and Sombra were waiting. He changed into his John Webber disguise. When it was dark, he left in the Chevrolet Impala that was on standby and headed for Wappinger. Rube and Sombra would leave an hour later.

At ten o'clock, the three men were in place on the hill that Peter selected previously, which had an unobstructed view of the warehouse about five hundred yards away. The entire compound was brightly lit by the spotlights, and the trucks were forming a queue that stretched outside the gates, all waiting their turn to pull up to one of the four loading bays.

The three of them spent about half an hour observing what was going on, and then Peter launched the first owl-drone. Holding a small box in its claws, it landed on the roof of a truck, waiting in the queue outside the gate in an area that was not reached by the spotlights. They waited a few minutes to make sure everything was okay after which Rube launched the second owl-drone onto the roof of a truck immediately behind the first one.

While they were waiting for their trucks to pull into the loading bays, they prepared and checked the rest of their equipment. Sombra made sure that he had good reception of the Wi-Fi signals from the inside of the buildings. He logged into the robot control unit with the administrator's credentials collected by the spyflies a few weeks ago and made sure he could see the controls on his screen.

Peter got the third drone ready. It was one of the old hummingbirds Roy had developed during Sword of Cyrus crisis, equipped with a small laser-cutting torch. He launched the hummingbird and steered it to the main power control unit, where he landed it on top of the box, waiting for further instructions. Finally, the two trucks pulled up to the designated loading bays and the doors at the back were opened.

They waited until they could see the robots on the screen as they approached the loading bay. Peter activated the hummingbird and latched it onto the thick black cable running out of the power control box. The robots were three yards away from the door when he gave Sombra the thumbs up. It was show time.

Sombra increased the speed of the approaching robots and steered them off track towards the piles of boxes at the doors. At the same time, Peter activated the laser-cutting torch on the hummingbird, and when the robots crashed into the boxes, the power went off, leaving the entire compound in darkness. The only lights came from the trucks and the moon.

Instant chaos erupted inside the warehouse. People were swearing and yelling at each other, truck drivers and crew were hollering at the staff, trying to find out what was going on. People inside were falling over boxes and robots until the manager shouted at everyone to stop moving while he attempted to get a flashlight.

Peter and his team had five minutes before the backup generator would start up. He handed the control of the hummingbird to Sombra to retrieve it while he and Rube maneuvered the owls off the trucks into the warehouse towards the boxes scattered across the floor by the collision from the robots. The owls dropped their loads, picked up another box each, and flew back to the roofs of the trucks.

Sombra had already retrieved the hummingbird and was busy swapping the RFID tag signals on the two boxes in the claws of the owls with those of the boxes left behind. He gave his companions the signal, and they launched the owls from the top of the trucks, steering them back to their position on the hill.

While the owls were on their way, Sombra completely disabled the RFID tags on the boxes they were carrying. As soon as they had the boxes in their hands, they would take the tags out and destroy them. Four minutes and thirty seconds after the power went out the three of them were smiling at each other while they held two boxes containing two hundred and fifty chips each in their hands. These were placed in Faraday bags and into their backpacks. The Faraday bags would protect the chips from any electromagnetic pulses and from any scanning devices looking for electronic circuits.

They had a few more things to take care of. All the

spyflies had to be extracted from the compound, and the relays Peter planted weeks ago had to be collected. With that all done, they packed all their gear and loot and left, Peter with one box of chips in his possession, while Rube and Sombra had the second box.

Back in the compound, the power generator kicked in, and the lights unveiled an incredible mess to the angry warehouse manager. The collision of the robots with the piles of boxes not only collapsed the boxes and scattered them all over the floor, but some of the boxes were also split open and the chips strewn everywhere. He had to order everybody out of the building while he and a few authorized staff members cleaned everything up.

It took them a very long hour to get back into operation. All that time, the manager was wondering what exactly happened. It puzzled him that the robots all of a sudden went haywire before the power tripped. However, he was under pressure and way behind schedule. The trucks were lining up outside, and the drivers were getting impatient. As far as he could ascertain, everything was back to normal. He would report the incident to his superiors in the morning and ask that they send out electricians to see if they could track down the cause of the electrical problem.

Before Peter and his comrades split up, he phoned the Rabbit Hole, where Sam and many others had been waiting in anticipation for what seemed like ages. When the call came, Sam put the phone on speaker.

"Good news, Sam. We've got it. Everything went well, exactly as we planned it." Peter's voice came through loud and clear for everyone to hear.

Sam was grinning broadly when he said; "I love it when a plan comes together. Job well done, boys! Excellent! The first battle of the war belongs to us."

Peter could hear the elation of the people in the background, listening to their conversation. "Okay, we're on our way now. I'll call you again in about two hours to tell you in detail how the whole thing went down."

Peter drove back to the safe house, removed his disguise, and returned to his car parked on the street. As he got into the car, he pulled the Faraday bag with the chips out of his backpack. He then placed it in a cleverly designed, hidden cavity behind the speaker in the door on the driver's side and headed back to Manhattan.

Rube and Sombra would hand their box to Owen the next night, and he would transport it to the Rabbit Hole. Peter would stay in New York until he received a message from the Rabbit Hole to confirm that Owen had delivered the first box to them, before he transported the second box he held.

On her return to work, Kelly took a keen interest in the technical side of broadcasting. She made contact with the head of the technical division at WONN TV and persuaded him to agree that she would be allowed access to the computer and control rooms and the staff working there. She explained that she wanted to create and broadcast a special edition of "The Edwards Dynamic" to show her viewers the history and development of the fascinating technology used in broadcasting today. The techies, who were always in the background and never got enough recognition for what they were doing, were all very happy to answer any questions she had and were most outgoing.

Slowly but surely, unnoticed, she managed to deploy the new generation spyflies throughout the entire WONN TV complex. At the Rabbit Hole, Sam and his team were delighted with the wealth of information they were busy collecting from WONN TV.

Peter met with Kelly a few more times before he got the call from Sam confirming that they'd taken delivery of the first box of chips. On the last night they had dinner, Peter accompanied her back to her apartment in a taxi. She invited him in for a drink.

The next day, Peter made the three-day trip to Mount Ararat in his car with a song in his heart. It seemed Kelly Edwards liked him! She'd invited him in for coffee and they'd continued to talk until after midnight, when he finally left her, saying he'd be in contact while away and looking forward to see her when he returned.

He could not believe what a lucky man he was.

Chapter Eighty-Four

THAT GLITCH MUST HAVE BEEN IRONED OUT

On the day after the execution of Operation Night Owl, an electrician turned up at the warehouse in Wappinger to investigate the electrical malfunction reported by the manager. He quickly tracked the problem down to the cable outside the main switch box and called the manager. He pointed the cable out to the manager and told him that it was obvious it had been cut. They both concluded that it must have been an inside job. The cable was fixed and the power restored but the manager was a worried man – the buck stopped with him.

One or more of his staff or the truck operators was a traitor. He asked for a face-to-face appointment with his superior to report the problem. A team of investigators was assigned and they turned up at the compound the same day the manager recounted the incident to his superior.

The investigators suspected the power cut was part of a plan to give the perpetrator time to get hold of some of the chips. However, they scratched their heads when an examination of the computer records showed that every box and all the chips were accounted for. In the end, they concluded that something must have happened that foiled the perpetrator's attempt. They closed their investigation with a recommendation that the compound's security system be upgraded to include the tracking of all staff movement through their implanted chips.

Consequently, the computer system was improved and the manager was now able to start collecting information about the movements of every employee and truck operator on the premises at all times. Next time an incident happened, they would know exactly how to track down the culprit.

The two boxes containing the fake chips landed at a hospital in Brooklyn, where they found that the first chip from a box would not activate after the implant. The patient was given local anesthetic and a second chip inserted, which also failed. The box was removed and put aside to be returned to the plant in China. The same process was followed a day later with another box when two chips again failed to activate.

All defective chips were gathered and shipped back once a month. Two months later, Guozhi, a quality control officer in China walked into his small lab, looked at the room in dismay, and sighed.

The boxes were stacked to the roof. He barely had space to work, he was completely drowned in boxes and work, and his manager wouldn't hire an assistant for him. Not only did he have to check all the parcels containing defective chips shipped to him from every country, but he also received a container with chips from the production line every half hour. Those chips from the production line received priority above everything else. They had to be tested and the reports send to the managers within half an hour of receipt.

He started the testing routine on the container of chips from the production line and while the computers were running the tests, he opened a parcel received from New York containing two boxes and read the enclosed report. "This is stupid!" he thought as he read the date and the hospital name on the one-line report that said the chips would not activate.

"That is why you send it to me idiot! I want to know what you did. What procedure you followed? Have you checked the activator? Why didn't you complete the prescribed defect report?"

He quickly opened the boxes, looked at the chips, and couldn't see anything suspicious. He looked up the date of manufacture and shipping and saw that these chips left the plant almost four months ago. He concluded that it must have been some glitch on the production line, but surely, that glitch must have been ironed out by now. He placed the boxes in the container marked for destruction; he didn't have time to waste on stupid operators who couldn't follow instructions and complete proper defect reports.

He followed the same procedure with each packet he opened, if it was not accompanied by a correct defect report, the box landed in the container marked for destruction. When the sender went to the trouble of filling in the form correctly, he would place the chips into small cylindrical devices about three times the size of the chips. There were ten of those devices attached to each line of computers on the bench in front of him. Then he would activate the quality check sequence.

The chips were analyzed by a computer program, which would run it through courses that tested each component individually and in combination with the other elements. The entire sequence took less than two minutes and required several activations and deactivations of the chip. The program would automatically generate a report, which was sent to the quality control team to review and act as required.

It was a monotonous and soul-destroying job. The only pleasure he had was to listen to the music playing through his headphones from his iPhone.

Chapter Eighty-Five

TO BUILD A PUZZLE WITHOUT SEEING THE PICTURE

Getting hold of the chips was one of the major milestones for the Rosslerites. They'd been working on that goal for months. It was with great expectation that they awaited JR and Mark's return from Mount Ararat with the box.

Roy and the rest of the technical masterminds, which included Raj, Rebecca, and Jack Walker – Susan's oldest son, a PHD in biochemistry – were all ready to dig in and unstitch those evil little devices.

There was a lot they had to discover. What technology was used? How was the chip controlled? How was the chip linked to the carrier's DNA? What mechanism was used to make it tamper proof? What power source did it use? Which body functions did it control and how?

After that, more questions - how was it linked to the Skywalkers? By their estimation, they had months of work ahead of them. They also expected they'd have to get outside help from medical scientists and other nanotechnology experts.

In the months and weeks leading up to the arrival of the

chips, Roy, Raj, Jack, and Rebecca had collected the names and details of leading nanotechnology scientists, seeking people who could advise them. This was handed on to Raj, who would contact his Tectus people and their hackers who would, in turn, gather information from sources that would give them insight into whom they could trust.

Salome and Daniel studied the information from the Spiderweb, which they'd brought with them in the hope they'd find a way to use it undetected. They then collected information about the biotech companies in which the seven members of the Supreme Council owned shares.

Once the chips arrived, all of this turned out to be very valuable information to help direct the focus of Tectus' collaborators.

There was a large audience present when Roy opened the box, picked out one of the chips with a pair of lab pincers and held it up so that everyone could see. The chip was half an inch long and the diameter of a grain of rice.

Sam commented, "It is incredible to think that such a small device can embody so much evil and cause so much suffering and destruction."

"How much information could be stored on a device of that size Roy?" Sarah wanted to know.

"Impossible to say until we have a chance to study it. Just to give you an idea, ten years ago, nanotechnology was used to put the entire Bible on a chip half the size of a grain of sugar. The Bible consists of a little over eight hundred thousand words. This chip is about half an inch. There are approximately twelve and a half million nanometers in that chip, and you can store ten hydrogen atoms in a nanometer," Roy replied, while placing the chip in one of the powerful 10th Cycle electron microscopes.

"Wow! That is staggering. So if I understand you

correctly, those chips by comparison can be as powerful as, if not more than, the laptop and desktop computers we have today," Sara said in amazement.

"A lot more than you would imagine. With the advent of quantum computing, the processing power of nano computers, as I suspect we will find in these chips, has exploded. Quantum computers are different from digital computers. They use the power of atoms and molecules to perform memory and processing tasks. They're thousands of times faster than the most powerful silicon-based computer you can think of. This little chip here has about double the processing power of all the computers here in the Rabbit Hole combined," Roy replied, to the astonishment of the onlookers.

"You don't suppose they would have left a user guide in that box for us?" Luke teased.

"Even if they did, Roy James wouldn't read it!" Salome laughed.

Roy and Raj answered a few more questions and then Daniel rounded everyone up, "Okay, let's give the techies a break so that they can get to work. I get the impression they have a lot to do, and we'll get plenty of opportunities to ask more questions later."

Roy asked Jack to set up one of the other 10th Cycle electron microscopes for his own use. The first thing they had to find out was what material was used to construct the outside of the chip. It didn't take them long to discover that the outside of the chips was made of titanium. This material had been in use for many years in human joint replacement procedures. It had proven to be safe for surrounding tissues and wouldn't cause any rejection or allergic foreign body responses. The chips were covered in a layer of silver atoms to prevent infections and inflammatory complications. They noticed that the shell of the chips had a few holes in it and on closer investigation agreed that those were probably ports through which nanobots would be released into the body.

Next, they had to get inside the chips to analyze the circuitry and functionality. Roy carefully removed the shells from the two chips he and Jack were studying and called Raj, Mandy, and the rest of the computer team to have the first look at the circuitry.

Raj and his team first wanted to find out how the chips were powered once inside the body. Thanks to the research information collected by Tectus' hackers and Rebecca, they had a very good idea what to look for. Unless the Supreme Council had access to new and secret technology, there were only two possibilities. The first and most likely would be the use of a biofuel battery made from carbon nanotubes, utilizing enzymes inside the body to convert glucose into electricity.

The second option was a battery system that would be charged by the electric current in the body. However, research showed that the second option was still in its infancy and not reliable or consistent. Any other known methods of powering biomedical chips inside the body used external sources, and they already knew that was not the case with these chips.

They soon found what they were looking for; a carbon nanotube battery, which meant the chip was powered by a biofuel battery as they'd anticipated. Apart from the energy source, they had a long list of features they knew had to be in the chip. Among those was a communications system, something similar to a two-way radio that would broadcast and receive signals. However, that was a feature they could find and analyze much better once they understood how the chip worked and how to activate it safely.

Other features on their list that they assumed would be present, were a GPS system that would enable the tracking of a person's movements and a credit or cash card feature, which would allow the carrier to pay for purchases, thus creating a cashless society as in the time of the eight Cycle. They also expected to find a plethora of medical features - biosensors that would be used for diagnosis, prevention and treatment. Nanobots were also high on their list.

While Roy, Raj and their teams were studying and mapping out each of the functions on the chip and how the components interacted, the rest of Sam's operational team put their thinking caps on and approached the problem from a different angle. They tried to map out the production process. They knew that the chips consisted of a number of components, each with a distinct purpose. This meant that different technology companies were developing and producing those components. The modules were made in different locations and shipped to the factory in China where the chips would be assembled and from which they'd be distributed.

With the help of Salome's Spiderweb and the shareholding information it contained, they were able to start identifying the technology companies involved in the production line. With the information they already had and that which they got from Tectus, they were able to gain insight into the latest research and development projects in those companies. That knowledge led them to the point where they were able to predict, with a high degree of accuracy, which features in the chips could be attributed to which company. Tectus could now infiltrate those companies and get the blueprints of the various components.

To help the Tectus members communicate efficiently, Raj created a separate space-mirror communications network for them. Three weeks later, valuable data started flowing in on a regular basis, as they infiltrated the computer networks and communications systems of the component manufacturers. The spyflies played a significant role in their success.

The process of discovering each little part in the chip and figuring out its functions required meticulous work and was painstakingly slow. It was as Roy explained to Daniel one day, "Like having to build a puzzle without seeing the picture in front of you. You will see the picture for the first time only when you have completed the puzzle."

Nevertheless, there was a team of dedicated and motivated people working on the project, and at the end of every day they could look back with satisfaction at their progress. It was just a matter of time before they would have the solution.

Chapter Eighty-Six

I HAVE AN IDEA

The Supreme Council was in session, discussing one of the standing and most important items on their agenda - the chipping program. They'd passed the halfway mark with the chipping of the world population – a point they'd reached with relative ease, thanks to the media. However, they understood they had very little left in their bag of tricks that they could use to persuade the rest of the people to volunteer for chipping.

Although they'd clamped down on Internet social media at the same time they took control, it was not entirely under their authority as the rest of the media was. That was something to which the council members did not take kindly. They were people who wanted to be in command at all times. Their Internet police were finding it impossible to keep a watch on all Internet activities. Trying to close down sites, delete posts, shut down servers, and threaten bloggers and social media users was becoming impossible.

Too much dissenting and provocative information was published, and it worried them that it was expanding. Their mobile and landline surveillance program revealed the same pattern of growing discontent among the population. It was something they had to nip in the bud sooner rather than later.

An analysis of the data showed that almost ninety-five per cent of the culprits were not chipped. It was as if the chip changed people into law-abiding citizens. Those statistics also provided the answer to their problem - all they had to do was to allow only the chipped to have access to the Internet, mobile, and landline communications.

On the other hand, they knew that although it might be easy and quick to implement with few technical challenges, such a move could be met with massive resistance from the public. One of the council members suggested that they implement the plan in two phases. During the first stage, they would make the services free to anyone who was chipped, and they'd use the media to help them sell the idea.

The second phase would be implemented later, when they were to start the enforcement of chipping. Everyone met the proposal with approval and instructions were given for implementation of the plan. The media would again play a significant role in this initiative. It would emphasize the numerous benefits that the chipped people were getting ranging from crime prevention to free education. They received free medical services, health benefits and tax-free status for government employees and now, free communications and Internet services.

The media trumpeted the big breakthrough in making the Internet a safe and secure place. People wouldn't be able to hide behind anonymity, it would be safe for children to use the Internet unsupervised. It would eradicate dishonest operations, and, of course, there would be monetary benefits for everyone. The chipped were much better off than the unchipped.

Since the last meeting, when Professor Barbara Cohen, director of the Science Advisory Panel, gave them a clear view of the progress they had made on the genetic engineering front, John Brideaux had conceived an idea. He wanted the professor and council members to know about it.

"Barbara, I have an idea that I would like you to hear, and if you think it's feasible, launch a project to look at how it could be implemented," John said.

"I am eager to hear about it, Mr. President," she replied.

"To overcome our challenge of indiscriminately sterilizing unchipped people with nanobots, would it be possible to develop a nanobot that would make the people very sick. If they don't get an implant within a particular time limit, that illness would eventually kill them? Of course, the only cure would be to get an implant," John explained with an evil grin on his face.

The council members and Professor Cohen loudly applauded their leader for this ingenious idea.

Professor Cohen answered, "Absolutely brilliant idea, Mr. President. That is entirely possible and could avoid the sterilization of people with a good genetic makeup, whom we actually want to produce offspring. "

The council instructed the professor to kick-off the project immediately and to report progress regularly.

Another critical item on the agenda of the council was their objective to create a new global monetary system with a single currency. It was a major operation that required a lot of planning and preparation.

The first step would be to announce another new

benefit for chipped citizens. They could now throw away all their cash and cards, because the chip would take care of all payments. It would not be necessary to carry money or cards around anymore, no more lost or stolen cards, no more identity theft. The media was going to have a field day with this new announcement.

The information about the new initiatives was always sent out to the media outlets a week or two in advance of the launch dates, to allow them time to prepare for the announcements. Thanks to the spyflies at WONN and Kelly's access to this data, the Rosslerites were getting the information at the same time as the media – and they were horrified.

Sam and his operations team were getting worried that the day when chipping would become compulsory for everyone was approaching fast, much faster than they have predicted. By their calculations, there were only a few more sweet tasting announcements that the council could make before they would initiate the final part of their plan that would see chips implanted into every living soul on earth.

When they received the information about the latest announcements that were coming, they foretold that infertility rates would soon skyrocket. Major changes to the monetary system would follow shortly after the replacement of cash and credit cards. The total collapse of the world's financial system was around the corner. That would be followed by the final push to chip all remaining people and the radical reduction of the world population.

Nonetheless, there was nothing more they could do to stop the trend, other than what they were already busy doing. They were working day and night to get the chips deciphered, which was the next and most crucial battle ahead of them. In order to aid Roy and his team's decoding efforts, Sam personally called Rube and asked him to take a message to the Tectus leaders to see if they could find a way to infiltrate the chip plant in China.

He requested that they designate some of their members to focus as much of their attention on that mission as they possibly could. A breakthrough on that front would be a colossal victory.

Rube didn't need any motivation; he understood the necessity and respected Sam Lewis and the rest of the Rosslerites. He knew that Tectus would help and assured Sam that he could count on them.

Chapter Eighty-Seven

THE PINCER PLAN

Peter arrived at the Rabbit Hole a few days after he got confirmation that the first box of chips had been delivered. He was pleasantly surprised to see how much progress they'd made in just a few days since receiving the first box. Sarah wanted to know how Kelly was doing and if he was obeying the terms and conditions of the sentence imposed on him. He was happy to say he had been a good citizen and that he hadn't failed in any of his duties.

Sam involved Peter in the operations team's research of the component manufacturers. He would contact Rube and Sombra when he was back in New York to see how he could assist Tectus to infiltrate the target companies and help them gather the required information.

Sam's operations team initiated *Operation Pincer*, the plan to set President and Mrs. Harper free. They reviewed the information they'd already collected through the spyflies and conversations with the Harpers.

With the help of Ben and Aaron, who were experienced with architectural drawings, they were able to recreate the exact layout and dimensions of the farmhouse and outbuildings. They gave the illustrations to their model building team, who created a house and farm to scale for them. They required an aerial view of the entire farm. Roy would equip a few of his zingers and owls with the necessary cameras, which Peter would deploy with the help of the Nashville Tectus agents who'd planted the spyflies before.

The operations team had a very good understanding of the routines of the presidential guards. They were quite surprised and relieved to discover that the guards were following a set routine, which had not changed in all the time since the spyflies were deployed, months ago. It seemed as if they were laid-back and didn't expect any surprises.

On the technology side, the Wi-Fi signals on the computer and surveillance networks were known, as were the computer login credentials for all of the guards. They knew the routines of exactly when, how and what the guards were reporting to the Washington security control center. They had voice recordings of the telephone reports that were sent in at the end of each day. Sam and Luke pointed out that the situation at the Harpers' residence did not differ much from what they'd seen and experienced in Boise.

Salome was alerted by that. "I am a bit troubled about the fact that they haven't changed their methods and security after the Boise incident. One would think they'd have figured out most of how that mission was accomplished and would have changed their modus operandi."

Luke replied, "You've made an excellent point there, Salome. It's apparent they have not figured out the spyflies and communications, but that doesn't mean they haven't figured out other steps. We can't assume anything. They could very well have a nasty surprise in store for us."

"I'll be surprised if they don't. We need to increase the number of spyflies and make sure we cover all rooms at all times. Once we have the additional spyflies in place, we need to assign some of our people here to monitor them carefully," Sam replied.

There was another significant issue to consider, and that was that the distance from Cookeville, Tennessee to Billings, Montana was more than one thousand six hundred miles by road. At a minimum, it was going to be a thirty-hour trip by car. It was not a safe enough option to evacuate and transport the Harpers to the Rabbit Hole by road.

They gave themselves a maximum of two hours from the time they would incapacitate the guards before the breakout would be discovered. There was a chance that it could take longer, but they felt it would be judicious to build their plan on the worst case scenario and made the assumption that they'd have only one hour – anything longer than that would be a bonus.

This analysis led them to the conclusion that the only viable option was to transport them by air. The distance from Cookeville to Billings by air was a little over one thousand one hundred and eighty nautical miles. Doug explained it was a distance that could easily be covered with a twin propeller light aircraft in about five hours without the necessity to refuel along the way.

The option of an airlift was on the table for discussion. They had to get a plane, or hire one, and that posed its own challenges. Not only that, they also had the question of who could pilot the plane, other than Doug, and how to avoid radar detection all the way from take-off to landing.

While Peter was listening to the discussions, he experienced a rush of adrenaline through his body. He and Owen had talked about this very idea, which was what Doug suggested a long time ago. That was for Owen and Alison to get private pilot licenses and buy a light plane, which they could use to commute between Nucla and Mount Ararat.

"I might have a solution for both those problems," Peter said eagerly. "As you all know, I've been planning to get out of New York after I completed my missions there, and to buy a property in this area to live on and to function as another safe house. With that in mind, Owen and I have been talking about the idea of buying a light twin prop, six-seater aircraft in partnership. Both of us are excited about the prospect of flying. I don't think Alison is as enthusiastic about the idea of becoming a pilot as Owen, but she definitely won't mind being flown around by any of us."

"So Peter, I understand that Alison seems to be okay with you and Owen's plans, but how does Kelly feel about it?" Daniel was smiling when he asked the question. He wanted to test Sarah's theory that there was something going on between the two of them.

Peter was caught off guard and began stuttering, "What does she …? Ahh… mhh … wait … yea well … hang on..." Then he stopped to get his dignity back and said with a bit more confidence, "She is very excited about the idea."

Daniel just smiled when everyone except Sam, looked at him, wondering where that came from, then realized what it meant and started laughing. Sam was grinning, he saw the dynamic between Peter and Kelly long before anyone else did, which is why he asked Peter to take her on those fishing trips. Although he was older than everyone in the room, he was the one with the most recent experience of being totally bedazzled by a beautiful woman. Among the people in the Rabbit Hole only Aaron had more recent experience than his, with Cindi sweeping him off his feet shortly after they moved into the Rabbit Hole.

Peter was a bit surprised to discover that everyone around the table already seemed to know what he only realized a few days ago - that Kelly liked him. He cleared his throat and with a bit of a laugh said, "Okay, I see there is another conspiracy going on here. Let me reveal it. I like her very much and hope the feeling is mutual. If it depended on me, I would ask her ..." he realized what he was going to say. He shut his mouth quickly and swallowed the rest of the sentence, causing everyone to explode into laughter again.

Sarah was right; I wish she could have seen Peter's reaction. She has missed a great moment. Daniel decided that he was going to re-enact that whole scene for her as best he could. And the best time would be during dinner when Peter would be present.

"Okay, you all had your chuckles at my expense now, but we still have a plane to buy and pilots to train," Peter said, trying to get out of the limelight.

Doug was more than happy to help Peter and Owen select the right plane and help them prepare for their certifications. He knew Raj had a few flight simulator games and applications on the servers, which would come in very handy in their training.

Daniel wondered how long it would take to get a private pilot's license. Peter explained it would take between forty and sixty hours of instruction to get a license for a single engine aircraft and another twenty to thirty hours to upgrade to a twin engine.

There were a few reputable flight training schools in Billings. If he and Owen put their minds to it and spent the time to get the required flying hours, they could probably complete it within two to three months. He would contact Owen later to discuss everything with him and report back.

The final issue that remained was what to do about avoiding radar detection for the duration of the flight?

Luke and Sam looked at each other and smiled. "Palladium?" Luke asked as Sam nodded his head.

Daniel and the others looked at the two of them, intrigued.

Sam explained, "Back in the cold war era, the CIA had a secret project called Palladium. It was designed to trick the Soviet radar and make spook aircraft appear on their screens, which they would then track while our aircraft was in a very different place and on a different course.

When the Soviets moved their radar operations to Cuba, we fitted one of our destroyers with the Palladium system and cruised in the waters around Cuba. This sent their pilots on a wild goose chase on many occasions while our planes were doing their surveillance in another location entirely undetected."

"We know that Roy already has the best possible radar-evading technology in operation in the owl-drones, which could be used to hide the aircraft from detection by electronic equipment during flight. The second part we need is a system that would give them a few spook planes that would send them on a snipe hunt. Something like Palladium." Doug concluded. With that, the first planning session came to a close.

It was time for afternoon Pilates, then a bit of fly-fishing, happy hour for the musketeers and then dinner. Peter missed Kelly on the fishing trip. Despite not having his mind on the task at hand, he still managed to return to the Rabbit Hole with two trout, which he prepared and handed to his hostess, Sarah.

During dinner, to Sarah's great delight, Daniel recounted Peter's revelation about Kelly, in minute detail. Peter, by now fully recovered from his awkwardness of earlier started questioning Sarah with a big smile on his face. "So, tell me more about this whole scheme that has been going on behind my back."

Sarah laughed, "Peter, I would not have believed it if anyone told me there was another person on this planet more maladroit than the three Rossler brothers around women they liked. Then I saw you with Kelly and knew that, yes, there was! It was very obvious that you needed a bit of help."

"What did you see?" Peter wanted to know.

"The girl is crazy about you and a blind man can feel with a stick that you are infatuated with her. However, for some reason you can't see how she feels about you, and you can't bring yourself to tell her." Sarah smiled while winking at Daniel.

"How long have you known all of this, and more importantly did you and Kelly talk about it?" Peter wanted to know.

Sarah was in her element, "I noticed the vibes a few days after the two of you arrived here. Yes, Kelly and I did exchange a few thoughts."

"If you ask me, Peter, it was more like an extended discussion and not just the exchange of a few thoughts as Sarah wants you to believe. You must remember my wife is the Rossler Foundation's official matchmaker!" Daniel laughed.

Peter spilled the beans. "To be honest with you, I love her. At the same time I'm scared out of my wits to tell her how I feel. I'm afraid I'll lose her if she doesn't feel the same, and I just blurt it out. She may not even want to be friends anymore! I've never met another woman that makes me so happy. There's nothing I want more than to be with her. As I almost said in a thoughtless moment in the meeting this morning, if it depended on me, I'd get in my car now, drive back to New York, and ask her to marry me. I know that sounds crazy. We barely know each other, but that's how I feel."

Sarah smiled, while she mentally ticked off another match in her record book. She just needed another short chat with Kelly. "Well, now you know there's nothing to be worried about. She's just waiting for you to say it."

After dinner, Peter spent more than an hour on the phone with Kelly. He told her about his fishing trip, and that it was not the same without her and how much he missed her. His heart almost stopped when she immediately replied, telling him how much she missed him and how much she would have liked to be there with him.

The next day, Peter called Owen and was able to report that he was very excited about the plan to start the pilot training and to buy an airplane. A day later, he went back to Mount Ararat where he and Owen finalized their flight training plans and started looking at suitable properties for him to buy. Of course, he was also keen to get back to New York as soon as possible. He had a lot to do, and besides, Kelly missed him.

Chapter Eighty-Eight

CHILLING DISCOVERIES

The information gathered and passed on by Tectus helped speed up the progress of the technical team. Two months after the Rosslerite group took delivery of the first box of chips, they were close to being able to activate some of the chips and start looking at how to neutralize the nanobots and disable the chips.

They quickly found the GPS part of the chip and the Wi-Fi frequencies it was operating on. They didn't have to activate a chip to find it. Roy found one of the components that he was sure would be used for communications and removed it. With the help from Raj and his team, once the component was removed from the chip and isolated, it could be activated and soon they knew exactly how it worked. At that point, they started looking at ways of over-riding and jamming the signals if it ever became necessary.

As they were moving ahead, Raj began building a computer-emulated model of the chip, using the code they'd swiped from the firmware during their analysis.

They made some bone-chilling discoveries. The first was

the infertility nanobot. This bot was founded on the same principles as an existing well-known contraceptive implant for women, which doctors would implant under the skin. It prevented pregnancy by releasing hormones that stopped ovaries from releasing eggs and by thickening cervical mucous. The nanobot, however, was much more powerful, and would permanently sterilize both males and females as soon as it was activated.

The second horror were the discovery of 'torture' bots which would send excruciating pain to the shoulders, face, elbows, and other areas of the body. Some of the bots would bombard the body with simulated electrical shocks and tremors, destroy brain cells, cause severe cramping in limbs as well as headaches and stomach aches. No doubt, these bots had only one purpose – to inflict pain – which was obviously aimed at merciless enforcement of civil obedience, whatever civil obedience meant in the new society.

The third shock came when they discovered functionality that would paralyze, damage, or destroy parts of the nervous system instantaneously. One of them, for instance, would paralyze certain brain parts and make it impossible for the victim to breathe. These bots were for purposes of exterminating people.

The team found the link between the chip and the carrier's DNA. Nano electronic biosensors were used to detect a person's specific biomarkers, which included antibodies, enzymes, DNA, diseased cells and foreign substances. The biosensors provided fast, exact and very specific measurements of the person's biomarkers and genetic makeup, which was then stored in the chip and in some of the nanobots.

They figured out that the mouth swabs taken before the

implant procedure were used to produce the individual's DNA sequence, which was then uploaded through the chip activator to the chip during the activation process. The chip's biosensors would analyze the person's DNA as soon as the chip was implanted, compare it with the DNA data received from the activator, and if it matched, the chip would be fully activated. Once the chip was activated, it would immediately release the killer nanobots into the bloodstream, where they would remain dormant until activated.

There were three scenarios that could activate the nanobots. Remotely, through a message from the Beast, or the moment it stopped receiving signals from the chip, or if there was a mismatch between the uploaded DNA data stored in the chip and that stored in the nanobots.

Roy and his team now knew where to focus their attention. The killer bots were roaming through the body at all times while receiving signals from the chip, and they stayed dormant as long as they received those signals. They had to devise a plan to neutralize the nanobots first, and then to deactivate the chip. They had a few options, the first of which was to deceive the nanobots by overriding the chip's signals and send it signals and DNA information from their own source.

That would keep it deactivated, however, it meant the killer bots would remain in the person's body. The big risk was that their signal source could fail, which would kill the person immediately. Another option was to recall the killer bots back to the chip, deactivate the chip and then remove it. That was if they were able to program the nanobots to follow such a command. The third and best option was to develop their own nanobot that would destroy the killer bots.

Before they could start live trials, there were some major obstacles to overcome. They didn't have the technology to analyze a person's DNA, and the chips could not be activated in the absence of human DNA. They could try to get blood and DNA data from one of the clinics. But then, even if they could get blood and DNA data, the problem was that once the chip was activated it would release the killer nanobots. If anyone were to be exposed to that blood, he or she would die.

Rebecca wondered, "How are they testing the chips at the manufacturing site in China? Surely they must have some quality control measures."

Chapter Eighty-Nine

NO BUTS, SAY IT

When Peter returned to Mount Ararat from his trip to the Rabbit Hole after delivering the second box of chips, he, Owen and Alison had a lengthy discussion about the latest plans. It was then they decided it would be better if Peter were to buy a half share in Mount Ararat and build a house on his part of the property. They would then jointly carry the cost of building a private airstrip and hanger to host their airplane. They called the Rabbit Hole and shared their plans, which were approved by the Steering Committee.

Peter returned to New York to deliver the additional spyflies and the owl drone for deployment at the Harpers' residence. Then he would meet with Rube to find out what assistance he could give them with their efforts to collect information about the chips.

Even though he yearned to spend his time in Montana with the people who'd become so important to him, being in New York had its compensations. It allowed him to spend as much time as possible with the woman he adored, who'd told him she missed him. Only when he could find a way to bring those opposing desires together would he be truly happy.

Owen had already enrolled at a flight training school in Billings and Peter at a school in New York. For each of them it would be a four-week intensive course, which would equip them with private pilot's licenses to fly single engine light aircraft, after which they would start the upgrade courses to certify them for twin-engine aircraft.

The spyflies, hummingbirds and one owl-drone were delivered to Rube via the taxi and briefcase swapping routine and were deployed as requested a few days later. Sam had more than enough volunteers, to constantly monitor every corner of the Harpers' farmhouse by working in shifts.

Rube and Peter had an appointment at a safe house for the Wednesday night. Tuesday, which was Kelly's day off, they had plans to spend the day together.

Peter did more research on light twin-engine aircraft, visited a few airfields to gather more information, and got a few test rides. On recommendation from Doug, they were interested in a six-seater, twin engine Baron G58 Beechcraft. It had a cruise speed of just over two hundred knots, which equated to about two hundred and thirty miles per hour and a range of close to one thousand five hundred nautical miles. That was the ideal plane for their purposes, current and future.

On Tuesday morning, Kelly and Peter met over breakfast and decided to spend the day visiting Central Park in the morning, lunch at McDonalds – a special and secret sin Kelly allowed herself only twice a month – then watch one of the latest movies, followed by dinner. By the time they came out of the movie theatre, neither of them felt like going through the trouble of dressing up to go to a fancy restaurant.

"I have an idea," Kelly said, smiling. "Why don't we go back to my place and cook our own dinner? You are such a handyman in the kitchen, I'm sure we can concoct something edible."

"That's a good idea, but be forewarned - I can only cook what comes out of cans or can be microwaved." Peter laughed.

They went back to Kelly's apartment, tried to make beef stroganoff, messed everything up completely, and almost set the fire alarm off in the process. This produced lots of 'Ooohs and Ooops' and peals of laughter. Finally, they ordered Chinese takeout. It was that or go to bed with empty stomachs.

Peter cleaned the dishes and sat down on the couch, and then Kelly came and snuggled into his arm. She looked up at him with a big smile on her face and said, "So, Peter Scott. Tell me what did you and Sarah talk about when you were there?"

Peter realized that Sarah must have spoken to her since he left. "Well, mhh, let me see, I can't remember all of it, but she said she liked the trout I caught. She also wanted to know if I was still obeying the conditions of my sentence imposed by the court ... let me see, what else was there..." Peter smiled as he teased Kelly, who clearly knew exactly what was said, thanks to Sarah's matchmaking ploy.

Kelly grabbed him by his ear and said, "Stop it! You know what I'm talking about!"

"Aha, got you! You spoke to Sarah since my last visit. Didn't you?" Peter laughed as Kelly started blushing.

"Well, yes. We had a short chat and exchanged a few thoughts." She giggled.

"Let me guess. When you say 'a short chat', that means it was more than an hour but less than two?" Peter gibed.

"Yes, something like that," she replied, now displaying a full-blown blush while she still had him by the ear.

Peter said, "Let go of my ear, and I will tell you everything."

"Just remember, I know everything that was said, I just want to check your version of it," she warned him.

"Kelly, I told her that I am in love with you but that I was worried to tell you how I feel, because I'm afraid I will lose you. I told her that I have never met anyone that makes me so happy, and that there was nothing I wanted more than to be with you. There you have it. Now you can kick me out if you want to," Peter said, his expression betraying his nerves. "I know it sounds crazy to tell someone who you've met so recently that you love her, but that's how I feel."

Kelly leaned back to look at him, her eyes sparkling with mischief, then held up four fingers, counted three down and said, "No, you left one part out. You've covered everything else. I'm waiting for that part."

Peter knew he was in for it now, and he had to spit it out, "Okay, okay. I did leave out something, but …"

"No buts. Say it." Kelly was enjoying every moment of it.

"I also said that, if it depended on me, I would get in my car, drive back to New York, and ask you to marry me." Peter stated in a serious tone while searching her face for any indications of how she felt.

"Yes, that covers everything. Well, I guess you must have changed your mind then, because you did drive back to New York in your car, and you saw me. But you haven't asked the question," Kelly replied while she snuggled closer to him.

Peter was breathless and speechless for a few moments. He took her face in both his hands, looked her in the eyes, and saw what he was looking for. "Kelly Edwards, will you marry me?"

"Yes! Of course I will. You were supposed to know that weeks ago! What took you ..." was all she managed to get out before he kissed her.

When they came up for air she whispered, "When did you know?"

He whispered back, "Before I met you."

"What! How is that possible? Are you kidding me?" she wanted to know.

"I'm the one who you were wearing that stunningly beautiful turquoise scarf for in Nashville, on the day when you had your interview with President Harper. In other words, to answer your question, it was the moment I first laid eyes on you." Peter smiled at Kelly, whose mouth was hanging open.

"I didn't know you were there. No one told me. Where were you? Where did you see me?" she wanted to know.

"You know the rules of the spy game and the principle of need-to-know. I was at the hotel where you were staying, and I saw you when you returned from the interview," he replied with a big smile.

"Okay, now it's your turn. When did you know?" he wanted to know.

"When you taught me fly-fishing at the Rabbit Hole, which is why Sam let you do all the teaching and he stayed away." She laughed.

They stopped talking and sat in a daze looking at each

other for a long time, enjoying it. Nothing else mattered - they were the happiest people in the world.

After a while, reality started setting in. They had a few decisions to make. They would keep their engagement secret to protect Peter from the public eye. Ring shopping would take place on Saturday, and Kelly would only wear the ring when in her disguise or when in his or her apartment.

Peter just laughed when Kelly commented, "I guess those are the sacrifices spooks have to make when they fall in love."

"Don't worry. When this mess is over, you will have the rest of your life to show your ring to the world," Peter remarked.

"Oh, yes, please, and when?" she said as they fell to enjoying a happy and contented night together.

Sarah could wait until tomorrow.

Chapter Ninety

THE CHINESE CONNECTION

Wednesday night, Rube and Sombra turned up at the safe house as agreed. Once they had a pen of silence deployed, they got right down to business. Rube reported that their information gathering operation was going well, and the good news was that they'd activated two of their hackers in China a few days ago, Gui and Jian. They were expecting to hear from them in a few days.

Peter questioned them about their method of communications with the Chinese hackers, to which they replied that they were using steganography techniques on websites in the Dark Net. The messages, even if intercepted, would not be compromised, because they only contained food recipes. The reader would have to know what the inclusion or exclusion of items meant, as well as what the order and quantities of ingredients meant.

He listened to them, asked for clarification on a few things, and in the end he was satisfied that they were using a safe method to send simple messages back and forth. However, once the hackers were able to infiltrate the plant's computer systems, the current communications method would not be suitable for sending the collected information back.

Rube grinned while he explained one of their online shops sold cowboy clothing and had just received an order from China for a few pairs of boots and belts with great big buckles. It took a few seconds for Peter to comprehend that the boots, leather belts, and buckles were fitted with spyflies and other gadgets before they were shipped.

Rube continued to explain that they didn't send the new generation spyflies that could be linked back to Raj via the mirrors. They were not keen on sharing that technology with too many people. Rube also explained they'd sent their contacts a few other technical gadgets, which they could use to send information back. The plan was that once the Chinese agents were able to get the information, he would buy something from their online store.

Peter was happy with their arrangements. He conveyed Sam's and the rest of the Rosslerites' gratitude for their help. He then gave them a quick update on the progress Roy and his team had made, thanks to the information they'd dispatched.

When Peter arrived at Kelly's apartment, the addictive aroma of a curry pulled him in and welcomed him. He was surprised. "You actually know how to cook?"

Kelly had a mischievous sparkle in her eyes as she put her arms around his neck. "Oh, yes, I know, but when I am trying to talk a man into asking me to marry him, I get nervous and forget how to do it. But then..." she paused, "You should also remember that I know how to defrost and warm up food after taking it out of the packet."

Peter laughed and said, "I get the impression it would be good for the two of us to take a few cooking classes before we leave New York. There are no takeaways at Mount Ararat or the Rabbit Hole, you know."

"That would be a lot of fun! I'll see if I can find a place we can attend in the evenings after work. With my connections, we might even find a cordon bleu school that might turn us into world class chefs." She laughed.

"Kelly, we haven't had much chance to talk about this, but are you sure you want to give up everything you have here and move into the rough country?" he asked.

"I can't wait for us to get out of this city and live out there! There's nothing that would make me happier than to be there with you. I had the best time – correction; that would be second best time of my life – out there with you a few weeks ago," she said.

"Care to tell me about the best time?" he wanted to know.

She put her arms around his neck again, kissed him, and said, "Peter, that time started last night."

The Chinese Tectus agents got their spyflies, studied the instructions that came with them carefully, practiced how to operate the gadgets, and tried to smuggle some of them into the manufacturing plant.

However, on their first attempt they discovered that the production line was a fortress. Workers had to take a shower, change into special disinfected clothes and gloves, and wear full-face masks, as well as present for a retina and chip scan before they could enter the production area. The production line area was sterile and completely isolated - many times more hygienic than a hospital operating room.

They managed to get one of their spyflies into the area and were surprised to find that the entire production line was automated. The only humans in the room were those checking and maintaining the robots.

They surmised, after a few hours of watching, that there was not much they could learn from looking at the robots. They retrieved the spyfly and started looking for the computer control room. They located that in another part of the compound and found it much easier to infiltrate. Soon they had three spyflies inside the computer center and were collecting information.

Rube reported the good news to Peter and told him that he expected to place his first order for samples of bamboo clothing from China within a week.

In the meantime, Peter's flight training commenced, which kept him busy almost full time during the day for the next four weeks. He enjoyed every bit of it - the real thing was much more exhilarating than he ever imagined it would be.

Upon arrival of the first consignment of bamboo clothing they'd ordered after getting the news that their Chinese colleagues had some information, Rube and Sombra examined the clothes. They found strands of nanofiber carrying the information neatly woven into the fabric. The information was extracted and passed on to Raj and his team, who got into it immediately.

The first batch of information from China contained

details of the exact assembly process and the sequence in which the components were fitted onto the chip. This was valuable information, which helped them to enhance their computer model.

The next bit of exciting information was the complete details of all the contractors who were involved in the development of the components. The bad news was that many of the contracted companies were not located in the United States. Some were in China and Taiwan, some in Japan, and a few in Europe.

Nevertheless, on the positive side, this information helped them get a much better idea of the makeup of the chips and precise information about which companies were involved in the component manufacturing. Tectus' hackers could now focus their full attention on those organizations.

They were still stuck on the issue of conducting live trials. A message was passed on to Gui and Jian to find the quality control center and try to gain access to it.

The two of them went to work and deployed a spyfly into the production area again to follow the process carefully. They knew that somewhere along the line, chips would be collected for quality control checks. On the second day of their surveillance, Gui pointed Jian to a small container close to the end of the assembly line and asked him to maneuver the fly closer. That was when they saw a chip dropping into the bucket every few minutes.

They stayed on it for a few hours and saw how the bucket with chips was removed by a robot and placed into a small box on the wall. The next time it happened, they saw that the first container, which they expected to see in the box, had disappeared. They'd discovered the quality control line; they now had to find the lab that was receiving those chips. The compound was an enormous place, so it took them two days, with three spyflies in operation, to find what they were looking for. Then they went to work.

Chapter Ninety-One

THE THINGS I SAW BEGGAR DESCRIPTION

The Tectus hackers had the time of their lives when they singled out the contractor companies one at a time, combined forces and attacked their computer networks from all directions with every tool in their arsenal. In some cases they managed to break in and collect all the information they wanted within hours, others took them a few days – nonetheless, they were moving forward in leaps and bounds.

Information was streaming into the Rabbit Hole much quicker than the technical teams could analyze and reverse engineer. It was not an issue, as Roy pointed out, "This is a nice problem to have, much better than having to deal with a lack of information."

Rube and Sombra were extremely pleased with the quality of the shipment of bamboo clothing samples they received and placed an order for a large quantity to stock their warehouse and ship directly to their online customers. Three weeks after Gui and Jian got access to the quality control facilities the shipment of bamboo clothing cleared customs in New York and Peter received a call from Rube, who sounded extremely distressed. He asked, almost demanded, an urgent meeting that same night.

Peter was on high alert when he walked into the safe house that night. His first observation of Rube and Sombra was that they'd seen a ghost or worst. The two of them looked sick.

"My friends, you don't look well. What's going on?" Peter wanted to know.

Rube replied, "That's because we are sick, Peter. We received the second batch of information earlier today. What we saw is the cause of our nausea. We wanted to show it to you before sending it to Raj."

"That sounds dangerous, Rube. What have you got?" a worried Peter asked.

"Be warned, what we are about to show you will make your worst nightmares look like a birthday party," Sombra replied. Peter noticed how his hands were shaking while he started his tablet.

Within ten minutes, anyone observing Peter would have reached the same conclusion about him; he looked sick, in fact, he was very ill. "My God! How is this possible! How could human beings ..." Was all he could stutter before he had to run to the bathroom.

When he returned, he looked at his companions and said, "I'll call Sam and prepare him for what's coming. We have to get this over to them now."

He phoned the Rabbit Hole. Sam took the call, immediately gathered that Peter wasn't okay, and inquired.

"Sam, I'm with Rube and Sombra. They have just shown me the latest information from China. It's the most horrific stuff I've seen in my entire life. There is no horror I can imagine that would even begin to describe what I have just witnessed." Peter's voice was trembling.

"Shit man, what are you talking about! What is it?" Sam was worried. It was clear that Peter was extremely distressed.

"You better have a look at it. Sombra is sending it as we speak. I suggest that you look at it before you decide who else should see this."

When the call ended, Raj had the files and handed Sam the laptop. There were more than six hours of video footage and over a hundred pages of text showing in detail what was happening at the quality control center. There were also many more files containing technical information. Sam was sick within a few minutes, but he managed to get through two hours of it before he woke Luke, Daniel, and Salome and took them to the meeting room.

Sam gave them a summary of what to expect and then turned on the video. The quality control lab was a twelve-story building. On the outside above the main entry, the words Science Advisory Panel Headquarters were clearly visible in English and Chinese. This was where Professor Barbara Cohen, head of the Science Advisory Panel of the Supreme Council, was stationed.

Nothing of Sam's introduction, or for that matter any warning, could have prepared them for what they were seeing and reading as the videos took them floor by floor through the building. It was not a quality control lab - it was a human experimentation center. There were a few thousand people kept like animals, tied to chairs and beds in soundproof cubicles that would stifle their screams and agony. Syringes carrying nanobots and cocktails of drugs, chemicals, viruses, and bacteria were injected into the helpless victims while their reactions were monitored, recorded, and analyzed. On one of the floors, they kept people of different races with the explicit objective of developing race and descendant-particular sterility and death causing chemicals.

Some of the chips from the assembly line were tested for quality by implanting them into the human subjects and activating them. After the implant, they would send signals to the chip to test that everything was working correctly. The victims' agony was clearly visible and audible as they were trembling, convulsing, vomiting and gasping for air from the effects of the torture bots. Relief was clearly visible on their faces as death mercifully set them free when the final button was pushed that would kill them.

In some cases the button was not pushed, the chip would be ripped out of the victim's body to make sure the killer bots were activated. The bodies of the dead were carried out and new victims were dragged into the cubicle for the next quality test.

Outside the building, trucks were lined up in two parallel lines; one line of trucks was waiting to be filled with corpses, while the other line delivered the doomed. One of the enclosed documents stressed the fact that the facility was in operation 24/7 and so were the lines of trucks outside. They had a seemingly endless supply of human guinea pigs.

Two floors were dedicated to experiments to find cures for various incurable diseases, such as cancer, Alzheimer's, Multiple Sclerosis, and others. The terminally ill were brought in and subjected to the latest untested drugs and treatment, which in most cases ended with their horrific death.

Much of their medical research was focused on the study of virus and bacterial infections. Victims were given injections carrying the viruses and bacteria and then the progression of the infection was monitored while the victims were being treated with experimental drugs. The deadliest viruses known to science, such as Ebola, Rabies, HIV, Marburg, Hanta, Dengue, Rota and various strains of Influenza, received top priority.

The documents retrieved from the servers and computers revealed details of every experiment that was in progress. The files from Professor Barbara Cohen's computer had the details of projects still in the pipeline.

The genetic engineering and cloning experiments were conducted on the fifth floor. When they got to the top floor, the opening scene had the four of them screaming with rage. It was filled with babies!

Daniel was on his feet hissing through his teeth. "God, what have I done? I am going to get Roy now. I want him to stop what he is doing and build me a nanonuke, and then I am going to Brussels. I have caused this. I should never have allowed that 8th Cycle project. I should never have trusted Brideaux. I have to rectify this. The blood of those people is on my hands and my conscience." Daniel's whole body was shaking.

Sam put his arm around Daniel's shoulder while Salome and Luke stood next to him. "Son, that is not true. That is not what happened. You are not evil. You were not negligent and you are not responsible. You carry no blame." Sam looked at Salome and gave her a slight nod to take over; she had much better psychological skills than he did.

She managed to get Daniel to sit and calmed him down. "Sorry about that," he said after a while. "Of course, we all feel the same, and yet, I'm the one throwing a tantrum."

"Don't worry about that," Salome said, with as much of a smile as she could muster while desperately trying not to run out and throw up. "That tantrum was on behalf of all of us."

They were all numb and silent.

Sam searched for something on the laptop and found it. "This is as bad as the World War II Nazi death camps. Here is what General Eisenhower said when the Nazi extermination camps were discovered. *'The things I saw beggar description. The visual evidence and the verbal testimony of starvation, cruelty, and bestiality were so overpowering. I made the visit deliberately, in order to be in a position to give first hand evidence of these things if ever, in the future, there develops a tendency to charge these allegations to propaganda.'"* When he stopped reading, Sam drew in a ragged breath.

Daniel regained his composure, "Sam, like Eisenhower, I want this place photographed, videoed and documented. Every file and every email must be collected; absolutely nothing must be left out. The world has to see this."

They all agreed with Daniel. The world had to see it. Sam undertook to ask Rube to send through this request to China.

Daniel asked the question on everyone's mind, "Who among our community needs to know about this and who doesn't?"

They decided that the full Steering Committee had to know and, for now, no one else. Their first reason for not wanting to show it to the rest of the adult population in the Rabbit Hole, was to spare their sensibilities. At some point, it may be necessary, but until there was a compelling reason to show it to others, they felt they needed more time to think through the possible consequences.

When Peter left the safe house, he had a dilemma. He knew he would not be able to hide his shock from Kelly, but he desperately wanted to protect her from the horror that he had just seen. Kelly was a mentally strong person, but this had nothing to do with a healthy psyche. It was something that would upset any normal human being, irrespective of gender or state of mind.

When he turned up at her apartment, he had his mind made up. She took one step towards him when he opened the door, saw his face, and said, "Peter, something's wrong. What is it?"

"Kelly, come and sit down with me. I'll tell you."

Kelly could feel his sorrow and huddled into his arm as he started talking about what he'd seen. She was in tears, her body shaking, when he came to the end and told her about the floor with the babies.

"Oh my God! Peter, we have to stop this insanity!" she cried. "I haven't even seen the videos and I'm sick. I'm not sure I want to see it. It must be terrible for you that you had to watch it."

Neither of them could go to sleep that night. They switched on the bed lights, found comfort in each other's arms and talked until sunrise, when she phoned her office to tell them she wouldn't be in that day. It was the first sick day in her entire working career.

They decided that it was time to start wrapping up their lives in New York. They knew their time in the city was rapidly coming to an end. The mountains of the Gallatin National Forest would soon be their home. Consequently, they decided to put both their apartments on the market that same day. They would rent a place close to her work. They still had more work to do, but the moment Roy and his team had the chip unraveled and they were ready to set

President Harper and his wife free, the two of them would move. Peter had already decided that he wouldn't want to let Kelly stay in New York while he was on that final mission.

At sunrise, everyone in the Rabbit Hole attended the daily Pilates session and had breakfast. Afterward, they went on their way to their daily tasks. Salome and Daniel had prepared Roy and Sarah for what was awaiting them at the Steering Committee meeting that morning. Daniel gave the attendees an overview of what he and the three others had already seen and warned them of the graphic and shocking nature of it. Even Sarah and Roy, who were forewarned, were shaking with fury when they reached the end.

The individuals in the group reacted no differently than those who'd seen this before. Roy wanted to start a nuclear war - he was ready to start building nanonukes and killer lasers. JR, Mark, and Doug wanted to gather a brigade of Marines. Rebecca, who had seen more human suffering than anyone in the meeting, could not stop the tears. Sinclair and Raj were pale and wordless.

Those who watched it before were revisited by the same nauseating feelings of a few hours earlier. There was just no way to not be repulsed by those scenes, no matter how many times they watched the video.

Strange enough, it was as if Daniel's outburst earlier had cleared his mind and helped him to think logically. "Roy and Raj. I suggest that you take the technical information and see if there is any useful information in there. I also propose that we consider sending those guys in China more and better equipment."

"Yes, I agree," responded Roy. "We should try to at least get the new generation spyflies to them. They could also do with the earphones and microphones, but I'm not sure about a mirror phone. We should think about that."

A short discussion followed, during which Sam, Luke, and Salome shot down the idea of sending new generation spyflies to China. They would rather accept the fact that it would take longer to find the solution than take the risk of compromising their communications system.

When Rebecca left the meeting, upset as she was, she managed to get herself to think rationally. She was part of the technical team - well aware of the progress that had been made and of the fact that they still had to resolve the live testing issue. The whole effort of reverse engineering the chips would be fruitless unless they could find a solution for that problem.

She got Jack, Roy, and Raj together. "I think we are quickly approaching the end of the road with our efforts to reverse engineer the chips. Soon we will have everything in place except for a solution to the problem of conducting live tests. We will be at a dead end, unless we resolve that problem."

"Any ideas, Rebecca?" Jack wanted to know.

"Not the solution if that is what you want to know. Nevertheless, I'm of the view that our Chinese collaborators got sidetracked when they saw what was going on in that place. I don't blame them for that, it would have more than sidetracked me and, I guess, any normal human being," Rebecca explained.

Raj immediately caught onto what Rebecca was saying.

"I agree, we need to get them to find the path of those chips that are removed from the production line for quality checks. Is that what you have in mind?"

"Exactly. I am ready to bet that if we find the place where they check those chips, we'll find our answer." she replied.

"Okay, let me have a quick word with Sam to clear it with him, and I will be on the phone to Rube." Raj said.

The technical team submerged themselves in the remaining technical data. A few days later, they had the complete picture of the puzzle they'd been working on for what seemed a very long time from the day they held the first box of chips in their hands. They knew exactly how each component functioned and had the videos to remind them of the effect of the nanobots. With the blueprints of the parts and nanobots, they started building their own nanobots that would neutralize or destroy those released by the chips.

Chapter Ninety-Two

THE PILOTS

Peter and Owen were the proud owners of private pilot's licenses for single engine aircraft. Alison and Kelly were taken on short flying trips at every opportunity and enjoyed it. The next step for the men would be to be certified in night flying and twin-engine aircraft before they'd be ready to purchase the Baron G58.

Peter had a pleasant surprise in store for Kelly when he asked her to take a long weekend and accompany him on a trip to meet two friends. She was not allowed to know the destination or the names of the friends. She played along and controlled her curiosity as best she could. Her inquisitiveness almost got the better of her when they turned up at a private airport just twelve miles from Manhattan, got into the two-seater Cessna and took off.

Two hours into the flight, she could not hold in her curiosity anymore and employed all her charm on Peter to tell her where they were going. He had to give in and tell her they were heading for Cape Cod for a weekend of brown trout fishing. What he didn't tell her was that Owen and Alison would be waiting for them as part of the first celebration of their secret engagement. It would be the first opportunity Kelly would have to show her ring to anyone other than Peter and talk about the man she loved with someone other than Sarah.

She enjoyed the flying so much she started wondering if she should also take flying lessons, but decided that it wouldn't fit into her current schedule while still working at WONN. She'd think about it again when they lived in Montana.

When they landed at the airport, Owen and Alison were there to pick them up, much to Kelly's delight. Owen and Alison had also traveled by plane all the way from Montrose, making stops along the way. They'd taken a side trip to include a visit to his 'outlaws,' as Owen liked to refer to Alison's parents. His first words to Peter were, "What a pleasant way to travel man! I don't think I ever want to sit behind the steering wheel of a car again. I should have become a pilot a long time ago."

That night, while having dinner, Owen said he wanted to tell Kelly about a conversation he and Peter had not too long ago. "You see Kelly; he phoned me one night to talk to me about farming and asked for my advice. I told him everything I knew. Then suddenly he said he had plans to go farming, but he reckoned it was something that he couldn't do without a wife. He wanted to know if Alison and I could help him find a wife, because he said he got the impression there was no perfect woman left in the world that would want to marry him. So, we set out to help the poor man fulfil his dreams, and had to go through this whole elaborate scheme just to get the two of you together."

Peter just shook his head when he heard how Owen had filled in a few details of his own.

By now, Kelly had Peter by the ear again, "Oh, I see. Is that how it happened? Come on I want to hear your version."

Try as he might, it was two against one; Peter could not get his version to sound believable. It was a relaxing and joyful weekend with Owen having them shouting with laughter at times with all his larks. They had no idea what a shock was waiting for them when they returned to New York.

The Supreme Council was in conference, discussing their plans to move the world to a new currency system.

"It's time that we hand out our last gift to the people," John Brideaux said with an evil smirk on his face, while looking around at the members of the Supreme Council.

"Mr. President, we are ready when you give us the word," replied the financial advisor.

The financial advisor explained the plan. They would launch a pilot program in one of the South Pacific island nations such as Samoa, Tonga or Fiji, monitor the results carefully and make changes as required. Once the pilot program was completed, they would roll it out worldwide. The first step would be to write off all debt for individuals in exchange for taking a chip. Those who already carried a chip would get the same benefit. All credit card debt, overdrafts, mortgages and personal loans would be wiped out overnight.

They knew the financial world would collapse into chaos when that happened; stock and money markets would crash. Every currency in the world would become worthless.

That was exactly what they wanted to happen. In the

ensuing chaos, they would introduce their new monetary system —virtual, electronic money, no cash — and their computers and chips would control it. That would make it impossible for anyone without a chip to buy or sell. The payment bots on chips would be activated and cash registers would be replaced with chip scanners to record transactions. Fraud, embezzlement and theft would be something of the past.

It was an elaborate and unscrupulous plan that required careful planning and timing, absolute precision and flawless execution. They expected resistance on many fronts, including chaos at banks and ATM machines from people trying to withdraw their money. Civil unrest was expected. They would have to make sure law enforcement agencies were ready to deal with issues. People lining up to be chipped would flood the chipping centers, therefore those facilities had to be reinforced with additional staff and police.

The media had a significant role to play in getting the initial announcement out and then getting messages out during the expected crisis. A few of the selected big media outlets had to be given advance notice so they had enough time to prepare and be ready for the big day.

With a well-planned project, the Council members were satisfied that the pilot program could be kicked off with no unexpected trouble.

Late on Monday afternoon, back at work after her long weekend at Cape Cod and shortly before Kelly was due to go home, the station CEO called an urgent meeting in the boardroom. On arrival, she immediately noticed that all of the most senior WONN staff members were present. Something important must be afoot.

In his opening address, the CEO announced how proud he was that WONN had been honored. It was chosen as one of only a few media outlets across the world to receive the information he was about to reveal to them. Before he went into the details, he issued a harsh warning to the members that this was for their ears only. It was in the strictest confidence until further notice. Their jobs and the station's future depended on their ability to keep it secret.

He then went into the details of the Supreme Council's plans to introduce their monetary measures to the world. Kelly was well aware of the Council's agenda and she knew the one world currency was in the pipeline, but she'd expected the announcement to happen a year or two into the future. She was watching the people in the room to try and gauge their reactions and body language. She was surprised to identify quite a few who were obviously troubled and some even agitated by what they were hearing.

She just hoped that the spyflies were in operation in the boardroom and doing their job. When the CEO finished, he allowed a few questions. The pilot program would be implemented in Samoa and would run for a maximum of two months. The rest of the world would follow thirty days after that. They had three months to prepare.

"Kelly, you have the most popular program here at our station, and it will be expected of you to contribute heavily to this initiative," the CEO told her.

"It will be my pleasure, sir." She allowed her face to smile and her mouth to speak while everything else inside her was in revolt.

When she arrived at their apartment, Peter had dinner ready. This was the result of their evening cooking classes, which they'd been enjoying so much. She told him about the meeting she just attended and when the announcement was expected. The two of them had discussed this scenario at length before. There were no surprises except for the timing.

"That means we have less than three months to get our ducks in a row, including the evacuation of President Harper and his wife. Do you think we'll be able to pull it off?" she asked.

"It's difficult to say. We're entirely dependent on a few technology breakthroughs now. My understanding is that there are only a few more things we need, but without them, we are still nowhere. I'll call Sam after dinner to find out if they made a recording of your meeting, and I'll find out what we can do to help." He said.

"I am not much of a guru when it comes to finance. However, I do know that in three months, our money will be worthless and we won't be able to buy anything," she commented.

"It's good that we sold our apartments so quickly. The property would be next to worthless within a few days after that announcement. Owen and I will have to buy that plane very soon and we'll have to make sure we have all the building material for our house at Mount Ararat," he said.

"Yes, that makes sense. I guess we also have to get rid of our stock portfolios and cash. What do you think?" she wanted to know.

"Oh yes, definitely. We have to sell those and buy precious metals, such as platinum, gold and silver. And we certainly won't give it to a bank for safekeeping," he said with a smile. "We just have to do it in such a way that it doesn't raise any suspicion. But you can leave that to me. I have a few good contacts in the financial world."

"We can't hide it under the mattress. We should think about where we can hide something like that." She smiled.

"I've just been thinking. You know I wonder if we should delay our plan to set President and Mrs. Harper free until after this announcement. The chaos that will follow could be the ideal distraction for us to execute Operation Pincer while all of law enforcement would be busy with crowd control," he mused.

After dinner, they called Sam and got confirmation that the Rabbit Hole group had the video of the meeting. Sam told them the Steering Committee had come to the same conclusions. All cash should be invested in precious metals, and any purchases that had to be made should be completed before the announcement. After the announcement, the only way to survive without being chipped would be through bartering. He also agreed with Peter's idea that it might be better to wait for the chaos that would follow the announcement to execute Operation Pincer.

Sam gave him an update on the progress made by the technical teams, and told him he was confident that a breakthrough was imminent.

Chapter Ninety-Three

MANDATORY DEATH PENALTY

Gui and Jian were inspired by Rube's plea to find the end destination of the chips coming off the production line for quality checks. The images of the suffering of those poor souls in that institution were etched into their minds, and they understood what the implication of a breakthrough on that front would be.

They were absolutely committed to finding it. Starting with mapping out every corner of the Science Advisory Panel Headquarters building, then room by room, they followed the people going in and out, carefully videoing and documenting everything happening inside. They reported their progress to Rube regularly through the Dark Net websites.

At the same time, the technical team at the Rabbit Hole focused their attention on constructing their own nanobots, which would be used to eliminate those in the chips.

Roy started working on a radar decoy system to install on the airplane that would airlift the Harpers, plus their own version of Palladium that would be used when they were ready to launch Operation Pincer. Sam and his team regularly revisited the Operation Pincer plans, poring over the new images and footage received from the additional spyflies and hummingbirds they'd deployed over the Harpers' farm, weeks ago.

They had a scale model of the entire farm, outbuildings, complete with roads, fences and gates. The model of the residence was updated long ago and they now knew the place better than most of the inhabitants did.

Salome remained worried about the 'trap' that she was convinced would be there. As they were speculating about what and where it could be she got a brainwave and shouted, "That's it! I think I've got it!"

"What is it, Salome?" Luke was first to ask.

"Everyone in that house and on that farm is chipped. I am convinced that's how they did it. They have sensors throughout the house that tracks every movement of the people and they know at all times who's there and where they are," she said. The realization made her voice shake. It had to be, and they'd almost walked blindly into the trap.

The rest of them looked at Salome and each other in astonishment. It was there all the time, right under their noses. Daniel called Raj and asked that he join them for a few minutes.

When he arrived, they explained Salome's notion to him. Raj just smiled and said, "Imagine the trouble we could have walked into, were it not for an astute ex-FBI agent in our midst."

He told them that he already had the frequencies the chips operated on, since they'd reverse engineered the GPS feature. But the spyflies had not yet been programmed to scan for that. He asked that they allow him a few hours to investigate. Late that afternoon, Raj called them to the computer center and showed them what they were looking for. Indeed, Salome had hit the nail on the head. There were chip scanners all over the place. Those scanners reported to a central computer, which was linked to the Washington Security Control Center. If someone without a chip in his body walked into that house, those who monitored would instantly know about it.

"How would you overcome that?" Sam asked. He expected Raj would probably have an answer ready.

"It is not going to be easy. We cannot pull the same trick we did in Boise when we recorded the activities and signals for a few days, then hijacked their computers and fed the recordings to them. They would know what we did there and would have countermeasures in place." Raj replied.

"Any ideas at this stage?" Daniel wanted to know.

"Nothing I am going to talk about, yet." Raj laughed. "Leave it to me and the team. We'll work it out and let you know. As Sam always says, 'where there is a will, there is a way'."

Jian pointed at the screen in front of them and said, "Gui, follow that guy walking down the corridor, let's see where he works. I've spotted him in the hallways a few times before, but have not been able to figure out what he does and where his workplace is."

Gui quickly moved the spyfly closer to the man and when he stopped in front of a door, where his chip was scanned to give him access, the spyfly landed on the back of his shoulder.

Almost immediately, the two of them realized this was the place they'd been trying to find for many weeks now.

They started recording immediately and managed to get two additional spyflies into the room as people came in to drop off new parcels or containers from the production line.

After two days of intensive observation of the man's routine, they were convinced they'd captured the entire process. They hacked into the computers on the workbench, intercepted and copied a few of the reports generated by the quality check software.

They had quite a bit of fun watching this man and his frolics while on his own, sometimes singing out loud, jumping up and dancing around to the tune of the music in his ears. To them it seemed as if he had those earphones permanently fixed in his ears, they never saw him without them.

They reported their discovery to Rube, who immediately placed an order for a few samples of the latest bamboo attire to be delivered via FedEx. The technical team was excited to receive the latest information. The discovery of the quality control room and the process was a significant step forward. The next challenge was to get a copy of the software and one of those devices into which the chips were inserted for testing. Gui and Jian were already working on that.

The two of them realized, because they were not chipped, it would be impossible for them to get into the facility. Even if they were chipped, it would be near impossible with all the security checks employees had to go through. Their only option was to get someone on the inside who would cooperate with them, but they knew no one there.

They decided to follow the man, who called himself Guozhi, they'd learned from the loud conversations he had with himself while alone in his lab. A spyfly was planted in his backpack, and when he went home, Jian and Gui followed him at a distance on their scooters.

Once they had his address, they deployed more spyflies and started monitoring all his after-work activities. Guozhi lived on his own in a small apartment. From their initial surveillance, it didn't look as if he had many friends. It seems as if he lived a lonely and mundane life. They were wondering if they should 'arrange' a date for him with one of the Tectus female agents to see if she could help to get them what they wanted from that lab.

They were just about to make the necessary arrangements to bring a bit of excitement into Guozhi's dull life when he surprised them. On the Friday night when he returned from work he acted excited, singing and dancing around his apartment while he dressed up. It was obvious he was on his way out. They followed him with great interest.

The next morning, although Gui and Jian were surprised with what they'd discovered about Guozhi's private life, they had what they were looking for. Guozhi was gay. They had graphic and irrefutable evidence on video, complete with sound.

Under the rule of the new government, homosexuality was a crime, and it carried a mandatory death penalty.

Chapter Ninety-Four

BLOW SMOKE UP THEIR SKIRTS

The Supreme Council's looming financial changes kicked everyone in Tectus and the Rabbit Hole into top gear. They'd decided that they wouldn't launch Operation Pincer before the announcement, as they wanted to use the distractions of the chaos that would follow in the wake of the proclamation at Peter's suggestion. However, they couldn't wait for too long after that. They were working against the clock to be ready before the announcement was made.

The technical team hadn't received new information from Gui and Jian since they reported they'd found the quality control lab. An analysis of the reports sent by them clearly showed that the chips were activated and deactivated a number of times during the quality check process. They knew the software running on those computers and the connected devices held the key to the elusive shutdown routine. The lack of news from China was frustrating and stressful.

The best Rube could get out of Gui and Jian was that their efforts had paid off. They'd made a breakthrough, but it would take about two weeks before they could expect to have the reward in their hands.

Daniel and the rest of the Operations Team paid Raj and his crew a visit in the computer lab to get an update on their progress with the chip scanners at the Harpers' house. They were not disappointed.

"As you know, we've discovered the frequencies on which the chips operate quite a few weeks ago. We also discovered that each chip has a unique thirty-two-digit number, which is sent to the chip scanner to identify the person. That number is embedded in the GPS module of the chip. Obviously, the reason for that is to know a person's exact location at any given moment," Raj explained.

"Sorry to interrupt, but I need to know how you were able to test that, especially since you can't activate the chips?" Luke wanted to know.

"You see, the chips are assembled from a selection of modules. Some interact with each other and some operate in isolation, such as the GPS module. Its only function is to report the carrier's location. Because it's a stand-alone module, in other words, it doesn't need the chip to be able to function, we were able to remove it from the chip and reconstruct it," Raj replied.

"Very interesting, Raj. We're all ears," Daniel said.

Raj continued. "Okay, so next we fabricated our own version of the chip scanner and tested it against the GPS module of the chip. It worked very well. In fact, we tested it with quite a few of the chips and were able to retrieve the chip ID numbers with ease from as far away as five yards.

"So now that we can read the chip numbers, what's next?" Sam wanted to know.

Raj smiled, "Well, we uploaded a small piece of code to the spyflies in operation at the president's house and retrieved the chip numbers of everyone in the house. Here is the list of ID numbers and the names of everyone."

"What! Come on Raj. You're kidding me, man! That's not possible. You really have those numbers? And the names?" Sam looked ready to dance a jig.

"I am not joking. We do indeed have the names and numbers. I can demonstrate it to you, if you want." Raj laughed.

"Sorry, I didn't mean it like that," Sam apologized. "It's just that I'm so technically challenged that these things all sound like fairy tales to me."

"No worries Sam, that's why you have a team of geeks to take care of those things." Raj grinned. "Shall I continue?"

Heads nodded all around for him to continue.

"Okay, so when we had that problem solved and were able to collect the data about the movements of everyone in the house in the same way their chip scanners do, we started recording that information.

We suspect that part of the security processes would be to make sure that they are not fed historical data as we did in Boise. They would have some program that would check to see what they are receiving was not sent to them before. Therefore, we used the recorded data of the people's movements and made changes to it, so that their actions were distinctive from anything sent before. We then compared and tested that against the original recordings to make sure the data we will be feeding them would be unique.

So by the time we go live, we will have enough unique movement data to blow smoke up their skirts for weeks." Raj concluded his explanation to an audience whose jaws had already dropped a few minutes ago and now broke out into laughter with his last comment.

Daniel looked at his companions and while he high-fived with Raj said, "You all of course *know* that I taught Raj everything he knows about computers!"

"Yea right! Of course, we all know that," Salome laughed.

In preparation for their move out of the city, Peter and Kelly decided it would be sensible if he went to Mount Ararat to get everything in place for their arrival.

He and Owen required just a few more hours of flight training to get certified for twin-engine aircraft and night flying. They were going to wrap that up in the next week, and then they would finalize the purchase of the Baron G58 Beechcraft as well as the construction of the airstrip and hanger.

Peter and Kelly had already decided what their house would be. Although they were financially well off, money wasn't an issue. Neither of them desired a luxurious home or lifestyle. The natural things in life, the beauty of fauna and flora, fly-fishing, freedom, healthy living, fresh air, and happiness were the things that mattered to them. They agreed they were going to live off the grid, produce their own food, and follow a minimalistic lifestyle. In any case, their personal wealth would mean nothing in a few weeks, anyway.

Kelly did some research and came up with the idea of building a house constructed from shipping containers, which would be eco-friendly, much quicker and easier to build than conventional houses, and a lot cheaper. Properly insulated, the house would be cozy in the winter and resistant to excessive heat in summer. Those houses could withstand winds up to one hundred and seventy-five miles per hour and would never collapse during an earthquake.

They were looking at designs and available kits when Kelly smiled and said, "We should look at a design that has at least four to five bedrooms."

Peter did not immediately get what she was alluding to, "Are you planning to host lots of guests?"

"No, one guest bedroom would be enough, but we will still need at least three more bedrooms," she chuckled.

"Why so many ..." Peter started and realized what she was talking about. "We haven't even talked about that. You will make me the proudest father ever! Kelly, it's absolutely fantastic to know we feel the same about having children."

"Oh yes, I can't wait to hold our babies in my arms and for the little pink feet pattering around our house," she said with a big smile as Peter put his arm around her waist and pulled her closer for a tender kiss.

"You make me so very happy," he whispered in her ear.

Peter would complete his pilot training during the course of the next week. And then he'd head for Mount Ararat to start the preparations and to help with the final planning of Operation Pincer.

A few days after Raj received the visit from Sam's operations team, Roy got his chance to show them what he and his team were doing. He explained they were working on their own version of the Palladium system that had been employed so effectively by the CIA during the Cold War era.

They already had the 10th Cycle radar evasion system ready, and he explained to them how it worked. It was contained in a metal box the size of a shoebox. When activated, it would make any airplane invisible to radar. It was already in operation in the owl-drones and hummingbirds – this one was just a bigger and more powerful version.

The next part of the project was the construction of a system that would create phantom airplanes, which would appear on radar screens in any location of their choice. The solution for that was actually very simple and easy, he explained, as everybody started laughing.

"What did I say now?" Roy asked, his eyes round and a slight tilt to his head.

"Roy, you're overestimating our intelligence. When ordinary human beings listen to you, nothing is ever simple and easy." Daniel laughed. "But, please continue. You might just surprise us all."

"Okay. Be ready for the surprise then. You'll see I wasn't joking about it." Roy smiled. "All we did was change some of the owl-drones and fitted them with a few gadgets, using the same technology Raj used in those GPS tracking devices in the vehicles of Sam's guards in Boise. That's it."

"Come on, Roy. It can't be that easy. There must be more to it," Salome said.

"Hang on, I understand what you said, but those owls are much smaller than an airplane. Their radar will pick that up, won't it?" Sam asked.

"No, don't worry about that. We've created an electromagnetic field around the drone that would make it look big enough on their screens," Roy said.

"Don't even try to explain how you did that. I am one hundred percent sure I won't understand." Sam laughed.

Roy continued. "Thanks to Rube and his friends, we have a map of the locations of each radar station in the

USA, including the frequencies they use and access to their computers."

Sam was impressed, "Well, the way I see it, thanks to these whiz kids, all we have to do now is map the entire plan out. After that, we start doing the walkthroughs, and as soon as we know how to shut those chips down, we'll be ready to go."

Chapter Ninety-Five

A NEW IPHONE

Guozhi didn't notice the two men lurking in the shadows when he arrived home. When he opened his front door, he was pushed from behind, lost his balance and fell to the floor, terrified. Struggling over onto his back, he stared up at the two figures dressed in black from head to toe, including their balaclavas.

When one of them spoke, the blood drained from Guozhi's face; it was a deep metallic voice, as if it originated from the inside of a big metal container. What he heard made his whole body explode in a cold sweat. "We have been sent by the Triad," the voice said.

He knew this was his last day on earth. He knew about the Triad and their cold-blooded killing of anyone who dared to cross their path. How had he upset the Triad? Now the reason was not necessary to know - he was about to die.

The second figure came closer, grabbed him by the hair, and pulled him onto his feet, groaning with pain. A foul smelling and -tasting piece of cloth was shoved into his mouth and secured with duct tape. The man almost dislocated his arms in the process tying his hands behind his back with the duct tape. They pushed him into the kitchen and made him sit down on a chair. One took a seat opposite him and the other the seat next to him. Gouzhi tried to talk, but he could not get a sound out. He'd already wet his pants, his terror was so great.

The two men didn't say a word. The one on the opposite side of the table just looked at him, while the one next to him opened a tablet PC and turned on a video. The man forced his head around and made him watch the video.

He tried to look away, but the man next to him waved his index finger as a signal to him not to look away again and turned his head back to the screen.

He was forced to watch three short clips. The first one was a compilation of the most gruesome parts of the treatment of people at the facility. The second one was of him at work in his lab. The third one was a compilation of a few very explicit sexual scenes between him and his lover a little over a week ago.

Ten minutes later, the video stopped, and tears of fright were running down Ghouzi's face. There was nothing about him these men didn't know. Fear made him overflow again and now urine was puddled on the floor. He had no doubt that these men were sent by the Triad, and he was certain they were going to kill him.

The man opposite him spoke for the second time. "Ghouzi, you have been found guilty by the High Tribunal of the Triad. We are the executioners. Do you wish to speak before we proceed?"

Ghouzi nodded his head nervously; he definitely had something to say.

"Good, you will get a chance to say something. Any noise and you'll die immediately. Is that understood?"

Ghouzi nodded in agreement, and the cloth was removed from his mouth. He kept his voice down and immediately started pleading and begging for his life; he would do anything they asked, if they would just spare his life.

The two men continued to frighten him for a while longer and then told him that the tribunal had authorized them to spare his life, if he would cooperate with them and do exactly as he was told. He didn't even listen to what it was they wanted him to do – he immediately agreed.

They took out an iPhone – the exact same model and color as his own – and handed it to him. Their demands were simple, if puzzling. He had to plug his new phone into one of the computers in his lab to charge it and make sure it was switched on while it was charging. Once it was fully charged, he had to unplug it and switch it off.

Then he had to remove the back cover of his new phone and place two of the cylindrical testing devices in the placeholders created for that purpose in the new phone. They told him he'd be watched every step of the way. He'd be contacted once the job was done, and he needn't worry, they'd know when he'd completed the job. He got a few more unsympathetic and very clear warnings about his health and his future if he failed in any way to complete his mission.

Three days later, Rube got the message from Jian and Gui. They had everything they wanted. The question was how to get it to him. They were a bit worried that the cylinders might be detected if they were sent as part of a clothing shipment.

Rube passed the good news on to Raj and undertook to get a message to the Tectus managers to see if they knew of anyone who could help. Within an hour, he had an answer back. There was a Chinese businesswoman in Los Angeles who owned and operated a very popular organic clothing store. She made regular trips to the factories in China, and she would be more than happy to purchase a few of the latest iPhones for her friends and bring them back with her the next week.

When the iPhone eventually arrived at the Rabbit Hole and Raj opened it, Sam smiled and said, "Just think about all the criticism the late Steve Jobs had to endure for outsourcing the iPhone manufacturing to China. The man was a genius, years ahead of his time. The world should thank him for the foresight he had."

"I agree with you, Sam. I've never been a big fan of Apple products, but after today I'm seriously reconsidering my stance on that." Daniel laughed.

Sarah wanted to know how the Tectus associates managed it. "Do we have any idea how our Chinese friends pulled this off? It wouldn't be easy to get into that fortress. It might be worthwhile to know. You never know when we might need to use similar tactics."

No one had the slightest idea. They would think about that later, but for now they had much more urgent work to do. All that mattered was that they had the final piece of the puzzle in their hands.

Chapter Ninety-Six

YOU MUST OBEY MY COMMANDMENTS

When the iPhone arrived at the Rabbit Hole, the implementation of Peter and Owen's plans were already in full swing. They'd bought their plane, which was in the hanger at the flight training school in Billings from where Owen graduated. It would remain there until they had completed the airstrip and hanger at Mount Ararat, the construction of which was already underway with an estimated completion within two weeks.

Peter and Kelly were collaborating via their mirror phones, talking and sending pictures and drawings back and forth to finally choose the spot for their house. It was a location with a beautiful view of the mountains and surrounding areas, a few yards from a small stream, and literally on the border of the Gallatin National Forest.

The five-bedroom kit home had already been delivered onsite, and the contractors guaranteed completion within four weeks. They had no requirements for telephone or power lines, and water would be provided by their well.

The Phoenix Agenda

Thanks to all the 10th Cycle technology available to them, they were going to be totally off the grid.

The Supreme Council's financial announcement, according to the latest directives given to their media partners, was five weeks away.

Kelly had given notice to the owner of their apartment and handed her resignation to the CEO of WONN. The latter caused an enormous upheaval. The CEO wanted to double her salary package, even offered her a promotion and unheard of benefits, but she politely declined. She explained that a severe health issue faced her, and that it would be impossible to continue. She was not lying about it; it was going to become extremely unhealthy to live in a city very soon.

She expressed her deep regret for the inconvenience her resignation would cause, and conveyed to the CEO that she would not like to burn any bridges. She would dearly like to come back, if she could overcome her health issues. This last request swayed the CEO, and he agreed to keep the doors open for her.

The news about her resignation leaked out quickly, and within days the media were rife with speculations about the reasons for her departure. There was even an inquiry or two directly from the Supreme Council. However, Kelly weathered all the storms around her. Within two weeks, things calmed down, and people accepted the fact that they would not see their favorite TV host anymore. She would arrive in Billings two weeks before the expected announcement.

Roy and Raj, with their teams, studied the cylinders and software from the iPhone received from China. Raj and his team's earlier access to the reports produced by the software helped them quickly gain an understanding of the code and how the program worked.

Roy and Jack analyzed the cylinders and learned their purpose and functions very quickly. Within a week of receiving the iPhone, the quality control process was mapped out. Every component in the cylinders was identified and associated with a function, except for one, which still escaped discovery – the shutdown routine.

Roy called Raj over to his lab. He had one of the cylinders loaded into the electron microscope and pointed Raj to it. "Have a look at that. What do you make of it? I'm at my wits end," he said.

Raj looked at it, zoomed the focus in and out a few times and then shook his head, "I have no clue what it is that I am looking at. Have you got any ideas?"

Roy replied, "Yes, I have a lot, but none of them makes any sense. The most logical one I can think of is that it's the on-off switch. The only reason I am thinking that is because it's the only part in this damn thing we haven't been able to identify. But if that is a switch, I have to say that I have never seen anything like it. I don't even know where to begin to figure out how it works."

Raj looked again and after a while he said, "It seems like a molecule consisting of three atoms, suspended in mid-air in the center of that nanotube. Is that what you saw as well? Or am I crazy?"

"No, you're not crazy, at least I hope not, because if you are, then so am I. That's exactly what I saw, and that's the cause of my frustration. What's the purpose of that? As I said before, we know that everything in that cylinder has been assigned a function, and that thingamabob is the only one we haven't assigned. The only thing we don't have is the off switch so that MUST be the off switch. Right?" Roy tried to justify his logic.

"I will agree with you only if you can eliminate the possibility that you could have missed the switch in any of the other components," Raj replied with a smile.

Raj could see that his friend was bone tired and suggested they both get some rest and tackle it again in the morning. They both left, but found it difficult to get their brains to stop working.

The next morning they were back to the problem, now joined by Ryan, Jack, and other team members. All had a look through the microscope and saw what Raj and Roy saw; a molecule consisting of three atoms suspended in mid-air in the center of a nanotube. They went through the components in the cylinder again making sure everything was accounted for. The only thing missing was the switch, which they knew *had* to be there. This, therefore, *must* be the switch.

By lunchtime, they were still scratching their heads. Sam, Luke, Salome, Sarah, and even Peter, who was visiting for a few days, turned up in the lab to find out what progress they'd made. They explained what they found and where they were stuck. "What do you think keeps that molecule in suspension?" Daniel wanted to know.

"An electromagnetic field," Roy replied.

"Would another, stronger electromagnetic field or pulse make that molecule move?" Daniel continued his questioning.

"Yes, definitely it would, but what are you thinking?" Roy asked.

Daniel explained, "I am just wondering if it is possible that if the molecule touches the side of the tube it could trigger the switch mechanism? But wait, I am way out of my league here. I have no idea what I'm talking about."

Roy looked up, stared at Daniel for a long while and started smiling, "You might be out of your league, but you just gave me an idea. I am now sure that's the switch and that molecule triggers the switch when it touches the sides of the tube. However, I don't think it is through an electromagnetic field or pulse. If that were the case, the chip could be switched off when people came close to any electrical devices with a stronger electromagnetic field."

Roy looked around the room as if to invite ideas. None were forthcoming, so he suggested to Raj they test an electromagnetic field to see if it moved the molecule. As expected it did, but it didn't trigger any reaction from the nanotube.

"I think there's something else that makes it move in a certain predetermined pattern, and that would trigger the switch," he murmured.

"What about sound?" Sarah wanted to know.

"That would ... shit! Yes, of course! That's it! You've got it!" he yelled. Then he ran around the table and kissed the flabbergasted Sarah full on the mouth, to the shock and surprise of everyone, who were shortly after rolling with laughter.

By the time they got their laughter under control, Salome matter-of-factly remarked, "Roy, my dear. You will definitely have to stop kissing women every time you make a new discovery. They're getting scared of you!"

Daniel tapped him on the shoulder and in a mock serious tone said, "I would like to have a quiet word with you, buster. See you in the gym at five."

"Huh, what?" Roy replied, acting as if he didn't know what just happened. He was already busy changing the settings on the microscope to focus on that nanotube. Within a few minutes he shouted, "Bingo! Gotcha!"

Peter, who had caught on to the humor of the people of the Rabbit Hole, shouted. "Ladies beware. Roy is on the loose again!"

Roy, however, had a better presence of mind than a few minutes ago. "Okay, don't worry, I've got it. There are conduits on the side of the tube wall. The molecule will spin, and when its orbit expands enough, it will land in those grooves and go to the bottom. When it reaches the bottom, it will trigger the switch. Like a bullet spinning along the grooves in the barrel of a gun."

"Raj, we need to find that sound file now," Roy said.

Raj and his entire team gathered around the computer he had with him, and within a few minutes, they found reference to a sound file in the code of the quality program. They located the file and opened it but heard nothing. They connected the cylinder to the computer, started the program and found the code that activated the sound file while Roy watched the switch closely under the microscope. A split second after the sound file was activated, the switch was in operation.

"There you've got it! Where is Sarah? I'd like to kiss her," he said with a broad smile on his face. Everyone burst into laughter again. Salome just shook her head, her face covered by one of her hands. Roy certainly had crawled out of his shell since she first met him and she liked it.

Though everyone was somewhat impressed, Peter was dumbfounded again. He still couldn't get used to how these people were able to take a problem head-on, and, through sheer brilliance, just make it go away.

"Do we have to know what is on that sound file? I mean do we have to try and listen to it?" Sam asked.

"Yes, we have to know that," Roy replied as he looked at Raj.

Raj tried a few times while he had earphones on and then mumbled something to the effect that it was most probably at a frequency inaudible to the human ear. He made a few changes to the sound player and file and all of a sudden, his facial expression changed from anticipation to shock and disgust.

Everyone was watching him. He slowly took the earphones off, turned the volume on his computer up, and said, "Be ready to be sickened."

I am John Brideaux
I am God
You must obey my commandments

The unmistakable voice of John Brideaux came over the speakers of the computer. The words shocked and appalled everyone.

"What a vile human being. That was the sound of evil." Sam articulated the words on everyone's mind.

Chapter Ninety-Seven

DOT THE I'S AND CROSS THE T'S

Finally, with the discovery of the chip's shutdown procedure, it was time to dot the i's and cross the t's. They had two weeks left before the announcement and at least four weeks to Operation Pincer.

Sam and his team decided that the final date for lifting the Harpers out would be determined once they were sure the conditions favored them, and they could execute the operation with as little risk of detection as possible.

Peter had a meeting with Rube and Sombra some weeks before he left New York when he briefed them about the pending financial disaster and the expected turmoil in the aftermath. He asked them to pass the information on to their Tectus members. The two of them had been urbanites their entire lives and were worried. He gave them all the advice he could, and told them that Owen was looking for someone to manage his farm in Nucla if they were interested. Initially, they were a bit skeptical about the idea of living on a farm so far away from the city lights. They said they'd think about it. But then, two days later they called

Peter and told him they were interested after all. They asked if he would talk to Owen about it.

Owen was more than happy for the two of them, with their partners, to manage his farm. He'd already sold all the livestock so there wasn't much to manage, other than to take care of the property and enjoy the views, fresh air, and the freedom of farm life.

The airstrip and hangar at Mt. Ararat were completed, and the Baron 58 was safely in its shelter. Peter and Kelly's container house was nearing completion; there were just a few more days of work. Kelly arrived at the Billings Logan Airport the day after Peter took delivery of the house.

In keeping with tradition, to her great delight, Peter carried her over the threshold. She was thrilled with her new home. It was much more spacious and comfortable than she'd imagined.

Two days after Kelly's arrival - one week before the announcement - Peter and Owen made a trip to Nucla. There they met with Rube, Sombra, and a few other Tectus members to agree on the final details of their plans. Using the Baron 58, it was a trip of a little over three hours for them instead of the more than thirteen hours by car that Owen was used to.

They arrived at the farm the day after Rube and Sombra, who'd come with two of the most senior members of Tectus. These were a former Navy SEAL, Dennis McMahon, and Eric Winchester, a former Colonel in the Marines.

When Peter and Owen arrived, they were surprised to learn that the four men, who'd never been to the Western Slope of Colorado, loved every moment of it, although it had been only twenty-four hours since they'd got there. Rube and Sombra were now actually excited about the idea of living on the farm. Dennis and Eric told them that they would be more than happy to swap places, if they ever wanted to change their minds.

They were all seated in the living room to commence the two-day planning session. First, Peter gave them a synopsis of the impending financial chaos and made sure they all understood what they should be doing to safeguard themselves and their loved ones, as well as the members of their organization.

Next, the details of Operation Pincer were discussed. Peter was the mission leader, and he walked them through the plan step-by-step, including the exact timing and the people involved. He invited Dennis and Eric to comment on the plan as he talked. Their military background was highly regarded, and their input would be much appreciated.

Tectus would make seven of their members available to assist Peter on D-Day. Rube, Sombra, and three others would help to operate the technical equipment while two others would be drivers. On D-Day minus one, some of the technical equipment would have to be positioned and tested. On D-Day, Sam and his operational team would have voice and visual communications with all team members onsite. The details of Plan-B were discussed, as well as the steps that would be taken if things went south and the mission had to be aborted.

Next on the agenda was the evacuation of some family members of the residents of the Rabbit Hole.

Tectus was in charge of Operation Fugere, as they named this mission, based on the Latin word that meant 'to flee'. Eric was the mission leader of this one. As Eric took them through the plan, it was clear that they also had their plots worked out down to the tiniest detail. They had eight families, a total of twenty-five people, to evacuate. Their operation would kick off the moment President Harper and his wife were airborne. They had made contact with each of the families and made sure they knew exactly what to do and were ready, willing, and able to go when they got the message. The families had been told to stock up on supplies to survive the anticipated chaos and shortages that would follow the announcement.

Operation Fugere was a complex mission that required the simultaneous evacuation of the eight families from eight different locations across the country. The families were to be transported to various safe houses and accommodated there until they could be moved to their final destination, the Rabbit Hole. That remained a secret to everyone. Not even the four Tectus representatives knew about the name or the location. They also knew not to inquire about it.

Eric and Dennis requested assistance from some of their former military comrades. There were many of them these days who were more than happy to help get rid of the new government. Peter was happy with their plans, as they were with the Operation Pincer plan.

Owen and Peter handed them a bag full of the latest technology equipment and communications devices, demonstrated everything to them, and gave them training videos and user guides to help them train their team members.

Chapter Ninety-Eight

NERO FIDDLED WHILE ROME BURNED

The Supreme Council's pilot program in Samoa was a resounding success. It was a small country and they managed the transition very well.

However, they miscalculated the reaction they would get in the rest of the world. They were pleasantly surprised by the enormity of the chaos they created. That was exactly what they wanted. The bigger the chaos and suffering, the better the conditions for them to step in and finally get control over all people on the planet.

The Supreme Council chose a Friday to make their announcement. All credit card debt, overdrafts, mortgages and personal loans vanished in an instant. The debt of those who were not chipped would be erased the moment the chip was activated inside their bodies. All people with a chip were debt free by the end of the announcement.

All monetary transactions would be handled through the chips and scanners. The Liberty Dollar was introduced. It would be accepted as payment for goods and services everywhere in the world, and no cash or cards would be necessary – or allowed. Chip scanners would process transactions.

Any business owner who would not accept the new currency was guilty of a crime carrying the death penalty. Similarly, all salaries would from now on be paid in Liberty Dollars only, and no other payment method was allowed. Any employer who didn't obey the directive would be guilty of a crime punishable by death.

They announced with pride that the Liberty Dollar was the first and only one world currency in human history. Nobody corrected them - the 8th Cycle, more than fifty thousand years ago, also had a one-world currency.

Immediately after the announcement, the jubilant media was onto it and pointed out that people should mark this day in their calendars. This was the first day they were finally liberated from the oppression of the fat cat bankers and financial institutions. This day would go down in the journals of history as the day when liberty and equality arrived; it was the end of poverty.

Across the world people were dancing in the streets - their excitement knew no bounds. These frenzied scenes of joy were broadcast on every TV and radio around the world. No one but those immediately involved noticed that the financial world had descended into utter chaos. Stock and money markets had crashed immediately and were shut down within hours, destined never to reopen again.

By Saturday, people woke up to discover that all paper money was worthless, all coin unacceptable, and they had no money. Banks shut down all their online banking facilities and ATM machines and closed their doors. No financial transactions were possible. Business owners immediately closed all operations and laid off their staff out of fear of falling foul of the new laws. Scores became unemployed overnight.

By Saturday evening, the media frenzy began to subside as billions of people found themselves jobless and penniless. By late Sunday, there were few joyful individuals in the streets and by Monday morning there were none. Reality had set in for the chipped as well as the unchipped, as they discovered that they were unable to buy or sell anything. They couldn't buy food, clothing, medicine, gas or any services, and they had no idea when they would be able to again.

By Monday, the first hungry people appeared on the streets begging for food, and their numbers increased rapidly with every passing day. Soon they became violent in their efforts to survive, and people locked themselves in their homes to stay out of the way of gangs of dangerous and hungry citizens. The doors and windows of banks were broken down, ATM machines were ripped out and smashed open in an attempt to get money, only to find out that the money was worthless, and there was nobody that would sell anything to them or indeed, had anything left to sell.

Shops were raided and food vanished quickly except in the warehouses, which became the next target. Desperation and hopelessness set in for everyone, chipped and unchipped. The questions on everyone's lips were, "Where are our liberators? Is this what liberty and equality looks like?"

Eight days after the announcement, vigilantes ruled the streets and neighborhoods of all cities and towns across the globe, creating violence and looting. Strangely enough, it became apparent that the impoverished parts of the world were much better off than the affluent. Poor people were used to struggling to make ends meet. They were much better prepared to handle hardship than the privileged.

Law enforcement agencies were inundated, understaffed and overworked. Tens of thousands of new police members would be chipped and deputized; every known security guard plus current and former military personnel were called up for police duty. Yet, despite the rapid growth in their ranks and expansion of the drone fleet, they were still unable to gain control and restore law and order. Killer bots were mowing people down in their thousands every day.

The drones would quickly sniff out the chipped amongst the offenders and activate the torture bots in their bodies, leaving them in excruciating pain with extreme cramps in their limbs and stomachs. The second time a chipped citizen was identified in the wrong place, the killer bots were activated. Tens of thousands of the chipped also died.

The media didn't report any of the misery and chaos. They were forbidden to do so. Of course, they didn't have to. Everyone out on the streets could see it for themselves, their empty stomachs dictating their feelings and beliefs. The media kept on playing only one tune repeatedly – just look at all the benefits of being chipped: free education, free medical, free phones and internet, a long and healthy life with no debt. By now, there were not many listening to them anymore. What was the use of all of those benefits if you were starving to death? The chip could not save you from starvation.

The brutal and inhumane police tactics were efficient at keeping the chipped off the streets, but they were the only ones being punished. Most of the unchipped got away unpunished, however, their limited 'freedom' came to a swift end when the police equipped the drones with new

The Phoenix Agenda

nanobots aimed at the unchipped. They were just killed indiscriminately and without warning when detected in any undesired location. Those who were able to escape detection by the drones, which many of them managed to do, were still free. The chipped had no such luck; their every move was monitored and punished at the slightest hint that they were not obedient.

The media was fighting a losing battle; they couldn't keep the people calm and motivated anymore. Their attempts to persuade everyone how incredible this new financial system was fell on deaf ears. Slowly but surely, they found that growing numbers of formerly devoted supporters of the new regime were going quiet and refused to be interviewed or contribute to the news.

Nero fiddled while Rome burned. The most fun-filled part for the Supreme Council was when they watched the exclusive daily footage, shot for them by their own camera crews around the world. They laughed and shouted like the barbaric and bloodthirsty crowds of Romans who found great entertainment at the Colosseum during gladiator fights, while helpless victims were torn to pieces by wild animals.

Only two of the Supreme Council members found no amusement in these daily horror shows of human suffering and despair. The two dissenting members made sure no one noticed their disgust. This is not what they envisaged for the new world. This was not liberty, equality, and fraternity. This was the human race at its lowest point of morality ever. It was barbaric and nauseating. Nevertheless, they remained quiet and veiled their feelings out of a very real fear that, if they objected, they might find themselves out on the streets amongst those participating in the death march.

"Look at that! Wait, turn it back a few frames, I would

like to see that part where the guy's head is taken off again," John Brideaux commanded the video operator; he had a ten thousand Liberty dollar bet on the winner. "Shit, it's thrilling; just look at all that blood." John Brideaux was having a good time and the council members joined in with their applause as they watched the man's head rolling away from his jerking, decapitated body.

The Supreme Council's special camera crews took great pride in creating daily entertainment for their enthusiastic audience in Brussels.

They named it after the very popular TV series from a few years ago, depicting a game where teenagers annually battled to the death for the benefit of their towns.

The camera crews would send out the word into different neighborhoods about a food drop and the location where it would take place – usually at a big stadium that could host many thousands of spectators. A few boxes of tinned food were dropped in the middle of the arena. That was the prize for the winner, food for their neighborhood.

The boxes were rigged with explosives so that no one would dare to rush in and take them. The explosives would be deactivated only when a clear winner emerged. The groups from each neighborhood would turn up with their nominated gladiators to fight each other for the food. The games would last for hours, and the blood and the dead would cover the arena. People saw and were repulsed, but they attended to support their warriors in the hope of getting some food if their fighters were victorious.

The Supreme Council watched and enjoyed it; they had no concerns about food, as they indulged in luxurious delicacies, prepared by the world's master chefs. Champagne, caviar, and exotic feasts were in abundance while they watched the melees and betting on the outcome of each one. The Supreme Council had a second stage of their plan in place, but they didn't want to activate it too early. They were still enjoying the spectacle and wanted the chaos and suffering to continue for a while longer. They were not satisfied that the level of desperation was high enough for the final part of their plan to be kicked off. They wanted more fear, more desperation and more chaos.

A small glitch happened on a live show of one of the major TV networks when a Roman Catholic priest agreed to be interviewed. He was briefed and coached in exactly what to say during the interview. However, shortly into the interview he stopped talking, looked straight at the camera and quoted from the Bible, Mark 13 verses 14 to 19:

"When you see 'the abomination that causes desolation' standing where it does not belong – then let those who are in Judea flee to the mountains.

Let no one on the housetop go down or enter the house to take anything out.

Let no one in the field go back to get their cloak.

How dreadful it will be in those days for pregnant women and nursing mothers!

Pray that this will not take place in winter, because those will be days of distress unequalled from the beginning, when God created the world, until now—and never to be equaled again."

The interviewer and camera crew were taken by surprise, so it took them a few minutes to realize what was happening and shut the cameras down. By then it was too late. The message had gone out to millions of viewers.

The priest, camera crew and CEO of the TV station were never heard of again. The TV station almost lost its license.

It was as if that priest's message gave some people a bit of hope, an escape from certain death. They started fleeing out of the cities to the countryside and the mountains in droves. They would drive their vehicles until they ran out of gas, abandoned them, and go on foot as far away as they could, many of them only with the clothes on their backs. Thousands upon thousands squatted on farms, in forests, and parks. However, for most of them it ended in death as they still had no food, no shelter, and now also no protection from hungry and vicious gangs roaming the countryside.

The desperation and hunger drove some people to cannibalism and the rest to suicide; those were the only two choices left. Family massacres became commonplace as people would rip out the chips of their children and spouses and then themselves, so that they could die and be free from the pain.

On a Friday five weeks after the announcement, the Supreme Council finally gave the thumbs up for the next item on their agenda. They started handing out limited amounts of rations at prepared distribution centers to all the loyal citizens only.

Loyal citizens were those who were chipped. Some supermarket shelves were stocked with food again, chip scanners were installed, staff was hired, and they were back in business. There were a few conditions though. Only the chipped could buy food, and only the chipped could be hired to work. The food was rationed to as much as one person required to survive for one day, which meant the whole family had to go shopping every day. Anyone caught sharing food with the unchipped would be punished severely.

At each shop and distribution center, a makeshift implant clinic and staff were ready to service everyone who wanted food. As soon as the chip was activated, the person could join the food line. Cargo planes, trucks, and trains were busy around the clock to move food and supplies to the distribution centers. Queues of people waiting for food and to be chipped stretched for many miles.

Tectus kept the Rosslerites well informed of what was happening in the world outside the Rabbit Hole. With the preoccupation of the police force and the chipping and food distribution requiring all the attention of the officials, the time was ripe for Operation Pincer.

Chapter Ninety-Nine

OPERATION PINCER

On the Saturday morning, forty-three days after the Supreme Council's announcement, when the butchery reached its climax, it was D-Day minus one. Owen, Alison, Peter, and Kelly landed at Upper Cumberland airport, eighteen miles from Cookeville and less than twenty-two miles from the Harpers' farm. They were disguised as two couples in their mid-sixties, all wearing sunglasses. The men were wearing wide brimmed hats and the women sunhats and headscarves. They informed the inquisitive supervisor at the airport that they were farmers from Georgia. This was just a short stopover, to experience the serene beauty of the lovely little town of Sparta and surrounding areas in White County. They would be leaving again the next evening.

Later that night, Rube, Sombra, and three of the Nashville Tectus agents deployed all the necessary equipment. They tested that everything was working correctly and linked the equipment up to the operations center in the Rabbit Hole. Peter met with them afterward and did a final walkthrough. They were all ready.

The Harpers were informed every step of the way. They knew what to expect and do during the entire operation. On D-Day, Peter did two more walkthroughs with them via the mirror phone on their Sunday morning and afternoon walks. At 10.20 pm, Sam and his operations team were all gathered in the operations center and in communication with Peter and his team. They did one final check to make sure that everything was working smoothly.

Rube had taken control of the network router inside the house, uploading the video and movement files to the computer connected to the Security Control Center in Washington. He was just waiting for the signal to swing into action. Sombra and two others had the mosquitoes, loaded with Immobilon, deployed and waiting for the signal.

At 10:30 pm, Sam and his team were satisfied that they were ready and gave Peter the green light. Rube switched the recording mode on all video cameras and microphones off and started feeding the pre-recorded files to the control center in Washington. There was only one person left to look after the entire country. Everyone else who usually operated the center was out in the streets on police duty. The team waited ten minutes to see if any alarm was triggered, and when nothing happened, Rube proceeded and switched off all motion detectors inside and outside the house.

Sombra and his assistants first neutralized the three agents who were already asleep and then coordinated their attacks on the remaining three. One was in the office reading a book and not paying any attention to the screens and computers as he was supposed to. One was outside on the porch having a smoke, and the third was watching a movie on TV in the family room. The three of them collapsed almost in unison as if they had practiced the move.

In the Rabbit Hole, everyone was listening and following every move on the farm more than one thousand one hundred nautical miles away. They checked the steps on their lists off as they were completed and reported by the team at ground zero, making sure that nothing was left out.

The door leading from the Harpers' bedroom to a verandah was not locked, and when Peter and Kelly walked in at 10:40 pm, the Harpers switched the bed lights on. Rube, Sombra and their three assistants came in through the same door right on the heels of Peter and Kelly and went into the house to tie up and gag the unconscious agents. They then set up the rest of the computer equipment to operate in automatic mode for the next four days.

"Mr. President and Mrs. Harper, I'm Peter. It's a pleasure to meet you at last. This is my fiancé, Kelly Edwards, whom I believe you have met before. We have to move quickly, but feel free to ask any questions you might have along the way."

"Thank God!" Esther Harper said as she wiped the tears from her eyes.

"Peter and Kelly, I'm overwhelmed, I feel the same as Esther. I think its best if you just tell us what you want us to do and questions can come later."

"Mr. President and Mrs. Harper, we first have to remove the chips. Then we'll help you pack your things and get you out of here," Kelly said as she asked them to lie down on the bed for the procedure.

Kelly moved over to Esther's side and Peter attended to Nigel.

Peter smiled as he explained, "This might hurt a little. Neither Kelly nor I have done this operation before.

Rebecca assured us she was confident that we're competent surgeons after the training she gave us. So please know we are sorry in advance if we cause you any discomfort."

"We're in your hands. Nothing can be worse than carrying that instrument of the devil in our bodies. Let's do it," Esther said.

Kelly and Peter put on surgical gloves, took out the chip deactivators constructed by Roy and Jack, and held them over the area where the chips were located for a few seconds until the green light showed. Then they injected each of their patients with a local anesthetic. When the injected areas were numb, they took out scalpels, made small incisions and pulled the chips out with sterilized medical pincers, placed them in cylindrical canisters, and then cleaned and dressed the wounds.

Both Peter and Kelly managed to hide their anxiety very well by making lighthearted comments all the time during the procedure. Not only was this was the first time either of them was required to inject and cut into another human, but it was also the first time that Roy's deactivation device had been used on a human body. Nigel and Esther didn't say anything, but they were both aware of the fact that they were the first to be unchipped and that there was a risk that things could go wrong.

Five minutes later, at 10:46 pm, the Harpers were unchipped and thunderous applause broke out in the Rabbit Hole when Peter reported that the Harpers were alive and well. The Harpers hugged both of their rescuers and started packing the few things they wanted to take with them. Peter and Kelly asked the Harpers to excuse them and said they'd meet them again later at the airport. There were a few more things to take care of. Rube and his team would be there shortly to give them a hand and get them to the van waiting about a mile away.

Rube and the rest of his team removed all traces of their visit, retrieving the spyflies, mosquitoes, and other equipment. Afterward, they went through to where the Harpers were waiting, introduced themselves, and helped them pack and move to the waiting van.

Peter and Kelly had gone to the unconscious agents, deactivated, and extracted their chips, placing them in cylindrical canisters. After they sterilized and dressed their wounds, they left a personal note for each of them in their hands, along with the canisters containing their chips.

Sam gave the drivers of the two vans waiting to transport everyone instructions to drive up to the farm entry road, switch off lights, and wait for their passengers. At 11.05 pm the lights in the Harpers' bedroom and the family room went off, while the lamps in the agents' office remained lit.

At 11:30 pm, two couples in their mid-sixties boarded their Baron 58 at Upper Cumberland Airport and moved to the end of the far end runway, where the pilot turned the plane around and stopped. He completed his pre-flight checks. While the pilot was busy, at 11:35 pm, Peter and Kelly got up out of the tall grass next to the runway where they were hiding and got into the plane unnoticed.

At 11:38 pm, the plane took off and headed south towards Georgia. At the same time, Rube launched an owl-drone in stealth mode, which followed the plane. Ten minutes into the flight, Peter called Rube and told him to switch the drone's stealth mode off while he changed to stealth mode in the Baron. As soon as Rube gave him the confirmation, Owen changed direction and set course northwest towards Billings, Montana.

The owl-drone would fly for four hours and then self-destruct by an explosion that would vaporize all onboard electronic components and every bit of the body of the drone. Peter called Colonel Eric Winchester and activated Operation Fugere. After ending the call with Eric, Peter explained to the Harpers what the operation was about. Esther responded with a prayer, "God, we pray that each and every one of those families will find favor in Your eyes. That You will deliver them from evil tonight the same as You delivered us."

Everyone on the plane agreed with her sincere prayer.

The travelers in the Baron 58 settled down for the flight to Mount Ararat before dawn. Kelly and Alison made sure Esther and Nigel were comfortable, and that they were not experiencing pain from their wounds. They offered them coffee and food and then sat back to relax – there was a lot to talk about.

Chapter One Hundred

OPERATION FUGERE

While the Harpers were on their way to Mount Ararat, Eric Winchester and Dennis McMahon orchestrated Operation Fugere with military precision, as was to be expected given their backgrounds. Sam and his team were following their progress and systematically helped them to double check that nothing was missed, the same as they did during Operation Pincer.

None of the families was under the same intense protection as the Harpers were. They were watched by one guard, which was posted outside their residences and would follow them everywhere they went. Their homes were bugged and phones and Internet were tapped. The Tectus agents had studied the routines of the guards and surveillance methods at each of the family dwellings. Allowing for the number of people in each family and the effort required, Eric and Dennis assigned a team of three to five Tectus members.

The teams were equipped with mosquitoes, spyflies and all the necessary medical equipment to remove chips. The training videos and user guides, compiled by Rebecca, Roy, and Raj, prepared them well for their tasks.

Each team had at least one ex-military person onboard. The families were primed and cooperated very well every step of the way. The younger children found the chip extraction procedures very frightening, but with the loving embraces and assurances of their parents next to them, most of them were quickly pacified. The evacuation from their homes took between twenty and thirty minutes for each family and, depending on the distance to the safe house, another forty to ninety minutes to a secure location.

All cell phones were destroyed and left behind. The extracted chips were placed in the canisters and taken with them to be delivered to Roy. The unconscious guards were also relieved of their chips and left with similar personalized notes in their hands as those at the Harper's residence. Cheers of joy erupted from the families and everyone else in the Rabbit Hole, as the news that their loved ones had been unchipped, evacuated, and brought to safety started flowing in.

At 2 am on Monday morning, to Salome's extreme relief, the final report came in. Her brother, his wife, and their two young children arrived safely at the Minneapolis safe house. They were the last family to reach their designated safe house and would be the first family to be moved to the Rabbit Hole, because they were the closest. Owen and Peter would airlift them to Mount Ararat within the next three days.

The remaining seven families would be moved over the course of the next two weeks, using various modes of transport arranged by Owen and Peter. First, they had to get to Mount Ararat and then to the Rabbit Hole where Ben and his public works team had been hard at it for long hours to prepare new quarters for all of them.

None of them knew where their final destination was.

President Harper could not control his curiosity anymore, "Peter, we have been guessing and wondering for months about this, but would you mind telling us where we are going?"

Peter replied with a big smile. "Not at all sir. We are taking you to Mount Ararat and from there to the Rabbit Hole."

Nigel hesitated for a moment, "Mount Ararat? In Turkey? You are not serious!"

Peter laughed. "No sir, not that far afield. Mount Ararat and the Rabbit Hole are all in Montana, not too far from Bozeman."

"What a relief! I was worried there for a while." Nigel laughed.

"What does it look like? Is it a farmhouse? Tell us more; we are very curious to know," Esther said.

Kelly explained, "Mount Ararat is a farm which we own jointly with Owen and Alison – a beautiful place. Peter and I have just moved in and have been enjoying every moment of it. It's just a few miles outside McLeod in the Sweet Grass County, about twenty miles southwest of Big Timber. All small towns."

"I've never been there, but it sounds lovely. What about the Rabbit Hole?" Esther wanted to know.

"Now, that's a different story. It's hard to explain. I have never experienced anything like it. It's a place one has to see and experience in person. I can tell you it is a cave system in the mountains of the Gallatin National Forest. I have been there twice and Peter a few more times and all I can say is it blew my mind away every time. I trust it will be okay if I don't tell you more than that. I really think you have to wait and see it for yourself. I won't do it any justice by trying to describe it." Kelly elaborated, without going into much detail. She wanted them to be surprised.

About three hours into their flight, Sam called Peter and gave him the good news that Operation Fugere was completed successfully and that everyone was out of harm's way. There was jubilation, not only in the Rabbit Hole, but also on the plane. Esther wiped the tears of joy off her face as she smiled and said, "Thank you, God!" while everyone nodded their heads in agreement.

Once they settled down after the exciting news, Nigel asked if they could continue the discussion they started earlier. "Please, tell us why Mount Ararat for the name of the farm?"

"Owen and Alison can tell you about the history of that much better than I can. They named the place long before Kelly and I appeared on the scene. We like the name. It is very appropriate as you will hear when Owen tells about it," Peter replied.

Owen and Alison recounted the whole chronicle from the time when Daniel and Mark knocked on their door late that night when they'd made the emergency landing on their farm in Nucla. Then continued right up to the point where they were on their way to the Rabbit Hole in the Baron 58 now.

They included the details of Sam and his family's rescue, the activation of Peter and Kelly, the contact with Tectus, and the invaluable assistance they were giving the Rosslerites. Finally, they told of the discovery of the space mirrors, Operation Night Owl when the chips were stolen, and the final breakthrough with the revelation of how to shut down the chips.

As the whole story unfolded through Owen's humoristic account, filled in by the others when required, the Harpers shook their heads in admiration. That this small group of people had achieved so much through their loyalty and dedication to their country, friends, and family was truly inspiring.

After listening to everything, Nigel and Esther agreed Mount Ararat was an appropriate name for the farm.

JR, Rebecca, Aaron, Cindi, and Mark made the trip to Mount Ararat as soon as they got the news that the Harpers were airborne. They took medical supplies, binoculars, zingers and owl drones equipped with surveillance cameras with them. On their arrival, Rebecca and Cindi went to the airplane hangar and prepared the place where they and the Harpers would hide until that night, when they would be taken to the Rabbit Hole.

The two of them remained there while JR, Mark and Aaron positioned themselves in different locations around the farm, from where they would have a good view of the surroundings. They would launch the surveillance drones a bit later to give them a better view so that Owen and Peter could be notified if it was safe to make the landing or not.

An hour out from Mount Ararat, JR contacted Peter and told him that everything was clear. They kept in touch until Owen landed the plane shortly after 5 am on the Monday morning, five and a half hours after they took off from Upper Cumberland airport. Owen taxied into the hangar while the Harpers had been lying low since they started the descent so that it looked as if there were only four people on the plane.

They all got out and were welcomed by the smiling faces of the five Rosslerites waiting for them. The Harpers were escorted to their quarters in a container at the back of the hangar, where Rebecca examined them both. First, to make sure they were suffering no ill effects of the chip removal, the flying, and the ordeal they'd been through since they were placed under house arrest.

The fact that the mission was almost over, and the realization that they could finally relax after more than forty-eight hours of high tension, allowed fatigue to set in. Owen, Alison, Peter and Kelly left for their homes while the Harpers and the rest all found a place to sleep for the remainder of the day.

Chapter One Hundred One

WE RESPECT YOUR CHOICE

By 9 am on Monday morning, while the Harpers and their rescuers were fast asleep over half a continent away, the first of the six agents who were guarding the former president opened his eyes. First, he became aware of a splitting headache, then that he was gagged and tied up. He had no idea what had happened. His last recollection was that he was standing outside having a smoke. He had no idea what day or time it was.

In moments, his heart was racing with panic. Something was terribly wrong. He started wrestling with the rope tied around his hands behind his back and after a while managed to free himself. He saw the little metal canister and envelope with his name on it, picked it up, and hurried into the house, where he found all his comrades conscious but still tied up. He helped to untie them, and a few minutes later the six terrified men read the letters in the envelopes addressed to each of them in person.

The Phoenix Agenda

We took the liberty of removing the biochip from your body. You are in no danger; we know how to remove the chips without causing any harm to you at all.

You can now choose what you want to do. If you wish to have the chip back in your body, please visit one of the implant facilities near you. They would be delighted to replace it. We apologize for any pain or inconvenience caused.

If you choose freedom, we suggest that you get away and find a hiding place where you can stay out of sight and the reach of the police and government. You should take the little blue canister and this letter with you, and bury it in a place where it can never be found. It contains the chip we took out of you.

When you make your choice, please remember what happened to the agents who failed to protect Sam Lewis, the former head of the CIA.

We respect your choice, whatever it is.

As they finished reading the letters, they stared at each other, too afraid to speak first. They knew very well about the horrific end that came to the Boise agents who failed in their duty, and they were now in the same boat as those ill-fated agents. If they decided to ask for the chips to be inserted again or stay on the farm, they would be dead in any event. If they left and went into hiding, they at least had a chance of survival.

The agent in charge of the group finally gathered enough courage to speak first, "The way I see it, men, is that we don't have much choice. Do we?" He looked around at them as they nodded their heads in agreement.

"Is it agreed then, we make a run for it?" one of them asked, just to make sure he understood correctly what everyone agreed to.

"I see no other option, unless you prefer to take your

chances with the mercy of President Brideaux," responded their leader.

Hearing Brideaux's name sent shivers down their spines. Within fifteen minutes, they were packed and ready to go. They left everything as they found it when they woke up. The more time that could pass between their departure and the discovery of the empty house, the further away they would be and the better their chances of survival.

In other parts of the country, eight more agents woke up with horrific headaches, untied themselves, read their letters, quietly thanked their mysterious liberators, and disappeared.

Chapter One Hundred Two

INDEED THIS IS THE PHOENIX

Shortly after darkness fell on a Monday night, the five Rosslerites along with Nigel and Esther Harper, left Mount Ararat. They arrived at the Rabbit Hole not long after midnight.

Every soul in the place was waiting for them. The euphoria that followed when the former president and his wife were led into the Robert Cartwright Town Hall was only matched by the time when Daniel and his friends arrived.

Tears of joy flowed freely, not only from the Harpers' faces but also from every other face in the room. When they all finally managed to calm down, Nigel took Esther's hand, stood up, and asked them for a moment. Everyone went quiet.

President Harper looked around him at all the people. He was without words for the first time in his life when it came to trying to express his feelings. The immense work they had achieved astounded him. Esther's and his rescue was nothing short of a miracle. It would be ages before he learned all it took to keep them safe as they were extracted from their home and brought here alive and well.

"Esther and I have been talking about this moment for many months. We actually prepared a speech for this moment. But there is nothing that could have prepared us for the events of the twenty-four hours that started the moment Peter and Kelly walked into our bedroom last night. There is absolutely nothing that could have prepared us for what we found here tonight. I cannot describe our joyful thanks for what you have done for us and all your families still on their way here.

"We are here to report for duty, not to receive Presidential treatment. We are here to work alongside you. We have come to this place to do our part in raising the Phoenix. There is not a task or duty that we wouldn't tackle. There is not a thing that we won't be prepared to do. We are here to support and assist you wholeheartedly in your effort.

"Our hands and our energy, our skills and our minds are available to you. It is an indescribable honor for us that you have invited us into your midst. From this moment forward, we would both like all of you, without exception, to call us by our first names and treat us the same as you treat anyone else here. It will be an honor for us to be part of this amazing family.

"We are astounded by what you have achieved, and we know we haven't even seen a fraction of it. We are astonished by your hospitality, your hard work, your dedication, and your loyalty - we would like nothing better than to be part of it.

"Indeed, this is the Phoenix. It has already been reborn and it is busy rising from the ashes of its predecessor. There is nothing that could be a greater honor for us than to be counted amongst you and to become part of the noble cause you have chosen.

"We thank God for you. May God bless all of you and your families and may God bless America and, indeed, the whole world."

The audience was on their feet in applause. Another round of embraces followed, and then Daniel and Sarah wanted to take them to their quarters so they could get some rest, but the Harpers didn't want to know anything about that.

"Daniel, my friend. You are not going to deny us the tour? Are you? We were told that everyone who stepped into this awe-inspiring place for the first time got a royal tour, which was led by Sarah. Esther and I would not be able to sleep until we have seen this whole place." Nigel laughed.

"Mr. Pres ...," Sarah began to say and remembered their request to be called by their first names, "Nigel and Esther, I am burning to show you, but aren't you too tired? You went through a lot the last day, not to even mention what you went through all those months before, or the ten-mile hike to get here."

Esther laughed. "We aren't that old, Sarah. We've just walked that ten miles and didn't even break a sweat. We also slept the whole day. We've seen only a little bit of this place and we want to see the rest. As Nigel said, we wouldn't be able to sleep until we've seen it all."

Many hours later, the Harpers were taken to their quarters, which were neighboring those of the Lewises. They were so excited and overwhelmed by what they'd seen they were unable to sleep. By six o'clock, they were still awake and ready to join Roxanne's morning Pilates session. After breakfast, they were invited to join the daily Steering

Committee meeting where they got their assignments. Esther, who was a practicing physician until she became First Lady, joined Rebecca's team and also the Gardeners of Gallatin because of her love of growing herbs.

Nigel was assigned to Sam's operations team and the Steering Committee. He also had a particular interest in construction, so therefore, his second assignment was to Ben's Department of Public Works. Ben explained that with the expected arrival of the rescued family members, there was a lot of construction work in progress, and they would welcome all the help they could get, irrespective of previous experience.

During the Happy Hour on Tuesday afternoon, Nigel got his induction into the rituals of the top secret society of the musketeers. After having two shots of Chateau de Grotte and one shot of honeyshine, he became a lifelong member of the exclusive, elite fraternity.

During the Wednesday morning and afternoon trips, he got his first two fly-fishing lessons from the members of his elite fraternity, and early on Thursday morning, he caught the first trout of his life. He was hooked on fly-fishing from that moment.

Esther immediately found camaraderie and friendship amongst her peers, Susan, Emma, Sally, Nancy, Martha and Bess. Within two days, she felt as if she had known them for years.

Chapter One Hundred Three

NO ILLUSIONS

On a Thursday morning at about 10 am, the Sheriff of Putnam County and his deputy arrived at the Harper's residence for their weekly visit. It took three minutes to comprehend what they were looking at, and for the sheriff to phone Jonathan Lucas, director of the secret services in the USA, to tell him what he found.

Lucas asked the sheriff to make sure that the news of the escape did not leak out to anyone under any circumstances. He would personally handle the situation from that point onwards. When the call ended, Lucas was shaking with fear. He'd assisted James Gordon to chip his predecessor, Robert Wilson, and was present when the six Boise agents were executed for their failure to guard Sam Lewis. He had no illusions about the fate awaiting him.

He looked around his desk, collected a few items, picked up his car keys, and left the office. Within an hour, he reached the outskirts of Washington. He'd already destroyed his mobile phone and disabled the GPS tracking device on his car. He was heading for Mexico, from where he would attempt to escape by boat to a secret hideaway in the Andes Mountains of Chile that he knew of.

By 1 pm, the security center in Washington noticed that the video and motion detector feeds from the Harper residence had stopped sending messages. The staff member reported this to his manager who immediately contacted the sheriff's office in Putnam County. The sheriff told him that the director of security, Jonathan Lucas, had been handling the matter since ten that morning already. The manager found that strange. As far as he knew, the feeds had only stopped working a few minutes ago. How did the director know about it almost three hours before the feeds went down? That was a question for his boss to investigate.

His manager immediately called Jonathan Lucas whose secretary informed him that Lucas had left the office shortly after ten and patched the call through to his cell phone, which went to Lucas' voice mail. He decided to call the deputy director of security. The deputy director was very surprised - he didn't have any knowledge about Lucas' involvement in anything related to the Harpers. Anything to do with the Harpers was a serious matter, and he should have been informed. He was worried.

When the deputy director couldn't get hold of Lucas either, he phoned the sheriff of Putnam County himself and got the shock of his life. For a few moments after the call ended, he contemplated a hasty departure. He knew all too well what happened to those who let Sam Lewis get away. However, after a while he managed to convince himself that he was not to blame for this fiasco. Nevertheless, he remained apprehensive.

At 3 pm Washington time on Thursday afternoon – 9 pm in Brussels – Liu Chen, the director of BOSS, answered his cell phone. Chen listened in absolute silence to the deputy director's report. When he finished, Chen instructed him to talk to no one about it. He would handle the situation from here and would call upon the deputy when necessary. He also told the deputy to make absolutely sure that the sheriff and his deputy kept their mouths shut.

Liu Chen had been present at James Gordon's chipping ceremony, and he had no illusions about the treatment that awaited him.

He turned around, looked at the naked woman in the bed next to him and said, "Anastasia, we have a lot of trouble."

Anastasia Oriov, the director of the Bureau of Information and Political Affairs (BIPA), despite the effects of the heroin shot she took earlier, could see that her lover was a troubled man. As he told her what happened, the blood drained from her face. By the time, Liu Chen finished his report, she was as pale as bleached linen. They stared at each other. Then Liu got up, put his clothes on, went to the bathroom, combed his hair, adjusted his tie, and walked back into the bedroom where he put his suit jacket on. He stood at the end of the bed, took out his 9 mm Beretta, and put it to his head. His last words before his brains speckled the wall to his left were, "Goodbye, Anastasia."

Anastasia looked at the mess and considered her options. She had nowhere to run and nowhere to hide. She had no illusions about what awaited her in the very near future. President John Brideaux was very clear about that the last time something like this happened. She opened the drawer of her bedside table, took the needle and syringe out, and filled it to the brim with a cocktail of heroin and valium. She found the big vein in her left arm and inserted the needle.

On Friday morning, the Supreme Council was in

session, but the seats of Liu Chen and Anastasia Oriov were empty. Nonappearance at his meetings was something John Brideaux hated with a passion. When he called a meeting, he expected people to be there, and anyone being absent without an excuse was more than his personality could handle.

He screamed into the intercom to his secretary, "Get hold of those two lazy bastards now. They most probably fucked the entire night and had too much drugs and booze. Tell them to get their asses over here immediately!"

Half an hour later, the secretary walked into the meeting room with a worried look on his face. "Did you get them? When will they honor us with their royal presence?" Brideaux wanted to know.

"Sir, I am afraid it's not good news. They were both found dead in Miss Oriov's apartment."

"Dead! What the fuck! Get the detectives onto it immediately and report back to me once you know what's going on." Brideaux ordered his secretary, turned back to the meeting attendees, and said, "Where were we?"

Senior inspector Jean Baptiste le Clercq stared at the scene in the bedroom of Anastasia Oriov's apartment as he tried to reconstruct the events that led up to the mess in front of his eyes. No forensic staff or anyone else was allowed to enter the room yet. Le Clercq saw no evidence of a struggle. The gun was still in the dead man's hand and the naked woman still had the needle and syringe stuck in her left arm. After fifteen minutes of observation and checking things, he concluded that it was a double suicide. There was nothing left but to try and find out why two of the most powerful and privileged people in the world would commit suicide.

He invited the forensic team in to come and do their

job, while he phoned Brideaux's Secretary to report to him that it was probably suicide and that the forensic team was busy collecting all the evidence. It would take a few days to gather and analyze everything before he would be able to report back.

When Brideaux got the note from his secretary, he read it and looked up to the council members and said with a grin on his face, "Well that's it then. Sounds like we have to get ourselves new directors for BOSS and BIPA to replace those two stupid assholes who killed themselves last night. Any suggestions?"

Two of the council members looked at each other in a fleeting moment of concealed disgust at Brideaux's reaction to the death of their colleagues. The man was a heartless and insensitive animal.

Nothing was reported in the media. Weeks later, people would learn that Chen and Oriov had resigned their positions and had been replaced.

Chapter One Hundred Four

THE VOWS

Midday on the Friday, Owen, Alison, Peter and Kelly had their gear packed for a weekend in the Gallatin National Forest. Owen and Alison were very excited for two reasons. It was going to be the first time they would see the Rabbit Hole, and they were invited to attend a very special occasion.

Kelly and Peter were excited to see their Rabbit Hole family again, but they were more excited about the fact that Saturday was their wedding day. Not only were the two of them going to make their wedding vows, but also Aaron and Cindi would be joining them at the altar to do the same. The people at the Rabbit Hole were also excited; a double wedding was not something that many of them had ever attended.

After dark, the four of them arrived at the Rabbit Hole and were welcomed by a jubilant crowd.

David, Salome's older brother and his wife and two girls had in the meantime been added to the numbers in the Rabbit Hole. Owen and Peter had airlifted them earlier in the week from the safe house in Minneapolis. Another twenty-one souls would be added to their numbers over the next two weeks.

Peter was pleased to see how well the Harpers had been received and how well they'd adapted to their new home in just a few days.

"Mr. President, I was wondering if you've made any good friends around here lately." Peter inquired, smiling as he remembered his thoughts many months ago about how well the president would fit in with the musketeers.

"Peter, first of all, please call me by my first name. Everyone here has been doing so since we asked them. Second, to answer your question; yes, I have made a few special friends, but it is top secret." Nigel laughed.

"I am an ex-CIA agent, Nigel, and I have top-secret clearance. You can tell me," Peter replied.

"Oh well, I guess I can trust you then. You see there is this top secret society here that call themselves the musketeers. It's an elite organization, and membership is strictly by invitation. Man, and that induction ritual is something else. I almost lost my voice and my breath. You have to be a tough man to get through that," Nigel explained as Peter laughed so much he had to sit down.

That night and the next morning, the Rabbit Hole was like an ants' nest as everyone was running around to get everything in place for the big event that afternoon. No one brought formal clothes with them when they moved to the Rabbit Hole. The wedding couples were happy to be married in informal clothes. Sushma, an ex-glossy magazine model and clothes designer, however, could not resist the challenge. She'd made two beautiful white dresses for the brides out of fabric Alison got and smuggled to her weeks ago without anyone knowing.

Early Saturday morning, the two brides were taken to Sushma and Raj's quarters where the final adjustments to their dresses were made, and they would be made up and pampered for their big day.

At two o'clock on Saturday afternoon, Felix Mendelssohn's wedding march started playing in the Robert Cartwright Town Hall. The guests all rose as two very proud men, John Mendenhall with Cindi at his side, and Nigel Harper with Kelly at his side, appeared in the doorway. In the center of the hall two more very proud men, Peter and Aaron, looked at their approaching brides in absolute astonishment.

Sam, who was a justice of the peace and therefore ex officio accredited to conduct wedding ceremonies, smiled as he looked at the couples with fondness. He remembered that it was not too long ago when his beloved Susan walked towards him in a chapel in Boise, Idaho. He was especially proud of the two agents who served him and their country so well, not only during all those years they worked for him while he was in the CIA, but in the recent months again.

The feasting and dancing went on into the wee hours of the next morning. Owen was the master of ceremonies and had them shrieking with laughter at all his witticisms and anecdotes. When the grooms made their speeches, they both remembered to thank Sarah Rossler for her help and guidance to find the loves of their lives.

Chapter One Hundred Five

ABSOLUTE POWER CORRUPTS ABSOLUTELY

On the next Wednesday afternoon, Jean Baptiste le Clercq received the forensic reports and studied them carefully. His first conclusion was correct. The traces of gunpowder on Chen's right hand and only his fingerprints on the weapon made it clear that he was the one who pulled the trigger. Only Oriov's fingerprints were found on the syringe, which made it clear that she was the only one who handled it. He was therefore satisfied there was no foul play involved. The two of them died within a few minutes of each other, most probably a suicide pact.

The question that remained was why did they do it? What drove them to such a drastic step? The blood analysis showed they'd both used drugs and alcohol on the night of their deaths. It didn't seem to be a good enough reason to commit suicide. He was stumped.

He looked through the list of their personal belongings and the accompanying photos but couldn't find anything that would lead him to the answer. There were no phone records among the evidence. He called the senior officer in charge of the forensic team and was informed that he required special clearance from the Supreme Council to access the phone records. Le Clercq phoned Brideaux's secretary and explained what he wanted. On Thursday morning, he had the phone records in his hand. The last call Oriov received was at six o'clock on the night of her death; Chen's last call came from Washington, less than an hour before his death.

He picked up the phone and called the number in Washington. Brad Johnston, deputy director of security in America, answered. Brad was a worried and very nervous man. He'd dealt with many crises in the last week. His director, Jonathan Lucas, had disappeared without a trace, and he was left to do two people's work.

The entire American police force and every security and law enforcement agency found themselves up to their asses in alligators because of the turmoil caused by the new financial system introduced by the Supreme Council. No one had time to look for Lucas. His phone never stopped ringing. It was one crisis on top of another, and he was tired and fed-up. He couldn't remember when the last time he'd slept was. Now he had to talk to a cop from Belgium whose French accent was so thick he could hardly comprehend what the man was saying.

Le Clercq had to repeat almost every sentence he was saying to Johnston, however, slowly he was getting parts of his message across. "Yes, monsieur, that is what I said. Directors Liu Chen and Anastasia Oriov are dead. I am investigating the reason for their deaths."

"Shit man, I don't know what you want from me. I was in Washington all the time. How the fuck can I help you solve a murder in Brussels?" Brad asked as he started to feel a little uneasiness in his stomach. He didn't know why, but he felt taking a superior attitude might help.

"No, no, monsieur, not murder, suicide. Both of them," Le Clercq explained.

"Even more so then. What the hell can I have to do with that? Can we please get to the point now? I have a lot more shit to deal with over here than you can ever imagine."

"Monsieur Johnston, you were the last person to speak to Director Chen on his mobile phone before he died. Between the end of your call and his death was less than an hour," Le Clercq said.

The penny dropped for Brad Johnston in that moment. "Oh ... my ... God! The mother of all fuckups!" Johnston screamed.

"Pardon, monsieur. What did you say?" Le Clercq asked. The phone went silent as he waited for Johnston to answer his question, but nothing came. "Are you still there monsieur Johnston?"

"Listen, Le Clercq. This is way above your pay grade and mine. I will call President Brideaux's secretary now. You can make your way over to him, and he can tell you what's going on if he wants to. I don't have any more time to talk to you." Johnston threw the phone down and dropped his head into his hands.

That was why Lucas disappeared. He understood the consequences for him when Brideaux heard about this. That was why Chen and Oriov suicided. They knew what was going to happen to them when Brideaux heard about this. It had been a week since he reported the disappearance of the former president and his wife. Brideaux and the Supreme Council were still clueless.

"What a complete and utter fuckup! Those who were supposed to take responsibility for this mess are either on the run or dead. I am all

that's left to take the fallout. How am I to escape this? What are my options?" A battle was raging in his mind while one cold shiver after another was trickling down his spine.

Brad Johnston knew he didn't have any more information than what the sheriff gave him. The Harpers had escaped, and there was no trace of the agents who were supposed to guard them. Was he supposed to know more? Was it his duty to get more information? He'd been told by Liu Chen to butt out and wait until he was called upon.

After a few minutes, he called Brideaux's secretary and told him what he knew and what he had done about the situation from the moment he learned about it right up until this call. He also gave him the sheriff's and his deputy's contact details.

When the call ended, Brad Johnston grabbed the muscles in his neck and shoulders to squeeze them in an attempt to get rid of the tension cramps. When he rubbed the muscle below his right collarbone, he remembered the chip and immediately stopped, he didn't want to disturb the damn thing and cause his own death. He then also remembered that he had nowhere to run and nowhere to hide and immediately abandoned all earlier notions of following in the footsteps of his missing director. In their department it was only Jonathan Lucas who was privileged enough not to be chipped, and he had used that privilege. How he hated the damn chip - how he hated to work for this government. He loathed every member of the Supreme Council. He detested this entire new world order, and above all was his total contempt for that animal, John Brideaux.

Three hours after his conversation with Brideaux's secretary, a horde of investigators, police, and officials descended in helicopters on the Harper's farm.

Four thousand three hundred and twenty-eight miles

away, in The Berlaymont in Brussels, the Supreme Council was in an emergency session. They nervously perched on the edge of their chairs as they expected to see their leader going mad at any moment. However, nothing was forthcoming; John Brideaux was as calm as a planted landmine.

"Sheriff okay, keep cool. Nothing will happen to you or your deputy. You did your job well, and you will be rewarded for that. Now, tell me what did you find on the first day when you arrived on the scene?" Brideaux said in a sweet and friendly voice. The call was on speaker so everyone in the room could hear.

The anxious sheriff explained in detail what he found and what he reported to Lucas and then later to Johnston. He made sure that he told them again that he didn't discuss the discovery with anyone, as he was ordered, and neither did his deputy.

"Great work, sheriff. I am proud of you." Brideaux said, to the immense relief of the sheriff and the bewilderment of the Council Members.

The councilors were looking at each other in disbelief. They didn't know this John Brideaux. Next, Brideaux asked his secretary to get hold of Brad Johnston and everyone in the room knew they would soon see the man they knew. Again, they were stunned.

"Brad, how are you doing? Sorry to trouble you. You are a very busy man, I know. Could you please do me a small favor?" Brideaux's friendly tone caught Johnston completely off guard.

When the call had come through and he was told who was on the line, he'd expected that his last moments amongst the living had arrived. He didn't know what to say and was stuttering. "Ah ... uh ... well ... Mr. President, I am very sorry about this big mess but ... ah ..."

"Brad, relax my friend, relax. Nothing to apologize for. You didn't do anything wrong. You did an excellent job. You are a real hero." Brideaux grinned. He liked it that people feared him.

Johnston regained some of his composure, "What is the favor I can do for you, Mr. President?" he asked as he started to relax.

"Can you please get me the list of the agents who have disappeared, as well as the list of all their family and friends? I take it you have that handy over there." Brideaux was still grinning.

"Yes sir, I have that right here. It will be with you in the next few seconds." Johnston replied.

Brideaux called his secretary and asked him to get hold of the manager of the Central Human Control Unit, known as 'The Beast'.

A few of the members realized what Brideaux was up to; most of them were however, too scared by his sudden streak of decency to think clearly and were still too puzzled to put two and two together.

When Anna, the manager of the Central Human Control Unit, arrived, Brideaux spoke to her and Boris, the acting director of BOSS. He remained very calm and collected. "Okay, here is what I want you to do for me. Anna, I want you to patch the screen of the CHCU through to that big screen there."

Next, he addressed Boris. "I want you to go with Anna and upload the names of a few people for me into the CHCU. I want the complete list of Anastasia's superstars. The full list of the Rosslers' family members and their employees' family members and, of course, Nigel and Esther Harper, together with the list that Brad Johnston has just sent us. Oh, and I almost forgot, the sheriff of Putnam

County and his deputy. I'll think about Brad Johnston and let you know if I decide to add him and his family's names to the list. Let me know when you're done. Oh, I almost forgot the important part. I want you to bring me the CHCU's control panel as well. Please join us for the party as soon as you're done."

He got on the phone with his secretary again. "I want you to arrange with the chefs to prepare a lot of food and drink. Make sure that we have lots of champagne, vodka, whiskey and wine. We don't want to run dry. Then arrange for at least twenty young and voluptuous women to join us. We're planning to have the mother of all orgies in this room tonight."

When he'd completed his orders, he looked around the room. "We haven't had ourselves any fun since the last food riot, which was over a week ago."

Almost everyone was smiling. They'd all figured out what their ingenious president had in mind, and most of them couldn't wait for the party to start.

"Okay, here's how we're going to do it. We will have a lotto. We will write down all those names on a piece of paper and throw them in a bucket. I have placed two million Liberty Dollars in the pool. There should be about a thousand people on that final list. Nigel Harper has a million on his head. His wife has two hundred thousand on hers, and each of the six agents who were supposed to guard them has fifty thousand on theirs. The rest of the people on the list will share the remaining half million equally between them. You see, that way, everyone is going to be a winner. Liberté, Egalité, Fraternité!" He received loud applause when he ended the explanation of the rules of the lotto. The party would be in full swing in an hour.

Eight hours later, across the globe, more than a thousand people, most of whom were famous and influential, were dead.

In the large meeting room of the Supreme Council, two councilors, the only ones in the room still on their feet, stood in a far corner looking at the disgusting scene of naked, drunk, drugged bodies scattered across the room in disgust.

One said quietly to the other, "In the last few weeks, I have reached the conclusion that Sir John Dalberg-Acton was absolutely right. Power corrupts, and absolute power corrupts absolutely."

Chapter One Hundred Six

SECOND WAR OF INDEPENDENCE

On the Monday morning after the double wedding, Sam welcomed Nigel to the operations team and started talking about the next stage of the rise of the Phoenix.

"We here at the Rabbit Hole agreed long ago that we will not accept the new world government and have firmly committed ourselves to destroy the tyranny they have brought to this world. By the grace of God, we have been successful at everything we have set out to achieve so far. I suggest we now consider our strategies for the final battle." With that motion, Sam opened the discussions.

Daniel was next. "Right in the beginning we made the decision that we have the best chance of winning this fight by outflanking Brideaux with superior technology. So far, it has proven to be the right decision. Our actions haven't required us to kill anyone, and I would like to see us continue with the same tactics."

Sam went around the table and got agreement from everyone. "Good, it seems to me we're all still on the same page as far as that is concerned then. Let's now discuss what our next move is and how to do it. Please put all ideas on the table, even if you think it is stupid. Resist the urge not to mention it for that reason. We want to hear everything - nothing is too outlandish for us."

Salome spoke up. "Luke was present a few days ago when we had a discussion about the killer nanobots. I am talking about those bots that were used to overpower security forces and nonconformists around the world. Those would probably be the same sort of bots used to kill Nigel's protection detail the day he and Esther were placed under house arrest. Let's call them the free-roaming bots," she said. She continued, "We need to find out everything there is to know about them. My suggestion is that we place that on the top of our list of things to do next."

"As long as those bots are out there and we don't have a way to neutralize them, everyone remains at risk. They're a major hazard to everyone, especially us. They aren't DNA specific, and they kill indiscriminately every human they encounter," Luke elaborated.

"We need more trained operatives to help us with undercover operations. When I look at how much we have been able to achieve since we activated Peter and Kelly, I suggest it's time to consider the activation of the two remaining non-existents. One of them used to live in Austin, Texas and the other in Los Angeles," Sam proposed.

Peter and Kelly, who were video conferencing into the meetings every day via the mirror satellite connection, agreed with Sam. Peter suggested they could help to activate those former agents with the aid of Tectus.

"I suggest we find out how we can get access to the Skywalkers and the Beast. If we get control of those and have neutralized the killer bots Salome mentioned before, we would have almost removed power from Brideaux's hands." Daniel added to the list.

Raj and Roy nodded. "Roy and I have been discussing that very idea for a while now. I think we must get the Tectus hackers to investigate that for us."

"Once we can get control of the Skywalkers and the Beast we can send a program update to disable all the chips or maybe just disable the killer and torture bots in the chips. This would render them harmless." Roy added.

"That would be ideal!" Sam exclaimed. "Do I understand you two correctly - we can deactivate the bots in the chips and then shut down the Skywalkers and the Beast?"

"I won't just shut them down," Roy laughed. "I intend to blow them all out of the sky! My trigger finger has been itching for a long time."

"Well Roy, nothing would give me greater pleasure than watching you do exactly that," Sam replied as everyone laughed.

"Lasers?" Daniel wanted to know.

Roy nodded. "Yep, I'm thinking we could employ our sky mirrors in a coordinated laser attack against the Skywalkers and take them all out very quickly."

"Except for Nigel, we've all watched those horrible videos of what's going on in Professor Barbara Cohen's Science Advisory Panel Headquarters at that plant in China. I would like nothing more than to see that facility and all chip warehouses obliterated." Rebecca said with hatred in her voice.

"What are you talking about Rebecca?" Nigel asked.

"Nigel it is the most repulsive thing I have seen in my entire life, there are no words that can describe what's going on in that place. Perhaps Sam and Daniel could show you the information we got from the Tectus agents in China. But be forewarned, it is exceedingly upsetting," she replied.

Sam and Daniel nodded their agreement with Rebecca's suggestion to show Nigel the videos.

"I know it's too early to make the final decision, but from what I've heard so far, it seems we'll have to follow a big bang approach. By that, I mean everything will have to be prepared and coordinated and then executed at once," Luke concluded.

"Yes, we'll have to get all our ducks in a row before we pull the trigger. The element of surprise is crucial, I think. I have to admit I can't wait to see the day we take down that slime-ball," Salome said as she recalled the disgust Brideaux stirred in her the only time she met him.

"My concern is that after the last carnage and starvation orchestrated by Brideaux and his disciples, many of the people who could have helped us will have been chipped. Although we now know how to remove the chips safely, in some cases we have to think about the possibility that we might not want to remove them or completely deactivate them," Daniel said.

Everyone was looking at him for clarification. "Daniel, I'm afraid I've lost you there. What do you have in mind?" Sam asked.

"What I'm trying to say is - now that people can't move around undetected, and they can't buy or sell, get food or medicine or any services without a chip in their bodies, none of them would be prepared to take the chance to work with us. My idea is that we should find a way to only undermine the killer and torture bots in the chip and leave the rest of it intact. That way, people will still have an active chip, and they'll be able to get by any scanners, get their food and medicine as usual, without having to worry about being killed or tortured. That's the only way we are going to get them to work with us."

Sam smiled. "Aha, I see what you mean. Good thinking Daniel. That means they really will be 'undercover' so to speak."

"Yes exactly. Roy and his team should have a look at how to override the current program to disengage the killer and torture bots without having to remove the chip. Of course, when it's done, they'll have to make sure the chip won't send a message to the Skywalkers and the Beast."

Daniel noticed the big grins on Raj and Roy's faces and realized they probably had a solution already. "You two go ahead and make my day. Tell me you already have it or know how to do it."

"You want to see a demo?" Raj laughed.

They explained that they had in fact already developed and tested the program to shut the chip down remotely. The first step in the process was to recall and then deactivate the killer and torture bots. To make the change to keep the rest of the chip active would take them less than an hour to do. The only thing remaining would be to make sure the chip wouldn't send a message to the Skywalkers, but even if it did, they were sure there would be ways to overcome that problem as well.

"We can shut it down from close-up or as far away as a mile, even more if we use the spyflies or zingers." Raj explained.

By now, everyone was ecstatic. Nigel just shook his head in disbelief. *I wish I'd a team like this around me every day when I was president.*

"Coming back to Rebecca's suggestion, are there any ideas how we could go about destroying the Science Advisory Panel Headquarters and chip warehouses?" Sam asked.

Peter had an idea. "Well, as you know, I've been to one of the warehouses. I'm not sure all of them would be as poorly guarded as the one I saw. Nevertheless, I've been wondering if it would be possible to use Roy's owls to drop explosives on the warehouses. The only issue is that I'm not sure the owls would be able to lift the weight of the explosives we might need."

Daniel caught Roy's eyes and saw the smile breaking across his face. "Peter, I suspect Roy can solve that little problem of yours. I'll let him explain."

Roy was already deep in thought and didn't hear them.

"Roy?" Peter asked but got no response. "Earth calling Roy! Roy James! Are you there?"

Salome elbowed Roy and startled him out of his daydream. "What?"

"Roy, tell us what you've been thinking. Where have you been the last few minutes?" Salome prompted.

"I have been thinking about nanonukes and chip warehouses," he replied.

"Mind telling us exactly what you've been thinking?" Daniel laughed.

"Well, I thought I heard Peter saying something about using the owls to drop bombs on the warehouses. I think there might be a better plan. I could build us some nanonukes, which we could plant at the warehouses. They will be no bigger than a pencil."

"Peter, does that solve your problem?" Daniel wanted to know.

"Yes absolutely." Peter laughed. "I always wanted to nuke something - now I might get my chance."

"Mr. President - ahh sorry ... that was force of habit - *Nigel* - you have been very quiet, any ideas from your side?" Sam looked at his former boss, still finding it odd having to call him by his first name.

"I've been listening to all of you for the past few hours, and I have to say, it's mind blowing to see you at work. Since the start of this meeting, my already high admiration for the courage and ability of this group has gone up several more levels. I am truly honored to be serving with you.

"I agree with what Daniel said in the beginning. We won't overpower them with force - we have to outthink and outwit them. I'm now convinced that's exactly what is going to happen. It's going to be as the Bible says, 'Not by might nor by power, but by My Spirit,'" he quoted from the book of Zechariah.

"While you have been talking, I also thought that we are in a situation very similar to that of our ancestors before the War of Independence. In the same way our forebears declared their independence from tyranny and injustice and took up arms to fight for it - we have declared our desire to be free and independent.

"A few key phrases from the Declaration of Independence spring to mind – 'all men are created equal', 'unalienable rights of Life, Liberty and the pursuit of Happiness'.' Whenever government becomes destructive, it is the right of the people to alter or to abolish it, and to institute new government'. 'Under absolute despotism, it is their right - it is their duty, to throw off such a Government, and to provide new guards for their future security'.

"We find ourselves in a second War of Independence,

this time not only for the liberation of the United States, but the entire world." Everyone applauded as Nigel ended.

After this, Sam suggested that they wrap it up for the day. "Raj and Roy will work on Daniel's suggestion. I'll brief Peter and Kelly about reactivating the other two agents. Salome and Luke can get in touch with Dennis McMahon and Eric Winchester to make sure we can count on the backing of Tectus."

Chapter One Hundred Seven

THE WAY OUT

The Supreme Council was still in a celebratory mood after the party a few nights ago, when they killed off more than a thousand of the world's nonconforming celebrities, while having a lot of fun in the process. Despite the fact that John Brideaux and the rest of the councilors were painfully aware the Rosslerites were behind the escapes and still at large, they all believed they got the last laugh when they killed the Harpers and the Rosslerites' family members.

The introduction of their new global monetary system was a huge success. In the weeks that followed the initiation of the project, driven by hunger and desperation, the bulk of the remainder of the unchipped received implants. The fact that very few of them did so voluntarily didn't bother the council in the slightest. The few who remained unchipped were those who managed to escape and set up a subsistence lifestyle in remote and hidden places far away from the cities. They would be dealt with soon.

Professor Barbara Cohen's birth control program was uploaded to the chips months before the economic changes were announced. The profile of the super human of the future was created and fed to the Beast. It was working its way through the list of people who were not allowed to produce offspring - sterilizing them all by activating the birth control routine in their chips and triggering miscarriages in the pregnant.

Within a few months, the population growth rate would show a negative trend. Within twenty years, the world population would dwindle to two billion mark - the ideal number that planet earth could sustain, according to the council's scientists.

President Brideaux was extremely pleased with the results of the new world economic initiative and Professor Cohen's contribution to birth control. He thanked and congratulated everyone for their hard work and dedication making those projects such a big success.

The new director of BIPA, Ashleah Borg, thought that with the successful completion of the chipping program, it was time for the Supreme Council members to start building a good image among the populace. She suggested that a few world trips would help to achieve that. Her submission was met with general approval from the members, and she was given permission to make the necessary arrangements for the trips, including informing the media about the schedule and purpose.

As the council members got up to leave the meeting, Ruben Weinstein walked over to Rafael Martinez. "You got time for lunch?" he inquired.

"Always amigo, always. One o'clock at the Comme Chez Soi?"

"Sounds good to me. See you there at one."

"Mr. President, Chief Detective Pierre Bertrand is here for his appointment."

"Show him in!" Brideaux barked back.

"Bertrand, give it to me in five minutes or less. I have a lot to do." he growled at the bewildered police officer.

"Yes, sir. As you requested, all councilors are now under full surveillance 24/7. All their phones are tapped, and their homes bugged. In my report, you will find the details of everyone - sexual preferences, partners, drug use, friends, meetings, extramarital affairs, and all activities of the past week. Is there anything else you want me to take care of?"

"Yes. I want to see a report like this on my desk every week. If you find anything that looks suspicious, you contact me immediately. Make sure no one knows about this, and I mean no one. Make sure the people working for you understand this as well. If this leaks out, I am going to push buttons, and yours will be the first. Is that understood?"

"Yes, sir I understand."

"We are done. Make sure you don't screw up, Bertrand. If you do, you might not be so lucky as to find your ass in Siberia, as a few others did."

Brad Johnston received a personal call from President John Brideaux to inform him of his promotion to Director of Security in America. A very unsympathetic reminder to make sure there were no 'screw ups' during his watch accompanied the call.

When Johnston placed the phone down, he wondered if he had the right to decline the promotion or maybe resign. From the tone of Brideaux's voice, he got the impression that would not be the case. It was an 'until death do us part' proposition, and he knew all too well death was what was going to part them unless he could find a way out.

As he had been doing hundreds of times the last few days, he sat back and considered his options. The answer, however, remained the same – with the chip in his body, he had no options other than suicide. The list containing the names of more than a thousand people killed on the night the news of the Harper escape broke served as an unambiguous notice of his hopeless situation, and it enraged him. What was infuriating beyond description was the rumor doing the rounds about the Supreme Council's bacchanalia while killing the unsuspecting and innocent people that night.

His troubled mind was raging with thoughts. *Think Brad Johnston, think. There must be a way out. You have been a security agent all your life - there must be a way out somehow.*

Despite his efforts to focus his thoughts, nothing was forthcoming by the time his phone rang. It was his secretary letting him know that his senior investigator was there for their scheduled appointment.

"Come on in Cathy." He waved Cathy Ballmer into his office and pointed her to a seat.

After the usual courtesies, he got straight to the purpose of the meeting. "Okay Cathy, what news do you bring me about the disappearance of the Harpers their agents, the Rosslerites' family members, and their security guards?"

"Mr. Johnston, I am afraid there is no progress to report. We have worked on the assumption that every one of them would be dead because of the activation of the kill routine in their chips. We haven't found one single body. No trace of them, not even rumors. We've checked every hospital, clinic, morgue, and graveyard in the entire country –

we're still none the wiser. We've questioned their friends, surviving families, and acquaintances - no results."

"That is bizarre - there were eight families, twenty-five people in the Rosslers' family group plus their eight agents, the two Harpers, and their six agents - in total, forty-one people. They're all dead, yet there are no bodies. Mr. Johnston, do you think there's a chance they could perhaps still be alive? I wouldn't know how they would have been able to escape death, but maybe it is a possibility we should at least consider."

"No don't waste your time on that," he said in a brusque tone. "They're all dead - you and your team have to find those bodies. Keep on digging. Something is bound to turn up eventually."

"Yes, sir, that's so, but..."

"Cathy, you have a chip. I have a chip. Do you want to flip a coin to decide who of us is going to take the chance to verify your theory? Those chips would not have missed anyone, take my word for it. Just look at this list. There are more than a thousand names on it. They are all dead, and that's been confirmed. It doesn't make sense that they're all dead but forty-one somehow miraculously escaped."

"Yes sir."

"You will have to excuse me - I have an urgent matter to attend to. Keep me posted with your progress."

When the door closed behind her, Brad had a big smile on his face - he could barely control his excitement. *Of course they're still alive! Cathy and her team have proved that beyond reasonable doubt. The question is how did they manage to do it? They found the way out.*

Despite the stress and anxiety threatening to drive him over the edge, Brad Johnston was certain of one thing. He was not going to let anyone know he believed there were forty-one live people on that list of the dead.

On his computer, he browsed to the top-secret folder about the Rossler investigation and typed in his access code. He firmly believed the answer he was looking for would be somewhere in those files.

Ruben Weinstein was the third-richest man in the world, just five billion dollars short of Rafael Martinez's hundred and twenty billion empire.

Weinstein came from a low-income family and humble beginnings. Hard work and perseverance made him a fortune in the offshore oil industry. Martinez, on the other hand, came from a rich family - he inherited a giant telecom company from his parents in his mid-forties and expanded it into the largest telecommunications provider in the world. Only John Brideaux, who'd accumulated more than two hundred billion, was richer than they were.

The two men ordered drinks and food and settled down for the discussion they'd both known they had to have, for some time now.

"Rafael I trust that what is going to be said here today will remain between us?"

"You have nothing to fear, amigo. What is said in Comme Chez Soi, stays in Comme Chez Soi." Rafael laughed.

"Well then, now that we have agreed about that, how can I put it?"

"No need, amigo. I can see you are not a happy man. If it makes you feel any better, neither am I. This is not what I had in mind."

"Yes exactly. We signed up to make the world a better place, to eradicate poverty, sickness, and inequality. Conversely, we have succeeded in creating a terrifying life of oppression, inequality, and hardship for everyone. I am deeply ashamed of what I have done. I regret every moment of it. I would have killed myself if I did not sincerely believe I could undo the evil I have committed." Ruben got tears in his eyes while he was talking.

"We have to do something to stop this madness, Ruben. I am on your side. But I think you know as well as I do the danger we are creating for ourselves and our loved ones. We will have to be very, very careful."

"No doubt about that. Nonetheless, I feel obligated to undo the evil I have helped to create. To that end, I will commit every resource I have available to me, if it costs me my life, then so be it. That would be a small price to pay for my evil deeds."

"I could not have said it better. Do you have any ideas?" Rafael responded with the emotion clearly audible in his voice.

"Not a specific plan yet, if that is what you are asking. I wanted to talk to you first."

"I have been looking for an opportunity to talk to you. I don't have a specific plan either but I am convinced with our combined means we can certainly find a way out. Like you, I commit everything I have to the cause, even my life if it's necessary."

The two men were relieved to discover their mutual feelings and trust. They decided to spend a few days to think about a strategy and compare notes at the next meeting.

A few miles away, John Brideaux's security detail delivered him to his luxurious residence. One of them opened the door for him, while the rest formed a guard of honor, saluting him while he walked past. He smiled. *I love this life! The absolute power in my hands! Feared by every human on the planet! I am God!*

When he walked into the house and saw the three young beautiful scantily clad girls waiting for him in his lair, he popped the second amphetamine tablet of the day. There was no way out. He had an all-nighter coming, and he would need the energy and the euphoria.

Chapter One Hundred Eight

GETTING THE WHEELS IN MOTION

"Jack Symonds is an ex-Delta Force operator. One of the best of the best ever produced by that elite Special Forces unit."

As Sam briefed them on their assignment in Los Angeles to activate the third non-existent, Peter and Kelly listened carefully.

"Wow, Delta Force! No one fools with those guys!" Peter exclaimed.

"You can say that again. It's going to be difficult to find him and convince him of who you are. He is a lone wolf with strange habits - probably what kept him alive so far. When I pulled him out of Delta Force to come and work for me, he already had five years of die-hard frontline experience. He's seen more action than most of us had hamburgers in our lives."

"Tell us more about his training and skills," Peter asked.

"He's gone through the most arduous training in the armed forces. He's highly skilled in counter-terrorism, counter-intelligence, recon, and taking down high-value targets. He's had sniper, small tactics, weapons, and explosives training and is an expert at Krav Maga, the Israeli military contact combat self-defense system. In his advanced Delta Force training, he also acquired skills in lock picking, unconventional demolition techniques, bomb making, and a variety of espionage skills including surveillance and counter-surveillance."

"Good grief Sam, this guy sounds terrifying, almost like one of those old Rambo movies!" Kelly laughed.

"Those are the training and skills Delta Force operatives get. He doesn't look like Rambo, I can assure you. He doesn't strike an imposing figure, and that is exactly what makes him so lethal. People always underrate him.

The night I met him he was with his girlfriend. Two guys, both of them almost double his size, insulted her. What happened next you only see in the movies - less than a minute later the two bullies had a broken arm and two broken noses between them, and Jack was finishing his beer as if nothing had happened."

"I'll take care that we don't make an enemy out of this man," Peter remarked. His dry tone emphasized the simple statement.

"Well, you'll first have to convince him that you aren't the enemy." Sam laughed. "He isn't an aggressive man by nature - he has a sound mind and strong psyche, highly intelligent. You don't have to fear him."

"Are you at liberty to tell us about the operations he was involved in?" Peter wanted to know.

"I don't mind telling you. With this new government, I am not bound by my oath of secrecy anymore, but I would prefer if we get him over to our side first. If I have his permission, I'll tell you. However, for now just take my word for it - there were a lot fewer bad people around, and the world was a lot safer when he worked for me."

"What is his personal background, and what was he doing last you heard of him?" Kelly wanted to know.

"The last time I had contact with him was a month before I retired. You two will remember that was also the last time I had contact with you. When I recruited him, he left the force and became an antique dealer. That was the ideal cover to allow him to travel all over the world in search of rare antiquities. His shop was on Camden Drive, in Beverly Hills.

"He grew up in the Laramie Mountains of South East Wyoming close to Cheyenne. He had an older brother, two sisters, and at last check, both his parents were still alive. He had a girlfriend at the time, whose name was Sue-Ellen."

Sam's briefing continued for a while longer until they were satisfied that they had exchanged all the necessary information. They decided that Owen, Alison, Peter, and Kelly would take a trip to LA to visit the Hollywood studio, where one of Owen's books was being filmed, while they were there.

Soon after the video conference with Kelly and Peter ended, Daniel called Sam and the rest of the ops team over to Raj's computer center for a demo of the deactivation of the nanobots.

The techies were beaming - they had good reason. With a computer emulation, Raj showed them how they were able to take an active chip, recall the nanobots, and destroy them while the rest of the chip continued operating as usual.

"What about signals going out of the chip?" Salome wanted to know.

"We have discovered and analyzed all the signal-generating events in the chip and found the one that would alert the Skywalkers of the inactivity of the nanobots. We had to make a small code change to the deactivation process. During the recall routine, a few lines of new code will be loaded into the chip's firmware, and that will guarantee it keeps on sending 'all-is-well' messages to the Skywalkers," Mandy explained with a big smile on her face.

Salome high-fived with Mandy as the rest of the audience gave her a big round of applause.

"Excellent work team!" Daniel congratulated them. "You mentioned earlier that you destroy the bots after you have recalled them. How do you accomplish that?"

Roy explained. "The nanobots are miniature robots that follow preprogrammed instructions. Thanks to the Tectus hackers, we already had every bit of code that controls the bots. All we had to do was change that code so that it instructs the bots to return to the carbon nanotubes from where they came. Once inside the tubes, the hatches are closed, and the bots are given instructions to self-destruct."

"Roy, you and Raj always make these things sound so easy," Daniel commented.

"It was not difficult, with all the work we have done - we probably understand these chips as well as any of Brideaux's scientists," Roy replied.

Luke summarized the significance of the achievement. "I'm stoked! This means we can go out and recruit helpers amongst the chipped. They can pass through any scanners, and no one will ever know because they will be under the ideal cover."

"It is as you say, Luke," Salome joined in. "However,

don't forget the chips still have a location tracking feature that will tell the Skywalkers where the person is at any given moment."

A long silence followed as the reality of Salome's remark dawned on them. Daniel caught the silent exchange of looks and raised eyebrows between Raj and Roy.

"Have you two perhaps forgotten to tell us something? Or should we convene a summary trial to find out?" Daniel looked at them with a blank expression on his face, struggling not to laugh.

Roy and Raj looked at each other, then at the group and then at the door.

"Don't even think about it." Daniel grinned. "I am much closer to the door than you are. Talk or face the consequences."

Everyone was staring at them. "Daniel what's going on here?" A worried Nigel wanted to know.

"Just hang on Nigel, you will find out in a moment," he said, pointing at Roy and Raj. "I suspect our two friends here have forgotten to tell us something very important."

Everyone's eyes turned to the accused.

Raj turned to Roy. "I have made a mistake like this before and got punished for it. It is your turn to take the rap."

"Ahh well, how can I put it ... ahh, mhh. Okay. We have actually solved that tracking issue of yours Salome. I am sorry, but we just didn't have the opportunity to tell you yet."

Roy looked like a little boy caught with his hand in the cookie jar. "Okay, explain what you forgot to tell us. We are all ears darling - mummy won't smack you." Salome started laughing.

"Raj and his team developed a program that overrides

the tracking feature and can make the chip carrier appear in any place we want. The same sort of thing we did with the GPS tracking devices in the vehicles of Sam's agents in Boise. Oh, and before Raj and I get into more trouble - we can also swipe the ID number from any active chip and use it in another."

When Roy finished the clarification, chaos erupted. Everyone shouted and cheered while Salome grabbed Roy and started kissing him passionately.

"From now on I am going to keep on forgetting things until I get a kiss like that!" Roy gasped when he was able to get a breath.

When the jubilation subsided, Nigel and Sam just looked at each other and shook their heads.

"These guys did all of that in less than twenty-four hours," Nigel whispered. "It's incredible isn't it?"

Sam nodded. Nigel, Sam, Ryan, and Luke left soon after. It was time for the musketeer's happy hour, and today they had something huge to celebrate.

Dennis McMahon and Eric Winchester dialed into the video conference requested by Salome. They still didn't know the position of the Rabbit Hole or the name of the place. As a security measure, it was agreed long ago that none of the Tectus members would ever ask or try to find out.

With the greetings and introductions out of the way, Sam started. "Dennis I believe you and Eric will agree that the teamwork between Tectus and the Rossler Foundation has produced spectacular results so far. We're here to find out if we can count on continued cooperation."

Dennis came to the point right away. "No need to ask, Sam. We would like nothing better than to work with you and your team. Tectus and all its resources are at your disposal."

"That's exactly what we were hoping to hear, and we are truly grateful for your help," Luke replied.

Sam continued. "We would like to invite the two of you to join the operations team and dial in via video conference during our meetings from now on. Would you be able to do that?"

"We were hoping you'd suggest that." Dennis smiled.

"We'd also like to know how the Supreme Council's latest insanity impacted he Tectus members and their families."

Eric replied. "Well Sam, the good news is that, thanks to the forewarning and advice from Peter, most of us came through it unscathed. Everyone including their families is still alive. The bad news is that nine of our members and their families were chipped. Although we are taking care of them so that they have food and shelter, we had to break all other contact with them. We were going to ask you for the necessary equipment to remove the chips and move them to secure locations. It wasn't easy to abandon them like that. You know our old military motto 'no one left behind'. But, in this case, we had no choice, we had to think of the bigger picture."

"Don't stress about that. We can help you. Salome can explain it."

Salome explained about the changes that Raj and Roy made to undermine the adverse features of the chips.

"That is a major step forward!" Dennis exclaimed when she finished.

"Yes that's indeed the case. But we will have to be very

careful not to start demilitarizing chips left and right. Doing that will cause a big security risk. If the authorities discover it, you can be sure new software will be downloaded to the chips via the Skywalkers immediately. That will be disastrous for us, as it will put us right back to where we started many months ago without chips," Salome warned them.

"I can see the danger. We will have to think it through carefully and get back to you for your advice and approval. Tell us what you have in mind for the immediate future and how we can help you?" Eric asked.

Sam gave them an overview of the brainstorming session a few days ago. "We've identified three major targets. First and most important is the free-roaming bots. We have to find out who produces them, where the manufacturer is located, and all the technical details. I take it you agree that as long as we can't eliminate those bots we're still up the creek?"

Eric and Dennis nodded their agreement.

"The next two targets are the Beast and the Skywalkers, which we believe are both controlled from somewhere in Brussels. We have to find out exactly where the control centers are and how those devices work. For all three of the targets, we need your assistance," Sam concluded.

"You got it," Dennis and Eric replied in accord, without hesitation.

"I have another important matter to discuss," Salome said. "We want to know if you can get access to the records of former security force and law enforcement personnel."

Dennis laughed. "I think I know where you are going with that. Yes, we can. In fact we already have access. It was one of our first operations. We're not only able to access the records - we can also edit them. Is that what you had in mind?"

"Exactly what I had in mind," Salome answered as smiles broke across Sam and Luke's faces. "I am sure that's going to come in very handy in the future."

"Well, as you are probably aware, many of our members are ex-military and police. It is important to make sure their names disappear from the books. Just let us know when you need that service. For you, there will be no charge." Eric laughed.

The discussions continued for a few more hours. By the end of the videoconference meeting, they'd agreed that Tectus would immediately mobilize a team of hackers to track down the manufacturer of the free-roaming killer bots and try to hack into their systems.

They would contact their members in Europe and launch an operation to start collecting information about the government offices and employees in Brussels. Over time, their agents would be provided with the necessary apparatus to expand their operations.

They would dedicate a team of hackers to work full time on breaking into the networks of the warehouses and start collecting every bit of information they could get.

Sam ended the meeting on a counselling note. "It is critical that we remain undetected until the very last minute. Therefore, it's important that you remain a small but effective organization. The more members you have, the more chance you have of discovery. If it's necessary to reassign some of your members or break contact with them, then do so. Only recruit new people if it is absolutely necessary because of a specific skill that neither you nor we have."

Dennis and Eric understood the importance of Sam's request, and had no issues with it.

Peter and Kelly went in search of Jack Symonds the day after they and the Bells arrived in LA. They soon discovered that Jack and Sue-Ellen, now married with two small children, had abandoned their shop a few weeks ago. The new financial system ruined their business overnight, as it did for so many others. On top of that, their shop was looted during the riots - people collecting valuables to barter for food and shelter stole everything. Their savings and livelihood vanished in just a few days.

Peter and Kelly drove out to Jack's home address, and parked a few blocks away. Each launched a spyfly and navigated it to the address while they remained in the car with tinted windows, which had been supplied by an LA Tectus member.

"Peter what do you think? The place seems to be empty. I get the impression there is no one living there at the moment."

"I got the same idea. Okay, let's bring the flies in and go back. I'll have to get one of Alison's extreme makeovers to come back and talk to the neighbors."

Later that afternoon, Peter returned in a different car, disguised as a man with long blond hair, blue eyes, thick black-framed glasses, and a limp in his left leg.

"Ma'am sorry to trouble you. I am looking for Jack Symonds."

"They used to live next door, but they moved away a few weeks ago. Didn't have much contact with them. I don't know where they went. But the old lady in the house on the other side knew them very well and might be able to tell you."

"Thank you, ma'am. It's very kind of you."

Peter walked around to the house, sincerely hoping that he wouldn't come to another dead end.

"Ma'am apologies for the intrusion. The lady two houses down said you might be able to tell me where I can find Jack Symonds."

"No trouble, son. Jack and his family left about four weeks ago after their shop was ransacked. They lost everything. The poor souls - and the little children - I feel so sorry for them. How do you know Jack?"

"Jack and I have been good friends since our school days. We haven't seen each other in years. I thought I would pay him a surprise visit while I'm in LA on business. By the sounds of it, things are not going well with my old friend?"

"That is definitely the case. They left here with nothing. It was not only the loss of their business. Jack got into some sort of trouble. Not sure exactly what it was, but he and his family were all taken away and implanted with those things in their shoulders. I also have one of them - otherwise, I won't get my pension. Jack and Sue-Ellen did not like those things in their bodies at all. Lovely girl, Sue-Ellen, and two lovely children. They always called me grandma."

Peter's heart dropped to the floor. Jack Symonds's case had just become a lot more complicated than he anticipated.

"Ma'am, any idea where they went?"

"I don't know the address where they live, but I have Sue-Ellen's mobile number. We phone each other every few days so I can talk to the children. Jack found a job at a factory, and she is working night shift at a grocery store."

"Would you mind giving me her number? I would really like to look them up and see if there is anything I could do to help my old friend."

"No problem. I am sure he'll be glad to see you again, and it would be very good if you have any means of helping them."

"Thank you, ma'am I really appreciate your help. Please don't tell them about me. I want to surprise them."

"Don't worry, son. It will be our secret." She smiled and winked at him.

As soon as Peter got in the car, he phoned Eric and asked him to track down the location of the cell phone. Early the next morning he and Kelly were at the address they got from Eric. They spotted Jack when he came out of the house to catch a bus to work. They launched a few spyflies, got them into the house, and hooked them up to recorders. There was nothing else to do but wait until they'd recorded a days or two of activity. They left to join Owen and Alison on their visit to the film studio.

On the second day they retrieved the surveillance equipment and studied the recordings. It didn't take long to come to the shocking conclusion that Jack and his family were in dire straits. It was painful to see how the family was struggling to keep body and soul together. Jack hardly ever said a word - he just stared into the void. It was clear that the children felt insecure, and Sue-Ellen was stressed to breaking point. There was not enough food in the house, and Jack looked like a defeated man, only a shadow of the man Sam described to them.

"Peter, when I compare what Sam told us about Jack to what I've seen and heard on those recordings I'm very worried. How much more can they take?"

"We'll have to move quickly. Unless you have a better idea, I'm going to approach Jack directly today. I just want to clear a few things with Daniel and Sam."

"That sounds soon enough for me. What's your plan?"

"We'll need Daniel and Sam's permission, but I'm going to suggest we get Jack and his family to Mount Ararat as soon as possible. Once there, we can decide about the rest."

"Good idea. It's a good thing they aren't under direct surveillance now. On the farm, we have enough food and accommodation for them and much better living conditions." Kelly had a faint smile when she thought how nice it would be to have the little boys around.

Owen and Alison were happy with Peter's suggestion. Daniel and Sam took less than thirty minutes to get the Steering Committee's approval.

That afternoon when Jack left the factory, at the end of his shift, Peter waited for him at the gate. "Jack Symonds is it?"

"Yes, who wants to know?"

"My name is Peter Scott. Can I have a few minutes of your time? It's very important that I talk to you."

"I have to catch that bus to get home before my wife goes to work."

"Believe me, Jack, it is not going to be a waste of time. I'll drive you home, and we can talk on the way. Is that okay with you?"

"Okay."

When they were in the car, Peter took out a letter and handed it to Jack. "It's from a mutual friend of ours. I'd like you to read it before I continue."

Jack looked at the envelope with his name on it and immediately recognized the handwriting. It felt like a very long time since he'd seen that handwriting, but as far as he knew the man whom that writing belonged to was dead. He was on alert and curious at the same time when he finished reading.

"Good. I've read it - it says I can trust you. I don't, and I don't know a Sam Lewis."

Peter was getting worried that the direct approach might not have been such a good idea after all. Jack was apprehensive.

"Jack I know it's weird but please hear me out. Sam gave me a few bits of information, which according to him, only the two of you know. I will report them to you and then you can decide what you want to do."

"I am listening."

Peter continued and related the details of a few missions that Jack worked on for Sam, including the three and four-word pass codes used on each. Jack stared out the window, emotionless.

There were just a few people in the world whom he'd ever trusted - Sam Lewis was one of them.

When Peter finished, Jack looked at him and said, "Stop the car. This is as far as I go."

Peter was devastated. *I've blown the whole operation.* Jack scribbled something on the back of the envelope when the car stopped dropped it on the seat, got out and walked away without saying a word.

A smile broke over Peter's face when he read the words. *'Tonight 9:30 in the park down the street from my house.'*

At exactly 9:30 pm, Jack appeared out of nowhere next to Peter where he was sitting in the dark, on a bench, under a big tree. "I decided to listen to what you have to say. Don't waste my time - say what you have to say so I can get back home."

Peter liked the fact that Jack didn't waste time on idle chatter. "In that case listen carefully to me, ask your questions, and make your decision." Peter smiled.

Jack nodded.

He gave Jack a brief overview of the Rosslerites' work and history including the escape of Sam Lewis, the Harpers, and all the families.

When he explained how they'd managed to counteract the chips, Peter noticed the first sign of emotion on Jack's face since he met him earlier that day. "You know how to get those fuckin' things out of people without killing them?"

"Absolutely. Piece of cake for us."

"Okay, what's the deal? What do I have to do to get that shit out of the bodies of my family and me?"

"Jack, there are no strings attached. We will neutralize the chips in you and your family irrespective of your decision to work for Sam again or not. Sam says it's a favor for an old and loyal friend. If you decide not to work for him, we will neutralize the chips and disappear out of your life. If you decide to work for him, we will do the same and move you and your family to Mount Ararat and set you up there."

Jack stared into the darkness for a long while. "Can I talk to Sam?"

"Yes, he is waiting to talk to you. Give me a second." Peter dialed Sam on the mirror phone. "Sam I have Jack here with me. He wants a word with you."

Jack listened to Sam for a while and said. "It's a done deal. When do we start?" Jack sounded almost excited.

"It will take a week to make all the arrangements. In the meantime, you can talk to your wife, resign your jobs, and pack what you need into two suitcases. Be ready at 10 pm next Wednesday night. Peter will be in touch the day before to confirm the final arrangements. You okay with that?"

"Can't wait. Let's do it." With that, Jack got up, gave the phone back to Peter, and disappeared into the darkness without saying a word.

"Sam, I have to say I can't remember the last time I met a man of so few words." Peter chuckled.

Sam laughed. "He has a way of getting to the point doesn't he?"

Since the financial desolation, a thriving black market had emerged that enabled people with the 'right currency' such as precious metals, gemstones, jewelry, and other valuable items to buy any product or services they wanted. It was illegal, but the police were treating it as petty crime and turned a blind eye as they had serious matters to attend to. They weren't going to make criminals out of people trying to stay alive, despite orders to the contrary from John Brideaux.

It was through those channels that some of the LA chapter members of Tectus acquired food, medicine, and other essential items and delivered them anonymously to the Symonds' house the day after Peter and Jack met.

Sue-Ellen was in tears when she opened the boxes she found on her doorstep when she got home from work in the early hours of the morning. She called Jack, and for the first time in weeks, she saw her husband smile.

"Sue, I have something to tell you," said Jack as he put his arms around his crying wife and pulled her close to him.

Brad Johnston spent every minute he had studying the Rossler files. The more days that passed without a single trace of the forty-one, the more he was persuaded that the Rosslerites had discovered a countermeasure for the lethal power of the chips. His and his family's freedom was locked up in that discovery.

However, nothing in the files gave him any clue how and

where to begin to find them. Most likely they were on American soil, but they could just as well be in Canada, Alaska or even South America. There was no indication. There were many files with information compiled by investigators who questioned, interrogated, threatened, and tortured people who knew anything about the Rosslerites. There were wild speculations, even reports from mystics and clairvoyants, but none had an inkling.

After countless hours, Brad concluded that he was barking up the wrong tree. He was not going to unearth the Rosslerites. He had to approach the whole thing from a different angle.

The next day he dictated a top-secret memo to all police chiefs across the country. There might be a chance that rogue scientists could discover a method to deactivate the chips. The police had to remain vigilant and make sure that all anomalies were brought to his attention immediately. Any discoveries of such a nature had to be kept quiet at all cost.

When Cathy Ballmer read the memo, she wondered if Brad Johnston had changed his mind. Nevertheless, she had her orders to keep on looking for forty-one bodies, and that was exactly what she was going to do. The quicker she could get just one of them, the quicker she could get off the timewasting assignment.

The Steering Committee was deliberating about the Symonds family. Should they be settled at Mount Ararat or the Rabbit Hole?

"With the changes to the chips' tracking features and the ability to broadcast a person's presence to fake locations

I see no danger in bringing them here. Or am I missing something?" Sarah argued.

"No problems that I can see Sarah," Sam replied. "However, be aware that Jack will have to keep his chip. Although it will be demilitarized, he will need to keep it in as we want to send him around on missions, so he must be able to pass through security checks without problems."

"That makes sense, but it doesn't stop them from coming here. Does it?"

"No, not as far as I can see," Sam replied.

Rebecca supported the idea. "I see no issues, Sarah. I agree with you. We can bring them all here, remove the chips and Raj can set up the diversions so that their locations are beamed to places far away from here."

"What do our security experts say?" Daniel looked at Sam, Luke, and Salome in turn.

"I can't foresee any issues either. I think it would be good to have them here. And it will be especially good for the children," Salome responded.

"Raj and Roy, are you confident in your ability to broadcast a false location? Are there any technical issues you can foresee?" Daniel asked.

They both shook their heads to the latter question.

"Good. It is settled then. Peter and Kelly will demilitarize their chips before they leave LA, fly them to Mount Ararat, and then bring them over to us," Daniel summarized the discussion.

"Kelly, you look a bit sad. Or is it just the screen resolution?" Sarah remarked.

Kelly laughed. "Nothing escapes you, Sarah Rossler! Yes, I am a bit sad, but I don't know exactly why. Maybe it's because I was sort of looking forward to having the two little ones around, you know."

Rebecca giggled. "Are you getting broody Kelly?"

"I guess that could be the case!" Kelly had a mischievous little smile on her face while Peter grinned from ear to ear.

"Okay, Peter, before you and Kelly go off to create a population explosion at Mount Ararat can you please see to it that Eric wipes out Jack's military record?" Daniel's final quip had them all rolling with laughter.

Jack and his family were ready when the van pulled up in front of their house at 10 pm the Wednesday night. Jack even looked a bit excited. They'd said goodbye to their neighbors earlier, telling them that Jack got a good job on a ranch in Texas.

All inside the van, Peter introduced them to Kelly and took off. About a mile away, he stopped and got hold of Raj. "Okay, Raj we're ready when you are."

"Let's do it," Raj replied.

Kelly explained to them what she was going to do. Jack indicated they were happy to carry on. She took the deactivator out and held it close to everyone's right shoulder for a few seconds until a little green light appeared on the device. Peter reported the progress to Raj, who was activating the signal tracking diversions as Kelly completed each person's chip. Three minutes later, they were back on the road, on the way to the airstrip.

Kelly made sure that she packed enough food and drink for the almost five-hour flight to Mount Ararat. Kelly sat in the back with Sue-Ellen, Jack was in the co-pilot's seat next to Peter, and the children were both fast asleep shortly after takeoff.

When they reached cruising altitude, Jack looked at Peter for a long while. "My friend, we will be eternally in your debt for what you did for us."

Sue-Ellen had tears in her eyes. "Thank you so much for the food and the medicine. You will never know how timely that arrival was."

"Don't mention it. It was the least we could do. I just wish we could have pulled you out of there earlier," Kelly replied with a warm smile.

"Okay, Peter. I guess you are now at liberty to give us the full picture. Do you mind telling us where we are going and what to expect?" Jack inquired on behalf of Sue-Ellen and himself.

For the next four hours, Jack and Sue-Ellen got their induction to the world of the Rosslerites. The two of them often voiced their disbelief in what they heard. Kelly and Peter just had to laugh as they remembered their own initiations.

When they landed at Mount Ararat and taxied into the hangar Owen, Alison, Sam, Daniel, Sarah, and Rebecca were waiting for them. A big applause went up when they stepped off the plane. Sam was the first person to hug and welcome them before introducing them to the rest.

Rebecca did a thorough examination on all of them. She was satisfied that they were all in good health with no need for any immediate medical treatment. They sat down to a king's breakfast, which Alison prepared and brought over to the hanger.

Rebecca couldn't help but smile as she saw Kelly sitting with both the little boys on her lap. She winked at Sarah and pointed with her head at Kelly. "She definitely has a mother's touch."

Sarah laughed. "You can say that again. She had little

Nicholas wrapped around her finger within half an hour after she saw him the first time."

Another few hours of talking followed before they all found a place to sleep until nightfall, when they would move over to the Rabbit Hole where another warm and sincere welcome and many pleasant surprises were awaiting them.

"Rafael my friend, what are your thoughts about our discussion of the other day?" Ruben asked after the server had taken their orders and disappeared.

"Amigo, I gave it a lot of thought. First, we have to make sure we remain in the background - we have to buy the expertise and services we need. I have been thinking how we could do it. We could easily take down the satellites and the Central Human Control Unit, which would destroy the whole empire. The problem is that we cannot do that until we shut down the chips first. You know what happened with the Eight Cycle. That is how they destroyed themselves. As you know, the only person that keeps the secret to the shutdown of the chips is John."

"How did it come to this? How did we allow a madman to become so powerful?"

"I have the same questions, amigo, but as they say, 'that is water under the bridge'. We can only change the future, not the past. We can now only remedy our past mistakes by doing the right thing in the future. What are your ideas?"

"I guess you are right about the past and the future – wise words. Well, with your control over the world's communications systems and having launched all those chip satellites, that and the CHCU should be an easy job as you said. But I kept on bumping my head against the same wall as you with the problem of shutting down the chips first. My idea is that we could hire our own scientists who can dissect the chip and find out how to shut it down."

"That would be the only way we could possibly do it. Unless ..."

"Unless what?"

"Well, many days I have been wondering about the Rosslers. Do you think they might have found a way to do it? If that is the case we have to try and track them down."

"Rafael, they are the most wanted people on earth. There are millions on their heads. No one has the slightest intimation where they are. All we know is that they are alive and busy with something. For what it is worth, we could talk to Brad Johnston, the head of security in America to find out what progress they have made to find them. But I have to say I don't think much would come from that."

"I suggest we don't ignore that opportunity. I agree with you, let's hire some scientists, and put them to work, but let's also try and find the Rosslers. You never know - they might just be able to save us a lot of time and trouble."

"That might be so, but if we find them, how do you propose we get in touch with them, and how are we going to establish our bona fides with them? I suspect it won't be as if we can walk up to them and say 'Hi we are Rafael Martinez and Ruben Weinstein of the Supreme Council. We would like you to help us take John Brideaux down', or something like that."

Rafael laughed. "Amigo, a few minutes ago you were worried about the past - now you are worried about the future. Let's see if we can find them first. Then we will see how we can contact them."

"Okay, I will set up a meeting with Johnston for next

week so that we can hear what he has to say about the Rosslers."

"Ruben, what do you think of Barbara Cohen?"

"That woman gives me the shivers! Why do you ask?"

"Same here, I don't know what it is that puts me off about her, but I don't like her."

"Do you think there could be other council members who feel the same as us?"

"Amigo, if there were any, I haven't noticed them. I am not prepared to take the chance to find out. The two of us are more than capable of handling this between us. Let's keep it like that for now."

Chapter One Hundred Nine

READY TO GO

The moment, Jack, and his family walked into the Rabbit Hole, they knew they had arrived home at last. It felt like the proverbial red carpet had been rolled out for them. Within a few days, they were settled in. Sue-Ellen and Jack quickly discovered that Peter and Kelly hadn't told them half of what they should have expected to see and experience. However, they had to admit that even if they'd been told, they would not have believed it at the time.

Soon after their arrival, Rebecca performed the little operation to remove the chips from Sue-Ellen and the two boys. Sarah took Sue-Ellen, who was a former mathematics and science teacher, under her wing. John and Jane Mendenhall were elated when she took up their offer of a teaching position at the Gallatin Unified School. Due to their similar ages, Nicholas and Aanya had two more best mates in Alex and Matt Symonds.

At the start of the next operations meeting, Jack was introduced to the Tectus leaders.

"Sam we have good news for you today," Dennis said with a big smile on his face as the introductions ended.

"We always welcome that type of news Dennis. Tell us about it."

"We found the manufacturer of the free-roaming bots. NaBoTech Enterprises, they are located on Silicon Hills in Austin, Texas."

"Now that is what I call good news. Excellent work guys!" Sam exclaimed while the others showed the Tectus leaders a thumbs up. "As Salome pointed out before, those bots are our number one target. What else do you know about them?"

"We've just started our surveillance activities. As can be expected, the place is extremely well guarded. We're collecting information about the layout and surrounding areas and the employees. We haven't penetrated the buildings yet. We'll be deploying more reconnaissance equipment over the next day or two and will keep you posted on the progress."

"I have an asset in that neck of the woods that could possibly be activated to help you with the work there. Can you use more help?"

"If this person has skills similar to your other non-existents, Peter, Kelly, and Jack, then yes, we can use that. How do you want to go about activating this person?"

"It will save us a lot of time if I brief you and Eric for the task."

"Do you mind giving us a name?"

"I guess you will need that sooner or later." Sam laughed. "Her name is Michelle Beckett. She is a ..."

"Former FBI forensics and electronics expert!" Dennis completed the sentence for Sam.

"What the hell ... you know her?" Sam was flabbergasted. "I am stunned! Tell me how do you know her?"

"It's a small world, Sam. She and her husband are the leaders of our Texas chapter! She's in charge of the NaBoTech operation." Dennis and Eric were grinning broadly.

"Well Sam, you have just saved us a lot of time indeed, this was the quickest reactivation of them all," Daniel quipped. "And to think how much trouble we went through with the other three while it could have been so easy!"

Sam recovered from his surprise and continued. "In that case, I know the operation is in good hands, and we'll get what we want relatively soon. She's an excellent operative. Could you please issue her with one of the mirror phones? I would certainly like to talk to her."

"No worries. We'll take care of that and let you know when she's connected."

"Well, that was all exciting stuff," Sam continued. "Shall we carry on with the rest of the agenda?"

For the next few hours, the team members discussed the progress they'd made with their assignments. Raj reported that he and his team had perfected the voice biometrics system and were ready to demonstrate it. Roy informed them about the progress he and his team had made with the construction of the nanonukes. He had them all laughing when he explained that unlike Raj, unfortunately, he would not be able to give any demonstrations. He also enlightened them about his research and work on the laser weapons, which he intended to use for destruction of the Skywalkers. Again, he apologized in advance for the fact that there would regrettably be no live demonstrations.

Rebecca gave them an update on the nanobot research. So far, they had identified two possibilities. The first was to build their own bots that would go out on a seek and destroy mission against the malicious ones. The problem with that option was they'd have to know where the malicious bots were being deployed and be ready there to launch the counter bots.

The second option was because the bots were, as Roy explained before, miniature electronic devices - they could be destroyed with electromagnetic pulses. She clarified that their work would remain speculative until they could get one or more of the bots and analyze them.

The last item on the agenda was Jack's first assignment. The few days he has been with them had given everyone who didn't know him before the chance to observe Jack. They all liked him. His demeanor instilled confidence and trust - he was a man of very few words, a good listener, and highly perceptive.

"Jack, we'll have to get you over to Brussels. We suspect that the Skywalkers and the Beast's control centers are located there. We desperately need access to those. Tectus has already started observations of the government facilities and employees. However, they don't have any of our equipment, which would enable them to expand their surveillance to the level we require. The first part of your mission will be to take the equipment to them and to help them set up their operations properly."

"Ready to go when you give me the word," Jack responded.

Sam had a little smile on his face as he remembered the operations this man had completed with so much valor. "Good. We'll meet again tomorrow morning and start planning the details. I think it will take us a few weeks to get everything in place."

Chapter One Hundred Ten

WHAT THE MEETING WAS ABOUT

Brad Johnston was on high alert when his secretary told him that she'd received a call, demanding that his schedule had to be rearranged to meet with councilors Weinstein and Martinez the next morning.

"Did they say what the meeting was about?"

"No, she said it is just routine. Nothing you have to prepare for them."

He managed to hide his apprehension. "Yes of course. No problem, happy to meet with them at any time that suits them."

At 9.30 am the next morning, a security detail arrived at his office and ordered him out of his office while they secured it for the meeting.

At 10 am, the councilors arrived with an entourage of security guards accompanying them to Brad's office. Soon after, Brad was collected from the waiting area, searched, and escorted back into his own office.

By the time he was introduced and took a seat in his

rearranged office, his nerves were on end. *What's going on here? What trouble am I in now?*

Everyone else was ordered out of the room, and counselor Weinstein started. "Brad it's just an informal visit. We sit there in Brussels in our ivory towers and don't always get information from the horse's mouth." He laughed. "We thought it would be good to visit a few of the senior officials while we are in America this week."

Brad started to relax a bit. *Maybe I am not in trouble.* "It's both an honor and privilege to be meeting you councilors. Is there anything specific you want to talk about?"

"I was wondering if you could give us a detailed account of what you know about the great escape." Martinez chuckled. "We only got bits and pieces of it, but it will be good to hear it from the man who discovered the whole thing."

Brad was back in panic mode. *Here it comes.* He licked his lips nervously, and Weinstein saw it.

"Relax Brad, there is no trouble. We just wanted to hear the full story. Those who were neglectful were punished, and the case is closed."

For the next twenty minutes, he gave them a detailed account of the events, including the time when he contacted President Brideaux's secretary. He also elaborated on the discovery of the escape of the eight Rosslerite families and their guards

The councilors listened quietly until he finished his narrative.

"Does anyone have an idea what happened to your predecessor, Jonathan Lucas?" Martinez asked.

"No sir. Unfortunately, he got a few hours head start and managed to disappear without a trace. At the time, the entire police force was occupied with riot control and crime prevention on the streets. We have a team working on his case, but I'm afraid they don't have any good leads."

"I am interested to hear more about the Harpers and the Rosslerite families. If I understand you correctly, you were saying that there were nine families, including the Harpers and all their guards, who vanished. By my calculations, that makes it about forty people. Is that correct?" Martinez inquired.

"Yes, sir. Forty-one in fact." Brad was becoming uncomfortable again and tried his best to hide it. This was a topic he didn't want to discuss if he could help it.

"I take it you have a list of all the people in America who were terminated during this event? Do you mind showing that to us?" Martinez asked.

"No problem. I have it right here." His hands were shaking when he picked the list up from his desk and gave it to Martinez. *If these two men have half a brain between them they'll quickly figure out what is going on.*

Martinez and Weinstein were pouring over the list for a few minutes. Brad's sudden change in behavior did not escape them. Martinez knew he was onto something - he gave Weinstein a quick look and continued the questioning, while Weinstein observed Brad's body language carefully.

"There are about five hundred names on this list. I see the bodies of all but the forty-one we have been talking about earlier have been found. Is there any explanation for that?"

"I made the same observation. My most senior investigator has a dedicated team working on it and reporting to me every week. They are in the process of following every possible lead, checking hospitals, clinics, morgues, cemeteries, interviewing friends, family, and acquaintances. I am sure it's just a matter of time before the bodies start turning up." Brad rubbed his nose.

Both of the Councilors were convinced they'd hit a nerve. Martinez decided to divert Brad's attention a bit.

"You said the families were all in different locations across the country at the time of disappearance. Is that correct?"

Brad rubbed his neck while he replied. "Yes, sir that is correct."

"From what you were saying, I got the impression they all escaped at more or less the same time - in other words, a coordinated effort. Who would have the organizational capability to pull off something like that without your elaborate security network knowing?"

Brad almost choked as he tried to swallow. *Are they going to hold me accountable for what happened on that deserter, Jonathan Lucas's watch?*

"I... I am... I think the only answer is that it was the Rosslers," he stuttered.

"Well, it is obvious they had something to do with it. After all, it was their families who were 'rescued'. Do you think they are capable of pulling off a stunt like this without any outside help?"

"Sir that is possible. As you know they are a very skillful group of people. It's highly unlikely that we wouldn't be aware if they got help outside their group. We know about every nonconformist group in the country and have tabs on them at all times. We've picked up many of their members and questioned them in the aftermath of these events and have come up empty handed so far."

Martinez decided to give Brad a few more inches of rope. "The Rosslers have been a thorn in our flesh since the very beginning. Can you tell us a bit more about the progress you have made in finding them?"

Brad relaxed as he thought he was off the hook. "We have a mountain of information on them. Again, we have a team of dedicated people working on their case. I have some of the information right here, if you want to have a look."

The councilors nodded for Brad to continue.

For the next forty-five minutes, he took them through the Rossler files, showing them the interrogation reports, photos, theories, and speculations.

"In other words Brad, you have no clue about them?" Weinstein's friendly manner from earlier had all of a sudden turned into a firm tone.

Brad was caught off guard. "To be honest, yes sir. That is the case."

Weinstein looked straight at him. "Okay let me see what we have here. You have no clue about your predecessor, Jonathan Lucas. You have no clue about the Rosslers - you have forty-one supposedly dead people but no clue where the bodies could be. You have no clue how they were able to escape. Despite the obvious evidence to the contrary, you insist on continuing to look for dead people."

Brad felt several cold tremors running down his spine.

Martinez grinned. "You see Brad, the problem is you are not honest with us. You know as well as we do those forty-one people are alive. Your own investigators have proved it. After all this time, they would surely have found at least one body. Nine families escaped from nine different locations at the same time, yet you maintain the Rosslers, a group of about forty-five people, amongst them a bunch of elderly, have pulled all of that off in one night. I am sure you are not that stupid.

"We came here to meet an honest and hardworking man, to congratulate you on your promotion and to encourage you to keep on doing good work. But I am afraid we will have to report to the Supreme Council that you are the wrong choice for this position," Weinstein almost snarled at him.

Brad was shattered. "I am sorry – please, let me try to rectify the mistake. I have a wife and three children."

"Not sure how you propose to do that, but let's hear it," Martinez said, giving Johnson a gap through which he hastened to step.

Brad was licking his lips and stuttering. "Councilors, please, believe me, it was not my intention to deceive you. I didn't want to give you unsubstantiated information. I truly don't have definite answers to the questions you have asked. But please consider that I have been in this position for just a few weeks now. It *is* my opinion that those people are alive. I have no evidence of it, and I don't know how they managed to do it..."

"We know that already. Stop beating around the bush. What have you done about it?" Martinez asked curtly.

"I have … ah … I have sent out a top-secret memo to all police chiefs to make them aware of the possibility that some of the chips could have been compromised. They are to report any irregularities to me immediately."

"Why could you not tell us about that? In addition, why does the Supreme Council not know about the fact that you believe those people are still alive? In other words, why are you withholding information from us?" Somehow, Weinstein managed to look furious while he was struggling not to smile.

Brad was about to have a messy accident in his pants. If he gave them an honest answer to those questions, he might as well jump through the window to his death. Either way the outcome was going to be the same. He just stared in front of him, the blood drained from his face, and he was speechless.

"What was your intention when you found a person who has a chip that has been tampered with? Who were you going to tell about it? Were you going to withhold that information as you've just tried with us?" Martinez continued to hammer him.

"Oh my God no! Never! I will bring it to the attention of the Director of BOSS immediately! I just don't want to bother him with unverified information and hunches at this stage." He was almost out of breath when he completed that reply.

Martinez and Weinstein looked at each other and Brad detected a faint smile on their faces, which confused the hell out of him. *Seconds ago they were grilling me in the flames and now they are smiling. Or are they the smiling executioners?*

"I think we have talked enough. It's almost time for our next meeting," Weinstein announced.

"Yes. I agree," Martinez got up.

Brad's state of confusion reached a dangerous peak when Martinez took a little recorder out his pocket. The red light was still on - he placed it on the table, and switched it off and sat down again.

"I have recorded our conversation. I guess you will agree that there is enough on that recorder to have your button pushed?"

Brad nodded his head in agreement - he had no illusions about the accuracy of that statement.

"We are going to give you another chance. I suggest you listen very carefully."

Brad nodded his head, as he didn't trust himself to say anything.

"About the matter of those forty-one people and the Rosslers, you will report to us first. If we ever find out that we were not the first people whom you spoke to when you got any new information, your days will be numbered. You will not talk to anyone, and that includes the Director of BOSS, until you have spoken to one of us. Is that entirely clear?"

"Yes sir, crystal clear."

Martinez took a cellphone, about the size of a box of matches, out of his pocket and placed it in front of Brad. "From now on, you will carry that with you wherever you go. It has been programmed so that you can do only two things - you call me or receive a call from me. Nothing else. It's a secure line."

With that, Martinez and Weinstein got up, shook hands with Brad, and left.

When the door closed behind them, Brad fell back into his chair. He was exhausted, and his mind was completely disordered.

At the next Supreme Council meeting after their return, the two councilors reported on their American trip and the meetings they had with various high-ranking officials. They made a point of telling everyone how impressed they were with the loyalty and support the council had among many of the officials, including the new head of security, Brad Johnston.

Chapter One Hundred Eleven

SILICON HILLS

True to their promise, Dennis, and Eric delivered a mirror phone to Michelle Beckett, and soon afterward, she and Sam had a long catch up. They came to a discussion of the NaBoTech operation.

"Do you have everything you need to get the job done?" Sam asked. "I have a few people available who can move around freely and have a bit of experience with this sort of thing."

"Thanks for that Sam. I might have to take you up on that offer shortly. For the next week or so, we'll be busy collecting information, but when the time comes to get hold of the bots, we might need that help."

"Good. Let's see what your surveillance efforts produce and take it from there. In the meantime if you could dial into our daily operations meeting and update us on your progress."

"No problem, happy to do that."

Once Michelle's team got the spyflies into the NaBo-Tech buildings, they made quick progress. Four days after the conversation with Sam, she reported that they'd managed to get into the internal computer network and collect a treasure trove of information.

"Yes, you heard me correctly. We have the design and manufacturing blueprints, the shipping process, stockpile locations, and everything else we might need - except of course the bot itself. I will be sending all the information over as soon as we're done with the meeting." Michelle smiled proudly.

"Sterling job, Michelle. Dennis, you've got yourselves one competent operator there!" Sam remarked.

Dennis joined in with the humor. "Absolutely Sam. No doubt about that. I'm glad we got to her before you did."

"The next thing will be to work out how to get hold of the bots. Michelle, you have seen the information. Any initial ideas?" Sam asked.

"Well, I'm not a field operative as you know, so it's dangerous for me to assess what's possible and what isn't. I can tell you though, as far as electronic security goes, they have the latest and greatest state of the art systems. Nevertheless, I'm confident with the information we've collected about the systems, we'll find a way to bypass that. Of course, that is if we decide that the plant is the best place to try and snatch the bots."

"I suggest we have a look at the information Michelle will be sending and see if some of the stockpile locations might offer an easier target." Salome suggested.

"Can't wait to get my hands on that information," Roy muttered.

Within half an hour after the meeting ended, the techies were poring over the NaBoTech information while Sam and the rest of the operations team were studying the manufacturing, distribution, and stockpiling processes.

The next morning Roy told the meeting that they'd studied the designs and were keen to get their hands on a few of the bots.

"What have you learned about the bots so far?" Daniel asked.

"They're relatively simple. They weren't designed to be tamperproof at all. They obviously have just one purpose, and that is to find humans and kill them."

"How does that happen? I mean what does it do inside the body?" Nigel asked in a soft voice as he recalled the dreadful day when he saw his security guards dying before his eyes.

"It targets the parts of the brain that regulate breathing. It destroys the nerves and arteries in the brain, and the person stops breathing immediately. It will cause severe muscle spasms and may produce blood at the nose and mouth," Rebecca explained.

Nigel's face was pale. "Dear God! That is exactly what happened to our boys. Roy, please tell me you know how to defeat those evil things. I don't ever want to see another human being die like that."

"Don't worry Nigel. We already know how to do that. They're mini robots preprogrammed with specific instructions. The quickest and easiest way to defeat them is to destroy the nano circuitry inside with an electromagnetic pulse. That's why I need to get hold of a few of them to work out how strong a pulse we need."

"How big an EMP are we talking about? Do you need a nuke or can it be done with something smaller?" Daniel asked.

Roy laughed. "As much as I would have loved to drop a few decent size nukes on them, it won't be necessary. You remember that one I tested on the warehouse in Denver.

Well, that one was about the half the size of a pencil. What I have in mind now will be the size of the tip of a pencil. It would fit into a spyfly. However, this one won't make a big noise, it will only generate a sudden high-intensity EMP and that's it. You won't hear a thing."

"Okay, I'm feeling better already. I was just a little worried you were planning to explode a nuke in the stratosphere!"

When the laughing receded, Jack, who had been listening quietly, started questioning Roy - to everyone's surprise.

"I take it the bots are inactive while in storage. At what stage are they activated, and how long do they remain active?" Jack asked.

"Yes, they're inactive while in storage. The operator activates them at launch, and they have a five-minute life-span before they self-destruct."

"How big an area will that EMP device of yours cover?"

"About four-hundred square yards, I'm sure of. Could be a bit more, but work on that to be safe." Roy replied.

"The spyflies can be remote controlled via the sky mirrors?"

"Yes, indeed."

"I guess the EMP will also destroy the circuitry of the spyflies? Is it likely that the spyflies might be discovered afterwards?" Jack wanted to know.

"No, don't worry about that. The pulse will vaporize the spyflies."

"I get the feeling you have a strategy in the making, Jack," Sam observed.

"Yea, I think the obvious thing to do is to plant the spyflies at the stockpile locations in advance of D-Day, hook them up to the sky mirrors, and detonate them when we want," Jack explained.

"That will be a job for Tectus," Sam replied while looking at Dennis and Eric. "They should start by collecting information about all the locations, and then we can look at how to deploy the devices."

"We'll get our people onto it immediately," Dennis confirmed.

"The only thing remaining is to get Roy a few of those bots now. We will have to give Tectus a few days to send back information about the stockpile locations before we pick a target." After his last statement, Sam concluded the meeting.

Chapter One Hundred Twelve

THE JOB INTERVIEW

As the information about the stockpile sites came in from Tectus, it became apparent that almost all of them were inside police stations. In those locations, it was going to be particularly dangerous to get hold of the bots. After long discussions with Michelle and studies of more video footage, the combined leadership groups decided to target the manufacturing plant in Austin instead.

Michelle, Dennis, and Eric had a plan to infiltrate the facility, which they presented to the operations team. This was scrutinized in much detail and given the go-ahead.

At midnight three days later, Bill Hockey, one of the workers at the NaBoTech facility, reported to the front desk for his shift. His chip had been demilitarized. Tectus had equipped him with a spyfly, micro earphones, and miniature microphone, all of which was hidden in his dreadlocks. He went through the sterilization area, placed the shower cap over his hair, and then took a shower. Next, he put on the full-body biohazard protective suit, which everyone working in close proximity of the bots had to wear at all times. As soon as he got out of the shower, he fitted the earphones and microphone.

While on a break at about 3 a.m., he got his chance when he was talking to one of his coworkers, Jason, who was working in the lab next to the production line where he was working. Michelle's team, who were following everything on a video screen about three miles away, swapped the chip ID's between them and gave Bill the signal that it was done.

Bill kept a close watch. As soon as he saw Jason leave for the bathroom, he walked past his desk in the lab, grabbed two tiny canisters with bots, and placed them in his pocket. He would hide those with the other gadgets in his hair later, when his shift ended.

The team outside swapped the chip ID's back as soon as Jason returned. They had to wait until Bill finished his shift at 8 am to get the canisters. The outside team started congratulating each other on a mission accomplished.

"Boys, I'm excited too, but don't relax too much yet. Keep a close watch until you have those canisters in your hands," Michelle, who was following everything closely from her home control center, cautioned them.

At 7:50 a.m., Jason started packing his equipment away and checking the canisters back into the safe. He discovered two of the canisters were missing. After a few minutes of intensive search, he was still empty handed and notified security, as procedures dictated.

In growing unease, Bill watched Jason through the glass window. The door was open, and he heard as Jason speak to the security manager. He hadn't known the canisters were checked in and out. But now it was too late - he was in trouble.

"We have a situation here! Jason discovered the disappearance of the canisters and told security!" Bill almost shouted into his microphone. Luckily, the full-face mask gave enough cover so no one noticed.

Michelle took over immediately and started talking to Bill. "Bill, listen very carefully. I know it's easier said than done, but it is of the utmost importance that you remain calm. You must act normal, or you'll raise suspicion. I can see you, so don't worry, just do exactly as I tell you, and everything is going to be absolutely fine."

"I'll ... ah ... try my best," he stuttered.

"Good. Now pack your stuff and be ready to leave. Don't rush it, just relax and act normal. There's enough time, nothing to worry about."

Bill managed to pull himself together and started packing his stuff while Michelle stayed in his ear and kept him calm.

"Excellent, Bill. Okay. Now I'm going to bring the spyfly to you and land it on your chest. Hide it, then get up, wave and say goodbye to everyone, and go to the change rooms. When you're in the shower, make sure you flush everything, including the canisters, down the drain. Don't try to bring any of the equipment out. Make sure they can find nothing on you. Don't worry, I can still hear you. I'm here all the way."

Bill's heart was pounding in his throat, his mouth was dry, and his palms were sweating.

"Looking good, Bill. I'm impressed - you look as cool as a cucumber."

Once Bill had all his stuff packed, he got up and headed for the change rooms. Many of his co-workers were getting ready to leave as well.

"Ok, go and take the shower and go home. We'll be waiting for you there."

Bill went through the end of shift routine, and as more workers who were either starting or ending shifts arrived, the change room filled with people. He flushed everything down the drain as instructed and started relaxing. He was getting more confident that he was going to get out.

As he walked past the front desk, towards the revolving door, the alarm went off. A voice over the public-address system ordered everyone to stop in their tracks and to remain where they were until further notice. No one was allowed to move from their current positions.

The sound of the alarm was battering his head, his ears were ringing, and his knees were shaking. He felt dizzy. He couldn't breathe - he had to get outside! The door was less than five paces away. He started running. He fell to the ground when he smashed his face into the reinforced glass that wouldn't move.

"Sam, we have a bucket load of trouble." Michelle started the conversation the moment Sam answered the phone.

"What happened?" Sam could hear the anguish in her voice.

"The NaBoTech operation went south. Our inside man was arrested."

"Shit, that isn't good news! Okay, get hold of Dennis and Eric while I gather the ops team. Let's go on video conference in five minutes."

Sam got the team, and five minutes later, they were ready to hear the full story.

"Okay, Michelle, give us the details," Sam requested.

"Everything went well until the lab assistant discovered two missing canisters. Bill forgot to tell us or didn't know that the lab staff has to check the canisters in and out at the beginning and end of their shifts. The lab assistant called security to report the missing canisters. At that stage, we decided to abandon the mission and instructed Bill to pack up his stuff, take a shower, and flush all equipment including the canisters down the drain. We followed him with one of the spyflies already on the inside and can confirm that was done.

"When he was about to leave the building, the alarm went off and he must have lost his nerve. He tried to run out of the building and slammed into the door, which was locked. Needless to say, the guards picked him up, cuffed him, and called the police."

"That is a bit more than messy, to say the least," Sam responded. The calm statement belied his inner consternation.

"Without a doubt. The issue is that the police might get it into their heads to activate the torture bots in his chip to make him talk and find out it's not working. I don't have to tell you what the implications of that could be."

"No, I think I can comprehend that well enough."

"Do you know where he's being held?" Salome asked.

"Yes, he's at the North Substation on Lamplight Village Ave. We have spyflies deployed and monitoring everything. They haven't started questioning him as yet."

"I get the idea he won't need a lot of encouragement to start talking," Luke commented.

"Yes. Unfortunately, that's the case. Of course, we all know that making a person talk is just a matter of time. In the end everyone talks."

"Is he a member of Tectus?" Daniel enquired.

"No. We enlisted him for this job because he worked there. Therefore, he has only seen the person who recruited him, and we've already moved him and his family into hiding."

"That's a bit of a relief to know that they won't be able to unstitch the whole organization." Salome pointed out. "Nevertheless, I'd hate to think we would just abandon him."

"Definitely not, the man worked for us, he took a risk for us. Therefore, we will not leave him behind. We are going to get him out," Sam stated while looking at Dennis and Eric. "You agree?"

"Unconditionally," they both replied as everyone else joined in agreement.

"Okay, in that case, let's have it. Put it on the table," Sam invited.

Discussions followed, and two hours later Jack concluded. "I see no other viable options. I'll go down to Austin to see what can be done."

"What do you need?" Sam wanted to know.

"Roy and Raj have all the gadgets I need. I'll go and see them. I need Peter to fly me down there."

"Peter. You ready for that?" Sam enquired.

"Yes, I'll start preparing for the flight and arranging for stops and fuel along the way."

"Eric, given your special ops background I'd like you to make your way there as well," Sam ordered.

"I was just getting worried you were planning to cut me out of the action." Eric laughed.

Jack looked at his watch. "I'll be ready to leave here in two hours."

It was late in the afternoon when Brad Johnston's desk phone rang - it was his secretary telling him that the chief of police in Austin, Texas was on the line for him.

He was not in any mood to hear yet another moping police chief, but it was part of his job to talk to him. "Put him through."

"Mr. Johnston I am acting on that top-secret directive of yours, which I received a little while ago."

"Michaelson, I send many of those things out. Be specific."

"I am referring to the one about chips not functioning as expected. The instruction said that if we find anything like that we were to call you immediately."

Brad felt a rush of excitement going through his body. "So say it, man, what do you have?"

"There was a security breach at the NaBoTech plant early this morning. Some of the canisters with nanobots went missing. One of the employees tried to run away when the alarm went off and was apprehended by the security guards. They called our North Substation, and we picked the suspect up. He refused to answer any questions. The investigating officer tried to activate his chip to help him speed up the process, but nothing happened. The chip was scanned, and it seems to be functioning correctly, except the pain inducing utility is not working. The investigating officer reported the matter to me."

"Where is the suspect now?"

"Still in custody at the North Substation. We're keeping him in solitary."

"Good job. Ok, keep him there. I'm coming down to Austin, and I want to talk to him in person. Keep him in solitary, and make sure everyone keeps quiet about this. Understood?"

"Yes, sir. When can we expect you?"

"I'll let you know, but it'll be sometime tomorrow."

When he put the phone down, Brad was wondering if he should call Martinez and Weinstein immediately, or if he should wait until he had the full story. Remembering what happened last time he withheld information from them made him reach for the mini phone in his pocket.

"Councilor Martinez, I got a call from the police chief in Austin, Texas. They have a person in custody who apparently has a chip that's been altered."

"What are you doing about it?"

"I'm on my way to Austin, sir. I will personally investigate and keep you posted."

"Good. Make sure no one else knows about this until you have all the information and have spoken to me first. Is that clear?"

"Yes, sir, one hundred percent."

Michaelson and the investigating officer met Brad Johnston at the Austin airport shortly after midday and took him directly to the North Substation. On the way, they briefed him on everything they knew and showed him the chip analysis report.

"Have you recovered the canisters?"

"No trace of them. Nothing on the suspect either. We have gone back and checked his movements through the chip monitor, but he was nowhere near the lab assistant's desk at all. The only reason we're holding him is that he tried to run. Other than that, we have nothing on him."

"Had he been away from his desk during his shift?"

"Yes, he went to the breakroom from 3 a.m. to 3:30 a.m.

and to the restroom from 4:06 am to 4:09 a.m. If he'd entered any of the unauthorized areas, security would have known about it immediately, and it would have shown on that report."

Brad knew how that could have been accomplished but was certain he was not going to educate them about it.

"And he is still refusing to talk?"

"Yes sir. I haven't put any pressure on him. I've been waiting for you to give me further instructions."

"No one else knows about this?"

"No, sir. It's only the three of us."

"Okay, I want him released into my custody, so I can take him to a place where I can have a private word with him. I think I might just be able to get him to talk to me. Any problems with that?"

Michaelson looked at the investigator with raised eyebrows. They both knew that wasn't a question - it was an order.

"No problem. I'll call ahead," Michaelson replied as he got his phone out and dialed the police station to make the arrangements.

When they arrived at the station, Brad made a few phone calls while waiting for the paperwork to be completed and his vehicle to be delivered.

"Jack and Eric have a look at this!" Peter called them over to the screen he was monitoring. "Looks like our boy has attracted high-level attention." He pointed to the man walking next to Bill Hockey down the corridor of the police station.

"Brad Johnston, the Director of American Security," Jack observed. "You're right about high-level attention."

Peter had spyflies following them, and as soon as they got outside, he landed one in Bills dreadlocks and moved it out of sight. The tracking team, who were on standby outside the police station about a mile away, followed the vehicle to a ranch about twenty miles away from the city. They gave Peter the location and left.

"Guys, I'm perplexed. Brad Johnston is one of the highest-ranking officials in this country. He arrives here without any security detail - he checks a suspect out into his personal custody and takes him to a farm where there is no security either," Peter commented. "Something's not stacking up."

"It is puzzling isn't it?" Jack responded. "Unless, of course, he doesn't want anyone to know what he's doing."

"Well, I guess we'll soon know what he's up to," Eric responded while he got the feed from the spyfly up on the tablet screen.

The three men took up position on a small hill, among some dense trees about three hundred yards away from the shed where Johnston and Bill were. They launched two more spyflies and steered them into the building.

"Son, do you know who I am?" Brad Johnston smiled as best he could when he started questioning the bewildered Bill Hockey, who was tied to a chair in the middle of the half-empty barn.

Bill shook his head.

"I am Brad Johnston the Director of Security in America. Now, I want you to relax, I don't intend to harm you. I want to ask you a few questions, and if you answer me honestly, you'll be free to go. I will personally drive you home afterwards. However, you will have to cooperate with me. Do you understand?"

Bill nodded his understanding. This was the best treatment he'd had in the past thirty hours. But he was still hesitant to talk to anyone. On the other hand, he also knew that at some stage, someone's patience was going to wear out, and he was going to be the one in pain.

"I brought you to this place so we can be alone. There is no one else here. No one can hear or see us. You can speak freely. So let's start with your name."

"Bill Hockey."

"Where do you live?"

"The southeast side of Austin."

"How long have you been working for NaBoTech?"

"About eight months."

"You see Bill that was not so difficult. Now, why did you take the canisters?"

"I didn't!"

"Come on, son, you promised to be honest with me. Try again."

"I didn't do it - I swear I didn't have anything to do with it."

"Son, I have a video here in my briefcase that shows you in the lab. Want me to show it to you?" Brad lied.

"I am not permitted to go into the lab area. If I did, security would know about it immediately." Bill tried to bluff his way out of it.

"Everyone's movements are tracked through their chips, but your chip has been modified. That's the reason the movement records show you have not been in the lab. But the video camera, which you didn't know about, saw you there. Right Bill?"

He didn't know about the video camera. In fact, no one knew about video cameras in the lab or the area where he worked. Where had they been hiding them? Bill knew he was in trouble.

Brad could see he'd hit the nail on the head. "Son, as you can see, I know all about it. I'm just trying to get you to work with me and be honest. You haven't been doing very well so far. Remember I can only let you go if you are honest with me."

"I don't want to talk anymore. I want a lawyer."

Brad laughed aloud. "Son, you have been watching too many old movies! I am your lawyer, your judge, your jury, and if necessary, your executioner. I am your only way out of this mess. Let's stop the games and get to the point."

Bill stared at him and realized what he just heard was precisely how it was going to be. He was out of options.

"We have now established that you took the canisters. Right?"

Bill nodded his head.

"What did you do with them?"

"Flushed them down the drain while I took a shower," he whispered.

"Why did you do that? Didn't you steal them for someone on the outside?"

Bill didn't answer. He just looked at Brad.

"Honesty son, honesty. Why did you do it?"

"I saw that Jason discovered the missing canisters and alerted security. I got scared and abandoned my plans to smuggle it out."

"There you go son! You see it's so much easier when you're honest. You keep on going like that, and you will walk out of here a free man."

Bill nodded.

"Tell me everything about your contacts on the outside. How did you meet, the names, how much were you going to be paid? Don't leave anything out. Remember I already know everything."

"It was just one person - he said his name was Red Butler. I don't think that was his real name. He asked me to help him get two of the canisters. He said he was going to sell them and share the proceeds with me. He said he would get payment in gold coins."

"Bill I told you to be honest with me! Let's get your story straight. I know you're lying, because I spoke to your friend before we came out here. Yes, don't look so surprised. He was arrested last night. He told me a very different story, and he was honest with me, so I have set him free. You are right - his name is not Red Butler, but that was about the only thing you were honest about."

Bill looked at Brad. He was almost sure that wasn't true, but doubt got the better of him.

Eric had seen enough and sat up. "Let's go kick this Brad Johnston's ass, and move our boy out, before someone else turns up here and makes it difficult for us."

Jack pushed him down. "Hang on buddy. You'll get your chance. No one else is coming. I want to hear more from our friend the director, here."

Jack got Sam on the mirror phone to give him a sit-rep. "Sam you won't believe what's happening over here. We have Brad Johnston questioning our boy in a shed on a farm outside Austin. He's alone, no one else but him and Bill. We've been watching all of it for about an hour now."

"What? Brad Johnston, the Director of Security? What the hell is he doing there?"

"We've been asking the same question, Sam. We don't have an answer yet. He's still questioning our boy, but has done him no harm yet. I'll make sure it doesn't come to that. We're going to hang on for a while longer before we move in. We'd like to see if we can find out more about his motive for this weird behavior."

"You're on the spot there Jack, I trust your judgment. Keep us posted."

"Tell you what, son. Let's come back to that a bit later. I would like to know about your chip that's been modified. Tell me who did it? When and how was it done?"

"Red did it two days ago. He had a little device with him when we met, and he held it to my shoulder. After a little while, a green light went on, and he told me that the chip was now harmless. I don't know anything else."

"Keep on going like that and everything is going to be okay for you."

Bill nodded.

"How did you get into the lab without the chip monitor detecting it?"

"I don't know how it works. I had a little earphone and microphone on me - Red was talking to me from the outside. When Jason went to the bathroom, I told Red and he said I was cleared to enter the lab. I went in, got the canisters, and returned to my desk."

"Okay, I think we're getting ..." Was as far as he got, before Bill saw Brad grab his neck and drop to the floor. He started screaming when he saw three men, with balaclavas over their faces walking into the barn.

"Stop it Bill! We've come to rescue you. This man will go with you to the road on the other side of the hill. There's a car waiting to take you away to safety."

Jack removed the handcuffs and pushed Bill in the direction of the door. "Go. You'll be taken care of. Don't worry about anything."

Eric quickly escorted Bill away and was back less than thirty minutes later, just when Brad was coming back to consciousness.

Brad moaned when he found he could not move his arms and legs because they were tied to the chair he was sitting on.

"Who? What the hell? Untie me you fuckin' dimwit. Do you know who I am or have any idea of what you're doing?" he demanded.

"Mr. Johnston your language." Jack smiled under the balaclava. "Yes, we know who you are, we know exactly what we're doing and you are about to find out what we want."

Jack held his mirror phone up to Brad so that he could see it. "You know what this is, Mr. Johnston?"

Brad shook his head.

"Let me explain. This little device is in control of the chip you have in your right shoulder. Now unlike Bill's chip, your chip is fully functional. I didn't have much training on using this thing, but what I have been told is that one of the buttons on here will activate the pain bots and another one will activate the killer bots. I'm not entirely sure which button is which, but don't worry we'll soon find out."

Peter had a hard time not to crack up laughing. Not only was that the most words he ever heard out of Jack's mouth, but he also learned that Jack actually had a sense of humor.

"Fuck you! You have no idea what you've gotten yourself into. The police will be here soon."

"Mr. Johnston, we will have to discuss your language at some stage soon. We have young people here. You can't swear like that, you're setting an awful example for them. As for the police on their way here, I don't want to be rude and call you a liar, but let me put it this way - you are having an adulterous relationship with the truth."

Peter and Eric had to walk a few paces away - they were about to ruin the whole thing with their urge to laugh at Jack's larks.

Back in the Rabbit Hole, Sam and the ops team were watching the whole thing on the screen. He had to mute the microphone when everyone burst into laughter for Jack's sudden, uncharacteristic streak of humor and loquaciousness.

"Ah, fuck you, you son of a bitch. What do want from me?"

"Honesty Mr. Johnston, honesty. That is what you wanted from Bill earlier. Is it too much to ask you for the same courtesy?"

Brad didn't answer - he just glared at Jack and the others' masked faces.

"I'll take that as a yes. Before I tell you what I want to know, let me just help you with a bit of background information. I think that will help us get to the point much quicker. We have been following you from the moment you landed here in Austin. We have a full recording of every telephone conversation you made today, and, of course, the entire interrogation of our boy, Bill."

"You're bluffing. I'm not an idiot."

The Phoenix Agenda

Jack winked at Eric, who walked up to Brad, opened his tablet, and started playing a video of the recording they made in the police station. They skipped a bit and played a clip of the questioning of Bill earlier. Brad tried to keep up the façade.

"Okay Mr. Johnston, tell us why are you on your own. Why have you moved our boy here for questioning? Why didn't you keep him at the police station?"

"I don't know what you're talking about."

"Oh, you know very well Mr. Johnston. But wait, I can see you need some help with this."

Jack waved Peter to him. "I didn't pay close attention when they showed us how to use this thing. Can you remember which one activates the pain bots? I think it's this one."

"I can't remember, but we're wasting our time with this guy. Let's push them all and see. Maybe he's lucky and we'll find the pain button before the killer button."

They were whispering loud enough so that Brad could hear them.

"Ah, okay, I guess you're right. I am getting tired, as well. I want to go home and get something to eat. I'm hungry," Jack said as he turned around and pushed a button on the phone.

Brad's eyes almost popped out of their sockets when an electric shock shot through his body and the muscles in his neck started cramping. He yelled, "Stop it, please, stop it, oh God, please!"

Jack looked at him and then at the phone and said, "You're a lucky man. I really didn't know what that button was going to do."

"What do you want from me?"

Brad's voice shook while a puddle of urine formed

below his chair. He was shaking with terror. This was his worst nightmare coming true. He'd always dreaded the day when his chip was going to kill him. He'd seen so many people killed and tortured by the chips - it was something he could not get out of his mind. Today was his turn. He had no doubt about it.

"I told you before. Honesty. Nothing else."

"Okay. I brought the boy here to question him because I don't want anyone else to know about this."

"You wanted to know how to modify the chips and you didn't want anyone else to know? Is that it?"

"Yes"

"You aren't going to tell me why?" Jack lifted the phone and moved his finger to the dials.

"No don't do that! Please don't. I'm trying to discover how it works, so I can get this damn thing out of the bodies of my wife and children and my own. I hate this government. I hate this job, and I just want to get away from it all."

"Now, that is what I call honesty, Mr. Johnston. At last, we're getting somewhere. So let me see if I have it have it right. You wanted to find out how to deactivate the chips and get them out of yourself and your family. You were not planning to tell anyone about it. Then you were going to run away and hide some place? Is that about right?"

"Yes."

"And you were not going to help anyone else? Not even your friends or family, nobody, it's all just about you, and yours, isn't it?"

"I don't know what I could do to help others. My family is precious to me. I didn't ask for this job, John Brideaux forced me into it. I had no choice. I want out."

"It sounds very selfish to me, Mr. Johnston. You see

somewhere on this device I have a button that could deactivate your chip. I can't remember which, but that doesn't matter. I won't do it for just anyone. I need people that will help their fellow humans to get rid of this government. So unfortunately, I won't be able to help you."

"What do you want me to do?"

"You've just told us that there isn't much you want to do."

"If you tell me what I can do to help, I will do it."

"Yeah, maybe we can talk about that later. I'm not so sure you're the type of person I would like to work for me. I have a few more questions."

Brad nodded.

Jack reached into his pocket, took Brad's mini cellphone out, and showed it to him. "I found this in your pocket while you were sleeping earlier. It has only one number on it, and if I'm not mistaken, +32 is the Belgian country code. Who will be answering when I push that quick dial button?"

Brad's face went pale. He shook his head.

"Oh, okay, I'll have to ask the person on the other side, then." Jack lifted the phone.

"Oh, my God, no! Please don't do that. I'll tell you. It's the number of Councilor Martinez."

"I see. Rafael Martinez, who owns the world's communications and satellite systems - and you have him on speed dial. Old school buddy, Mr. Johnston? No, wait that can't be. He's from South America, and you're from North America. Geography was never my strong suit. You'll have to explain the friendship to me then. Just remember, you're still in the job interview. I have not yet given up on the idea of employing you." Jack tossed the little phone in the air and caught it as Johnston turned even paler.

Johnston began talking fast. "About three weeks ago,

Councilors Martinez and Weinstein came to see me in my office while they were on a trip to America. They questioned me at length about the Rossler Foundation, the recent disappearances of their family members and former President Harper and his wife. They are of the opinion that the people who disappeared might still be alive, despite the activation of the killing sequence in their chips. They believe the fact that none of their bodies has turned up proves their theory."

"The Rosslers? I've heard of them. Aren't they the bunch of outlaws who stole a lot of money and vanished? Rumor has it they're holed-up in some ancient lost city somewhere in the Amazon jungle. Wild goose chase, if you ask me."

In the Rabbit Hole, Sam's ops team was screaming with laughter. "I need to have a fatherly chat with Jack Symonds when he gets back here," Sam commented dryly.

Johnston bristled. "Well, I happen to agree with the councilors. The fact that none of the bodies of those forty-one people, including their security guards, have turned up, while the bodies of more than five-hundred others in America, who were terminated at the same time, are all accounted for, makes a strong case for that."

"I see. Yes, that does make some sense. So what's that got to do with this little cell phone?"

"Martinez gave it to me. It's a secure connection. I was instructed to make sure he's the first person to know the moment I have any information about the Rosslers or find anyone who has a chip that has been modified."

"And did you do that?"

"Yes, I phoned him yesterday. I told him I was flying to Austin to investigate a report about such an incident and would let him know as soon as I am aware what is going on."

"I guess you have a call to make, then. You don't want to keep the councilor waiting. You have all the information now, don't you? Or could there be something else you wanted to know before you make the call?" Jack extended his hand with the phone to Brad. "Want me to untie you to make the call?"

"Well, that's a bit weird. What do you want me to tell him?"

"I suggest you are honest with him. Tell him you found the chip meddlers, and that you have proven the theory could be correct. There are in fact people that know how to deactivate parts of the chip and even remove it without causing harm. Also, tell him you have offered your services to those people, and if they make you a job offer, you will have to leave his employment. That's what I would do."

Peter and Eric were struggling to control themselves, Nigel was shaking his head, and the others were crying with laughter.

"Okay, wait I see you're a bit nervous to talk to Martinez. Let me call him for you and speak to him. I am sure he'd enjoy hearing how we do it. I'll be able to explain it much better than you can." Jack moved his index finger to the dial pad.

"No don't do that, man! You might as well kill me yourself."

"No? You don't want me to call him, and you don't want to call him yourself. In that case, you have to explain to me why the world's communications and offshore oil tycoons are meddling in the affairs of BOSS. Why would they have instructed you to bypass the Director of Boss, your direct supervisor?"

"I'm not sure why. I've been wondering about that, and my theory is that they want to go against the Supreme Council. There's no other logical explanation."

"What made you think that?"

Brad gave them a full account of the meeting with the councilors and explained how the conversation was recorded up to a point. How the recorder was switched off, and he received his instructions and the mini phone off the record.

"Oh, I see. So they have you by the short and curlies, then."

"Yes."

"Okay I have decided to make you a job offer. But it will be on a trial basis until I'm happy with your performance."

"What do I have to do?"

"You will stay over for another day or two here in Austin. Tomorrow morning, we'll meet again to finalize your job description and compensation. At the meeting tomorrow morning, you will have three of those canisters with you, and will hand them to me. When you have done that, I will deactivate the pain bots in your chip. How does that sound to you? "

"I'll do it. Where and when will we meet?"

"Don't worry. We'll let you know."

Jack untied him and handed all his personal belongings back. "I suggest you make that call to Martinez soon. Oh, I almost forgot to tell you. I think it's important you know that while you were asleep we, made a slight modification to your chip so we can hear everything you say and know where you are at all times. I hope you don't mind - it's for your own safety."

Brad didn't know if the man was bluffing or not, but

when he looked down at his wet pants, he decided he wasn't going to take a chance to find out.

"No problem. I will get the canisters and wait to hear from you about the meeting tomorrow."

When Brad left, Jack, Peter, and Eric got to their car and drove off to the safe house. They'd planted eavesdropping devices, provided by Raj, in Brad's two cellphones and were able to listen to all his conversations.

"Excellent job team!" Sam commented. "We didn't know you were so verbose Jack! However, I have a serious matter to discuss with you."

"What would that be?"

"The Rosslers a bunch of outlaws who stole money and living in the Amazon jungle? You have some explaining to do when you get back here, my friend. I have got a lot of very unhappy people around me at the moment." Sam managed to sound serious.

"Okay, I'll prepare myself for that."

"We're all looking forward to watching the sequel tomorrow." Sam finished the call.

As soon as Brad got to his room at the hotel he phoned Martinez.

"Councilor Martinez, I'm in Austin and thought I should give you an update."

"Go on, I am listening."

"Sir, the initial assessment by the police was correct. The chip was modified. The modification resulted in the deactivation of the pain and killer bots."

"Do you know how it was done and by whom?"

"All that the suspect could tell me was that a device was

swiped across his right shoulder, and that apparently did the job. He had no idea how it worked. Someone whom he met only recently did it. The police have been unable to identify that person yet. I will be staying down here for a few more days to help them find that person."

"You do that, it's critical that you find that person. We have to know how it's done. Keep me posted."

Peter smiled. "I think Johnston is right. That conversation almost convinced me that Martinez and Weinstein are working on a scheme to get out. If they were legit, they would have gone openly and directly to the plant in China to get the information they want. They're definitely hiding something."

Jack nodded. "Yep, I agree. They're up to something."

At 8:15 the next morning, while Brad was having breakfast, the waiter dropped a note on the table when he served the coffee.

9:00 a.m. at the Wilderness Coffee shop on Congress Ave.

Brad arrived five minutes early and ordered a coffee. By 9:15 a.m., he was getting worried and started looking around. The server approached and took his empty mug away. "Anything else I can get you, sir?" she asked as she dropped a note on the table.

It was a new address, about five miles away - he had to be there in half an hour. Three hours later, four relocations, three more coffees, and heart palpitations from all the caffeine, Brad walked into a motel room ten miles outside the city. Two men with balaclavas over their faces were waiting inside. They scanned and searched him, and told him to sit down.

"You found the place okay, Mr. Johnston?" Jack asked.

"Not too difficult, but was it really necessary to send me on a wild goose chase all over town? You can trust me. I'm not being followed, and will not give you away. I really want to work with you."

"Mr. Johnston, listening to your conversation with Councilor Martinez yesterday afternoon gave me no reason to trust you. You weren't honest with him. Were you?"

"Ahh, well, what else could I say?"

Jack ignored his question. "You have the canisters?"

"Yes, I have." He took three canisters out and placed them on the table. "Listen, about that conversation with Martinez, I couldn't tell him what had happened. If I did that, he would have pushed my button, and I would have been dead."

"I don't think so. I got the impression Martinez wants you to bring him the technology that can deactivate the chips. He doesn't wish to ask the scientists working for the Supreme Council, although he has access to them. Why do you think he'd rather find another way to do it?"

"I told you. I think he and Weinstein might have plans to rebel against the Supreme Council."

"Therefore, he won't be pushing your button. You are their only hope. Do you agree with that?"

"I never thought of it that way. I am just too shit-scared to take any chances."

"Okay. I promised to make a few alterations to the settings of your chip. So just sit still while I do that." Jack got up and held the device close to Brad's right shoulder, making sure he could see the lights. When the green light came on, he stepped back. "All done, the pain bots are inactive. Martinez will still be able to kill you if he decides to push the button, but I can guarantee that you won't piss your pants again."

Peter had to drop his head so Brad wouldn't see him laughing, while Sam had to mute the microphone in the ops room.

"Let's talk about your next assignment and your compensation."

"Wait, hang on! What about the killer bots, and what about my wife and children?"

"Well, that brings me to your compensation. We are not a wealthy organization. Since the introduction of your government's new fiscal arrangements, business is atrocious. We don't have money to pay you. All I can offer you is the modification of your and your family's chips as payment. My suggestion is for every assignment you complete successfully, I will make a change to the chip of the person in your family that you choose. Your chip's killer bots will be the last to go. How does that sound to you?"

"What do you want me to do?"

"Arrange for the two of us to take a trip to Europe, including a visit to Brussels, where you will catch up with your two esteemed friends. The reason for your trip is to get a better idea of the policing and law enforcement methods in Europe. Brussels will be one of the stops on your journey. I take it a man in your position can easily arrange that?"

"You are going with me? Why? I don't even know your name, nor have I seen your face. I will be able to arrange the trip, but taking you along might be a problem."

"You will know all in time, Mr. Johnston, even my name

and my face. Just be patient. In the meantime, make the arrangements."

"I think I should be able to organize that without too much trouble. What should I say to the councilors? Why do I want to meet with them?"

"You will have information about the forty-one missing people and the deactivation of the chips that you want to show them."

"I'll make arrangements as soon as I get back to Washington. The only remaining problem is I'll have to give Martinez an update in the next day or two and I don't know what I can say so he doesn't become suspicious."

"You see Mr. Johnston, that's the problem when you start lying - you have to keep on lying, and sooner or later you get caught up in your web of lies. Maybe you should play for time, tell him that the investigator is following up on all the leads, and it could take a long time to see any results. You are returning to Washington, you have the full cooperation of the police chief, and he will keep you informed."

"That might keep him off my back for now I hope."

"Just remember, hope is not a strategy, Mr. Johnston. I think we're done. I was just wondering if it would be necessary to remind you that I can also push your button and, of course, those of your family?" He held his cell phone up.

"It's not necessary. I understand that well enough." Brad replied with a grim look on his face.

"Have a safe trip. We will be in touch."

Chapter One Hundred Thirteen

WAITING FOR THEM TO ARRIVE

When Jack arrived back at the Rabbit Hole late in the evening of the next day, he received an idol's welcome from the ops team. He could not get the three canisters out of his bag quick enough for Roy, Raj, and Rebecca, who immediately rushed off to the lab with them.

Jack was relieved to see that his derogatory comments about the Rossler Foundation during his interrogation of Brad Johnston, apparently didn't cause any permanent psychological damage to his friends.

For the next few days, the ops team went into overdrive to prepare the file for Johnston and make Jack's travel arrangements. The technical team was occupied with the analysis of the free-roaming killer bots and the solution for its deactivation. Tectus was busy working out their strategies to plant EMP devices and nanonukes in target locations in preparation for the final day.

Jack and Peter kept a close watch on Brad's communications and other activities, making sure that he showed no signs of double-crossing them. As soon as they learned that the arrangements for the European tour were in place, they got Tectus to deliver a message to set up a meeting to finalize the plans.

Brad arrived at the address in a quiet neighborhood on the outskirts of D.C. a few minutes before 10 pm.

"Come on in, Mr. Johnston." The voice, he recognized immediately - it was the first time he saw the face. "I am Simon White. Now you've seen my face and know my name. You will have to excuse my companion here. You have met him before, but unfortunately, he is a very shy sort of person and asked to remain anonymous." Jack smiled as he pointed to Peter's balaclava covered face.

Brad laughed. "Well, I guess I don't need any introduction. I am glad we are on better speaking terms now than our previous encounters. Please call me Brad."

"I prefer that we keep our relationship friendly but formal. That way we won't get confused about our roles."

Brad nodded his head in agreement. "You're right, Mr. White. Maybe it's better that way."

"Good. Now that we have the formalities out of the way, let's get on with the plan. I see you have booked a very nice trip for us. Five days in Brussels, then London, Paris, Rome, Prague, and Berlin. I'm excited!"

"You will have to give me a bit more detail about your involvement so I know what to expect and plan for it," Brad said.

"You're forgetting yourself, Mr. Johnston. May I remind you that you aren't the one in charge here? You aren't in a position to make demands. And I'm sure you understand the principal of 'need-to-know' and the importance thereof in our line of work. Here's what you need to know for now. I'll give you the information about the forty-one missing people and the process of modifying the chips that I promised. I've included a little bonus about the Rossler Foundation. You will be presenting it to your friends, so I suggest you study it carefully, and tell me if you have any questions. Luckily, we don't need passports and travel documents. These chips make it so much easier to travel around these days." Jack pointed to his right shoulder.

The surprise on Brad's face was obvious when he came to the realization that Jack was chipped.

"Like I said, the chips do have some advantages." Jack smiled.

"Well, I would much rather prefer the disadvantage of not being chipped."

"According to your itinerary and meetings schedule, you will have dinner with the councilors on your last day in Brussels. That suits me very well."

"How do you know ... huh ... don't worry, for a moment I forgot you know everything I do." Then he realized what he'd just heard. "Wait, hang on there. You're going to the dinner as well? How the hell ..."

"Yes, of course. I wouldn't miss it for the world. I take it you can organize that?"

"I will see what I can do."

"You'll have to do better than that. Do I need to remind you that the deactivation of one of your family member's chips depends on that dinner invitation for me?"

"Understood."

Jack smiled and continued. "At that meeting you should present to them what's on the flash-drive. I will be listening."

"You still haven't explained your role in all of this."

"I am a security consultant and special investigator – a former FBI field agent that worked for a special top-secret branch in that organization. You have contracted me to advise you about the Rossler Foundation, the missing people, and the chips. I am the author of the information on the flash drive. That's why you brought me along with you."

"And if they decide to run a background check on you?"

"Then all three of you will know that I am not lying. I told you before - I choose honesty. It has always served me well."

"To end with, I just want to confirm that a man of your stature does not have to go through the usual customs and security checks?"

"Yes, that's correct. I assume you'll be taking some special luggage with you then?"

"No, you will be the one with the special luggage. I will give it to you at the airport."

Brad nodded.

"Familiarize yourself with the information on this flash-drive. The flight to Brussels is about seven and half hours. We'll have plenty of time to talk about any questions you might have."

"Thank you. I'll see you at the airport in ten days." Brad shook hands with them and left.

During the first hour of the flight back to Mount Ararat Peter and Jack were quiet. Their thoughts about the danger that Jack was walking into kept their minds occupied. The mission relied on Brad Johnston, who was a selfish man. A man who was cooperating with them only for his own advantage, he didn't care about anyone else. More worrying was the fact that Johnston's cooperation was driven by his belief that he had no choice, since the killer bots in his chip were still active and his belief that they held the button that could kill him in their hands. He was not motivated by patriotism, or the will to be free, or to help his fellow humans. Brad Johnston was the weak link in the chain and a dangerous man.

"Jack, I suspect we might have the same concerns about this whole thing. Can you see any other way we can do this? Once you get on that plane with Johnston, there's no turning back. We still have ten days to pull out and find another way."

"Peter my friend you must have read my mind. I have my concerns, and Johnston ranks right at the top of my list."

"And mine."

"That man will sell his mother to the highest bidder. I know his type - he will work with whoever offers him the best deal. The problem is that he is the only person that can get me close to Martinez and Weinstein."

"I agree with that, but we're making big and risky assumptions about those two. We believe they're looking for a way out, based only on their strange behavior during their dealings with Johnston. There could very well be some logical explanation for that, and we might not know until it's too late."

"Well, I'm as troubled as you are, but as you said, we have ten more days to change our minds and abort the mission."

"It would have been very helpful if the Tectus agents in Brussels were better equipped, so they could get close to our friends the councilors. A bit of inside information like that would have helped us make the right decisions now."

"You've just given me an idea. I'll have five days from the time I arrive in Brussels until the dinner. If I can get a few Tectus people activated quickly, and we concentrate all our efforts on the councilors, we might just be lucky enough to collect some useful information in that time."

"I'm feeling a bit more comfortable with that idea. It will be better than going to that meeting on a gut feeling alone. You might just have the validation of our theory or the warning to disappear and get on the first plane out of there."

"Let's convey our discussion to the rest of the ops team when we get back and see what they can contribute. Tectus can give their people over there sufficient warning about my arrival and what would be expected of them."

Jack had eight days back at the Rabbit Hole with his family and to prepare for the dinner appointment should it be decided that he would attend. The operations team spent many hours looking at the mission plan from all possible angles, debating the alternatives and escape plans. Their conclusion, despite all the precautionary measures, was that it remained a daring undertaking with many unknowns and uncertainties. Therefore, it was decided that Jack would have the only and final say in the decision to go ahead.

Roy and Raj equipped and trained him with their latest and best gear to take with him for his own and the Tectus agents' use.

Five days after the meeting with Jack and Peter, Brad had gathered enough courage to call Councilor Martinez. He explained that he had hired a highly skilled special investigator, a former FBI agent, and that his work had produced some good results so far. He explained that he would be bringing the man, Simon White, with him on the trip to Europe and recommended that they should meet him.

Martinez immediately gave Brad a dressing down. "Brad, you will have to stop doing this. One day, and that day is not too far away, I will lose my patience with you. You went out and hired this Simon whatever his name is and didn't tell me until now?"

"Councilor, I am very sorry about that. I didn't think you would mind. The man has an impeccable record, one of the best FBI special investigators there was. In the short time he has been working, we have made more progress on the missing people and the Rosslers than anyone else has."

"What has he discovered?"

"I have a report from him, which I am studying at the moment. It looks like he has discovered evidence of an underground network of people closely linked with the Rosslers and the missing people. He also uncovered some clues to the locations the nine families escaped to, clues that all other investigators have missed. I firmly believe if there is anyone that can get to the bottom of this, it would be him."

"Who else knows that he is working for you?"

"Only you and me, sir."

"Make sure it stays that way. Understood?"

"Yes, sir."

"Bring him along to the dinner. See you in a few days."

Brad let out a sigh of relief when the call ended.

At Mount Ararat, Peter and Kelly smiled when Brad's call with Martinez ended. "I reckon we just got another strong hint that the two councilors are working on something that they don't want their colleagues in the Supreme Council to know. What do you think, Peter?"

"Yes, that certainly seems to be the case. Let's get hold of Jack and send him the recording."

No one was surprised when Jack told the ops team on the sixth day that he had given it due consideration, and despite the perilous situation, he wanted to proceed.

On the morning of the eighth day, in the last ops meeting Jack would attend before he left for Europe, Nigel wanted the last word. "Son, during my time as president I had to send people into harm's way, too many times. It was always one of the most difficult tasks of my presidency. Today I feel like I am doing the same thing again. It brings back memories that I would rather not have. I have been thinking through this carefully, and I want you to give me your word of honor that you'll do as I am going to ask you."

"Yes, Mr. President?" Jack could not get used to the idea of calling his former commander in chief by his first name. Nigel ignored it. This was a serious moment.

"If by lunchtime on the day of the dinner, you have not received confirmation of the bona fides of those two men, you will go to the airport and come back here to your family and friends. New opportunities will present themselves to us at the right time. Do I have your promise?"

"Mr. President, but ..."

"No buts. That is an order."

"Yes, sir. You have my word." Jack was standing to attention.

"Good. In that case, son, I am happy for you to go, and may God bless and protect you."

It was a somber group of people who wished him well the night he walked out of the Rabbit Hole with JR, Mark, and Doug.

Since their arrival, he and Sue-Ellen had been quickly welcomed into the group of families of former military service members. Jack was pleased to know that Sue-Ellen had made good friends with their wives, and that she and the children would be in good care while he was away.

Sam was the last person to shake his hand. "Jack, you and I have come a long way. You are a treasured friend. I want you to come back alive. That is more important to me than this mission is. You know our rule, 'if in doubt leave it out.' I want you to look me in the eyes and tell me that you will do as Nigel Harper told you this morning."

"I will do that."

"Okay, Jack. It's all over to you now. God bless."

Jack met with Brad at the airport as agreed, and while they shook hands, Jack swapped the identical briefcases so swiftly that Brad didn't even realize it happened.

They were booked into first class, and there was enough space around them to be able to talk without being overheard. Nonetheless, Jack made a quick scan with his phone to satisfy himself there were no surveillance bugs.

"Mr. White, I studied your report. It contains explosive information. Where and how did you get hold of that?"

"I told you I'm a special investigator - that's what we do."

"The information about the technology used to get those families out was amazing. I'm baffled that our investigators couldn't figure that out."

"Well, you had to know what to look for to be able to figure it out. They obviously didn't."

"What's the story with the video clips and images of people being tortured? Why did you put them in your report, and where did they come from?"

"You mean to tell me you don't know?"

"What is it that I'm supposed to know?"

"That's the work that the Science Advisory Panel does at that chip manufacturing plant in China under the leadership of Professor Barbara Cohen."

"Good God! No! That can't be true. It's impossible!" Brad had gone pale in the face. "How do you know that? How did you get those videos and images?"

"I told you. I'm a special investigator. That's what we do - we collect information. You've only seen a few minutes of it. I have more than six hours of video footage and over a hundred pages of text showing in detail what's happening at that place."

"Fuck, man. I'm sick just to think that I'm an official of a government that can do something like that."

"I hope you're beginning to understand how important this mission of ours is, Mr. Johnston. There are thousands of human guinea pigs in that place. They are tortured and killed in their hundreds every day as we speak. You see - this mission is not just about you and your family. There is a much higher purpose than just you and me - it's about everyone there and the billions of us who have been chipped."

Brad was staring in front of him slowly nodding his head as the gravity of Jack's words settled in his mind. "Do you think it is a good idea to show that to the councilors?"

"Well, if they don't know, I reckon it's time they do. If they do know, I would certainly like to know how they feel about it."

"I agree, but the problem is disgusting as that video may be, that the councilors' feelings about it has nothing to do with your investigation. They might get upset if we present them with information they didn't ask for, especially if they already know about it."

"We will see how they react. I suspect they have no idea about this."

"Let's talk about the Rosslers. Do you really think they're hiding somewhere in Mexico? What lead you to that conclusion?"

"I had a good look at the Harper's escape, and I got the idea that they were airlifted out of there. Therefore, I studied the radar reports of the air traffic for that time and found there was quite a lot of activity going on at the time. However, there was one report that got my interest. It was about a light plane that flew south late at night and then went off the radar close to the Mexican border."

"I have never heard anyone mention Mexico as a possible hiding place. Alaska, Canada, and South America - all those places have come up in speculation, but none had any concrete evidence to back it up. It might be worth following up on that idea of yours."

"As I've said before, you guys are barking up the wrong tree. You are giving the Rosslers much more credit than they deserve. As far as I'm concerned, they've chosen a prepper lifestyle and just want to be left alone. That's why they've only helped their family and friends. If they had any intentions of overthrowing the government, they would act very differently."

"That could be so, but it doesn't explain how their families escaped the killer bots."

Jack laughed. "You've already forgotten that the chips can be neutralized and removed."

"Are you saying you're the one who helped them?"

"No, I am not saying that. What I'm saying is that it's possible some of the people I work with could have."

Brad knew he was not going to get more information, and he changed the subject.

"We have an invitation to a cocktail party at Councilor Martinez's house - I take it you already know that?"

"Yes, I brought a special suit for the occasion."

As they settled in their hotel rooms in Brussels, Jack went to Brad's. "I'll stay out of your way for the next few days until we meet with the councilors. I'm going to look up a few old friends."

When he walked out the front door of the hotel, a taxi driver lifted his eyebrows and asked, "Mr. White?"

Jack nodded and got in. After an hour-long sightseeing tour of Brussels, making sure they were not followed, the driver dropped him off at the safe house, where a few of the Tectus members were waiting for him.

Guillaume Francois was the leader of the Western European chapter of Tectus. He introduced himself and his three companions in a thick French accent. Jack soon realized that all of them were native French speakers and were struggling to get the conversation flowing.

"*Pouvons-nous parler en français?*" he asked in perfect French to the surprise of everyone.

"Yes, thank you. We'll do better in French." Guillaume replied in his native language, with a bit of an embarrassed smile.

Jack opened the briefcase, and for the next few hours, he showed the four enthusiastic agents how to operate all of the surveillance equipment. He explained what his immediate objectives were and how important it was to get as much information as possible about Weinstein and Martinez within the next four days. Guillaume got a mirror phone, which he would use to keep Jack posted with progress.

By the time Jack left them, they were all inspired and ready to get their new toys in operation as quickly as possible. Early the next morning Jack was pleased to hear from Guillaume that the two councilors were under full-time surveillance at their homes, offices, and in their vehicles. He reported to the Rabbit Hole and also used the opportunity to speak to Sue-Ellen and the kids for a while.

The first day and a half went by without producing much useful information, other than finding out about the security, as well as what the councilors' houses, offices, and family members looked like. In operations of a different nature, this would have been good information, but Jack was on the hunt for evidence that would give him the sign that he could appear at the dinner. The councilors were living a protected but otherwise routine life, as far as he could see.

On the evening of the second day, things took a different turn when Guillaume hooked Jack up to his screen via the mirror phone and showed him a few video clips.

"What do you make of that?" Guillaume asked. "It looks like our councilors are already under surveillance."

Jack replayed parts of the clips a few times, stopped and studied the images closely. "Excellent catch Guillaume! They are definitely being followed, and I am willing to bet on it that their phones are tapped, and their houses and offices bugged as well."

"The million dollar question, as you Americans say, is who is doing this and why?"

Jack was worried that the councilors might already be in trouble. "Two possibilities I can think of quickly. The two councilors are suspected of something, and someone is collecting evidence. The other possibility is that all councilors are under surveillance, which means someone is paranoid about being stabbed in the back or is collecting dirty secrets to use against them in the future. No reward for guessing who that someone could be."

"John Brideaux," Guillaume mumbled. "There are a lot of street stories in Brussels about that man's crazy behavior. I wouldn't be surprised."

"Okay, Guillaume, here is what I want you and your team to do. Use the spyflies in the houses and offices and scan for all the bugs. Draw maps of the houses and offices and plot exactly where the bugs are planted. Then get a few of your people to put surveillance on the rest of the council members so we can find out which of my theories are correct."

"No problem, Simon. I will get that in place right away and let you know how it goes."

Jack reported the discovery to Sam, who agreed that if their expanded surveillance showed Martinez and Weinstein were the only ones with taps on them, he would abandon the mission and go back home.

By the evening of the fourth day, Jack and Guillaume were on the phone to discuss the day's catch.

"Two topics to discuss, Simon. The results of the surveillance of the other council members and a breakfast meeting between our two friends tomorrow morning."

"Let's talk about the councilors first," Jack suggested.

They studied the latest video clips and got confirmation that the entire Supreme Council was under the constant scrutiny of the Brussels police department's undercover agents.

"Now we know two things for certain. One, John Brideaux is cracked and paranoid. Two, Martinez and Weinstein have not been singled out for special attention," Guillaume concluded.

Jack smiled. "This is good information. I am going to

make a little presentation out of these images for our two friends. I'm sure they would appreciate my concerns about them."

"I would like to have a spyfly on the wall at that meeting, Simon!" Guillaume quipped.

"We aren't out of the woods yet. I must have confirmation about Martinez and Weinstein's inclinations by midday tomorrow, or I'm going back home, and we will have to wait for another opportunity. It would be a pity if I have to do that. On the other hand, my coming here has at least served the purpose of setting you guys up with the right equipment for the future."

"Yes, undeniably. Maybe you will get what you want during tomorrow's breakfast. It will be the first time we are able to find out what the two of them talk about when they are together."

"If they're actually on their own, then yes, there is a good chance for that."

"We have everything ready. The flies are already waiting for them to arrive." Guillaume laughed.

Chapter One Hundred Fourteen

A FACT-FINDING MISSION

At 7:30 the next morning, Councilors Weinstein and Martinez seated themselves at a table in a private area reserved for special guests at the Hotel Le Plaza.

Two spyflies blended perfectly into the folds of the dark blue curtains less than three feet away from them. The video screens in Guillaume's apartment displayed crystal clear pictures to him and Jack as they were watching the councilors place their orders. The sound was perfect. Sam and the ops team were linked up to Jack's computer, holding their breaths.

"Amigo, you remember the cocktail party at my house tonight?"

"Wouldn't miss it, my friend. Not that I like partying so much, but I am rather looking forward to talking to Johnston and his special investigator. I did a bit of research on him. He has an impressive record."

Martinez laughed. "You should have told me - it would have saved me the trouble of checking him out as well. I am interested to see Johnston's report and to hear what White has to say."

"Rafael, I am just worried that we are chasing after something that will lead us nowhere. It feels as if our plans are taking too long. We have to try and speed things up."

"Amigo, the Japanese have a saying, 'isogaba maware' it means 'make haste slowly'. It means you should advance and grow, but you must do so with the utmost thought and care. We will be of no use to anyone if we can't stay alive and help to complete the defeat of that madman and his cohorts."

Jack and Guillaume pumped their fists in the air with glee. In the Rabbit Hole, the ops team looked at each other incredulously. They could almost not believe what they'd just heard.

Nigel looked up and whispered, "Thank you God."

In Brussels, Weinstein continued, oblivious that his words were being broadcast halfway around the world. "Wise words, my friend. Very wise words. It's just that every day when my conscience accuses me of my evil actions in the past, I am forced to think how to make it good again and right now would not be too soon for me."

"Amigo, for now we have done what we could. Our scientists have the chips and will find the answer eventually. We have control of everything else we will need. Once we can beat the chips, things will move much quicker. In the meantime, there is also the possibility that we could find the Rosslers. We know they already have the solution. That incident in Austin a few weeks ago has proved it. I am placing a lot of hope on finding those people soon."

"I remain skeptical. Although I agree, it would be ideal if we could get in touch with them. I am still not sure how we are going to introduce ourselves and win their trust.

The Phoenix Agenda

Somehow I don't think they would be too keen to be seen in public in the company of two members of the Supreme Council!" Weinstein laughed.

Daniel could not help himself. "You can bet your ass on that! But after what I've just heard, I am so keen to meet you guys that I'm thinking of throwing a private party here at the Rabbit Hole and invite you two over." Luckily, Sam had the microphones muted.

"I told you before. We will know how to deal with that issue once we have established contact with them." Martinez grinned.

"Let us hope we can get that done soon. But I have to say I am not holding out much hope that Johnston will be the man that will be able to do it. Maybe his ace investigator could do it. We will know better after our meeting tonight."

Martinez nodded.

"That Austin incident has reminded me that we will also have to find a way to eliminate those deathbots. As you know, they have been distributed all over the world."

"I am sure if the scientists can find a way to beat the chips, they will also find a way to beat those bots. But you are right. That would be one of the obstacles to overcome."

"Well Daniel, it looks like the attendance of your private party has just become compulsory for the two of them," Nigel remarked, only half in jest.

The ops team would replay that recording many more times just to confirm they hadn't gone crazy. That they had, without a doubt, found knights in shining armor who would help them to get over the final hurdles to the finish line.

Jack was back in his hotel room, busy unpacking his bags when Sam phoned to confirm that the dinner was on.

Councilor Martinez's villa was an impressive and elegant place in peaceful settings with magnificent views and over a park of about twelve acres. It boasted nine thousand square feet of living space, reception rooms opening onto a stunning terrace, seven bedrooms, seven bathrooms, a lift, caretaker's accommodation, and a seven-car garage.

Rafael Martinez and his wife welcomed Brad and Jack when they arrived. After half an hour of standing around making small talk with the guests, Ruben Weinstein arrived at the group where Jack and Brad were standing.

"Good to meet you, Mr. White. Brad speaks very highly of you. I'm looking forward to catching up with you later." He smiled as he moved on to mingle with the others.

By 9 pm, all the guests but Brad and Jack had left. One of the house staff showed them to Martinez's study. Jack activated the pen of silence in the side pocket of his jacket while they were on their way - he knew of at least three bugs in that room.

Martinez and Weinstein were waiting for them and showed them to their seats after handing them each a drink.

"Brad, it is good to see you again and kind of you to have accepted the invitation tonight. We have been looking forward to hearing what news you bring us from America." Martinez smiled.

From where Jack was sitting opposite Brad, he could see the nervousness on his face and the slight shaking of his hands when he took the reports out of his briefcase.

"Councilors, I brought this for you. It was authored by Mr. White. As I have explained over the phone, I brought him along with me, in case you want to discuss anything in more detail." He handed them each a copy.

Weinstein placed his on the small table next to him and said, "Thank you for that, I will study it carefully later. I am thinking it would be good if you could give us a summary of what we will find in the report."

Martinez nodded his agreement as he put his report down.

Brad took a sip of his drink - his hands were still shaking. It was obvious to Jack that Brad was anxious. They must have put the fear of God into him during that first meeting.

Jack wanted to get to the point - he didn't care much for all the bogus niceties while everyone, except Brad, knew full well what was important. "Councilors, please accept my apologies in advance, but if you would bear with me for a moment, I would like to make a suggestion."

"Please go ahead, Mr. White," Martinez replied while Brad visibly relaxed. He could not stomach another inquisition - it would be better if White did the talking.

"Why don't we rather discuss our common goals? I know we have the same concerns about the world out there. Why don't we talk about what must be done for the billions of people out there living in the most horrendous conditions, with chips in their bodies like animals? People are killed and tortured out there, while we are sitting here in luxury. My suggestion, Councilors, is that we talk about that."

Both Martinez and Weinstein went pale with fury. No one dared speak to them like that. "White, listen here. I will give you three minutes to explain yourself, and then I will call security."

"Councilors, I am not worried about that, I can assure

you when you have heard what I have to say, you will be grateful."

"You had better start talking, White, my patience is growing thin." Martinez barked.

Brads' face had turned a strange shade of blue as he was struggling to breathe. It looked as if he was on the verge of a heart attack.

Jack smiled as he looked at him and said. "You okay over there, buddy?"

Brad nodded his head, but it was clear he was not okay. However, Jack had to continue. He'd keep an eye on his companion to make sure he didn't get worse.

"Good. Where were we? Oh, yes, you are waiting for an explanation. So let me do that, then. I work for the Rossler Foundation. I am here on a fact-finding mission to investigate the possibilities of a joint venture with you gentlemen. My understanding is that there are some common interests, and that a joint venture could be advantageous to both sides."

The two councilors' mouths hung open in shock and disbelief as they looked at each other and Jack. Brad was making strange noises as he sat forward and buried his head in his hands.

"Excuse me for a moment gentlemen, my friend here is not well. Let me just check what's wrong with him. I will be with you in a sec." Jack got up and walked over to Brad, placed his hand on his shoulder and whispered, "Buddy you must be strong now. Everything is going to be okay. Just hang in there. You are going to be a very happy man soon. Sit up, take a few deep breaths, and relax. Everything is going to be good."

"Apologies for that. I think he should be okay now." Jack was still smiling.

Sam and the ops team were biting their nails as they watched the event unfolding. They were worried. The councilors were fuming. Had Jack pushed them too far?

Weinstein was furious. "White, you think you are smart. You will not walk out of this place a free man tonight. You can take my word for that. If you have anything sensible to say, I suggest you get on with it. Your time is running out."

"Good. I see you don't believe me. I can understand that. Let me help you get over your doubts by showing you a few things." He opened his briefcase, took his tablet out, and placed it on the coffee table in front of him.

The councilors leaned forward on their chairs.

"Did you know that you are being followed by the Brussels police department, and that your houses and offices are bugged?"

Jack's question hit them between the eyes - they looked around the room nervously. Martinez tried to keep his pose. "Come on, White, that is impossible!"

Jack smiled - he was waiting for them to step into that. He started the slide show and gave it to them, warts and all. He was watching their expressions and body language as he talked. When he got to the last slide, he was looking at two very distressed councilors.

Weinstein was still a bit skeptical. "You are telling us there are three bugs hidden in this room, yet you are not worried to talk in their presence." He thought he had Jack trapped.

Jack took the pen with the little blue light out of his pocket and placed it on the coffee table. "No, I am not worried to talk as long as I have that with me, and that light is on."

"Don't tell me you are recording our conversation!" Martinez shouted.

"No, I am not recording it." Jack grinned.

"White, have you had too much to drink?" Weinstein growled.

"Okay, gentlemen let's do one thing at a time. First let me explain to you what that pen does. It suppresses any bugs in this room, and it will not let any sound out of a circle ten yards around us. I will demonstrate that to you later if you are interested. Now if you will please follow me, I'll show you the bugs."

Brad was still not feeling well and preferred to remain seated. Jack took them around the room and showed them the bugs. Martinez wanted to pull them out, but Jack stopped him. "Don't do that. The police will immediately know that you found them, and that will blow your cover."

They returned to their chairs with changed demeanor.

"These are the maps of your houses and offices with the exact locations of the bugs. However, as I have said, you should not remove them under any circumstances. Leave them where they are and learn to live with it."

"Simon, this is disturbing information." It didn't escape him that Martinez was calling him Simon all of a sudden. "I want to know how you got that information."

"Councilors, I will explain that to you in all the detail you want. But for now, can we move on to the real purpose of our meeting?"

"As you wish. Let's continue then," Martinez said.

"As I have said before, I work for the Rossler Foundation, and I am here to explore the possibilities for a joint venture."

"What makes you think we are interested in working with them?" Weinstein asked.

"Your conversation over breakfast this morning."

The two councilors were speechless. Weinstein was the first to get his voice back.

"You mean to say you listened in on that conversation?" He was a worried man. If Jack could do it, others could do it.

"Yes I did, and I heard every word of it, I have it here on the tablet, if you want me to refresh your memory."

"I don't believe you. Show it to me," Weinstein demanded.

Ten minutes later the councilors stopped him – they knew he was not bluffing.

In the Rabbit Hole, the ops team took their first deep breath and sat back to watch the rest of the show. Jack was about to hit them with one more nasty revelation.

"Gentlemen I don't want to waste your time, but I was just wondering if you know about the work of Professor Barbara Cohen's Science Advisory Panel? I mean, have either of you been to their headquarters in China?"

"We know about the research she is doing. She reports to the Supreme Council, and we get regular reports from her, but neither of us has been over there yet. Why do you ask?" Weinstein replied with hesitation, as he suspected there was another nasty revelation coming up.

Jack found the videos and started playing them without saying a word. He sat back and watched the two men's torment growing to the point where they both shouted. "Stop it!"

"Are you sure it comes from SAP?" Weinstein was shaking.

"One hundred percent. You have only watched a few minutes of it. I have about six hours of video footage and over hundred pages of documents."

Weinstein and Martinez were sick as they looked at each

other and nodded. It was time to trust this man and have a serious discussion.

For the rest of the night Jack explained to them what the Rosslerites had achieved and what help they required. Jack revealed his real identity, and they were all on a first-name basis. The councilors had many questions, and they also shared everything they had with Jack and Brad, who'd finally recovered from his shock and was participating in the conversation.

Shortly before sunrise the next morning, Martinez recapped the main points of the discussions.

"Ruben and I will give you all the help you need. You just tell us what, when, and where, and we will take care of it. Access for your technical people to the Skywalkers, as you call them, in addition to the CHCU and all communication satellites will be arranged.

"You will provide us with the technology that will enable us to demilitarize chips so that we can use it until the day we are going to deactivate all chips through the Skywalkers. You will provide us with the blueprints of your EMP devices and nanonukes, which we will build and plant at stockpile locations and warehouses outside America and any place that you can't reach.

"Have I missed anything important?"

"No, I think that's about it for now. I brought along a few gifts for you, compliments of the Rossler Foundation." Jack laughed as he took out the two pens of silence, two mirror phones, and a dozen spyflies that he placed on the coffee table.

"I see you came prepared and sure that the meeting was going to go down like it did." Ruben laughed.

"After listening to your breakfast conversation I knew what to expect."

Jack demonstrated how to use the equipment and then lectured them for almost thirty minutes about security.

"You should stop having face to face meetings - use those phones I gave you. Make up a reason for a disagreement between the two of you and make sure a few people see that, so there is a logical explanation for why you are not seen together anymore. If you are going to demilitarize chips, be very careful. You saw what happened in Austin the other day. Although it turned out to be a blessing in disguise, it could have turned out very different for us."

Ruben, Rafael, and Brad paid close attention while Jack coached them and reiterated the importance of them not removing the bugs from their houses and offices.

Back at their hotel, Jack was packing his bags to catch a flight back that afternoon. Brad was sitting on a chair, watching him. He was still a bit shell-shocked from the events of the past ten hours.

"Jack, you son of a bitch! To think all this time you had me convinced you were an honest man."

"Well, I have been more honest than you. At least with the councilors that is."

"What do we do now? What is it you want me to do in all of this?"

"You finish your European tour as planned and when you get back to America, we'll meet again and discuss the way forward. Remember this is only the beginning. We have a mountain to move before we are ready. You are going to play a big role in that."

"I will do my part."

"Good to hear that."

"I guess you want me to give you a name now?"

"What name?"

"The name of my family member whose chip you will demilitarize. That decision is impossible to make. I love them all. I would like them all to be free - can't choose anyone above the other."

Jack smiled. "Brad, don't stress about that anymore. I will see to it that all of your family is taken care of as soon as I get back. As far as your own chip is concerned, I deactivated both the pain and killer bots that day in Austin."

"You bastard! You had me living in fear all this time that the councilors or you might kill me! Why didn't you tell me?"

"Needed the guarantee of your cooperation, Brad."

An hour later, they had coffee in the hotel lounge and shook hands. Jack left for the airport, and Brad continued his scheduled tour.

When Jack walked back into the Rabbit Hole late the night he arrived home, he only had enough time to embrace his wife and children before he was dragged off to the Town Hall where the entire group was waiting. They were on their feet in applause the moment he and his family appeared.

Chapter One Hundred Fifteen

A NEW JOIE DE VIVRE

There was a new joie de vivre amongst the Rosslerites since Jack's return. The next morning, an encouraged ops team gathered in the war room to start the preparations for the last item on the Phoenix Agenda. All of the major obstacles that slowed their progress in the past were now surmountable.

Roy and Raj with their technical teams engrossed themselves in the technical preparations, while the rest of the ops team commenced the development of a detailed plan with timelines and responsibilities.

A ruckus ensued one morning when Mark indicated he had a request.

"Let's hear it." Sam invited him to speak.

"I speak on behalf of all the former military personnel and a few others here in the Rabbit Hole. Our request is that we be implanted with demilitarized chips, so we can get out of here and be part of the preparation work going on outside. We believe that ..."

Daniel did not give him a chance to finish. "Over my dead body."

"No, wait, Daniel, let him finish," Sam demanded. "I'd like to hear all of it." He nodded for Mark to continue.

"Well, what I was about to say was that we have the skills and experience that's required on the outside now. We can work with Tectus and help them."

Daniel had calmed down a bit, but was back on it immediately when Mark finished. He couldn't forget how he felt during the first Antarctica expedition, when they believed the expedition members were all dead. He'd blamed himself for sending his youngest brother to his death.

A heated debate followed, but Mark stood his ground, and in the end, Nigel suggested that the matter be voted on at a community meeting.

That night in the Town Hall, Sam explained the request from Mark and others.

"Before I put that to the vote let me just see how many of you here are prepared to do what these men want to do?"

Sam was not entirely surprised when everyone put their hands up including the ninety-year-old Bess Rossler, Nigel, and Esther, although Bess's hand in the air had him smiling.

"Well, the bad news is you can't all go. The good news for those who stay here is that we have more than enough important work for you to do."

When the laughter receded, he continued. "So I take it, then, that you are all happy for these men to go and do as they suggested?"

Bess stood up. "No, Sam, I don't think we are happy for them to go. But if they have something more important to do on the outside, they should be allowed to go. One of them is my grandson, and I know the danger the boys are getting themselves into. We have all made a commitment to do our part in this - those men are only asking to be allowed to do their part."

When the old matriarch sat down a few moments of silence followed before everyone started clapping hands. The matter was settled. Mark and his comrades were smiling.

Daniel and Sam were standing next to each other as the people were leaving when Nigel approached them. "Daniel, I have to say that grandmother of yours is a gracious lady. With a group of people like this, we can conquer the world."

"That's exactly what's going to happen very soon, Nigel." Daniel beamed.

The next morning JR, Mark, Doug, Peter, and two others reported to the clinic for the chipping procedure, accompanied by spouses with miserable looks on their faces.

"Oh, how I hate John Brideaux for this," Rebecca whispered. Her hands were shaking a little as she performed the small incisions and inserted the chips.

She left JR for last, and when she finished, she stood back, wiped the tears from her eyes, and looked up at her husband. "Joshua Rossler, you come back to me - alive - you hear me?"

JR took her in his arms and whispered. "I love you more than anything else in this world Becca. I will be back - alive - I promise you."

Six proud but sad wives embraced and encouraged their husbands as everyone watched in silence. The scene in front of them was yet another reminder of the seriousness of their situation.

Martinez and Weinstein gave their support and cooperation exactly as they'd promised, and more. With the additional resources, Tectus was able to expand their operations into the rest of the world. Martinez's control over the world's communications gave them an enormous boost in their efforts to access government networks to extract vital information.

Roy and Raj had the time of their lives when they got access to the Skywalkers, the Beast, and the communications satellites from Martinez.

Mark, Doug, JR, and others were welcomed by Tectus and immediately placed in charge of teams of former combat veterans, ensuring that all apparatus were positioned at all the chip warehouses in America, Canada, and parts of Mexico.

They were under strict orders not to appear in public, and if they absolutely had to, they must be properly disguised to pass by the facial recognition systems. None of them ever liked the idea of leading from behind, but they understood the dangers of being recognized.

Brad Johnston had a lot of time for soul searching after Jack left him in Europe. When he arrived back in America, he was a changed man - he definitely had a different outlook on life and his fellow human beings. He was ecstatic to learn that Jack had kept his promise and modified the chips of his entire family. He would keep his promise by doing his part when he was called upon from time to time to get the police out of the way of Tectus operations. He also got the help of Tectus to help identify members of the current and former law enforcement community. Across the country, these people would be useful in establishing and maintaining law and order when the current government was finally defeated.

During one of the musketeers' happy hours, Nigel raised a matter he had on his mind for a while.

"The way things have started to fall in place lately, I'm convinced that the day of our freedom is fast approaching."

"Let's drink to that!" they shouted. Everyone lifted their mugs in a toast.

"I was wondering if you guys have given some thought about what happens after we have dethroned John Brideaux?"

"I have been thinking a lot about that." Sinclair laughed. "I like this place, and I've been wondering if the new government will allow me to live the remainder of my days out in this place with my wife and buddies."

"Hear, hear!"

"I don't know about the rest of you, but I had the best time of my life in this place with you and my family here. I can't think of a more idyllic lifestyle." Ryan remarked while the rest of them lifted their mugs with honey-shine in another toast.

"I feel the same as all of you, but that isn't what I was talking about." Nigel was serious. "We will have to think about elections and forming a new government. We'll need a new president, Congress, and Senate. There's a lot we'll have to do."

"Thinking of running for president again, Nigel? You'll get all our votes. With everyone else's in this place it should give you a hundred count head start on any competitor," Sinclair joked.

"No, my time is over. I have no intentions of running for any office ever again. I am going to retire right here with the rest of you. Wouldn't have it any other way."

"So what are you thinking, Nigel? Who do you think will make a good president? It must be someone that will, on his first day in office, sign a Presidential decree that allows the musketeers to live here in this place as long as they please." Luke smiled.

"I don't want to influence you, so why don't we all write down the name of our candidate, and I will keep it until the time comes to reveal it?"

They all nodded, and Nigel gave them each a small piece of paper from his notebook. Later that night, in the privacy of their quarters, Nigel opened the nominations, showed them to Esther, and they both smiled broadly – it was unanimous.

The ops team carefully plotted the progress of the field teams and slowly built the D-Day plan, which according to their estimates would be ready for execution in about three months. It was a multi-faceted and complex operation, requiring painful meticulousness. The sequence of each of the stages, the timing, who, what, where, and how had to be mapped out and considered many times over. There was no room for error.

With the increased level of activities, there was growing concern amongst the ops team that the potential for discovery was also rapidly increasing. Some were wondering if it wouldn't be better if they speeded things up. However, Nigel was the one who reminded them of Martinez's wise words – 'Make Haste Slowly.'

Two and a half months had passed since Jack's return from Brussels when Roy and Raj reported that the technical preparations were complete, and they were ready for the first walkthrough. Another two weeks of fine-tuning, walkthroughs, and demonstrations followed before the ops team was satisfied that everything was ready to commence execution.

It was D-Day -3.

Rafael Martinez, Ruben Weinstein, and Brad Johnston all received their final instructions and knew what they had to do. For the next three days, every step in the plan was rehearsed twice a day.

The ops team agreed it was important for everyone in the Rabbit Hole to be able to see what was happening during the last stages of the operation. Everyone had worked for this day, and everyone was going to see the fruits of their labor. Raj installed a projector screen in the Robert Cartwright Hall and hooked it up to a video camera in the war room.

Chapter One Hundred Sixteen

INFORM HIM ABOUT IT

It was D-Day. Sam got the final confirmation from everyone who had dialed in via video conference and mirror phones.

He tapped Raj on the shoulder, "All yours, son. Give them hell."

The code for the shutdown routine of the chips had been uploaded to the Skywalkers weeks before. Raj typed the command, and a few seconds later, he looked up to Sam. "It's done - all twenty-four of them are downloading the shutdown sequence to the chips across the globe. In forty minutes, it will be completed."

Sam walked over to Roy. "You're on next, son. You can take out the bots now."

Roy leaned forward and pushed the button that would shoot a laser signal to the four mirrors, fifty-five thousand miles away. The signal would be distributed to more than one thousand five hundred locations where the free-roaming bots were stockpiled. Spyflies equipped with EMP devices would be triggered. Twenty seconds later, he looked at Sam.

"No return signals from any of the spyflies. The bots are

history and so is the plant in Austin. Good job, Tectus." Roy smiled as he showed Dennis and Eric on the screen a thumbs up, followed by thundering applause.

"Raj you can send the telephone messages out." Raj nodded and got busy. Within the next twenty minutes, his voice biometrics system would have called every chip warehouse manager on the planet. It would be the manager's superior instructing him or her to vacate the premises immediately due to an imminent bomb explosion.

Everyone was quietly watching the screens. Nigel was sitting next to Daniel, whispering. "This is way above my little brain. We are in the middle of a raging battle, and there is no noise, no explosions, no deaths, and what's inconceivable is the enemy doesn't even know they are getting their butts kicked."

"Much better than the old battlefields with all their blood and guts, wouldn't you say?" Daniel smiled. "I don't have the stomach for that anymore. Maybe I'm getting old."

"Ah, buffalo bagels! You are in the prime of your life. There's a lot you still have to do for this country."

Raj reported that the calls to warehouses were completed.

Sam nodded to Roy. Roy looked at Peter sitting next to him and said. "Okay, Peter this is the moment you've been waiting for. Let's start at the top of the list - those would have been evacuated by now."

Peter held his index finger up. "Oh man, this finger of mine has been itching for days - this is going to cure it."

Within minutes, they got the first confirmations from Dennis and Eric, who were in contact with their people observing the warehouses. Soon the video clips would stream in showing the explosions. These were the first visual evidence of the battle that was going on.

"There you go, Nigel. There are your explosions." Daniel laughed. "Feeling better now?"

"Yeah, now we're talking business."

When they got to the last target on the list, Roy called Rebecca over. "Rebecca I saved this one for you. Will you please do us the honor?"

Rebecca had a big smile on her face as she pushed the button that would leave the China chip manufacturing facility and the Science Advisory Panel Headquarters in ruins. When Dennis got confirmation from the China agents, triumphant cheers went up and again when the video clips arrived a few minutes later.

Raj had entered the access code for the CHCU, the Beast, and uploaded the code that would activate its shutdown routine. He gave the thumbs up when he got the confirmation back that the code was activated.

In Brussels, the technicians on duty in the CHCU control center looked at their screens in disbelief. This had never happened before. The CHCU was programmed to restart once a week only, and that happened automatically - they had no control over it. The CHCU had gone through a restart two days ago. Something was wrong, and they got on the phone to their supervisor. He would be there in half an hour.

Sam stood next to Roy. "Okay, I told you nothing would give me more pleasure than to watch you blow those Skywalkers into oblivion. Here I am - show me."

Roy looked at him and said, "There was a slight change of plan. Instead of you watching me do it, I will be watching you doing it. What do you say?"

"Well, I couldn't ask for more. That will give me great pleasure. What do I have to do?"

"See those twenty-four red dots flickering on the screen?

Click on them one at a time. Every time you click, it will disappear in a few seconds. When that happens, it means it's destroyed. Think you can do it?"

"Son, move over let me give you a demonstration for a change."

The destruction of the Skywalkers was the final step in the process. With them out of the way, the Supreme Council's reign would finally be over. This was the moment they'd all worked and prayed for all these many months.

Nigel started counting down aloud as Sam clicked the red dots, and soon everyone joined in. "One down, twenty-three to go. Two down, twenty-two to go..." their voices reached a crescendo when they all shouted, "Twenty-four down!" All were on their feet cheering.

John Brideaux's new world order had finally come to an end. All that remained was to inform him about it.

Chapter One Hundred Seventeen

THE SCREEN WENT BLANK

Nigel Harper looked at all the faces around him. Not too long ago, he would not have believed it if anyone told him this moment would arrive in his lifetime. His and Esther's rescue was still fresh in his mind, and so was the pride and honor he felt to work with this group of people in front of him in the months that followed their rescue. For the rest of his life, this moment would become his most cherished memory.

He was about to face the world and the Supreme Council. Thanks to Rafael Martinez, everyone in the world in front of a TV screen or radio would see and hear him. He could see all the members of the Supreme Council in their meeting room, and he knew they could certainly see him. When Raj lifted his hand, he was on.

"Ladies and gentlemen of the Supreme Council and everyone across the globe watching and listening, my name is Nigel Harper. I am a former president of the United States. I am now going to address the Supreme Council, but what I have to say is of utmost importance to every citizen of our planet."

John Brideaux was in the middle of a sentence when the big screen came on. Everyone turned to look, and silence descended as they recognized the face of the man they'd killed a few months ago. When Nigel started speaking, many of them almost jumped out of their chairs. His voice was so loud and clear it was as if he was in the room with them.

Across the world, people grabbed their remote controls and raised the volume as their programs were interrupted.

"Mr. Brideaux, I apologize for not making an appointment. The reason for the interruption is to inform you of an important event that took place during the past hour."

Brideaux was on his feet. "You're dead." He screamed, "You're fucking dead. I know you are! This is a trick." He swung around and addressed the members, "Those bloody people are at it again. It's a fake." He waved his hands around and repeated, "It's a fucking fake, don't believe it."

One of the council members had the remote control and attempted to disengage the screen.

Nigel responded, "I have to inform you, Mr. Brideaux, it will not be possible to 'turn me off'. You and the council have to hear my message."

Brideaux sunk halfway back into his chair and then jumped up again. He ran to the screen and stared at Nigel in horror.

Nigel looked back at Brideaux coldly. "Today we have taken away all of your power and control. People of your ilk will never reign again. The horrors you have visited on the people of the world ended an hour ago."

Brideaux was shaking his head, his hands in front of him as if was trying to fend off something while he slowly walked backward away from the screen.

"Your satellites are destroyed. The Central Human Control Unit was shut down and cannot be restarted. All chip warehouses were reduced to rubble, the entire stockpile of killer bots destroyed. Every chip in every human body has been deactivated. Your day has run its course - it's over."

"You fuckin' imbecile! You liar! No one can do that! I am God. I am the only one who can do that. I am God! You must obey my commands!" Brideaux had a wild look in his eyes.

There were many ashen faces around the table and someone vomited.

"Today the world was delivered from your monstrous, savage, and disgusting ploys of madness."

In the background, Nigel heard the sound of the fire alarm and the announcement for everyone to evacuate the building. The council members jumped up and rushed to the heavy wooden doors, but they were locked. No one could escape.

Nigel had a faint smile on his face as he continued. "Ladies and gentlemen, please return to your seats. We are not finished yet. The alarm was just to get everyone else out of the building so we can continue without interruptions."

The councilors slowly returned to their seats, their heads hanging in defeat. Brideaux was sitting on the floor in the far corner of the room. His eyes were wide and bloodshot.

"Just to prove to you that all I have said has happened is true, let me show you a few short video clips."

The screen went blank for a few seconds before filling with images of the explosions at the warehouses from around the world. The councilors watched in stunned silence as they saw the destruction of their empire, while sounds of jubilation erupted across the globe.

"I have left one of those clips for a bit later. I first want to show everyone what was really happening at that facility before we destroyed it. Before I continue I will issue a solemn warning to all viewers except the Supreme Council, of course, that what I am about to show you is disturbing in the extreme. I advise that sensitive viewers don't watch for the next five minutes, and under no circumstances should children be allowed to see this."

Again, the screen turned black for a second, and then the views of Professor Barbara Cohen's Science Advisory Panel headquarters in China came on. It was with pleasure that Nigel saw many of the councilors beginning to cringe. That most of them had no idea how far Brideaux and Cohen had taken their power hungry drive was clear as they were forced to see for themselves what they had implemented.

Nigel's face appeared on the screen again, "That, ladies and gentlemen, was the research work of Professor Barbara Cohen's Science Advisory Panel. I am glad to tell you it no longer exists and never will again." He played the last clip showing the explosions that turned the place into dust.

In the corner, Brideaux was on his feet and beginning to squawk. It was an ugly sound, and an awful sight, as foam gathered at his lips and nose. He was jerking in a strange dance of fury that seemed as if his joints would no longer hold him together. He was waving his gun at the councilors, screaming incoherently as everyone stared at him in fear.

When he tried to lift the weapon to his head, Rafael, and Ruben rushed forward to stop him. "It's not going to be that easy John Brideaux!" Rafael shouted.

The first shot hit Ruben in the chest and threw him to the ground. The second shot grazed Rafael's left arm before he managed to reach Brideaux and wrestle the gun from Brideaux's jolting hand.

The doors swung open. Five men with black balaclavas walked in and told everyone to remain seated. One of them stood almost six inches taller than any of his comrades. It was this man who walked slowly towards John Brideaux and stopped two paces short of him. He removed his balaclava.

"Told you we would meet again." He had a grin on his face.

"JR ... I ... I ... should have ... killed you," Brideaux slurred, as his trousers grew dark with urine. He was beyond controlling even the fundamental elements of his body.

Professor Cohen sank to her seat, pallid. All had fallen to dust, and she was powerless. Her last sane thought was *Please don't let me wet my pants.*

One of the masked men went across to where Ruben was lying on the ground, checked for a pulse, and shook his head. He moved his hand over Ruben's smiling face and closed his eyes.

"You son of a bitch! You killed my best friend!" Martinez screamed with fury as he grabbed Brideaux by the throat.

JR jumped forward and pulled his hand away. "Stop it. There will be no more killing. It's over."

Everything went quiet as the dazed councilors stared at each other and John Brideaux in the corner.

Nigel's voice startled them. "Jack, Chief Detective Pierre Bertrand informed me that he and his men are waiting outside to escort you and the councilors to the airport. Air Force One is waiting and ready to take off as soon as you arrive. Have a safe trip. We will wait for you in Washington."

Jack nodded to his men. They moved forward and started to handcuff the councilors.

Nigel continued. "To everyone who has been following these events, I will sign off shortly, but before I go, I have a few requests. Please let us all remain calm and civilized as we rebuild our planet. There rests an enormous duty on the shoulders of every one of us to rebuild our society and our lives. We will only succeed if we can respect each other. What has happened to us must not be allowed to ever happen again. Work with your police, offer your help to those in need, and take care of each other. I will talk to you again in ten hours.

"May God bless us in our undertaking."

The screen went blank.

Chapter One Hundred Eighteen

THERE IS A TIME FOR EVERYTHING

Around the world, chaotic scenes of jubilation were erupting as people woke up to the news that they'd been liberated. Bonfires and fireworks lit up the night skies as people streamed out of their houses onto the streets, dancing, and singing. The events that took place at The Berlaymont in Brussels earlier were not only the main news - it was the *only* news that was broadcast in all countries, on all stations. The news media had been replaying the recordings and speculating about the future for nine straight hours when Air Force One touched down at Joint Base Andrews in Washington, D.C.

Brad Johnston did his part as he'd promised. Hundreds of police recruited in advance and sworn in the past nine hours were present. Banners with messages of welcome and gratitude accompanied by the thundering noises of bliss coming from hundreds of thousands of people greeted Jack and his team when they appeared at the top end of the steps.

Chief Detective Pierre Bertrand and his men remained

in the airplane to keep a close watch over the thirteen Supreme Council members until Brad's police would take over.

Rafael Martinez was amongst them. He'd requested not to be given any special treatment for his role in the demise of the Supreme Council. He had no misapprehensions about his part in the creation of the worst human disaster since the dawn of the 11th Cycle. He was deeply remorseful and repentant about everything he did – his actions of the past few months were testimony to that – yet he was prepared to accept the justice that would be measured out to him.

Nigel and Esther Harper were waiting at the bottom of the stairs. Next to him stood Daniel and Sarah, Sam and Susan Lewis, and the rest of the Rosslerites. They had tears of joy in their eyes as they looked up to the five men who'd taken the Supreme Council into custody – the numbers of the Rosslerites were full again.

Jack and his team were embraced by their waiting loved ones and then Nigel harper walked over to the podium while every news camera in the world followed him.

"My fellow Americans and citizens of the world. A very wise man once wrote the following:

There is a time for everything, and a season for every activity under the heavens:

a time to be born and a time to die,
a time to plant and a time to uproot,
a time to kill and a time to heal,
a time to tear down and a time to build,
a time to weep and a time to laugh,
a time to mourn and a time to dance,
a time to scatter stones and a time to gather them,
a time to embrace and a time to refrain from embracing,

a time to search and a time to give up,
a time to keep and a time to throw away,
a time to tear and a time to mend,
a time to be silent and a time to speak,
a time to love and a time to hate,
a time for war and a time for peace.

Today is the beginning of the time to be born, to plant, to heal, to build, to laugh, to dance, to gather, to embrace, to search, to mend, to speak, to love, and above all it is time for peace."

The crowd was absolutely quiet until his last words reached their ears and their minds. They began to chant – "Harper for president, Harper for president!"

Nigel held his hand up and the crowd went quiet again.

"My friends, there is also a time to come and a time to go. I had my time. I am an old man, and the days that God has granted me to remain on this earth are few. It is my time to go. Our country and the world need new leaders to take us into the future. We need people who get courage from their deeply-held beliefs - people who will not waver in the face of adversity."

The crowd exploded in applause, while Nigel waited for them to calm down and for the musketeers to do as they'd agreed.

Daniel and Sarah didn't know what was happening when the musketeers and their spouses who formed a half circle around them moved closer and gently started pushing the two of them towards the podium five yards away. They looked around in bewilderment at the smiling faces. They were holding on to each other as their legs began to feel jittery.

"Sarah what's going on?"

"I have no idea, Daniel."

When they were close enough, Nigel took their hands and pulled them towards him and the microphones.

"It is today my privilege and honor to introduce to you two of those people. They are half my age, but over the past few months, they taught me two things:

One. Our present circumstances will not determine where we will go; it merely dictates where we will start.

Two. Never doubt that a small group of thoughtful, committed people can change the world. Indeed it is the only thing that ever has.

I present to you Daniel and Sarah Rossler, the next President and First Lady of the United States of America."

Next in the Rossler Foundation Mysteries Series

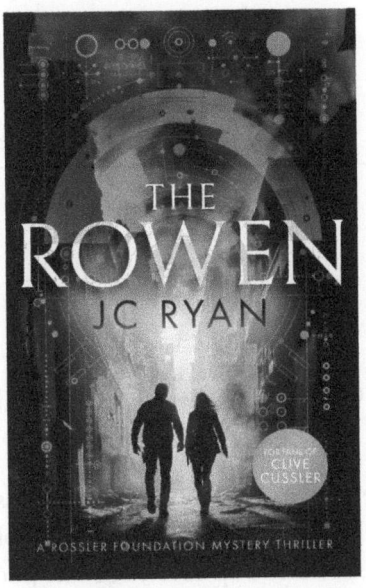

vinci-books.com/rowen

In a world reborn, new threats emerges. The battle for freedom rages on.

The Rosslerites, led by Daniel and Sarah Rossler, have just achieved the impossible: overthrowing the despotic One World Supreme Council of John Brideaux. But their hard-won victory is short-lived as two malevolent forces conspire to drag humanity back into the abyss of tyranny.

Turn the page for a free preview…

The Rowen: Chapter One

THE EARTH WAS SHIFTING

June 30, 1908, Podkamennaya Tunguska River in Siberia, Russian Empire

Shadows appeared in the complete darkness as faint light began to illuminate what was hidden in the blackness. Rows and rows of neatly lined up silver, egg-like pods reflected the dim light making it slightly stronger than it would have been otherwise. Each elongated pod rested horizontally on a sturdy stand and had a small panel on one side, some with glowing lights, and some without. On one of the pods the lights on the panel were bright and flashing, and with a quiet hiss, the transparent top of the pod began to move. It slid halfway down the eight-foot length of itself revealing the body of a man, dark hair, and a clean-shaven, chiseled face. The man moved, sitting up, revealing a well-muscled upper torso and arms, bearing the scars of many battles.

Emerging slowly from his pod, he blinked in the dim light, the skin of his bare chest prickling in the crisp air. He found himself in a large, cavernous room and felt uneasy.

Looking around, seeking the source of his disquiet, he eyed the other pods in the room as his memories flooded back.

Ligator! Where is Ligator?

As the commander, the awakening routine had been programmed to activate Ligator's pod and awaken him first; then it would be up to him to decide if he should awaken his second in command.

Where is Ligator?

He stared at the pod next to his and saw that it remained sealed, its control panel lights still dark.

Ligator's pod must have malfunctioned.

Another wave of anxiety hit him. The wake sequence was programmed to trigger only in two instances—when a new and advanced human society found them or when there was an imminent natural threat that could destroy them.

Which one is it; clever humans or a threat from nature?

I must get to the control room to see what has triggered the waking cycle.

He disconnected the tubes and wires connected to his body and climbed out of the pod. The pods were designed to sustain life while the body was in a deep, near-death sleep, for up to a hundred thousand years. Necessary sustenance and periodic stimulations to keep the muscles strong and moveable, ensured the person would awaken invigorated and alert.

He looked into Ligator's pod; there was only a small pile of what looked like dust and debris—no body. He took in a sharp breath.

Ligator is dead. I am in command now.

How long has it been? It must be less than a hundred thousand years but...

He shivered as he approached the lockers on the far

wall. He was looking forward to the warmth of coverings and the security of his weapon.

He opened the airtight locker where his personal items had been stored before entering the pod and dressed in a black shirt and black pants— the uniform of a soldier of the Eighth Cycle. He sat on the nearby bench to put on his boots and then returned to the locker for his weapon.

The small silver and black cylinder, about an inch in diameter, fitted easily and comfortably in his hand. It was a powerful weapon that accurately fired an invisible, deadly pulse, capable of incinerating a target, leaving only a heap of ash with no chance for re-animation. It was a close-quarters weapon—ideal in a facility like this. For now, there was no need to retrieve one of the long-range weapons.

Feeling warmer and more secure in clothes and with a weapon in hand, he headed for the control room after triggering the awakening cycle on a pod across from his. It was standard procedure to always have at least two officers in every operational detachment at all times.

Soltan is intelligent and capable. I'll promote him to second in command—he will serve me well.

By the time he left the pod room the lights had come to full illumination, allowing him to see clearly. He moved quickly but cautiously through the deserted hallways.

If someone has entered the facility, where would they be?

Pausing frequently to listen for voices or sounds of movement, he worked his way toward the central hub. The emptiness and absolute silence, almost hurting his ears, left him with an eerie, surreal feeling.

The closer he got to the central complex without detecting any sign of life, the tenser he became.

Where are they?

Are they hiding?

Why would they hide if they think this facility is deserted?

He slowed as he entered the large hub and then even more as he approached the corridor leading to the control center—every muscle in his body on alert, his weapon raised and ready to fire.

Warily, he stole down the corridor, stopping every other step to listen and check behind him. Finally, he reached the door to the control room and leaned against it, listening for noises in the room but hearing only silence. An apprehensive tingle started at the base of his spine and worked its way up his back, making the hair on the back of his neck prickle.

I don't like this.

Something is wrong here.

Gently he tested the square, palm-size gray pad next to the door. As designed, it responded to the pressure of his hand and he saw the door start to move. He took a step back and raised his weapon.

He checked the corridor again.

It's too quiet in here.

Stepping over the threshold, his eyes darted around the room—nothing. He moved forward. Nothing out of the ordinary caught his eyes, but then this wasn't his installation—he didn't know much about it. Every one of them, including the captured scientists and civilians, had been put into the deep sleep cycle shortly after attacking and overpowering the facility. There had been no time for them to familiarize themselves with the place.

One by one, he examined the multitude of panels, screens, switches, and lights.

Something is wrong. What is it?

He felt a tingling sensation under his feet—it grew

stronger, and suddenly he lost his balance as the floor moved under his feet.

The Earth is shifting!

Regaining his feet, he noticed a green light glowing on one of the panels on the wall to his left. Approaching to examine, it appeared to be a monitoring and control panel. There were four tall, rectangular displays side by side on the panel that appeared to be some kind of gage. Each display was divided into four equal vertical sections holding four similarly colored lights. Blue at the bottom followed by green, amber, and red at the top.

To the left of each gage, corresponding to the colored lights were labels with numbers. Next to blue was 0 – 1, green was 1 – 2, Amber 2 - 3 and red was labeled 3 – 4. A narrow line, probably made of metal, hovered horizontally over the colored lights and appeared to be made to move up and down the stack in response to some stimulus.

Below each rectangular display were a set of dials that he surmised were used for making adjustments to whatever the displays were monitoring.

On the first display, the one to the left, the light was green; on the others, the lights were blue. The line on the first gage hovered over the middle of the green section. His eyes darted to the other gages, similar to the one he just inspected. The needles on them were all hovering near the bottom of the displays in the lower portion of the blue sector.

The only one that's different is the green one; Why?

He paced the room, clueless, checking gauges and equipment. Returning to check the first gauge after every few paces, he noticed it continued a slow climb through the green sector toward the amber sector.

The Phoenix Agenda

I'm a soldier, not a scientist. How am I supposed to know what to do?

There is some kind of threat lurking—that much I know.

"There are no other humans here. It must be another type of threat then," he mumbled.

He checked the green gauge again, noticing it had moved up again, almost touching the amber section now—that spurred him into action.

Returning to the pod room quickly, he checked the panel on Soltan's pod noting that the cycle was progressing without problems.

Although Viktor knew the deep sleep procedure was technically sophisticated, it was fairly simple to enact, even for a layperson. He recited the process mentally just to be sure he would recognize a problem if one arose.

A person entering the deep sleep was placed in a pod and hooked up to an intravenous drip that released an anesthetic to render the person unconscious before a very cold fluid with a high concentration of oxygen filled the pod, and the person began breathing it.

A drug was then administered to stop the heart, and the blood siphoned from the body and stored, in a frozen state, in a container inside the lining of the pod. Artificial blood, filled with nutrients that would keep the muscles strong and joints flexible, was put back into the body to slowly circulate throughout for as long as it remained in the deep sleep.

Finally, micro electrical stimulations, continuously sent to the brain through tiny electrodes that penetrated the skull at the temples, kept the brain unconscious but alive and ready to function when the person awoke.

When awakening someone out of the deep sleep, the process was reversed. The liquid inside the pod, the chemical inside the body, and the person's real blood would be warmed; the electrical stimulation would increase in strength, and when the liquid in the pod reached the specified core body temperature, the artificial blood would be removed and replaced with the person's real blood.

The liquid in the pod would drain out and be suctioned out of the lungs. Then the heart would be restarted through electrical and chemical stimulation while brain wave stimulation continued to increase.

Soltan would be awake soon—which was not soon enough, but he knew he could not interfere with the process. Not unless he wanted to turn Soltan into a pile of dust like the hapless Ligator.

I need another brain here to help me figure out what is happening.

But Soltan is a soldier, he probably understands as much as or less than I do.

He turned and approached a pod at the far end of the room, hesitated for a moment, and pressed the button to begin the awakening cycle. It would take time for the woman to regain consciousness and be able to leave the pod—all he could do was wait.

"Don't want any more dust heaps, especially not this scientist. We need her now." He muttered as he started pacing impatiently again.

How long have we been asleep?

What is happening outside?

Or perhaps I should first ask; what has happened outside while I was asleep?

This L'gundo scientist might have the answers to those questions.

Soltan, a tall, blond haired man whose physique easily matched his in comeliness and strength, emerged from his pod.

"Viktor," Soltan shouted from inside his pod, "good to see you!"

Viktor moved quickly to Soltan's pod when he heard it opening, "good to see you too my friend."

"Do you know how long we've been asleep? How long have you been awake? Where are the others? Where is Ligator?" Soltan fired off a barrage of questions.

Shaking his head, Viktor replied, "Ligator's pod malfunctioned, he is dead. I've only been awake a short while, so I don't know how much time has passed. You are the second to awake. There is a problem in the control room—the pressure is rising in something, at least that's what I think is happening. Do you know anything about the technology in this place?"

"No idea—I'm a soldier like you. I can fight, destroy, and kill—I don't know how to fix things. Do you have any ideas?" Soltan said as Viktor assisted him to climb out of the pod.

"I don't know anything about the equipment in this installation. I've started the awakening cycle on one of the L'gundo pods; the woman scientist we captured when we took control of this place. She should know what the readings mean and what actions to take."

While the awakening cycle on the woman's pod progressed, Soltan followed Viktor as he strolled among the one hundred pods, carefully checking the status on each of them. Viktor was pleased to find that only Ligator's and two others had malfunctioned.

When the familiar hiss announced that the awakening cycle for the L'gundo woman was complete, he drew his weapon and carefully moved toward it just as the cover came fully open.

He drew in a sudden breath as a dark-haired woman sat up exposing her stunning, bare upper body to his view. Viktor swallowed hard, barely noticing her beautiful lips and brown eyes as he focused on her perfectly shaped breasts, staring at the nipples, hardened from the cold. He felt his groin respond to the beauty and fitness of her young luscious-looking athletic body as she clambered out of the pod. She was a little on the shorter side of average height with well-muscled legs and hips, firm buttocks, and luring skin that looked too soft and smooth not to touch.

She turned to face him and, recognizing him she frowned, hatred and anger immediately washed over her face.

"You," She hissed through her teeth.

"Yes. Me." Viktor replied as he leveled his weapon at her. "There is a problem in the control room—the pressure is rising in something. I need your help."

"How long—"

"I don't know. I've only had time to check the equipment and wake you and Soltan up."

She gave the tall, dark haired man a withering look, hate radiating from her eyes. "You are the one called Viktor, are you not?" She hissed.

With a slight incline of his head he answered, "Yes, I am Viktor."

She exploded in rage. "You and your soldiers came in here and killed everyone, including my son. Then you reanimated us and put us into the deep sleep. Where is my son? And what makes you imagine I would want to help you?"

"The reason you will want to help me is simple—if you don't, we might all be dead soon, this time forever, and that includes your son."

"Where is my son? Where is the rest of my team?"

Viktor pointed to the pod next to hers, "Your son." He said and then waved his hand at the rest of the pods in the row, "The surviving members of your team. And we," he pointed to Soltan and himself, "are the only ones who have the code that can start their wake-up routine."

"Then start it," the woman snapped.

"Yes, of course, I will—" he paused for a few moments, smirking, "just as soon as you have resolved the technical problems, and not one moment before. Understood?"

She glowered at him. "Well, *Viktor*," she emphasized his name with hostility, "in that case—I am Telestra, and I suggest you let me put on some clothes, and we go have a look at the problem."

Two more worrying earth trembles shook the place while Telestra was busy reviewing the data retrieved from the control room.

Soltan had forced his way into the storage area, and one of the sealed food storage boxes. He brought back packages of preserved food. He and Viktor were sitting at the round, white, marble table in the control room eating from bowls that contained a green colored mushy looking substance.

Telestra joined them at the table. "What is that?" she asked indicating the green mush that was rapidly disappearing into their mouths.

"Vegetables," Soltan responded, "ugly, tasteless, and nourishing vegetables."

Without looking up from the food in front of him, Viktor added, "Between the chemical preservatives and the flash freeze-dry process it leaves everything tasteless. By the time they get through pulverizing it with the vitamin additives, you can't tell what you're eating. But it keeps you alive and..."

When he looked up from his bowl, Viktor noted

Telestra's worried expression, paused mid-sentence and asked, "What's going on?"

"This installation was built at this location because of the subterranean volcanic activity that occurs here. All the power for the facility comes from the hot gasses released by the magma from the mantle. Those gasses flow through the four natural fissures that occur here and our equipment harnesses the gas, controls the flow of it, and utilizes it to generate power to the facility. One of the flow regulator valve mechanisms has failed, and pressure is building up in the other fissures as a result."

"What does this mean?"

"It means that if that regulator isn't repaired, and very quickly, there will be a devastating explosion and this installation will be blown into pieces; very small, very hot pieces, as a new volcano is born."

Soltan stared at her—alarmed. "Can you repair it?"

"Definitely not by myself; the pressure is already dangerously high in fissure three and starting to rise in fissures two and four. I'm not sure if it can be stopped in time."

"What do you need?" Viktor asked.

"I need my colleagues; they know how to operate this equipment. Did you happen to leave any of them alive?" she asked sarcastically.

Viktor clenched his jaw and narrowed his eyes at her. "There are some."

"Then I suggest you wake them up so we can get to work." She had a slight grin when she added, "unless you want to be dead—forever."

Viktor stood up and moved as if to examine the gauges again. *If I wake up more of the L'gundo, will Soltan and I be able to keep control?* He weighed his options while pacing the room.

Telestra went back to the control panel and studied the gauges.

Soltan joined him and matched his steps. He whispered, "I think we'd better wake the L'gundo scientists."

"That goes without saying. The challenge is maintaining control over them after they have been awakened." Viktor spoke softly and slowly. "Go to the pod room and wake twenty of our soldiers. When the soldiers' wake-up cycle is halfway done, start the cycles on ten of the L'gundo scientists. Stay there and when our soldiers are awake, apprise them of the situation and give them their orders. But don't wake up her son—under any circumstances."

"On my way," Soltan acknowledged, turning to leave the control center.

Telestra wiped the sweat from her brow. It was already too hot in the fissure access area. She had been examining the malfunctioning mechanism and thought they were going to be lucky if they could save the installation. She had already concluded that they would probably be unable to stop the explosion. Her highest priority was to wake up her son and as many as possible of her team and then try to escape.

I need my son, and I need my team, and I need them now! She thought with frustration, but there was no hurrying the awakening process—doing so had ghastly consequences as they had learned while developing the process. She had seen the dusty remains in two of the pods on her way out of the pod room earlier.

She slowly walked the edges of the access area weighing her options—working on a plan. Wondering if she had considered everything—maybe she *could* stop the explosion.

But she wouldn't know that without having her team around her. The rock walls of the fissure access cavern were a stark contrast to the immaculate white walls of the rest of the facility. Here in this rough, dirty, cavern was the raw power that provided them with clean, comfortable living spaces and all the energy they needed to run the facility. Staring at the rock walls and knowing the fissures that were behind them made her marvel, not just at the force of the Earth itself, but the ingenuity of her ancestors who learned to harness the power of a forming volcano and tame it for their use.

These fissures are just the tip; they extend down for hundreds of miles to the mantle. Gas that was stored as a fluid, more than 1,800 miles below the earth's crust, was seeping through the mantle into the fissures. If not for my ancestors learning to control the flow of the gas, it would have grown to become a volcano, spewing toxic gasses and molten lava onto the surface of the planet.

As another tremor rolled through the Earth, it was a relief to hear the stumbling footsteps of her colleagues, herded by the soldiers. Her heart dropped when she noticed her son was not amongst them.

"Where is my son?" She asked fiercely.

"He's not a scientist." Viktor retorted. "He will be awakened only when you and your team have fixed this problem. Now get on with it."

Telestra's eyes were filled with fury as she fought against the impulse to jump on Viktor like a tigress and rip his throat out.

Her team, blinking and confused, gathered around her to hear what she had to say. There was no time to talk about anything else. Viktor stood nearby leaning against the rock wall, arms folded over his chest.

Slowly she got her emotions under control and started talking to her team. "Here's the situation. Due to a shift in the fissure, most likely caused by the recent tremors, the flow regulator valves in Fissure One have been crushed in a closed position—blocking all flow."

The entire team looked alarmed, instantly recognizing it could not be repaired. They began talking nervously among themselves.

Soltan and some of the soldiers saw their anxiety and looked to Viktor for his reaction.

Viktor presented a calm front to his men, but he felt the muscles in his gut tightening. *If the L'gundo are this worried, it must be more critical than I thought.*

"Settle down everyone, settle down," Telestra commanded. "Fissure Three is amber, and Fissures Two and Four are green. I need you to organize yourselves into four teams." She gave them a few moments to organize themselves into the requested teams.

"Team one." Two people stepped forward. "Look at Fissure One and see if you can find a way to open those flow regulator valves." The two team members looked at each other in disbelief. The regulator was crushed—it could not be repaired. What was she thinking? They would have to look for alternatives.

"Team two." Three people stepped forward. "Work on releasing some of the pressure from Fissure Three." They looked at one another in dismay. This was a dangerous assignment and almost certainly meant death. Should the pressure reach critical levels while they were inside the fissure they wouldn't have time to… well, they just wouldn't have time for anything.

"Teams three and four," four people stepped forward in

sets of two. "You work on Fissures Two and Four, coordinate with Team Two to try to divert some pressure from Fissure Three and funnel it through Fissures Two and Four. Dekka and I will go up to monitor and assist you from the control room."

She saw Dekka look at her sharply, but she didn't acknowledge him—she hoped none of Viktor's men noticed. Dekka wasn't a geological scientist; he was a biomechanical engineer who worked with nanotechnology. If there was an explosion, the control room might survive, and if it did, she would need his expertise.

Viktor snapped a look at her, suddenly alert, "No! All of you L'gundo will stay down here and work; none of you are going to be allowed in the control room."

Telestra rounded on him, "Excuse me? I thought you wanted help with this problem."

"You will all work from down here." Viktor snapped. He didn't like being challenged in front of his men.

"Do you or any of your soldiers know how to interpret the readings on our equipment and make the necessary adjustments as they are needed?" She snapped back.

"No. But you can monitor and make adjustments from here." *Soldier mentality—give them command, and it goes to their head.*

"Look, Viktor," she fairly spat the words at him. "That is *not* an option. The equipment can be adjusted from here, but the main controls, readouts, and programmed adjustments are in the control room—the two *have* to be worked in conjunction.

"You are going to *have* to allow at least the two of us into the control room—there should be four of us, but two is the bare minimum."

Viktor hesitated. He didn't want the L'gundo to have

access to the control room. He didn't know enough about it and wasn't sure what they might be able to do with what was accessible on the many panels. "You, Telestra, may work from the control room, but no one else."

"I assume you like the idea of a hot molten lava-lined casket then, because that's what this place is going to be for all of us."

"I think you are making more out of this than it really is to trick us and regain control of the installation."

"You are a fool!" she exploded in exasperation.

"Then explain the situation to me so that I can understand it."

"We don't have time for this!"

"We will make the time."

"Fine, send Dekka to the control room so he can get started, and I will explain this to you." *I just hope Dekka will be able to fake his way through it for a few minutes until I can convince this idiot.*

Viktor nodded his agreement. "Soltan, take a soldier with you and take Dekka to the control room. Monitor what he does and if he tries anything stupid—kill him, and I mean kill him forever."

Telestra and Dekka looked at each other in disbelief and shook their heads. Then Dekka turned and followed Soltan and another soldier as they left for the control room. "Good luck," Dekka mumbled, "you're going to need it."

"Teams, get moving!" Telestra said as she glowered at Viktor.

The teams scattered to the nearby lockers and under the watchful eyes of the soldiers, gathered their equipment, donned their protective suits and headed into the fissure accesses.

"Alright, Viktor, here's a quick science lesson for you,"

Telestra was furious, and she made no attempt to hide her disdain as she spoke measuredly. "This facility collects and disperses highly volatile gasses from the magma in the Earth's mantle. This is done by sealing off and controlling the gas released from the four natural fissure vents that are present here. The flow regulators are what control the flow of the gases and thus the pressure in each fissure.

"If the flow is not regulated properly to control the pressure it will cause a devastating explosion.

"There are four zones, or pressure levels, and a color associated with each one. In the normal operational zone, the pressure level is between zero and one and is colored blue. On occasion, more power is necessary, and the pressure is allowed to rise to level two, this is the warning zone and colored green.

"The danger zone, between level two and three, is colored amber. The only time the pressure reaches this level is when something has malfunctioned. If the pressure reaches level three, red, a blast is imminent.

"Right now, the pressure in Fissure Three is approaching level three, the red level. If you have paid any attention to what I've just told you; can you tell me what that means?"

Viktor didn't reply, he grabbed her arm, turned, and dragged her toward the control room.

Telestra watched in horror as the pressure in Fissure Three reached the mid-point of level three. She had no idea what was preventing the explosion, but she was now sure it was coming.

The Phoenix Agenda

"Get them out of there!" she screamed. "Get them out of there!" Her fear for her colleagues and friends working in the fissures was palpable.

"No. Keep working. You have to stop this!" Viktor yelled.

The argument had started a short time ago when Fissure Three had reached level three. Telestra and Dekka both knew they were fighting a losing battle and had tried to reason with Viktor but to no avail.

Dekka shouted, "There is no stopping this you idiot! The ground tremors have caused physical shifts in the fissure, there is no way of unlocking those flow regulator valves, and the relief systems are at maximum capacity."

Viktor grabbed Dekka by the front of his shirt with his left hand and clenched his other fist to punch Dekka in the face, but the sound of rumbling stopped him as the tremor rolled under their feet and through the rock walls, stronger than ever before.

"The explosion is about to happen! If you don't get them all out of there, they will die! Get them out and seal off the facility or we will all die!" Dekka yelled.

Viktor glanced over at the pressure gauges. Fissure Three's indicator was red—in the blast zone—Fissures Two and Four were both amber and nearing the red line.

"Evacuate!" He shouted. "Then seal off the facility."

Soltan repeated the command over the intercom. He, Viktor, Telestra, and Dekka watched on the video feed as the scientists and soldiers scampered out of the fissure access area.

Telestra gave a sigh of relief, but it was premature. Another tremor rumbled through the ground, and she saw the telltale signs near the opening of Fissure Three. A soft glow had appeared, and although she couldn't hear it, she could see on the faces of those remaining in the access area that they could hear the hiss and pop as the gases began to ignite.

"Run!" she screamed.

The Rowen: Chapter Two

A BRIGHT FLASH CAME FROM THE SKY

The forest is unusually quiet, lifeless. Petya thought as he shouldered his rifle and paused to listen for the sounds of animals. He heard nothing; no birdsong, no scuttling of small animals in the underbrush, not even a breeze stirring the leaves of the trees. *I haven't seen or heard any animals all morning—strange.*

Sunshine brightened his brown hair and warmed his thin face and arms. Petya was small for his age, but he was a skilled hunter, never failing to bring home food to help feed the family. Not many thirteen-year-olds were as dedicated to helping their families as he was; his parents took great pride in him.

He left the house in Moga Village early this June morning, to hunt for game near the Tunguska River. By sun-up, he had traveled nearly three miles.

Standing on a rocky ridge, he surveyed the area around him for any sign of wildlife. The forest was a dark summer-green, as it should be this time of year, the sky a beautiful blue—unblemished by clouds.

There should be a breeze and birds soaring on the currents. Where is everything?

Then the ground shifted under his feet. It was the third time this morning he had felt the tremors. This time it seemed stronger than before.

Perhaps the tremors are frightening the animals, and they have all gone into hiding.

As he picked his way across the ridge, an unfamiliar feeling of fear started to spread through him.

What's wrong with me?

There is nothing for me to fear out here!

He continued to move, stumbling as another, stronger, tremor rolled through the ground. A sudden impulse to run like a frightened animal filled him despite his earlier assurances to himself—he quickened his pace. The fear in him grew into terror; he broke into a run as if driven from the ridge by an invisible force.

Just as he reached the edge of the forest, a bright flash came from the sky turning everything red—the sky, the earth, rocks, and trees. He heard a rumbling sound in the distance that quickly grew in volume; the ground began to shake violently. The wind picked up, quickly growing to hurricane force as Petya staggered toward the shelter offered by the large trunk of a fallen tree.

Diving to the ground next to the trunk, he noticed a burning pillar of fire in the sky and felt the air grow warmer, becoming hot as it blew over his body. He heard several loud booms like huge cannons, followed by the deafening roar of thunder. The ground continued to shake forcefully, and the wind whipped around him. He saw trees blow over in the distance.

What is happening?

Petya scooted closer to the trunk and found a depression

into which he quickly slipped his thin body, with the huge old tree as a shelter over him. Feeling a little safer, he closed his eyes against the searing light and covered his ears to shield them from the frightening noise.

After what seemed like an eternity, the shaking ground quieted, the wind slowly began to die down, and the roaring subsided.

Just as he was crawling out from under the trunk he heard several more loud bangs, looked up, and saw blazing objects raining down from the sky landing around him. A small piece hit his arm, and he yelled out in pain as it burned through his skin. He quickly scrambled back under the tree trunk hoping it would continue to protect him.

Fires were burning in the distance causing a glow in the sky.

Will this never end?
Is this the end of our world as the prophets predicted?

Grab your copy...
vinci-books.com/rowen

About the Author

JC Ryan is a bestselling author renowned for his intricate espionage, archaeological thrillers, and conspiracy mysteries. With over 30 acclaimed novels, including the popular Rex Dalton K9 Thrillers, Rossler Foundation Mysteries, and Carter Devereux Mystery Thrillers, Ryan has captivated readers around the globe.

Drawing from his diverse professional background—as a military officer, lawyer, and IT manager—Ryan creates compelling narratives that skillfully blend historical accuracy with thrilling adventure. He is celebrated as a master storyteller, known for crafting riveting plots, meticulous historical details, and engaging, multidimensional characters. Ryan's meticulous research lends authenticity and depth to each story, immersing readers in richly constructed worlds filled with intrigue, suspense, and adventure.

Fans of David Baldacci, Lee Child's Jack Reacher, Tom Clancy's Jack Ryan, Nelson DeMille's John Corey, Vince Flynn's Mitch Rapp, Mark Greaney's Gray Man, Gregg Hurwitz's Orphan X, Robert Ludlum's Jason Bourne, Daniel Silva's Gabriel Allon, Brad Taylor's Pike Logan, Brad Thor's Scot Harvath, James Rollins' Sigma Force, Steve Berry's Cotton Malone, and Dan Brown's Robert Langdon will find JC Ryan's novels equally compelling and unforgettable.

When not writing, Ryan enjoys spending time with his college sweetheart, whom he married in 1978. They are proud parents of two daughters, have two sons-in-law, and are grandparents to two grandchildren.